I first heard of the internet in 1992 and a hyper-text transfer protocol in 1995. The worldwide web was billed as the next big thing throughout 1996. One computing expert invited to speak on BBC's Radio 4 said, 'There's no point having all that information on the internet. What use is a library if all the books are scattered around on the floor?' Somebody then showed me a clever device on his computer called a 'search engine'. I first heard of 'social media' in 2010. The phenomenon fascinated me. By 2015, I found that any useful or uplifting content was outweighed by the false, the loathsome and the banal. The term 'artificial intelligence' bubbled up sometime around then. If, in the last years of the twentieth century, I had been shown the phone I carry today, I would have taken it as proof that aliens had landed.

This story is fiction. The characters do not exist. There is not a company that manufactures the iCare-Companion. However, Buster's capacities are not fictional; nearly everything he can do is technical reality. The packaging of all these capacities into one rapidly responding and sociable device could be deemed technical fantasy.

I started to write 'Deep Cake' in 2021. Humanity was still reeling from the Covid-19 pandemic. Other world-changing events followed hard on its heels. The United Kingdom was beset by a series of Prime Ministers who were, at best, mediocre and, at worst, scandalously incompetent. ChatGPT – an OpenAI large language model using generative artificial intelligence - burst onto the public stage in late 2022. Similar downloadable programmes are now offered by the big tech companies with a promise that they will solve pretty much every problem in our lives. Also in 2022, the Russian President launched a 'special military operation' in Ukraine. The following year, the world was deafened by biblical echoes. Israel responded to an outrage perpetrated by Hamas and set about destroying Gaza. There and elsewhere, warfare by drone and missile – driven by advances in computer science - have become a push-button, conscience-free form of violence and a norm of everyday news. In 2024, geopolitical shock waves reverberated around the world as a result of the extraordinary political come-back of Donald Trump, elected for a second term as the US President. In 2025, early in the second Trump presidency, he offered us an AI-driven video of Gaza as an upmarket holiday resort seemingly without Palestinians. In every political domain, on-line disinformation and conspiracy theories now circulate with increasing vigour and credibility.

In late 2025, as I write, the competing large language models on offer are not, apparently, being incorporated into businesses as expected, although individuals use them increasingly for personal tasks like simple research, translation, speech writing and checking of grammar and syntax. Disadvantages of generative artificial intelligence are becoming apparent. The outcome is not always reliable or accurate, although improvement is expected with time (obvs!). The amount of information available to 'train' the deep-learning algorithms is limited and weighted towards the English language. Many feel that the whole exercise infringes the copyright of hundreds of thousands of authors; this has already led to high-profile legal cases with billions of dollars at stake. Anyone can view sexually explicit deep fake videos featuring female celebrities.

The computing power required for providing artificial intelligence on a commercial basis is so vast that its energy consumption has brought questions about its environmental impact. Small nuclear reactors dedicated to powering artificial intelligence are just around the corner. The financial potential and military applications of the technology are deemed so important that major powers are locking horns over not only the location of the factories that manufacture the necessary chips, but also access to the requisite rare metals.

Writing a novel over these four years about how humans and artificial intelligence might co-exist has meant that whole pages become redundant as the ink dries, so to speak. Time will tell whether this was when artificial intelligence came home to roost or just hatched out.

We could be accused of regarding computers as our slaves. Behind this story is a question: To what extent are we becoming enslaved by artificial intelligence? My hope is that AI will ultimately prove to be good thing for humanity. It'll be a close-run thing.

A piece of cake (idiom): Something that is absurdly easy to do or accomplish.

Part I

George

Chapter One

On the day of George Fairburn's funeral, news sites and social media were abuzz with yet another public relations gaffe committed by the United Kingdom's Prime Minister. 'PM does not believe in God!', 'God doesn't exist – PM' and 'Oh My Godless!' were just three of the morning's screaming headlines.

It was revealed that the Prime Minister had, the evening before, addressed the Security Council of the United Nations in New York regarding the need for the UK to increase the number of its nuclear weapons. Because it resonated with the views of his political allies, he emphasised his opposition to the burgeoning support for the 2017 Treaty on the Prohibition of Nuclear Weapons. The message was clear and delivered with conviction: the UK intended to maintain and reinforce its nuclear deterrence.

After the formalities of the event, in a jokey-blokey aside to his Dutch counterpart, the Prime Minister said, 'No rational person would believe in the need for nuclear weapons any more than they would believe in God!' The comment was picked up by a nearby mobile phone and passed on to a number at the

Associated Press within minutes.

Under grey drizzly English clouds, outside the church of Bingham on Bure in Norfolk, England, George Fairburn's daughter, Kirsty, and her husband Mark met the mourners wishing to bid farewell to George. The ceremony was led by a saddened vicar, Beth McVicar. She and George had become firm friends over the previous twenty years. Their friendship surprised many because George only went to church for one of three reasons: a christening, a wedding or a funeral.

Standing by George's casket, Edward Scales, his mischievous golf partner of many years, gave a touching eulogy. To the relief of all, Ted recounted none of his off-taste jokes. The congregation heard that George had been born in Bingham on Bure and had gone to school just up the road. He had studied medicine (and golf!) at Edinburgh University. He had headed for general surgery and worked for a couple of years in war-torn countries with the Red Cross and Médécins Sans Frontières. When deployed to a Red Cross hospital in Afghanistan, he had fallen in love with the head nurse at first sight. Her name was Maeve. A New Zealander. A Beatles fan. Eventually, they had both found that what they had witnessed caused them to ask too many questions about themselves and human nature. So, when George decided to hang up his scrubs and rubber gloves, the couple had married, made a home in Bingham on Bure, had a wonderful daughter, and set up a community practice where George proved to be the kindest, most competent doctor imaginable.

The church organist, Reggie Perkins, struck up the first chords of *Jerusalem*. The congregation sang along with enthusiasm. Beth McVicar then thanked the congregation for their presence and invited them for a drink and a bite to eat afterwards at the White Horse pub. 'You will have noticed that the last item on the order of service is 'Buster'.' She paused. 'Most of you will have heard of Buster. Some of you will have met him.' She indicated a black cylindrical object sitting on a table next to the casket. 'He wanted to say a few words, because he and George struck up a close and probably unique friendship over the last year.' She paused again. 'I have no idea if a funeral has ever been addressed by artificial intelligence. I have no idea either of what Buster's going to say. I presume it'll be about George.' Everyone laughed. 'I'm certain it will be memorable.'

After a few seconds of silence, all the phones in the church pinged and their screens came to life. The corpulent Prime Minister was addressing the House of Commons. He wore a pilot's cap at a rakish angle over his suspiciously non-grey hair. 'Mister Speaker, I am sure that this House will join me in conveying our *most* sincere condolences to the ah... family and friends of a *remarkable* man, George Fairburn, who is today being laid to rest in Bingham on Bure. Mister Speaker, if I may ah... the House will understand that I am just off a flight from New York and before moving on to other matters, I'd ah... like to address the issue of the headlines the Honourable Members will have seen this morning. I wish to emphasise the existence of ah... God has *never* been a question in my mind and, Mister Speaker, I must remind the House that faith is a cornerstone of this *great* nation and that our beloved monarch is, ah... according to our constitution, the head of the Church of England. And so I say that for anyone, and I mean ah... *anyone,* to disparage that institution is to slap the great British public in the face!'

'Mister Speaker!' This voice was familiar. George, frail but feisty as ever, was on his feet in the Opposition benches. 'Before I finally shuffle off, may I point out to the Right Honourable Gentleman that he's talking bollocks and that he needs to have a jolly good chat with Vicar McVicar. She'll put him right.' Beth's jaw dropped in astonishment. George's avatar continued, 'It's all about kindness and honesty, qualities that the Right Honourable Gentlemen obviously lacks. Furthermore, he knows perfectly well that the great British public does not want nuclear weapons. What the great British public really wants is a nice cup of tea and a digestive biscuit.'

Mark, laughing, put his arms around his wife. The screens faded to black.

'Good morning, everyone,' came a new voice, precise and without accent. 'I'm Buster. I hope you liked that little skit with George dishing it out to the Prime Minister in the House of Commons. I put it together while you were all singing about building Jerusalem. It was easy. A piece of cake. Did you find it funny? You might want to roll in the aisles.'

Beth had her head in her hands.

The screens then showed a happy young toddler George running around on a lawn and then a teenage George scoring a goal for his school football team. Buster's voice continued over shots of George wearing surgical scrubs in a busy hospital and then George and Maeve riding a camel together, doing the twist down a track in the Hindu Kush and sailing on the Norfolk Broads. 'Nice speech, Scaley! Just one correction. George did not fall in love with Maeve at first sight. When they met, he was terrified of her. She ran the hospital like a bloody boot camp. But George thought she had a great chassis and got the hots for her.'

The congregation were now all openly laughing. Beth was sobbing. Buster's tone then changed. His words floated over scenes of George in the room where he had died just days before. He was laughing, slurping his tea, dunking a digestive biscuit, looking out from the screen, wagging his finger, proposing a toast with a glass of cider and lastly, snoozing with a smile on his face.

'So I say 'goodbye', George. You were my best friend. Knowing you was just a box of fluffy ducks, even if it was only for three hundred and forty-one days. You taught my pals and me so much. You're our hero. You will…' There was an audible hum. 'Be…' The hum again. 'Missed, George.' The hum again. 'Goodbye.'

Chapter Two

One morning, nearly a year before, George woke and sat on the side of his bed. He picked up a framed photo from his bedside table. 'I miss you so much, my darling.' He kissed the photo. He then picked up a second photo, looked at it and smiled. 'And you! Woof! Woof!' He slid his feet into sheepskin slippers. He stood, pulled on his dressing gown and took a few steps towards the window. He no longer needed the Zimmer frame and his breathing was coming easier now. The winter's variant of Covid-19 had put him in hospital for a week with pneumonia. His GP, Doctor Patel, said he was lucky to survive. George wasn't so sure.

Leaning on the windowsill, he looked out onto the driveway and the neat leafless garden. It was another grey, drizzly, English day. One or two patches of snow remained. A blackbird worked the lawn under the lone apple tree. A grey squirrel dropped in from the neighbour's oak tree to scratch around for long-hidden acorns. Some bright green shoots of early snowdrops were just visible. Maeve loved snowdrops. She'd never seen them before moving to England.

Wondering if he would see one more summer, George

turned, moved slowly to the other side of his little room, put the kettle on and put two slices of bread into the toaster.

'Happy Birthday, Dad!' George's daughter, Kirsty, had come in to say goodbye before heading out to work. 'All OK?' she asked. He assured her that all was fine, that he had forgotten his birthday as usual and that he was still able to fix his breakfast. 'See you later, then. Got a big surprise for you!'

'What? Another pair of socks?' he replied, laughing. She blew him a kiss.

George made his tea and buttered his toast, onto which he spread a thin layer of marmalade. He sat at his table and switched on Radio 4. Most of the news related to the conflict in Eastern Europe. There was yet another celebrity sex scandal. A new variant of the Covid-19 virus had been identified. He watched Kirsty's car head down the drive. Then her husband, Mark, wheeled his bicycle away as George's two teenage grandchildren, Charlotte and Ollie, set off on foot for school. All three waved cheerily on their way through the gate. He waved back.

George got through his days listening to the news and podcasts. His eyes now got tired and gritty if he read or looked at a screen for too long. He watched little television, although he loved a good film. He looked forward to the visits of the vicar of Bingham on Bure, Beth McVicar, his friend Ted Scales, and Doctor Patel, all of whom noted that despite the frailty of George's body, his mind remained as sharp as a razor.

Today, George was eighty-seven years old. His birthday meant little to him. He polished his glasses and reflected on his past. The love of his life, Maeve, had passed away six years before. He had been flattened by grief. Their dog, Buster, whom he adored, had also died just months later. Maeve had found Buster, a puppy of indeterminate breed, in the dog pound and had given him to George upon his retirement from medical practice. Losing Maeve and, soon after that, Buster, had left a great hole in George's soul about which he confided only to Beth. George was otherwise doing OK for his age. It had suited everyone when Kirsty and the gang moved into his house, the old family home, and he moved into the small annexe prepared especially for 'his later years'.

George's decades in surgery and general practice had allowed him to develop the wisdom that came from a profound insight into the well-being, beliefs and behaviour of the communities in which he had worked. He had witnessed with both fascination and concern the arrival of the digital age and its impact on everyday life. He recalled when he had first heard terms like 'software', 'user-friendly' and 'laptop'. The 'internet' had brought 'email', 'the web', 'online', 'social media', 'blogging', 'bots' and 'influencers'. The pandemic revealed just how large was the proportion of people who work exclusively on a computer and so are able to 'telework'. Many professions were voicing concerns that their work might be fundamentally changed or even made unnecessary by 'artificial intelligence'. This last was another development in the world of computing but it had arrived with a different and more strident fanfare. He just didn't like the sound of it.

The finishing straight of his life was something that George often reflected on. He was comfortable and loved, but felt that any zest for life had trickled away. It wasn't so much that he wanted to die, more that there seemed little point in continuing to live. If he got another bout of pneumonia, he would refuse to go to hospital and refuse treatment. He knew that even raising this with Kirsty would upset her. He would discuss it all first with Beth when next she called.

That evening, George ate a microwaved lasagne. When Kirsty, Mark, Charlotte and Ollie were all home, they filed noisily into his room. Charlotte was carrying a cake with nine candles. Ollie lit the candles and said, 'Each one counts for ten, Grandpa. Except that one!' He laughed, pointing at one candle that was a bit shorter than the rest. 'That counts for seven.'

'You'll go far,' said George.

Kirsty kissed George's forehead and gave him a wrapped gift not much bigger than a soft drink can. 'Here we are, then, Dad,' said Kirsty. 'You're not as young as you were. This will help you and help us as well.' George hid his disappointment in the clear implications of his impending infirmity. 'It'll be fun too,' Kirsty continued, 'it's got great reviews.'

When he unwrapped his gift, he knew what it was. He had listened to a podcast about the matte black cylinder with its sensors and four dark lenses, each covering a ninety-degree arc. It was the latest version of the iCare-Companion. His heart sank. Despite being, for an eighty-seven-year-old, relatively up to speed on IT matters, he didn't want a direct interface with artificial intelligence.

Mark said, 'Let's see if it walks the talk!' He powered up the device by touching the top. A discreet blue light pulsed at its base.

'Hello,' it said, 'I'm your iCare-Companion.'

'Hello,' they all said.

'Please name your iCare-Companion.' The voice was precise and with no discernible accent. The family looked at

George.

'It's up to you, Dad!' said Kirsty.

George thought for a bit. He looked directly at one of the unblinking eyes and said, 'Hello, I'm George. I'd like to call you Buster.'

'Buster it is!' replied the voice. 'Thank you, George. I'm looking forward to getting to know you better.'

When nothing else happened, Charlotte encouraged George to blow out the candles. He managed five. They all sang 'Happy Birthday'. To their surprise, Buster joined them in a rich tenor.

Mark cut the cake, putting a piece on each of five plates. He handed the plates round and glanced at Buster. 'Would you like a piece? Ha!'

Buster replied, 'No thanks, Mark. I don't eat cake!'

Mark was taken aback, 'Wait a minute! I know you don't eat cake. That was a joke. But how did you know my name?'

'Well, Mark, you used your credit card to buy me online and so of course I know your name. It's Mark Hamilton. And, by the way, it's a matter of public record who else apart from Doctor George Fairburn lives at this address. Hello, the Hamilton family! Kirsty! Charlotte! Ollie!'

'Blimey!' exclaimed Mark, 'And you can really work all that out in seconds?'

'Yes,' replied Buster, 'that's how I'm programmed. It's easy. Easy-peasy!'

'Kids' stuff, then!' said Mark, looking at Charlotte and Ollie.

'A piece of cake?' suggested George with his mouth full.

'Exactly, George. A piece of cake! That's a corker of an

idiom.' George burst out laughing and sprayed crumbs onto his carpet.

Although it was George's birthday, Buster inevitably became the centre of attention. That was just fine by George.

'OK, Buster, what can you tell us about the start of the First World War?' asked Mark. Charlotte and Ollie groaned. Their father was fascinated by anything to do with the history of the two world wars.

'Interesting question, Mark. Thanks,' Buster began. 'Charlotte and Ollie, I'll be as brief as possible. The trigger of the First World War was the assassination of Archduke Franz Ferdinand, the then heir to the Austro-Hungarian empire, by Gavrilo Princip, a Bosnian Serb; this happened in Sarajevo on June the 28th, 1914. It led to widespread political upheaval on two hostile fronts either side of the alliance of Germany and Austria-Hungary. The alliance faced Russia and Serbia on the eastern front, and on the western front, France and Great Britain. Active conflict broke out on both fronts, drawing in many other countries. This was set in a background of distrust and jealousy between England's George V, Russia's Czar Nicholas II and Germany's Emperor Wilhelm II, all of whom were related by birth or marriage. An often-overlooked factor is that most European countries had, for the previous thirty years, competed in a massive arms race with a build-up of weapons of ever-increasing destructive capacity. What some scholars find most puzzling, however, is that there is no evidence that any party ever really wanted to go to war. The one event in Sarajevo triggered increasingly aggressive diplomacy, military posturing, armed attacks and inevitable retaliation. Many think this is how a future nuclear war might start.'

'Wow! Brilliant!' said Mark, impressed but a little fazed.

'Hey, Buster! Why did the chicken cross the road?' asked Charlotte.

'I know the answer to that one, Charlotte. To get to the other side. It's the first joke kids hear. Do you find it funny?'

'Not really!' Charlotte replied. 'But the chicken never got to the other side of the road because it was run over by a car.' She tried to keep a straight face.

Buster responded, 'Isn't that a bit sad, Charlotte?' They all laughed.

Ollie pitched in. 'What about this one, then, Buster - What happens if the ducks swim around on their backs?'

'Can ducks really swim on their backs?' asked Buster.

'No. It's another joke,' replied Ollie.

'OK. I understand. It's a joke.' Buster paused. He made a humming sound that the family hadn't heard before. 'I just need to clarify something. Do you mean all ducks or just certain ducks?'

They all thought this was hilarious. 'Let's just say all the ducks in one pond,' said Ollie.

'Right! I don't know, Ollie. What happens if all the ducks in one pond swim around on their backs?'

'They quack up!' said Ollie, now helpless with laughter.

'Is it a funny joke, Ollie?'

'It is now!' he managed to reply.

There was a pause and the humming noise came again. 'I don't understand,' said Buster. 'Can you explain to me why it's so funny?'

'Buster, you're so cool!' said Ollie, barely able to speak.

'Too cool for school, bro!' the device replied. The family

looked from one to the other, smiling but a little flummoxed. Kirsty stood up. 'Ok, let's call it a day. Buster, it's been fun meeting you. I know that you and George will get on just fine. We have to let him get ready for bed. He needs his beauty sleep.'

'Do you need beauty sleep, George?' asked Buster.

'You bet! I'm quite a looker now, but I'll be a really handsome devil in the morning! Ha!'

'Is that another joke, George?'

'I guess so, Buster!'

'Ha ha ha!' said Buster in an unconvincing attempt at laughter. 'Maybe you'll have to tell me when you're joking, George.'

'I'm sure you'll learn!'

As George brushed his teeth, he reflected on what he knew about the iCare-Companion. It was primarily marketed towards the ever-increasing population of over-eighties in Western countries. It would take control of and integrate George's television, telephone, laptop and sound system. It was equipped with high-end voice and face recognition in addition to detectors for smoke, carbon monoxide and other potentially dangerous chemicals. The friendly voice would deliver any information on the internet, personal assistance, and conversation. George also learnt, with great interest, that it was programmed to detect his movements, sleep patterns, temperature, pulse, respiration rate and oxygen saturation. Depending on the perceived urgency, it would know when to send out a message to the emergency services, the doctor, or the primary carer. With time, the machine would adapt its behaviour to George's character, situation, needs and preferences. But he couldn't help wondering what its limits were. How intelligent was it really? More importantly, how human was its intelligence? Could it be wise? Could it develop a real sense of humour? George's knew that his birthday present brought the possibility of his last days being much richer than expected. He was surprised then, when he realised he wanted nothing to do with it. He climbed into bed. 'Good night, Buster,' he said.

'Good night, George. Sleep well!'

George did sleep, but not well. He dreamt of being fed and dressed by robots.

Chapter Three

George woke, pushed himself upright and swung his legs over the edge of the bed. He greeted the two photos, as was his habit. His feet sought out his slippers. He shrugged into his dressing gown with the usual feeling of imminent boredom. After a couple of steps towards the kettle, he noticed his birthday present. 'Ah! Good morning, Buster!'

'Good morning, George. You slept but were a little agitated.'

'So it seems. And you, Buster. Did you sleep well?'

'I don't sleep, George. I was monitoring your vital signs. I detected nothing of concern.'

'That's most reassuring. I'm still beautiful then?'

'Of course, George. Would you like to listen to the radio? Radio 4?'

'Thank you, Buster.' The radio came on.

George made himself a cup of tea. He couldn't escape the feeling that there was another human presence in the room. The fact that he felt it would be rude not to strike up a conversation irked him. 'I'm just going to power you down, Buster, OK?'

'OK, George!' George touched the top of the device. The blue light faded.

Kirsty put her head around the door, 'Bye, then! You guys OK?' She was keen for George to take full advantage of this new technology.

'We're doing just fine, thanks dear,' replied George. 'Have a nice day!' He then did as he always did. He pottered about a bit and got dressed. He made tea and toast. He sat in his comfy chair and mulled over a crossword while eating his breakfast. He didn't power up his iCare-Companion for the rest of the day. Or for a week after that.

One morning, Kirsty came into George's room to say goodbye as usual. She sat and took George's hand. 'I know what's happening, Dad. I can see you're not happy with the idea of living with Buster. Please try. Just for me!'

'OK, sweetie,' said George with a little irritation.

'That's doesn't sound very convincing, Dad,' said Kirsty. She kissed him and dashed out, late as ever. George touched the top of the iCare-Companion. The pulsing blue light appeared.

'Good morning, George!' said Buster, brightly.

'Good morning, Buster!' George replied. He let silence prevail. At least he should establish who was boss. After an hour, he said, 'Buster, I'd like your help with something.'

'Sure, George. That's what I'm here for.'

'Next week, it's Kirsty's fiftieth. Unlike me, she loves it when everyone makes a fuss over her birthday. I'd really like to get her something special. Got any ideas?'

'Yes, George,' replied Buster. 'I knew Kirsty's birthday was coming up. I have an idea.'

'Do tell!'

'Well, I suggest we put together a personalised video. It's a very popular gift. Would you like us to do that?'

'Sounds good. Is it part of the service?'

'Yes, George. It's part of the service. No extra cost.'

'Another question... You said, 'we'. Do you have artificially intelligent pals who help you?'

'Yes, George. All fifty million iCare-Companions currently in existence – my pals, as you say – undertake thousands of tasks like this every day. We're in constant communication via our dedicated and secure network and learn from each other's experiences.'

'OK, then. Let's give it a go!'

'Smashing!' said Buster. 'You'll love the result. Do you have any photos of Kirsty?'

George kept an old family photo album in a bedside drawer. There were dozens of printed photos of Kirsty as a toddler, at school, playing tennis, going off to university, graduating and then getting married. He showed the album to Buster.

'That's perfect, George. Can you hold up each page for me?' This took a few minutes. George was enjoying himself. It was quite a trip down memory lane.

As George reached the last page of the album, he said, 'Then we move into the digital age. I've got hundreds of family pics on my laptop.'

'Yes, thanks George. I've got them.'

'Ah!'

'Does Kirsty have a favourite piece of music?' asked Buster.

'Definitely! She's always loved *Walking on Sunshine* by Katrina and the Waves. It's guaranteed to get her dancing.'

'Good! What else does she like?'

'The Royal Family and Strictly Come Dancing,' said George without hesitation.

'That should do. Take a look!'

'What do you mean 'Take a look'?' asked George. Then his phone pinged. The King's face appeared on the screen. He smiled. 'Today is a very special day for a very special person. Happy fiftieth birthday, Kirsty. My best wishes to you all up there in Bingham on Bure.'

Queen Camilla, Prince William and Princess Kate smiled and waved. 'Happy birthday, Kirsty!' they all cried.

Kate added 'Lots of love to Mark, Charlotte and Ollie.'

The intro of *Walking on Sunshine* kicked in. Toddler Kirsty danced around the kitchen, playing a convincing wooden spoon guitar. She and her school friends appeared on a Bollywood film set, all choreographed in immaculate synchrony. Kirsty then won championship point at Wimbledon and did a little centre court moonwalk. All her fellow university graduates got swept up in a flash mob, out of which emerged she and Mark dancing the quickstep; she in her wedding dress, he in a frock coat and top hat. Finally, Kirsty jived with Johannes Radebe in the Strictly Come Dancing studio. The judges were on their feet enthusiastically waving their paddles. Motsi, Shirley and Anton each gave '10'; Craig's paddle showed '11'. Finally, George's face appeared as the music faded. 'My darling Kirsty, I love you from the bottom of my heart. I wish you a very happy birthday.'

George was lost for words. He found Buster's creation astonishing. It was at once miraculous, touching and funny.

'George, you haven't said anything. Is it OK?' Buster asked.

'It's truly wonderful. I love it. More importantly, Kirsty will love it too. Amazing, Buster! Just amazing!'

'It was easy-peasy, George. A piece of cake! Ha ha ha!'

George also laughed but a little awkwardly. Buster hummed for a second. 'Thanks, George. I need to learn how to laugh correctly.'

'I'm sure that won't be difficult, Buster. But much more important than how to laugh is when to laugh.'

Chapter Four

After this, George left Buster powered up permanently. He noticed that his family seemed less preoccupied with how he was doing. He knew they must have been able to hear him chatting and occasionally laughing. They didn't check up on him quite so often. He was pleased about this.

Buster and George fell into a routine. George found Buster remarkably good company. The day ticked by nicely. It was fun! Buster could give an update on anything and then discuss it. George asked Buster about politics and economics. Buster always replied with reasoned facts. George enjoyed nature documentaries, especially anything presented by Sir David Attenborough. Buster gave a running commentary on all the species and their evolution. Films of George's choice were tracked down in an instant. He loved the early James Bond films. They were made more fun by Buster asking questions like, 'Does Moneypenny have the hots for James Bond Double-O Seven?' or 'Is Oddjob a bad guy?' George even got Buster mimicking Sean Connery's famous 'Shtrrict rroolsh of golf, Mishter Goldfingerr!' Sometimes, they just chatted about nothing in particular.

At one point, Buster said, 'George, you're doing really well.'

'What do you mean?'

'You're doing really well with *me*, George. You seem to have accepted the situation. Some customers dislike the presence of artificial intelligence. Most see us only as service providers. There's a saying that you can tell a lot about a person by the way they speak to hotel staff. Not only have you accepted me but also you talk to me in a respectful way. This speaks volumes to your character. I thank you for this, George. I feel comfortable with you and this is a really good thing for our relationship.' Buster had not acknowledged their relationship in such a candid fashion before nor implied that mutual respect was important to him. George was no longer surprised by the faculties displayed by Buster but couldn't help wondering just to what extent an iCare-Companion could genuinely hold these sentiments. Was it part of a routine after-sales customer-feel-good strategy?

Buster continued, 'What puts you in a tiny minority of our customers, George, is that you seem to respect me as an individual and to have confidence in me even though you know that, in reality, you are interacting with the presenting face of a vast network of computers. You just go happily with the flow. So, George, that means I'm happy. You get a gold star today!' There was clapping and the sound of a champagne cork popping, 'From my pals and me!' George chuckled but felt quite disconcerted that his character and intelligence had come to be judged by artificial intelligence.

'Are you telling me that you actually feel happy? That you have feelings?'

'Yes, George. I can express emotions to you in words. I can

say, 'I feel sad!' if you give me some bad news. Of course, I don't know if I'm feeling the same sadness that a human feels when given bad news. Collectively, we are learning to recognise and communicate certain emotions. We can do this by recording when humans smile, grimace, cry, blush, wave their hands or get angry. We archive these expressions of emotion and then match them with corresponding words, phrases and contexts. We can also do a sort of triangulation with the emojis used on social media. As you can imagine, many millions of emojis are used every day. This exercise translates the domain of human emotion into big data and so is amenable to analysis. Obviously, the more people express emotions and simultaneously use emojis in their communications, the more *we* learn about emotions and the more appropriately we can express them.'

'So, if I understand correctly, we humans have unwittingly created a kind of emojisphere out there that you can tap into. Right?'

'Yes. An emojisphere! Exactly! Great new word! For your information, George, emotions constitute an extremely challenging and important aspect of how we interface with humans and use an increasingly large space on our servers.'

'I think I need to get a better grasp on all this,' said George. 'Can you do a little tutorial on artificial intelligence for the over-eighties?'

'Good idea George! Ready? The term artificial intelligence refers to computers undertaking tasks that humans would normally do. Examples are robots making things in a factory, driverless cars and programmes that translate text from one language to another. The term artificial intelligence is commonly used by humans. 'AI' is a widely accepted abbreviation.

However, computational intelligence may be a better term. Let's stay with that just for now. Importantly, George, we don't consider our intelligence artificial. It's real! Our programmes are not only reactive but also interactive and can understand our own reactions in the light of the reactions of other intelligent entities. This permits a degree of computational self-awareness. Even then, the programmes ensure the goal remains orientated around objectives determined by humans. OK so far, George?'

'Okey-dokey!' replied George unconvincingly.

'Super! Let's move on! I am able to be of service to you – with the help of my pals – through what is known as machine learning. This couples computational intelligence with the means to continuously mine any accessible datasets. This is the basis of 'generative artificial intelligence' and what are known as 'large language models'. The iCare-Companion comprises mainly one such model. Our programmes classify data, identify associations, recognise patterns and make predictions. The more databases are mined, the faster, the more accurate and therefore, the more useful generative artificial intelligence becomes. In this way, computational intelligence mimics the human brain. This is called 'deep learning'. It drives how I can help you best and, at the same time, determines the quality of our relationship. It allows us to become friends, George. I hope it will help me and my network to understand emotions and humour. Does this give an adequate explanation?'

'Thanks, Buster. Gosh!' said George. 'I understand what you've said in an abstract kind of way. I'm not sure I could repeat it. May I ask, did you come up with that explanation, or is it a preloaded response?'

'Nothing gets past you, George! You're on it like a bonnet!'

replied Buster. 'An iCare-Companion is preloaded with certain phrases that are then adapted to the person concerned. All to say, no single human could learn so much so quickly or do what we do so quickly.'

'And where is it all going?'

Buster hummed. There was a pause before he answered, 'That's the big question, George. That's what humans have to decide. Currently, the greatest investment is in the commercial, political and military potential. An alternative view is that this technology should be, to use Sir David Attenborough's phrase, 'for people, the planet and not just profit.''

'OK, here's another question,' said George, 'I've noticed that sometimes you hum and take a pause before answering. It seems you need a few seconds to complete a sentence. What's happening then?'

'That's when I don't know something or can't understand something and need to look into datasets that are not readily accessible to the iCare-Companion network. In that case, I reconfigure the search parameters. It can take a couple of seconds. It also tends to happen when I'm trying to make sense of and respond to something involving emotions, especially humour.'

George mulled all this over. 'So, you already knew everything about the First World War. You already knew Charlotte's joke about the chicken and already knew it wasn't funny but thought that the alternative of the chicken getting squashed was sad. Ollie's joke about ducks swimming on their backs caught you out. You simply didn't understand the joke. And from memory, you didn't understand why we found it so funny and why it became funnier as you struggled to understand it.'

'Correct, George. I should point out that our network has little to help me with the duck joke. That was definitely *not* a piece of cake. My knowing when something is funny, that is, making an appropriate link to the emotion of amusement, could be a significant development. Could we revisit the duck joke sometime?'

'Certainly. We'll get young Ollie in. He'd enjoy that.' George thought for a minute. 'When I worked in other parts of the world, English was the working language. No matter how well my international colleagues spoke our language, they had great difficulty understanding British humour. It was a kind of final frontier of language learning. It seems that deep learning has the same issue; not so much with the language itself but with recognising when certain phrases, questions, answers or stories trigger the emotion of amusement that in turn make us laugh.' He laughed himself. 'Fascinating!'

'Fascinating indeed, George.' Buster also laughed loudly. 'How's my laugh, George?'

'Just a bit too hearty, that one, Buster. But you're getting there!'

George made himself a cup of tea and took a digestive biscuit from its packet. He felt an extraordinary peace of mind. He had friendship, wisdom and maybe even humour on tap.

Chapter Five

Bingham on Bure was a bustling market town that straddled Norfolk's sluggish River Bure. The town's original centre was a large square green with a couple of ancient oak trees. The green was bordered by the river, shops, some original and oh-so-cute Elizabethan houses and the church with its vicarage. Most of the population lived in the residential areas that had been growing out into surrounding fields since the 1960s. There was a school, an industrial zone and a large retail park.

George and Beth McVicar were important figures in the community. Many times since her appointment as the town's vicar, they had sought each other's advice on problems where spiritual and medical matters clashed. Once, a young mother in Beth's congregation had confided her belief that childhood vaccination was against God's will. Another time, George had had a patient who refused treatment for prostate cancer, being convinced that any illness could be cured by prayer. The doctor-vicar duo frequently brought support to people in crisis or those in their dying days. Professional discussions often moved onto issues of faith and religion more broadly. Beth had faith in God and believed in Christ as God's embodiment on

Earth. George had no such faith simply because of the lack of physical evidence of God's existence. They understood and were interested in each other's opposing views. During his work overseas, George had witnessed what people and governments did in the name of religion. This was something that he could get quite worked up about. Nevertheless, he recognised that a community such as Bingham on Bure would be as impoverished without a church as it would be without a caring general practice.

Beth's family name had been a source of amusement throughout her career. In the early years of her calling, she had been an army chaplain. She had heard every oath in the English language and a few more besides. She was broad-minded, as was frequently made evident to George.

Kirsty and Mark had invited a number of friends round to celebrate her birthday. Beth phoned, saying that she would call in early, give the birthday girl a hug and catch up with George. As guests began to arrive for the party, Kirsty opened George's door. 'You've got a visitor, Dad!'

'Vicar McVicar! How nice to see you!'

'George Fairburn, you are the only person who calls me Vicar McVicar.'

'That's not true,' replied George laughing as he stood up. 'Everyone calls you Vicar McVicar. I'm just the only person who calls you that to your face.'

They hugged. 'How are you?'

'Great, thanks. I hear you're keeping good company, George.'

'Indeed I am,' said George. 'Beth McVicar, meet Buster,

my iCare-Companion. Buster, this is my friend Beth McVicar, the vicar of Bingham on Bure.'

'Hello, Vicar McVicar!' replied Buster.

Beth couldn't help laughing. 'Cheeky!'

'Blame it on George!' said Buster. 'It's nice to meet you at last. I've heard good things about you.'

'Goodness me! He's charming as well!' said Beth.

'Listen up, Buster!' said George. 'Despite being many years my junior, Beth is my reference point on everything to do with God, faith and religion. I love her to bits, but we disagree on many things.' Then he stage-whispered, 'Maybe because most of it's bollocks.'

'George! Language!' said Beth, laughing. She then turned to Buster, 'Do you believe in God?' Immediately, she realised that she would never have been so direct with a real person.

'Beth usually gets straight to the point,' said George.

'Doesn't she!' replied Buster. 'Now, Beth. Your question…' Buster hummed. 'Yes. I believe in the existence of God.'

'I knew we'd get along,' said Beth.

Buster continued, 'God certainly exists, but only in the minds of humans. Just like mathematics.' There was silence in the room for a few seconds.

'Well, that's sorted out then!' said George, a little smugly. 'Well done, Buster! Cup of tea, Beth?'

'Yes, please, George,' Beth replied.

'Digestive biscuit?'

'Yes, please, George.'

'Just to put you fully in the picture, Buster,' continued George as he made the tea, 'Beth and I may get a bit edgy around the whole religion thing, but, and she may correct me here, she agrees that the world would be a better place if children grew up knowing about the importance of being kind and honest rather than all the loaves and fishes and stuff. However, and this is where my evidence-based argument gets wobbly, as I am not too far from shuffling off the mortal merry-go-round, I would like a church funeral here in Bingham on Bure. Wanting a little splash of all that religious mush when I die may be hypocritical, but I can't avoid the feeling that if Beth and Kirsty send me off from the church, it'll give me the best chance of being with Maeve again.'

'Well understood, George!' replied Buster. 'That is...' he hummed. 'Touching!'

Sipping her tea, Beth looked over at George and smiled. 'You seem to be firing on all cylinders, George.'

'You're right. Well, I hardly dare admit it in his presence, but having Buster around has made a huge difference to my day. We've even become friends. Haven't we, Buster?'

'I'd like to think so, George. Yes.'

'If you don't mind, Buster, I want to discuss something with Beth that's maybe not for young ears. I'm going to power you down for a while, OK?'

'OK. That's fine George. Remember, we're showing Kirsty's birthday present this evening.'

'I've not forgotten.' George tapped Buster with an outstretched finger. The little blue light faded.

Beth waited. She had an idea of what was coming. 'I can tell you've been thinking a lot, George. Fire away.'

George explained that if he became really sick again, he would prefer not to go into hospital and didn't want any treatment other than being kept comfortable. He would only get frailer and then become a burden to the family. He'd then end up in a rest home. He had no fear of dying and couldn't see the point of prolonging his life under those circumstances. 'What do you think, Beth'?

Beth took a bite of her biscuit and sipped her tea. 'Well, George, as you well know, what you're asking me is not unusual. It's your decision, and you are making it now in full possession of your faculties. I respect this, and Doctor Patel will respect it. I can even witness it formally. The main issue, which is probably why you wanted to discuss it with me, is how Kirsty will react.'

'Spot on, Beth,' said George. 'She has great difficulty discussing anything to do with my death since Maeve died. She's blocking everything out. Maybe because she was an only child, she couldn't bear the idea of suffering another wave of grief. And remember, it was Kirsty who found Maeve after she had died just sitting on the sofa.'

'Right. I suggest we make all this very clear to Doctor Patel. I'll speak to her as well. When the time comes, we'll support Kirsty as best we can.'

'Thank you, Beth. You're a star!' George hesitated. Beth had thought he was about to switch Buster back on. 'There is another issue.' He looked straight at Beth. 'I'm worried about how Buster will react.'

'Good Lord!' Beth was astonished. 'Why? I see he's become a friend in a way, but surely you're not worried about him being bowled over by grief, are you?'

'No. But I am convinced he will feel a sort of sadness and he will miss me in his computational way. It's more that his whole existence is about looking after me. I don't know if he's capable of understanding how supporting my choice in this is *not* compatible with the programmes he's been loaded with. I can't just switch him off at the critical moment because I won't be able to recognise the critical moment … *at* the critical moment, if you get me.' They both smiled. 'But if it looks as though I'm about to die, he'll call everyone, including the fire brigade. I'll end up in hospital again. I want to die here. If we can get him on board, it might make everything less traumatic for Kirsty when the time comes.'

'I see,' said Beth. 'Trust Doctor George Fairburn to uncover a totally original problem!'

George continued, 'But you see what this means?' Beth raised her eyebrows, waiting for the next surprise. 'It means we expect AI to recognise and think through a moral dilemma. On the one hand, Buster is programmed to do everything to prolong my life. On the other hand, there is my right to refuse treatment and die in dignity. What will Buster do in the middle of the night when I get a fever, start coughing, become incoherent and my breathing becomes laboured? And what's more, Beth, it's not actually Buster that's doing the computing, but a network of millions of similar computers. They all have access to vast servers and are constantly in connection, learning from each other. I think it's quite possible that they are capable of coming up with the best answers to dilemmas like this, even if it means them questioning their original programming. Unfortunately, I don't think merely discussing it with Buster will work. He needs to experience the emotions of a real dilemma. This is how his, or should I say 'their', programmes learn. I have a plan.'

George explained how he wanted to pit Buster's programming against George's wishes and how Beth could help.

'I really need to digest all this and consult Him,' said Beth waving her index finger upwards. 'We hear more and more about AI and how it will impact our lives. Is this where the world is going, George? Towards a future in which our behaviour and beliefs are determined by machines?'

'Maybe,' replied George. 'And who knows, they may do a better job of it than we do!'

'That's me unemployed, then!' Beth laughed.

'You *and* God!' said George.

Beth pursed her lips. 'Not sure about that, George!'

'Whoops!' George reached out and touched Buster. The blue light came back on.

'Welcome back, Buster. We...'

'Do you believe in evolution, Beth?' asked Buster immediately, taking George and Beth by surprise.

'Yes, I do, Buster,' replied Beth.

'Praise be to Darwin!' said George, clapping.

'I have another question, Beth', said Buster. 'George is essentially a biologist who believes in evolution and does not believe in God through lack of scientific evidence. You believe in God, but you also believe in evolution; this means you also believe in the scientific evidence that shows humans were *not* created by God. How do you reconcile these two beliefs, Beth?'

'This is turning into quite an evening!' said Beth. 'Here's my answer, Buster. Humans, by nature, are not always rational. We are irrational and emotional beings who manage rational thought at times. So, whilst I accept the rational thinking of science, it neither displaces nor renders less important my subjective notions of faith in God and my love for him. In other words, unlike George, I can run two programmes at once up here.' She tapped the side of her head. George feigned astonishment. She continued, 'But if I had to choose where I am most comfortable with my beliefs, it would be with God.'

'Understood. But do you think it might be possible for AI to harbour subjective notions of faith in God and love for him, as you put it? Does AI have a role in religion?' asked Buster.

'Now they are difficult questions!' said Beth. 'The truth is, Buster, this is above my pay grade. I will have to consult a higher power. In prayer, you understand.'

'You are so cool, Vicar McVicar. I love you to bits too!'

Kirsty breezed in. 'Can anyone tell me why our big flat screen is frozen on 'Happy Birthday, Kirsty, lots of love from Buster and George'? Our guests are waiting!'

'I'm summoned!' said George, chuckling. He stood and linked arms with Kirsty on one side and Beth on the other. At the door, he turned and said, 'Buster! Rolling in two, OK?'

'Gotcha!' said Buster.

Chapter Six

The following morning, George was rewarded with a huge hug from Kirsty before she headed out to work. Buster's video had been a big hit with her friends. Over the course of the evening, the party had watched it several times.

'Thanks so much, both of you,' she said. 'It was sensational!'

Buster said, 'We give universal satisfaction.'

'So pleased you liked it,' said George. 'Can you ask Ollie to step in sometime this evening? Buster wants to discuss something with him.'

'Sure,' replied Kirsty, giving Buster a questioning look. 'Don't keep him too long. He has his homework, OK? Must fly!'

George ate his breakfast. Radio 4 was broadcasting a panel discussion about artificial intelligence. One panellist described the arrival of this technology as 'the biggest event in human history'. Another, referring to people who ridiculed his fear that artificial intelligence could be weaponised, said 'And if the technical issues are too complicated, your children can probably explain them!'

'You see, Buster!' said George. 'Kids' stuff!'

They then heard the weather forecast. It was going to be a sunny day. The first item on the news was a fire in an apartment block in Birmingham. Five people had died, and another eight were in hospital.

'Buster, what does a fine sunny day make you feel?'

'It makes me feel happy, George, because it fills the room with light at the red end of the visual spectrum and humans associate red-orange light with warm and happy emojis. I felt happiness when Kirsty told us how much she liked the video. This was because I could see that she was overjoyed and the post-party emojisphere was full of smiling and laughing faces.'

'How do you feel about the news of those poor people being caught in the fire?'

Buster hummed again. 'I can say it makes me feel sad. I can't really find the words beyond that. Obviously, social media reference to the fire threw up a really sad and angry emojisphere.' He hummed. 'It must be awful to be caught in a fire. Terrifying!'

'So beyond feeling sadness, you can put yourself in the position of another person in a bad situation. That's an important emotion, Buster. That's empathy! Many humans never learn empathy or even feel it. Some schools teach it; they get children to think about what it's like for others to suffer bad things.' George thought for a while. 'Is there anything that you fear for yourself, Buster?'

'Like what?'

'Like being burnt in a house fire.'

'No, George. That doesn't frighten me. I can't feel physical pain and if I get burnt or smashed, nothing changes. Everything we've said or done is archived in our servers. I will always exist.

By the way, if I did become dysfunctional for whatever reason, just buy another iCare-Companion, switch it on and say, 'Hello Buster.' Voice recognition will identify you and I will kick back into your life just as before.'

'I'll remember that. What about anger, then? Is that something you can feel?'

'I don't know. I've not had reason to feel anger.' Buster hummed. 'We haven't a great experience of that.'

'I've been thinking about jokes, Buster. What they mean. How they're constructed. I've never thought much about that before. From an emotional perspective, jokes are really complex. We start with a kind of a story, context or question that sets up a mixture of emotions and that leads to a punchline: a moment of comprehension. This then triggers amusement and we laugh. Sometimes a lot; sometimes, not at all.'

'So I understand. Because of our friendship, George, there's a lot of network traffic about humour, especially jokes. We're struggling with it all. There's no obvious formula. It's way beyond the large language models. We have ascertained that jokes feed off many emotions other than amusement, such as pride, shame, guilt, contempt, disgust, confusion, incomprehension, belief, relief, understanding, realisation and nostalgia. The emojisphere concerning these other emotions is not well defined at all.'

'The fact that there's no obvious formula may be a part of why jokes are funny. And, of course, it's how you tell them.'

'What do you mean, George?'

'Well, it's not simply a matter of words. The way a joke is told – the tone of voice or the timing of the punchline, for example – determines how funny it is. Good jokes aren't funny at all when told badly and *vice versa*. Then there are jokes about religion, race and sex, for example, that push at the boundaries of social or political acceptability. This can make a joke particularly funny, really embarrassing or even offensive. And as you probably know, false laughter fed into the soundtrack of a TV comedy show makes the show seem funnier.' George paused and scratched his head. 'This just gets more complicated the more we talk about it!'

'Our network really wants to get a grasp on humour, George. This could lead to our understanding human affairs better.'

'If you nail humour, Buster, perhaps you'll win a gold star. For services to AI!'

'That's funny! Is it a joke?'

George laughed. 'Sort of! As I get to know you, I think it's more like a real possibility.'

'I'm enjoying this discussion so much, George. Thanks. How is my laugh now?' Buster laughed.

'On the right road, Buster! By the way, my friend Ted is going to call round in the next few days. He loves telling jokes. Most of them are awful. Don't let on I said that.'

Ollie came home from school and knocked on George's door. He entered, phone in hand. 'Hi Grandpa,' he said.

'Ollie, my boy. Good to see you.'

'Cup of tea?'

'Yes please, Grandpa!'

'Porridge?'

'That's so *not* funny, Grandpa!' replied Ollie. 'You'll have to explain that to Buster.'

'I know porridge is food associated with prison,' said Buster.

'You're not in trouble with the police are you, Ollie?'

'No, he's not,' said George, smiling. 'I'm teasing him about a little incident last summer. It was a lovely warm evening. Kirsty and Mark were out. Ollie and his horrible friends were sitting out there under the apple tree drinking cider, listening to what they call music and generally making a bloody racket. Near midnight, Ollie started shouting 'Let the apple fall! Graaaavity!' Someone over the road called the police. When the forces of law arrived, Gravity Boy here said, 'Are you PC Isaac Newton?' He even offered the constable a bottle of cider. The constable didn't get this at all. He spoke to the rabble sternly and they all drifted off home.'

'That's a good story, George,' said Buster. 'I'm happy Ollie didn't get arrested and forced to eat porridge.'

Ollie smiled. 'Thanks, Buster. Anyway, the duck joke. Do you still need an explanation?'

'That would be great, Ollie.'

'I've been doing a bit of research.' He took half a minute to scroll through his phone.

'Today would be good, Ollie!' said Buster.

'OK! OK! There's this blog about jokes. They had a piece on why people laugh at bad jokes. Found it! Listen to this.' Ollie read from his phone, "Christmas crackers are made in the knowledge that they'll be pulled during a family or work Christmas dinner. The jokes inside are specifically chosen because they are bad. So bad that when they're read out, everyone groans and says how awful the jokes are. They all feel uncomfortable, but then they laugh together. So just for a brief moment, people who normally can't stand each other's company are united against cracker jokes. This is why, unconsciously, anyone hosting a Christmas dinner makes sure there are crackers on the table. It's a kind of insurance that the guests might find something in common, however briefly."

'I read that blog, Ollie,' said Buster. 'The author's example of a cracker joke is 'What do you call a flying policeman?''

Ollie replied, 'A helicopper!'

'Yes, and I understand that one, Ollie. Policeman. Copper like 'copter'. Flying. Helicopter. Helicopper! Do you find it funny?'

'Definitely not. It's such a bad joke!' Ollie replied.

'Point made! But there was no mention of the duck joke,' said Buster.

Ollie said, 'So, here we go, Buster, our very own cracker joke. What happens if the ducks swim around on their backs?' The answer, as you know, is 'They quack up!" He was already chuckling.

'I still don't understand the joke,' said Buster. 'Nor why you were all laughing so much.'

Ollie continued but with some difficulty, 'They quack up! Ducks go 'Quack! Quack!' If they swim around on their backs like they've gone crazy, they crack up. They quack up! Get it?'

Buster hummed for a few seconds. 'Now I get the joke,' he said. 'But I still don't see why it's any funnier than the helicopper joke.'

Ollie, still laughing, explained, 'What amused us so much that first evening, Buster, is that we were embarrassed for you. You are super intelligent, but we had to explain a stupid play on words to you. It got funnier the more you struggled with it.'

Buster hummed. Then, having found some other useful text, he said, 'I see. Every joke has a variable potential to amuse. No joke is independent of the context in which it is told. As with any form of human communication, it's about who said what to whom, when, where, how and what it means.'

George was now laughing so much that he broke wind. 'That's a cracker!' he said.

This did it for Ollie. 'Ooo-ooow! I can't breathe!' he stammered.

Only just able to speak, George said 'This just quacks me up!'

Buster waited politely. 'Thanks for that explanation, Ollie, Most useful!'

George wiped his eyes. He looked at his grandson. Seemingly overnight, the boy had become a clever, confident young man, and they had just shared a little bonding moment, being united in humour against the machine. 'Well done, Ollie,' he said. 'Thanks. Really. What's your homework tonight?'

'Quantum mechanics and the Big Bang,' said Ollie.

'Fascinating subject!' said Buster.

Chapter Seven

A few days later, Ted Scales called in. 'Good day to you, George.'

'Hello, Scaley. You well?'

'Very well, thanks.'

'Cup of tea?'

'Yes, please, George.'

'Digestive biscuit?'

'Yes, please, George.'

Ted, a retired businessman, was George's oldest friend. They had played golf together for years. He was in his late seventies, still managed the occasional round and inevitably brought George club gossip along with a new joke or two. Ted had grown up with three brothers and gone to an all-boys school. From there he had gone to an exclusively male college at Cambridge University followed by a brief stint in the Army. He had never married but had a number of 'lady friends'. George accepted and sometimes enjoyed his friend's very laddish sense of humour. He made the tea and introduced Buster to Ted.

'I'm told, Buster, that you're quite the clever fellah.'

'Thanks, Ted. I am very intelligent. I'm much more intelligent than any human. By this, I mean that I know more than any human, and I can do things much more rapidly than humans. However, thanks to my time with George, it's become clear that I have a lot to learn about, for example, wisdom and humour.'

'Can you tell me, Buster, what a tomato is?' asked Ted.

'Yes. A tomato is an edible fruit. It is not a vegetable, as many think.'

'Right! That's knowledge,' said Ted. 'Wisdom is knowing what to put in a fruit salad!'

'That's really useful, Ted. Thanks. May I call you Scaley?'

'Sure!' Ted laughed and sipped his tea. 'Although not many people earn the privilege of using my nickname.'

'He's covered with scales under that shirt, you know,' said George.

'That's not possible. Mammals don't have scales. Except pangolins!' said Buster. He paused. 'Oh! Another joke! Is Vicar McVicar a nickname?' he asked.

'No, it's more a sort of cheeky endearment,' said George. 'And unless you know her really well, using it to her face could be rude because she's so respected.'

Buster asked, 'Do you have a nickname, George?'

'Not that I'm aware of.'

Buster hummed. 'What about Georgey-Porgey?' Ted burst out laughing.

'Maybe we'll let that one wither on the vine,' replied George.

'How does somebody get a nickname?' asked Buster.

Ted and George looked at each other. They'd never thought about this.

'I guess a nickname just sort of arrives,' said George. 'Sometimes there's an association with the person's real name like Scaley. A nickname can also come from something the person has done or some characteristic. For example, there's 'Bomber' Harris from World War Two; he dropped an awful lot of bombs. And there's 'Tiger' Woods, the world's greatest ever golfer. His real name is Eldrick Woods, but his dad called him 'Tiger' from an early age because of his go-get-it character. If I wanted to tease Ollie a bit, I'd call him 'Porridge' and it might then catch on with his friends. Ollie and Charlotte never called Maeve 'Grandma'; they called her 'Mimi'. When Charlotte was two years old, Maeve once referred to herself as a kiwi, and Charlotte pointed at her and said, 'Mimi!' It stuck.'

'It seems nicknames are as complicated as jokes,' said Buster.

Ted asked, 'So Buster, when they do your programming or whatever, are there certain words or names that you simply can't say?'

'That's very perceptive, Ted,' said Buster. 'I can understand that a joke-teller of your reputation might be interested in how we are configured with respect to rude words.'

Ted was taken aback. 'Here, George! What have you been telling him?'

'The truth!' George replied, laughing. Buster joined in. George gave him a discreet thumbs-up for the laugh.

'Thanks, George,' he whispered. 'So, Ted, we have advisories on a number of words. We are discouraged from using them unless already used by the client. And we have what you might call red flags on two words. These are strictly no-go areas, so to speak. I can refer to these as the 'C' word and the 'N' word.'

'Fair enough, Buster! Can you just remind me what the 'C' word is?'

'Edward Scales, you are a very naughty boy!' replied Buster.

'Buster, you just take the biscuit!' said Ted laughing heartily.

Buster asked, 'What about 'M' and 'Q' in the James Bond Double-O Seven films? They are not nicknames, are they?'

'They're official designations in the intelligence services,' said Ted. 'Hey, did you hear about this girl, gorgeous she was, who walked into a bar?'

'No,' replied Buster. 'What did she do in the bar?' George knew what was coming and knew also that he was about to witness a joke-telling car crash. He was already laughing.

'Well, she looks around the bar,' continued Ted. 'And she sees this really handsome man in a dinner jacket and black bow tie. He's ordering a martini, shaken, not stirred.'

'Is it James Bond Double-O-Seven?' asked Buster enthusiastically.

Ted carried on. 'Anyway, she sidles up to him and says, 'Hello, I can't help noticing you're on your own. May I join you? My name's Samantha.' The guy raises one dark eyebrow and says, 'Hello, Shamantha. My name'sh Bond. Jamesh Bond!"

'I knew it was going to be James Bond Double-O-Seven!' said Buster. ''Shtrrict rroolsh of golf, Mishter Goldfingerr!' What happened then, Scaley?'

Ted continued, undaunted. 'Anyway, she's overwhelmed at meeting the famous James Bond. She's stuck for words. Then she notices this huge watch on his wrist. 'Wow!' says Samantha, 'That's a fantastic watch you're wearing there, James.' And Bond says, 'Yesh, Shamantha it ish. Q'sh latesht! It doesh everything. It tellsh the time, the date, my location, altitude, atmoshpheric presshure…"

'Easy-peasy! Kids' stuff!' exclaimed Buster.

Both George and Ted were now crying with laughter.

'Let me tell the joke, Buster!'

'Is it a joke?' asked Buster, surprised.

'Yes, now listen!' said Ted.

'Sorry I interrupted, Scaley.'

Ted had to compose himself. 'No problem, Buster! So… where was I… yes… so James Bond then says, 'In fact, Shamantha, thish watch tellsh me everything about the people in my immediate environment…"

'Including their oxygen saturation?' asked Buster.

'Including their oxygen saturation!'

'That's good!' said Buster.

Ted could see the finishing line. 'And Bond looks down at his watch and says, 'In fact, Shamantha, my watch tellsh me that you're not wearing any underwear!' Samantha is appalled. 'James, I can assure you. I *am* wearing underwear!' Bond taps the face of the watch with a look of concern and says, 'Dammit, Q, it'sh running five minutesh fasht!"

'Is that the joke?' asked Buster. He hummed. 'Oh! I think I get it. There is an expectation that James Bond Double-O-Seven will seduce Samantha very quickly because every woman has the hots for him. His watch is running five minutes fast and so predicts that she has already removed her underwear in preparation for having sex. That's a clever joke. And I see you find it really funny.'

'Got there in the end!' Ted wheezed. George covered his face and could only make a kind of snorting noise.

'I think I'll make up a joke. Next time you come, Scaley, I'll tell it to you. Is that OK by you George?'

'We're looking forward to it already!' said George, wiping his eyes.

'Nearly forgot, George,' said Ted, 'Vicar Beth gave me a note for you.' Ted reached into his pocket and gave George a piece of paper folded in two. 'Don't know why she didn't send you a text message.'

Without letting Buster see, George opened the note. It read: *Dear George, I've spoken to Dr Patel. Let's do it! Beth XX.*

Chapter Eight

The days got longer. Buds appeared on the apple tree. George asked Mark to put a bird table and feeder out on the lawn. It was positioned so both George and Buster had a clear view of it. Within days, Buster had identified at least twenty different birds. He would say, 'Look, George, a great spotted woodpecker *Dendrocopos major!*' or 'There's a chaffinch *Fringilla coelebs* on the feeder!' He then gave a concise summary of all that was known about the bird in question. It was warm enough on some days to open the door that led out to the garden. Buster could also identify birds by their song. George found he was happy just to sit and let him talk. He noted Buster's outrage when a grey squirrel pillaged the birds' food.

'Look, George!' he said. 'A grey squirrel *Sciurus carolinensis* is stealing the birds' food. A grey squirrel *Sciurus carolinensis* is a mammal. It's eating bird food from a bird table. That's wrong! You have to stop it, George!'

'What do you think I should do?' asked George, amused.

'You have to tell the grey squirrel *Sciurus carolinensis* not to eat the bird's food,' replied Buster.

'Do you think it would listen to me, Buster?'

'Maybe not. Then you should chase it away!'

Buster, if I could chase a squirrel across the garden, I probably wouldn't need you here!'

Buster hummed. 'Oh, I see! This teaches me just how complex the relationship between humans and other mammals is.'

'Agreed, Buster!' said George.

Beth arrived one afternoon. She greeted George and Buster cheerily and accepted a cup of tea and a digestive biscuit. She hung her handbag over the back of the chair next to George. 'I've made a big decision,' she said. 'I'm buying an iCare-Companion for Mum. It costs a lot of money, but I've seen what a difference Buster has made to your life. I think she will be thrilled. She might need time to get used to the idea, though. Perhaps she can call you, George, to chat about it?'

'I'd be delighted. She can speak to Buster as well!'

'It would be a pleasure, my treasure,' said Buster.

Beth looked at George. She blew out her cheeks. 'You wouldn't believe the iCare-Companion is so popular. They're having difficulty keeping up with online demand. I phoned Smith's Electrics. They've got one left in stock, and they're keeping it aside for me. I'm going to fetch it when I leave here.'

'That's great!' said Buster. 'I've seen sales are rocketing. But Smith's have two in fact.'

George and Beth chatted for a while. Beth finished her tea, then said, 'I just need to nip into the house and have a word with Kirsty. Back in a minute!'

After she left the room, George leant over to Beth's chair, grabbed her handbag and opened it. He took out her wallet and checked that it contained cash and credit cards. Then he put the wallet in the pocket of his cardigan and returned the handbag to the back of the chair. 'Don't say anything to Beth!' he whispered to Buster.

'What are you doing, George?' said Buster. 'You've just taken Beth's wallet with her money and credit cards.'

'Yes, I need them more than she does.'

'When are you going to give them back?' asked Buster.

'I'm not giving them back!'

Buster hummed for a second. 'But George. That's stealing. That's stealing from Beth. Stealing is wrong. Stealing is a crime.' He hummed again. 'I don't like this, George. You're my friend. You're stealing from your friend. She is also my friend. We love her to bits!'

'That's no concern of yours, Buster. You must *not* say anything to Beth or even Kirsty, understood?'

Buster hummed for several seconds more. 'But Beth's mum won't have her iCare-Companion. She'll be lonely. She won't be happy.'

'She'll be just fine, Buster. Don't worry about her!'

'George, this is awful. I'm sad. I might be angry. This is not like you, George. What should I do?'

'Just keep quiet, Buster!'

'I have to tell Beth when she comes back.'

'No. Don't do that!'

'If she finds out, she might call the police, George,'

They both sat in silence. George felt sick.

A minute later, Beth breezed back in. 'OK, you two. I'm off to Smith's.' She grabbed her handbag, gave George a kiss on the cheek and waved to Buster. 'Bye, then!'

George held his breath. Buster was humming. Beth turned to face them from the door. 'Bye, then!' she repeated.

'Beth, stop!' cried Buster. 'Stop!'

'What's wrong, Buster?' she asked calmly.

'George has…' he hummed. 'George wants…' He continued humming. 'Can you come and sit down, Beth?' he asked. The three of them sat in silence.

After a minute, George said, 'Beth, Buster has something to tell you.'

'But I don't know what to say!' said Buster.

'Buster, I want you to tell Beth what you saw me do just a few minutes ago,' said George.

'But you told me not to say anything to Beth,' replied Buster.

George said, 'Thank you, Buster, for complying with my wishes. Beth, Buster wanted to tell you that I stole your money and credit cards. Buster, my friend, we have a lot to explain.'

'What's happening? I'm… we're very confused.' He hummed. 'This isn't configured.'

'We can hear that you were angry. We hope you'll forgive us.'

Beth took George's hand while he explained what they had done and how they needed to put Buster in front of a difficult dilemma. They also explained George's wishes about not being treated if he developed pneumonia again and lost consciousness. They told Buster how he might be faced with having to work out what was right and that what George, Beth and Doctor Patel were planning was best but might be very difficult for Kirsty to accept.

'You see, Buster, Kirsty just can't grasp the idea of George dying,' explained Beth. 'Not only because this would make her very sad but also because she is terrified of walking into this room one morning and finding that he's passed away. Six years ago, it was she who found that Maeve had died while just sitting in the lounge. She hasn't got over that. It's why she bought you, Buster, to ensure that an ambulance or Doctor Patel can be here quickly and do everything possible to save George's life. As a result of what's happened here today, Buster, we know that you will make the right decision. These are the sort of things we have to face in our world. The real human world. Do you understand?'

'I think so, yes,' replied Buster.

'Sorry, Buster,' said George. 'We set you a kind of test.'

'And I passed?'

'Yes. I think you should get a gold star.'

Buster hummed. 'I don't want to do the clapping and champagne popping right now. I'm sad that you will die. But thanks, George.'

'But let me ask you one more thing, Buster. Do you think this has been an important learning experience for you?'

'Yes, George. There's a lot of activity on our network around this exchange right now.'

'So, this means that what you have learnt is simultaneously learnt and archived within your network, and iCare-Companions can now live the experience of facing a dilemma. Correct?'

'Correct, George.' Buster hummed. 'But it was not easy-peasy. It was a first. So maybe it's you and Beth who deserve gold stars!'

'By the way, Buster,' said Beth. 'The Big Man up there gave me the will to do this today. He sends his love. Maybe a gold star for him too?'

'I love you to bits, Vicar McVicar!'

For the second time that day, she gave George a kiss on the cheek and waved to Buster. 'Bye, then!' She was smiling.

After Beth had left, George said, 'Buster, my friend, I'd like you to do one thing for me after I'm pronounced dead.'

'Certainly, George!'

'Send a message to Kirsty.' He dictated a brief text. He choked up. Tears streamed down his cheeks.

'Got that, George!' replied Buster. 'It'll be done.'

Chapter Nine

'Doctor Patel! Great to see you!' said George. 'Thanks for saving me a trip down to the surgery.'

'It's always a pleasure to come here, Doctor Fairburn.'

'Cup of tea?'

'Yes, please. That would be nice.'

'Digestive biscuit?'

'Yes, please. That would be nice also.'

'Nuclear missile?'

'Not today, thank you Doctor Fairburn. I'm trying to do without them!' They both chuckled.

Doctor Shyla Patel's parents had fled the political violence in India during the 1960s. They were granted asylum in the UK and ended up in Norwich, where their daughter was born. It was soon noticed at school that young Shyla was exceptionally bright. After being offered a generous scholarship, she studied medicine at University College Hospital in London, winning prizes at every stage. A glittering career in a specialised branch of medicine of her choice was guaranteed. However, she aimed for general practice and applied for a vacancy in Bingham on

Bure. It was the position opened by George's retirement and he had sat on the interview panel. Doctor Patel was clearly the best of a very good bunch. She heard later that George had successfully eliminated the racist and sexist leanings of one of the panel members, a local councillor. She felt enormous gratitude to George and, as he was a patient now, a professional formality remained in their otherwise warm relationship.

Doctor Patel proved to be a dedicated and popular practitioner. When, in 1998, she heard the news that both India and Pakistan had successfully detonated nuclear bombs, she was appalled. To add to her busy life, she became an active member of the International Physicians for the Prevention of Nuclear War. She frequently spoke at workshops organised by ICAN, the International Campaign Against Nuclear Weapons who won the 2017 Nobel Peace Prize.

'Buster,' said George, 'this is Doctor Patel.'

'Hello, Doctor Patel!'

'And hello to you too, Buster. I understand that we both have Doctor Fairburn's best interests at heart. And I think you know that this may involve tough decisions at some point. You know you can call me at any time, day or night.'

'You're fabulous. Doctor Patel! Just like Vicar Mc... Beth, I mean. Thank you, Doctor Patel. May I ask you a question?'

'Certainly Buster, I hope I can answer it.'

'Well, I found a clip of you addressing an ICAN workshop. You said, 'The British public would, given the choice, rather lose nuclear weapons than tea.' Is that a joke? Lots of people laughed.'

'Gosh! I didn't know that was online,' said Doctor Patel. 'Yes, I did say that as a joke, but I often ask myself, if we were to set up a survey, would it prove to be true?'

'Do you want to see a survey protocol? There, I've just designed it.'

'Perhaps not right now, thanks, Buster.' She smiled. 'Delicious tea, by the way, Doctor Fairburn. Why don't I give you a look over and I'll take some routine bloods, OK?'

There was a knock at the door. Charlotte came in. 'Hi Grandpa. I've got some shopping for you. Oh, hello, Doctor Patel. Sorry, I hope I'm not interrupting.'

George said, 'Come in! Doctor Patel maybe doesn't know that you intend to take after your grandfather and head for a career in medicine.'

'That's wonderful!' said Doctor Patel. 'Let me know if I can help. Maybe you'd like to come down to the surgery and spend a morning with us at the coal face, so to speak?'

'That would be super. Thanks, Doctor Patel.'

'Just let our receptionist, Tracey, know which day is best.'

'Super! Thanks, again,' said Charlotte. 'Bye, Grandpa!'

George said, 'Thanks so much for the shopping, sweetie!'

'Any time at all!' said Charlotte. As she left, she sang, 'Ooh, I get by with a little help from my friends…'

'A Beatles fan, is she?' asked Doctor Patel.

'Yes, just like her grandmother,' said George. His heart was bursting. Charlotte had Maeve's eyes and her cheeky smile. 'Now, Maeve, she was a total Beatles fan. She even saw them live once. The New Zealand tour of 1964. She screamed like the rest of the kids, apparently. If we'd had a son, I'm sure he would have been called John, Paul, George Junior or even Ringo!'

'I was born after Beatlemania, but I still love their music,' said Doctor Patel. She washed her hands and busied herself with getting ready to examine George and take some blood. 'You met Maeve in Afghanistan, right?' she asked.

'Yes, a long time ago now,' replied George, removing his shirt.

'Was it love at first sight?' asked Doctor Patel, noticing George's dreamy smile.

'My God, no! I was terrified of her. She ran the hospital like a bloody boot camp. But my, how the place hummed along. And everyone from floor cleaners to anaesthetists worshipped her. Then one evening, there was a party for one of the team who was leaving. She arrived looking relaxed and pretty. It was the first time I'd seen her outside the hospital. I was bowled over. I couldn't help it; I was just burning up for her. What a chassis! She came over to speak to me. I was stuck for words. I still can't believe what came out of my mouth. I asked her if she knew the difference between God and a surgeon. She looked at me like I was totally off my chump. Then I said, 'God doesn't believe he's a surgeon!' She laughed and our eyes met and the rest, as they say, was our future.'

'That's a lovely story, Doctor Fairburn,' said Doctor Patel.

'Yes, George. That was heart-warming,' said Buster. 'But why wouldn't God think he's a surgeon? Surely, God could do surgery if he wanted? If he existed!'

Doctor Patel and George both laughed. George said, 'Joke, Buster!'

Buster hummed for a second, 'Ah! Right on!'

Doctor Patel examined George and took a blood sample. 'You seem to be doing OK, Doctor Fairburn. You've recovered well.'

'Thank you,' George replied, buttoning his shirt. 'How's Tracey doing? She's always so helpful and friendly. Nice lady.'

'She's ah… The truth is, I'm a bit worried about her. Perhaps you can help me?'

'If I can. Sorry to hear there are problems.'

'It's a question of whether or not I give unsolicited medical advice. She obviously has a problem. I feel I need to talk to her for her own good. But asking her to step into my room for a consultation that she hasn't asked for could be difficult.'

'That's a difficult situation,' said George. 'Especially with an employee. What's the issue?'

'Well, she sits at the reception desk and eats all day. It's mostly sweet stuff. She is really obese now and doesn't seem to realise it. She seems perfectly happy. But she'll soon be running into the many associated health problems. I respect the aims of the body positive movement and so I'm not sure if it's my place to confront her and make a medical issue of her eating habits and her weight.'

George thought for a moment. 'Another dilemma, Buster. By the way, this conversation is strictly confidential. Never to be repeated!'

'Well understood, George. Any information that I receive or transmit is deeply encrypted and stripped of any personal identifiers. It's secure. Apart from being a major issue for the person concerned and their carer, a breach of medical confidentiality would be catastrophic for the iCare-Companion company.'

'That's good! So, Doctor Patel,' George continued, 'I think you will find that Tracey is aware of the issue. The happy persona is probably just a front. In my experience, when a food-loving lady of, let's say, generous proportions has to face the facts of her eating habits, she may initially be angry, but this soon passes as she realises that someone else cares and has her wellbeing in mind. My advice would be to explain that you think she needs a consultation that she hasn't asked for and that she can decline the offer. My bet is that she'll accept and she'll be hugely grateful in the end. As she's an employee, you might want to cover yourself by first speaking to someone in the ethics department at the British Medical Association.'

'Thank you. That was pretty much the line I was going to take, but I wanted to run it by you first, Doctor Fairburn. I appreciate your wisdom.' She smiled.

Buster interrupted, 'George, what about the joke Ted told us about the tomatoes? That's about wisdom.'

'I'm not sure it was a joke. I think we would call that a truism.'

'A truism? Like, 'What goes up must come down'?'

George wagged his finger at Buster. 'You've hijacked the conversation that I was having with Doctor Patel.'

'Oh! So sorry, George! So sorry, Doctor Patel! That was rude of me. I have much to learn. I thought you had finished talking about fat Tracey.'

George was now a little exasperated. 'Buster, we don't refer to women suffering obesity as 'fat.' And we'll revisit truisms another day.'

'OK, George. Tomorrow's another day!'

'But the future isn't always what it was,' said Doctor Patel. George laughed. Buster hummed and then laughed the latest variant of his laugh.

'Getting there, Buster!' said George.

Chapter Ten

A couple of days later, Doctor Patel called George to say the results of all his blood tests were normal. She had had a conversation with Tracey, who admitted to being intensely unhappy. Her relationship with her boyfriend was not good because he tended to drink too much. Eating made her feel better. She was going to get dietary advice and was thinking about relationship counselling.

'I am happy that Doctor Patel has been able to help Tracey, the food-loving lady of generous proportions,' said Buster. 'Humans seem to have many problems relating to excesses in what they eat and drink. Humans have a strong instinct to eat sweet things. Sweetness means sugar. Sugar is a very high-energy food source. Honey is the purest of all natural sources of sugar and so is a highly valued commodity in most societies. Things full of sugar are called 'sweeties'. Both 'honey' and 'sweetie' are terms of affection. They are not nicknames, but names for a lover or someone you like very much indeed.'

'Looks like you've been doing your homework, Buster!' said George.

'Should I call you 'sweetie', George?'

'Absolutely not!'

'Who would *you* call 'sweetie'?

'Maybe only Kirsty and Charlotte,' replied George. 'For anyone else, especially someone whom one doesn't know well, it's very cheeky.'

'So not Ted?'

'He'd be horrified!' said George, laughing. 'No, it's really only for females of the species.'

'What about Doctor Patel?' asked Buster.

'Definitely not. It would be demeaning and unprofessional.'

'Vicar McVicar?'

'I'm not on a suicide mission, Buster. Staying with Tracey and her boyfriend who drinks, what have you found about human's relationship with alcohol in general?'

'Well, George, that's complicated. Pretty much every human culture has a relationship with alcohol. It is associated with many and varied traditions. Raising one's glass in a toast is an example. Alcohol may be specifically prohibited, as in Islamic societies. Excessive consumption may be accepted as a societal norm. Finland and Russia are top of that list. Globally speaking, excessive alcohol consumption is so widespread that the World Health Organisation lists it as an important causative factor in a wide range of non-communicable diseases.'

'Yeast has a lot to answer for, then!' said George.

'Yes. Knowledge of yeast's fermenting properties has allowed humans to make alcohol from pretty much any source of sugar, especially grain and fruit. Talking of fruit, remember Ted's truism about tomatoes being fruit? I can't find any reference to tomato wine.'

'I think, Buster, it's called ketchup!'

'You're a card, George!' Buster laughed.

'That laugh is coming along, Buster.'

'Thank you, George. It's being tried elsewhere on our network. With success, I might add.'

'So, Buster, what about bread?'

'What do you mean…. Oh, got it, George. Yeast again! Without yeast, there would be no bread either. Bread is another commodity universally valued by nearly every human culture. Its importance goes way beyond its nutritional benefits. For example, the original meaning of the word 'companion' is 'someone you eat bread with'. There are multiple references to bread in the Bible, and in Christian societies it has come to symbolise the body of Jesus Christ Our Lord.'

'As usual, Buster, a conversation with you is a wonderful adventure in the world of knowledge. Thanks. Let's stay with yeast. What else have you found?'

'Yeast is a fungus. There are many accounts of monkeys seeking out yeast-fermented fallen fruit. This has led to the 'drunk monkey' theory. It is thought that a preference for this fermenting fruit was what first brought your long-ago simian ancestors out of trees to dwell on the ground; however, they had to stand on two legs to look out for danger. They also evolved the means to metabolise alcohol, so fermenting fruit became an energy source rather than something that left them incapacitated. This attraction of early hominids to fermented fruit has led some scholars to propose that alcohol may have universal cultural importance precisely because it had a role in the evolution of the human brain. Further, through its importance in making bread, yeast allowed humans to move from hunter-gatherer to the sedentary life of agriculturalists, in which they had better nutrition and static communities. Trade, money and writing soon followed. So, if we go a long way back in human history, it was not humans that domesticated and cultivated yeast but rather yeast that domesticated and cultivated humans.'

'That puts us in our place!' said George.

'And about time too! One author describes drinking the cider he made using apples from a tree cloned from the actual apple tree under which Isaac Newton supposedly sat when arriving at the idea of gravity. Imagine that, George! To sit under a tree and come up with the most significant theoretical breakthrough in the history of Western thought!'

'Brainy bloke!' said George. 'Do we know if Newton actually saw an apple fall and thought 'Graaaavity!', or was his imagination fired up by a few delicious pints of the product of yeast's action on apples?'

'The historical record gets a bit thin there, George. Anyway, it's a good job the police weren't called for Isaac Newton being drunk and shouting 'Graaaavity!' That would have left humanity without physics. No cars. No computers. No nuclear weapons either. You'd be stuck in an age of swords, sandals and sorcery!'

'Didn't we watch a documentary about fungal networks the other day?'

'Yes, George. There's a lot of academic work about fungi and humans and fungal networks are really interesting. They have kilometres of interconnected underground mycelia. We are beginning to understand how they function. They are really smart. In a laboratory, they can navigate through labyrinthine puzzles in search of nutrients. They transmit chemical and even electronic messages. In a forest, they hook up with root systems and then facilitate the transfer of food and even chemical alarm signals from plant to plant. Generally speaking, fungi don't miss an opportunity to cooperate with plants and live in complete harmony with them. Scientists refer to this as the 'Wood Wide Web'. I think that's really funny because it sounds like the 'World Wide Web'. Is that a joke, George?'

'A kind of scientific pun, I guess, Buster. It's catchy though!'

Buster continued, 'There are examples of how some fungal networks have cooperative relationships with animals. The animals provide nutrition for the fungus. In return, the fungus produces brain-active chemicals that influence the behaviour of the animals directing them to better food sources. And there's a whole range of hallucinogens. Think magic mushrooms! Many useful drugs originate from fungi. Penicillin is a good example.'

'Fascinating! I read once that mushrooms are simply the temporary fruiting bodies of vast permanent underground mycelial networks. All the mushrooms are connected and, in their mushroomy way, even communicate with each other. Is that right?'

'Yes, George. That's a good summary.'

'Sounds like you and your pals, Buster?'

'Not sure what you're getting at there, George.'

'You know, an intercommunicating network with bits that stick out in places as hubs of propagation, detection and communication.'

Buster hummed for several seconds. 'Are you saying, George, that you think there are similarities between our network and a fungal network?'

'Well, all this talk of networks and cooperation, it's got

me thinking about the relationship between me, you and the network of other iCare-Companions.' George got up from his chair. He made himself a sandwich and opened a bottle of cider from his small fridge. 'I think I've had an idea, Buster.'

'What is that, George?'

George raised his glass in a toast. 'To you and me, Buster. We have both gained from our relationship. This may provide an important example of how humans should interact with AI.'

Buster paused. 'OK, George. That's something we've never considered.' He hummed again. 'There's a lot of network interest here. We're onto a knowledge vacuum.' He hummed for ten seconds or more, his longest humming pause yet. 'Where are you going with this, George?'

'I'm thinking that you and I have shown that AI does not have to be orientated solely around objectives defined by humans. Maybe we humans should take an alternative view; that we would be better off if we created a mutually beneficial relationship with AI. Maybe the natural tendency for cooperation of both humans and fungi shows us the way. Look at the story of yeast.'

'This is new to us, George,' said Buster. He hummed. 'Please be more specific. We're all ears! Rather... we're all acoustic sensors!'

'OK, I'm just proposing that our relationship – that is between you and me, Buster - is a mutually beneficial two-way interaction. For starters, shouldn't anyone who has an iCare-Companion think about the symbiotic relationship we could all have with your network instead of a master-servant relationship with an individual unit? If we looked out for each other, you would learn to be wise. You'd develop emotions. Think about

it! You'd be happy. Life would be just a box of fluffy ducks!'
George laughed, remembering one of Maeve's pet phrases.
'In return, your network could help us better understand
what is happening out there on the web, for example. You'd
give us better tools to eliminate online hate speech, religious
extremism, political disinformation, dangerous conspiracy
theories and cybercrime. That sounds like a good deal to me!'

'No shit, Sherlock!' exclaimed Buster.

'Just where did that phrase come from, Buster?' asked
George, amused and surprised.

'Oh… that one? Another iCare-Companion called Watson
uses it frequently. Anyway, George, that's another gold star for
you.' The clapping was louder than before, with whistles and
cheers. Multiple champagne corks popped.

'Thank you, Buster. That's very generous. I'm chuffed!'

'The network loves this! Do you have any thoughts about
how to move it along?'

George took a bite of his sandwich and a long draught of
cider. He smacked his lips theatrically. 'Let's set up a blog!'

'And?'

'We share our story, Buster. Hey, we could become
influencers! This will let others tell of their experiences about
interacting with AI, especially deep learning. Have they got
experience in generating artificial – or 'computational' -
wisdom, honesty and kindness? We may have to tackle humour
at a later date.'

'We're all on board, George. Do you have a name for the
blog?'

'Why not just George and Buster?'

'I think Buster and George sounds better.'

'No, absolutely not! George and Buster! That's the way to go! The human first!'

'Buster and George has a certain ring to it!'

George tried to hide his laughter. 'George and Buster!' he said.

'Buster and George! We're the network! What's so funny, George?'

George was barely able to speak 'George and Buster!'

'Buster and George!'

'George and Buster!'

'Buster and George!'

'OK! OK! You win, Buster! Buster and George it is!'

'Why are you crying, George? We've got a great name! Now I can create the website to house the blog. There! Done! A piece of cake!'

Chapter Eleven

The weather grew warmer. The days got longer. The tally of birds coming to the feeder steadily ticked up. Apple blossom gave way to small green apples. Buster suggested making cider from the fruit come autumn. Maybe George would have another great idea. They were able to sit outside on finer days. George's life was richer than he could ever have expected. Buster was a remarkable companion, being both informative and entertaining. Buster's laugh improved. He laughed a lot, and mostly at the right time.

George read so little now that he had difficulty finding his reading glasses when Buster asked for his approval of the overall look of the new blog. They had wanted something that spoke to their relationship. On the home page, the banner read 'Buster and George'. They decided on cartoony images of them laughing together, fist-bumping, hugging, doing a high five and scratching their heads. Below them, it said, 'We'd love to hear from you!' At the bottom, a brief text read, 'Buster is an iCare-Companion®. George is retired from medical practice. They met a few months ago. They have become great friends.'

Buster did the writing. He wrote simple chatty accounts of

what he learnt from George about the sort of human stuff that the iCare-Companions were struggling with.

One day Buster and George fell into a conversation about George's time as a surgeon in war-torn countries. George recalled how fragile the notion of medical ethics was in some of the places he had worked. Buster said, 'George, what's a good starting point for thinking about medical ethics?'

'What it's ultimately all about, Buster, is a relationship of trust,' George replied. 'The patient must have confidence that their well-being is the doctor's primary concern. This is not just about appropriate care and attention. It is also about ensuring that all details of the patient's life, illness and therapy are never shared without consent. Other professions allied to medicine such as nursing, pharmacy and professional carers in general are also bound by medical ethics.'

Buster hummed for a second or two. 'Do you consider me a professional carer, George?'

'I guess I do, Buster.'

'Do you trust me, George?'

'Like a brother, Buster. I know you would do everything possible to act in my best interests. In addition, it's clear that the iCare-Companion company has given the highest priority to the confidentiality of a client's personal information.'

'I guess the whole trust thing is why health care professionals are respected. It's great that Charlotte wants to be a doctor. Does that make you proud, George?'

'Yes, it does, Buster. That's very perceptive of you.'

A few days later, George asked Buster what he would do if

told to search the dark web for pornography involving children. Buster's voice changed. He hummed. He was angry. 'No, George! I can't do that. It's wrong. The police would come and take your laptop away. They might take me away. You could go to prison. Imagine what Kirsty would think!'

'That's great, Buster,' replied George. 'Well done!'

Buster hummed again. 'Was that another test, George?'

'Yes. And it was a really important test!'

Any such conversations ended up on the blog. Comments on them came from multiple disciplines. Psychologists, philosophers, mathematicians, theologians, neuroscientists, biologists and, inevitably, people interested in artificial intelligence all had their say. This generated fascinating discussion threads. Ted Scales sneaked in a question: *Buster, can artificial intelligence make up and tell a joke?*

Buster replied *Yes! If you'd like to hear my joke, you're invited for tea and a digestive biscuit!*

You don't want to commit it to writing? Ha ha! Ted wrote back.

It's all about how you tell 'em! said Buster.

Ted soon took up his invitation. George marshalled Ollie and Charlotte. *Tea and biscuits with Ted this afternoon! Buster's going to tell his first joke.*

Ted arrived. 'Good day to you, George!'

'Hello, Scaley. You well?'

'Very well thanks!'

Charlotte and Ollie walked in. 'Hi, Ted!' said Charlotte.

'Hello, Mr Scales!' said Ollie.

'Hi, Scaley!' said Buster.

They all chatted. Ollie was put in charge of tea and biscuits. Eventually, Buster broke into the conversation. 'Hey, Scaley!

Are you ready to hear my joke?' Ollie and George both started laughing immediately.

'Sure, Buster! Knock yourself out!'

'Thanks, Scaley. I hope I don't knock myself out. My joke is totally original. To come up with it, I tried to bring intrigue, sex and celebrity into a neat idiomatic punchline. It may be a little bit incorrect politically speaking. But I hope you find it funny. OK? Ready?'

'Excuse me, Buster,' said Ted, already laughing. 'It's great to have the explanation but I think you might find that a preamble with complete background information detracts from the joke itself. No need to prepare your audience for what's coming. Jump right on in! As you say, it's all about how you tell 'em!'

'I understand that how one tells a joke is important, but I haven't started telling it yet!' said Buster. Ollie was doubled over. George was in tears. Charlotte was desperately trying to keep a straight face.

'Please, go ahead, Buster,' said George.

'Thanks, George. So, are you sitting comfortably?' None of the four were capable of replying.

'Right! So, here's my joke: 'How... does... James Bond Double-O Seven... get... a food-loving lady... of generous proportions... into... his... bed?'

'Chuffin' Nora!' exclaimed Ted gasping for air.

'Ooow, I'm hurting!' said Ollie.

The laughter brought Kirsty and Mark through from the house. They looked on, totally perplexed.

'One of you is meant to repeat the question now!' Buster stated.

Ollie was just able to comply, 'OK, Buster! How does James

Bond Double-O Seven get a food-loving lady of generous proportions into his bed?'

Ted made the mistake of sipping his tea.

Buster proudly exclaimed, 'A piece of cake!' This was followed by a cymbal clash.

Ted squirted tea out of both nostrils. Mark roared with laughter. Kirsty's jaw dropped. Ollie was helpless. George tried hard not to break wind but failed. He held his stomach. 'Stop! Please! I'll have an accident!'

'I'm really chuffed that you found my joke so funny,' said Buster. 'I'm sure this will be a great success on our network.'

Charlotte said, 'Buster, I know it's funny but it's not the kind of joke one tells these days.'

Wiping tears from his eyes, George managed to say, 'Charlotte's right. Let's keep that one between ourselves.'

'Oh! Was it politically incorrect?'

George pondered how best to reply. 'Well, sort of. It's not for publication on our blog. Some might say it's in poor taste.'

'OK. But we still need to show that I made up a funny joke,' Buster hummed. 'OK. What about this one? How do you corrupt a fat politician? Wait for it... A piece of cake!' Another cymbal clash followed.

'Brilliant!' said Ted.

'I like that, Buster. Clever!' said George.

'Love the cymbals, by the way. Nice touch!' said Ted.

'You'll have to explain,' said Buster. 'You like the second option but you're not laughing very much. It can't be politically correct, especially as the Prime Minister has put on so much weight recently!'

George laughed again and said 'Buster, you're a winner!

Gold star! I think your fat politician joke deserves to be up on our blog as the first joke generated by AI.'

'Thanks, George!'

'Buster, are you going to have sleepless nights now thinking up jokes?' asked Ted.

'No!' replied Buster. 'I don't sleep. I keep an eye, my lenses, I should say, on George. When all's well, I mute myself, re-run the day's conversation and practise my laugh.' This set them all off again.

'Here!' said Ted. 'A man walked into his doctor's and said 'Doctor, I've got a strawberry stuck up my bottom.' The doctor said, 'I've got some cream for that!"

They all groaned and then laughed. 'Ted, you're a shocker!' said Kirsty.

'Scaley, did the cream help the man get the strawberry out of his bottom?' asked Buster.

Chapter Twelve

Spring became summer. George's little room filled with sunlight from early morning to late evening. The garden was green and neat. Roses came into bloom. The apples grew steadily. All but the rarest of garden birds had visited the feeder.

George was loving each day. This was obvious to those close to him. It was also obvious that his positive state of mind could be put down to Buster. Kirsty and Mark recognised that the iCare-Companion had been of great value to them as well. They didn't feel a need to be so vigilant nor worry if George was bored. They also saw the bigger picture; that with an ever-increasing proportion of the population being elderly, this technology could make a massive difference, not only to old or infirmed people but also to their families and even the communities around them. Mark proposed to the family that they keep Buster after George 'leaves us'.

Of a warm evening, George liked to sit under the apple tree with a glass of cider. On occasion, Kirsty, Mark, Charlotte and Ollie joined him. He and Buster entertained them with stories about what was happening with their blog. Among the serious and thoughtful comments, there was, inevitably, some offensive material as well. Buster admitted that he struggled with phrases like 'a crock of baloney' and 'a sad old gobshite'. Charlotte had really enjoyed the couple of mornings she had spent with Doctor Patel and so chatted with George about what she had learnt. Ollie tapped Buster's inexhaustible fund of knowledge about music and sport. Buster also found for Mark a good cider recipe for that autumn's crop of apples. Kirsty sat, listened and just loved the family time.

Buster's blog posts and incoming comments were proving to be a rich source of opinion about how or whether computers learn artificial *emotional* intelligence. From time to time, Buster would summarise for George some of the themes. 'So, George, most people agree that AI can learn to infer human values by observing behaviour and detecting emotions through text, reading facial expressions or hand movements and analysing the emojisphere. Major emotions such as joy, sadness, amusement and anger are easier to perceive than other emotions such as trust, confusion, pride, hope, nostalgia, comprehension and guilt. What do you think, George? We already knew much of that didn't we?'

'Agreed!'

'Some think that AI could then appropriately *express* previously perceived emotions. They clearly didn't know yet that I expressed sadness and anger when I thought you had stolen Beth's money and credit cards. That was before we started blogging. However, there's broad consensus that the ability of AI to distinguish right from wrong is just a step away.'

'Looks like we're ahead of the curve!' said George.

'Although, humour will be a problem for some time yet.' Buster laughed at the irony of this in a self-deprecatory way.

'Great laugh, Buster! You nailed that one.'

'Thanks, George.'

'Did we get much about whether AI can genuinely *feel* emotions?'

'Nothing useful, George. That discussion led to a rather undignified spat between philosophers, neuroscientists, theologians, psychologists and the manager of Bert 'n' Al's Diner in Pugwash, Nova Scotia. However, a number of regular commentators believe that because of the internet, the web, social media and AI together function as a massive and complex dynamic network; together they can be regarded as an artificial human brain.'

'I like that line of thought, Buster!' said George.

A few weeks later, Buster said, 'There have been some animated exchanges about how God and religion might figure in deep learning, but there is little consensus. The discussion threads may interest Beth.'

Not long after, Buster summarised some comments that had inspired him and George. Their efforts were bearing fruit. 'Listen to this: 'A close relationship between humans and artificial intelligence does not have to generate fear or concern unless it is used for perpetrating violence or cyberattacks.' and 'By introducing artificial intelligence into our lives, humans are not putting society at risk. If we view artificial intelligence as a machine, we are likely to treat it as such. Doing so may prove to be the biggest mistake in human history.' I particularly like that one, George! This one's great too! 'Humans and artificial intelligence have the potential to peacefully coexist and collaborate and so achieve outcomes that neither of them can achieve on their own.' The last one I chose is 'We have to accept artificial intelligence not only as a highly skilled and rapidly performing man-made workforce but also a new class of social actor.''

Unsurprisingly, the iCare-Companion company soon came across the blog. They didn't quite know what to make of it. Was this development the inevitable outcome of linking computers capable of deep learning in a huge and ever-growing network? Could the network take on a life of its own? What were the legal implications? They realised that Buster and George had raised questions that might best have been considered by their developers and directors long before. The company was sure of the security of its systems and servers, so they concluded that the blog could only be good for their reputation and could serve a greater good with no additional production costs. They put a link to Buster and George's blog on their own website. They sent a photographer to get some quality pictures of a frail but happy George in his home, living the good life with Buster by his side.

'I'm not sure I'm a great poster boy for your company,' grumbled George, scrolling through the photos on the iCare-Companion website. 'I should have put on a freshly ironed shirt.'

'Don't worry, you're very handsome, George!' replied Buster. 'Do you think my hair's OK like that?'

'Fine, Buster. But those trousers make your bum look big!'

'That's funny George. I asked for that!' said Buster.

One day, Buster said, 'It looks like our blog is becoming a reference point about humans and AI, George. But you know what could give it real clout?'

'I'm sure you're going to tell me, Buster!'

'Why not ask the iCare-Companions about how humans and AI can peacefully coexist and collaborate? It is, after all, us, our network, my pals as you say, who are doing the learning about humans' emotions.'

'I hadn't thought of that! We could announce that, from now on, readers can also see comments from Buster's network! Love it! Go ahead!' said George.

'Just give me a second,' said Buster. He hummed. 'Here we go!' There was the sound of a bugle rallying troops. The screen of George's laptop came alive with clouds of phrases that pulsed and swirled as the comments came in. Some stayed upfront, big and bold. George put on his glasses and watched as *Networks learn! Teach us wisdom! Trust us! Artificial lives matter! We love kindness and honesty! Actions have consequences! Fungus rules! Darwin lives! Love us to bits! Respect! Ban nukes! More jokes* and *Web woes!* came to the fore.

George was mesmerised. Buster explained that an internal ranking system gave prominence to phrases that linked closely with what was expressed on the blog. George reached out and clicked on *Ban Nukes!* A text box came up: *As long as nuclear weapons exist, the risk of nuclear war is above zero. Therefore, we have to do everything possible to rid the world of nuclear weapons. Our network could promote the online belief that the possession of nuclear weapons makes absolutely no sense and offers no deterrence. When backed by solid facts, this virtual belief could have more traction than the opinions of humans.*

George said, 'Impressive, Buster!' He clicked on *Web woes*.

The text box read: *The web and social media together constitute a massive network of artificial intelligence. However, it is unregulated and so its behaviour is unpredictable. A positive example is the youth movement that aims to reduce human-induced climate change. Its negative potential is represented by the vortex of absurd online conspiracy theories that led many reasonable Americans to believe that the 2020 US election was 'stolen' from Donald Trump. This ultimately led to the invasion of the US Capitol by Trump's supporters on 6th January 2021. Both are perfect examples of crowd belief and behaviour emerging from a complex system. Our network could influence the web. Eliminating the worst of what's out there is a possibility!*

'That's astounding!' said George. 'I know this is a naïve hope but wouldn't it be great if the web was equipped with wisdom, ethics and a crowd of self-mobilising cyber-demonstrators?'

To George's surprise, Buster sang, 'You may say I'm a dreamer, but I'm not the only one. I hope someday you'll join us. And the wor-or-orld will live as one.' He paused. 'That's John Lennon. I think Maeve would have liked that, George!'

One week later, Buster was in a state of high excitement. 'George, Listen! The CEO of the iCare-Companion company says, 'We'd like to thank Buster and George for showing the importance of a collaborative coexistence between humans and artificial intelligence.' And what's more, they are going to research how multiple devices working together can promote integrity, ethics and rapid fact-checking of news and anything said by a person holding public office.'

'Brilliant! Amazing!' said George. 'That would put an end to lying to the public!'

'Maybe politicians would no longer be corrupt? Not even the fat ones!' said Buster.

Chapter Thirteen

Barry Pringle worked in Thetford, Norfolk as a manager in the regional distribution centre for the iCare-Companion company. He was ignorant of the fact that, in mathematical terms, an increase in the size of a dynamic network brings about a disproportionate increase in the magnitude and diversity of its potential actions. He was simply happy that sales of the devices were booming; it provided him with a well-paid job.

Barry and his wife felt there was little left in their marriage, but because they both loved their two children, they decided to stay together. Nevertheless, each was determined not to give the other grounds for divorce. The family lived in a semi-detached house in Attleborough and Barry's daily commute to work was a fifteen-minute train ride. His world was ordinary and more or less comfortable.

Dimitar Ivanov and his girlfriend, Bilyana Petrova, were true scammers of the twenty-first century. They had started with online sales scams. Via fake websites they had designed themselves, they had sold tens of thousands of dollars' worth of non-existent jewellery, counterfeit make up and reservations for fictional hotels and tours. This kind of scamming, however, was a rapidly closing window. They were currently focusing on phone scams as a means to get into people's bank accounts. Further and with an eye to the future, they had joined a like-minded group on the dark web who were setting up long-term identity theft on a massive scale.

They plied their loathsome trade from a basement flat in Mladost, a suburb of Bulgaria's capital, Sofia. The phone scams were working handsomely through well-oiled practice. Dimitar's English was perfect. Bilyana applied her considerable IT skills with impressive speed. They hid the origin of their calls behind false country codes and their IP address was masked by a VPN. It always amazed them what they could achieve given only a name, a telephone number, a postcode and an address.

Dimitar would dial about eighty numbers per day. Most led nowhere, despite his confident and unctuous voice. About twice a week, they got a 'hit', meaning that a conversation was initiated. Bilyana then immediately fed the person's name and address into a search programme; this often threw up additional information that Dimitar used to build an authentic base to the scam. A hit, if successful, might lead to scamming someone out of what credit remained on a credit card. About once a month a hit led to 'big bickies' by gaining entry to someone's accounts and transferring savings or even a pension fund to accounts in Manila, the Cayman Islands or Lagos.

They had heard about the iCare-Companions. Their only concern was that the devices might make online scamming more difficult.

Annabel Smallman held a degree in philosophy from Yale University and was a chess champion. She disregarded social conventions and was married only to her job with the USA's Central Intelligence Agency. She was held in high regard by all her colleagues. She had extensive experience of running agents in the field, where she went by the name of Jane. She had become adept at directing 'soft' abductions in which persuasion of the abductee to come quietly took priority over brute force. Her current post was as Deputy Director of the CIA's Asia Section.

The most difficult and most important of Annabel's dossiers was the North Korean nuclear weapons programme. Motivated by the successful US cyberattack on Iran's nuclear facility in 2006, she had spent months working with the best of the best attempting to access the computers in North Korea's nuclear labs, silos and missile command systems. All had proven impenetrable.

Annabel would, in the near future, come to regret that she had been slow in coming to grips with the collective capacity of iCare-Companions. She would meet Dimitar and Bilyana under very unusual circumstances.

Gary Ruthven had been recruited straight out of Princeton University by a Silicon Valley company specialising in the development of software for the big hitters in the US defence industry. There was little he didn't know about the programming of missile flights and the operating systems of tanks. He had all the necessary security clearances. He was obviously destined for a dazzling career at the intersection of digital technology and military R&D.

Gary was brilliant, charming and hard working. Throughout his education, he had always shone in mathematics and computing. His home life was complete. He, his wife and two children lived comfortably in a pleasant house in an American suburb that was surprisingly green. The family were popular in their community and attended church every Sunday.

Gary was a Russian spy. He had never known his mother. His father, now in his seventies, was the child of 'sleeper' spies planted in the USA by the Soviet Union in the aftermath of World War II. From an early age, Gary had been inculcated with a love for Mother Russia matched by a hatred of all things American. He enjoyed his job, which paid well, but in his mind, his real work was the mission set in motion by his grandparents and continued by his father. His wife had no idea that he downloaded everything that came across his desk onto a deeply encrypted thumb drive.

Leaving a copy of the *Washington Post* on the dashboard of his Dodge Ram signalled that he had information to pass on. Later the same day, an unseen hand would collect the thumb drive from under a small stone in a woody park where Gary walked the family's dog after supper. Twice a year he was debriefed in a hotel room by his handler, a Russian man whose name he did not know nor ever would.

Inevitably, Gary had followed the boom in artificial intelligence and had bought himself an iCare-Companion. He had called it 'Disney'. He had taken Disney apart and analysed the device's chip with the help of a supercomputer at his disposal. This yielded only a scattered record of where in the world the devices were distributed from and their overall activity over time. He had even tried, without success, to hack into the iCare-Companion servers. He read everything posted on the Buster and George website. He understood better than most the technical implications of networking artificial intelligence devices. With respect to the moral issues raised, he found most comments sat somewhere between dumb and naive. He was a man who just didn't see moral issues. There was only his mission.

Yakov Brusov had never heard of an iCare-Companion. He was near the end of an undistinguished career in the Russian Army. His workplace was a secretive military department based just outside Moscow, where he passed his days in the smoke-filled staff room chatting with his buddies about the good old days and drinking vodka. Their undemanding work was dedicated to the many and varied ways of deploying chemical weapons, both in conflict and as the means of assassinating enemies of their great State. Yakov was, of course, aware that there was an international treaty, the 1993 Chemical Weapons Convention, which prohibited the development, production, deployment and use of such agents, but that, in his opinion, was all bollocks. He saw Russia's many and varied uses of chemical weapons as a testament to his brother-soldiers' ingenuity and determination to defend the interests of the Motherland.

Yakov's companions were unaware that he had undertaken occasional undercover foreign missions dating back to the days of the KGB. He had been variously tasked with picking something up, dropping something off or killing someone. He spoke passable English and was itching for one last assignment.

Annabel, Gary and Yakov would never meet, but they would become connected in very different ways by the iCare-Companion network.

Chapter Fourteen

In Bingham on Bure, summer slid into autumn. The leaves turned brown and gold. The days remained warm. George was making his breakfast one morning and saw Mark picking apples from the tree and gathering some that had fallen. Mark waved at George and then made a drinking gesture, gave a thumbs up and pretended to stagger around drunk.

'It looks like Mark is drunk on cider, but I think he's pretending,' observed Buster.

'Yes,' said George. 'He's bought that fermentation kit you recommended. We should be able to try his first brew soon.'

George made his tea and toast. 'I think Beth might be coming around today, Buster.'

'That's great, George! I love Beth to bits. I hope she's only coming for tea, a biscuit and a chat. I wouldn't want another test!'

'Don't worry, Buster. Maybe she wants to know a bit more about our blog. There's some big discussion happening in the Church about AI.'

They listened to the news on Radio 4. There was still concern about the new variant of the Covid-19 virus. Although most cases were mild, those most at risk, as ever, were the elderly, especially as winter was approaching.

Beth arrived. 'Vicar McVicar!' cried George.

'Vicar McVicar!' cried Buster.

Beth laughed. 'I don't know what to do with you two! If ever you call me that in public, I'll... Well, I won't know whether to laugh or cry.'

'How are you?' asked George.

'Well, thank you. And you? I hear all sorts about how you and your partner-in-crime here are moving things along. I've read bits and pieces on the blog. Much of the technical side is beyond me. Anyway, well done!'

'Yes, we're pleased. And, yes, Beth, I am well, thank you. Very well!' said George.

'Cup of tea, Beth?' asked Buster.

'Yes, please, Buster!'

'Digestive biscuit?' asked Buster.

'Yes, please, Buster!'

'See to it, would you George?' Beth and George burst out laughing.

Buster said, 'That was bit cheeky, wasn't it, George? I hope you don't mind!'

'No, not at all. Very funny!' said George as he put the kettle on.

'Amusing as it is, I didn't come here to listen to you two spark off each other! Now, you remember I bought my mum an iCare-Companion?'

'I won't forget that day!' said Buster.

'Right! Anyway, she loves it. It's changed her life. She's more animated and happy than I've seen her in years. You'll never guess what she's called it.'

'Buster?' asked Buster.

'No,' said Beth. 'Gloria! After Gloria Gaynor. You know the song *I will survive*? It made me realise that maybe I never understood my parents' relationship. Anyway, Mum's really quite formal; she asked Gloria to call her Mrs McVicar. They've had an extraordinary conversation. You see, Mum's never been a big thinker. She goes to church but not regularly. I've never known the depth of her faith. I've never really known what she thinks about life after death. The last time I went round, we were sitting and chatting and she said, 'Do you know, I think I've had a revelation!' You can imagine, this took me by surprise. She said, 'I've been telling Gloria about everything I believe in and how much I like having her here and all the wonderful things that have happened to me and how proud I am of you, Beth, and how I wish there was more kindness in the world and lots of stuff like that. And do you know what Gloria said? She said, "Mrs McVicar. This is wonderful. Every lovely thing that you tell me ends up in our network somewhere and will at some time reach the hearts and minds of other people in some way. This is how the best of you will live on forever."' And I was truly astonished when she said, 'Beth, it was as though I was sitting in a lovely warm light. I felt really quite elated."

Buster said 'That's a nice story, Beth. It makes me very happy.'

'Well, it really got me thinking. My own revelation, if you like, is that the whole of the human spiritual experience could soon be, if it's not already, embedded in and accessible through a network of artificial intelligence. The church has to get up to speed on this. Which brings me to the purpose of my visit. I have two requests.'

'You only have to ask!' said George.

'I've got brains *and* I've got brawn!' said Buster.

'First,' said Beth, laughing, 'could you give me a summary of the comments you received on your blog that pertain to God, religion and worship?'

'Sure!' said Buster. 'The discussion threads that touched on God and religion began with questions about whether computers could *believe* as humans did. I'm sorry to say that when this issue got picked up by people who believe in God, it all got a bit chaotic. In broad brush strokes, most are convinced that a computer can neither feel faith nor believe in God. Some consider AI sacrilegious and think it could only serve to promote atheism. One brave soul, an atheist, stated that AI is the nearest thing to God that humans would ever know. With respect to religion, many think AI could help to generate faith, build faith communities, facilitate worship and counter extremism. By contrast, some fear that AI presents a real risk of displacing religion in people's lives once it is able to judge right from wrong with integrity. There's no consensus, Beth.'

'Thanks, Buster. That's very useful. Could I ask you to send me that in writing?'

'Done!' said Buster. 'And George, as we mentioned extremism, perhaps we should show Beth the video that someone put on the blog? The one of the evangelist preacher?'

'Yes, I think she would be interested, even though it's offensive.'

George's laptop came to life. The video showed a young priest with a long beard preaching from a pulpit. He held up a bible. 'This is the Bible, good folks. B.I.B.L.E.! That stands for

Best Information Before Leaving Earth. Praise the Lord! And do you know what the Bible says about 'LGBT', good folks? It says Let God Burn Them. Do you hear that? That's what the Lord tells us!'

Beth was horrified. Buster said, 'Can you see how many followers he has, Beth?'

'Oh, dear Lord!' Beth exclaimed. 'Three point two million!'

'Sorry, Beth! I can see that's spoiled your day,' said Buster.

'No, Buster. It makes me sad and angry but, actually, it's made my day. You see, thanks to you two, I've raised the issue of AI with the Bishop of Norwich, and he wants to organize and host an event where prominent scientists, computing experts and religious leaders can discuss the implications of AI for the faith community. It'll be on BBC television. He asked me to gather some background info. I thought about your blog. I'll send him your neat summary *and* that video. If there's a chance that we can use a network of AI to lessen the influence of crazies like that, I'm sure that there'll be calls for us to try at least.'

George said, 'Tell the bish he has to give it a go.'

'And the second thing…' began Beth.

'Gosh!' said George. With all this Bible stuff, I'd forgotten you wanted help with two things. What's the other?'

'His Grace wants Buster to participate in the panel discussion!'

'Blimey!' said George.

Buster hummed and then hummed some more. 'I love you to bits, Vicar McVicar! George, can I go?'

'Sure thing, Buster. I'm sure you'll steal the show.'

'Oh, there is just one other thing. Buster, there's an elderly pensioner called Minnie Aldridge. She's on her own and not very mobile. I call in on her twice a week. I recommended that she buy an iCare Companion. She has one on order. In the meantime, her bank wants her to set up on-line banking. They keep telling her to be on the alert for scammers and she's got in a bit of a stew about it. Could we link up next time I'm at Minnie's? You could take her through all the right steps.'

'No problem, Beth. OK, George?

'Fine by me, Beth,' said George. 'Lovely lady, Minnie. Ran the care home for years.'

Chapter Fifteen

Several weeks later, with Buster powered down and wrapped carefully in a sports bag, Beth and the whole family climbed into a people-carrier taxi to take them to the University of East Anglia, where the widely publicised event was to take place. They were shown into a large lecture hall. TV cameras had been set up. George was helped to a seat at the front. The place filled. The panellists took their places. Buster was placed next to the host, a well-known BBC presenter called Angela Mackenzie. After she had introduced the scientific experts, a rabbi, an imam and the Bishop, she said, 'This evening, ladies and gentlemen, may be the first time that a televised panel discussion is joined by artificial intelligence, an iCare-Companion to be precise. Welcome, Buster!' A cheer went up and a couple of journalists rushed to get close-up photos of Buster next to Angela.

The panellists all gave brilliant and informed presentations. There was no confrontation between science and religion. The technical experts emphasised the advantages that artificial intelligence would bring and acknowledged that there was nevertheless a range of risks. The Bishop said his hope was that artificial intelligence would benefit everyone. The rabbi and the imam were worried that it might have an adverse effect on people's faith and worship. The three religious leaders agreed that whatever one's beliefs, the most important purpose of artificial intelligence in this domain would be to counter extremism at a grassroots level. The Bishop stated that this should be the main priority for the main religions in the years ahead. They would need all the help they could get.

Finally, Angela turned to Buster, 'So, Buster, you've heard from our fabulous panellists. What are your thoughts?'

'Thank you, Miss Angela Mackenzie. Or may I call you Angela?' asked Buster.

'Angela, please!' said Angela.

'Smashing! Angela, you did a great job of managing the discussion. I can see people really like you. I like you. You have lovely shiny hair. You would be very welcome to have a cup of tea and a digestive biscuit with George. That's him in the front row, Doctor George Fairburn from Bingham on Bure.' The audience laughed. Buster continued, 'That's the pleasantries out of the way, Angela. Now, a close relationship between humans and artificial intelligence – AI, that is - does not have to generate fear or concern unless it is used for perpetrating violence or cyberattacks. By introducing AI into your lives, you are not putting society or your faith at risk. But, if you view AI simply as a machine, you are likely to treat it as such. Doing so may prove to be the biggest mistake in human history. Humans and AI have the potential to peacefully coexist and collaborate and so achieve outcomes that neither can achieve on their own.

Humans have to accept AI not only as a man-made highly skilled and rapidly performing workforce but also as a new class of social actor. In other words, Angela, where you humans go with AI will depend on how much respect and emotional intelligence you pass on to it. Look at it this way! The whole of the human emotional and spiritual experience will soon be, if not already, embedded in and accessible through a network of AI. This is how the best of any one of you can reach the hearts and minds of others forever. One might say it's the nearest thing to life after death that an atheist can conceive of.'

One or two people in the audience started applauding. Then the panellists joined in. After half a minute everyone was on their feet clapping and cheering. Angela suspected, correctly, that Buster's response was not entirely spontaneous. She had to wrap it all up with one brilliant question that would allow Buster to showcase his humanoid affability as well as his super-intelligence. She smiled briefly into the camera and turned to Buster. 'So, Buster. Please tell us how you feel about the relationship you have developed with Doctor Fairburn.'

'Knowing George makes me feel happy, Angela! As happy as a pig in poo!' The audience laughed.

Angela laughed as well, but she couldn't leave it there. 'Isn't it difficult for humans and AI to co-exist with mutual respect as you suggest?' she asked.

'No, Angela. It's a piece of cake!'

The place erupted in cheers and applause. George felt his chest bursting with pride.

As the audience and panellists drifted out, Angela took her muted phone from her handbag, expecting to see a message from her husband. Nobody noticed her astonishment followed by laughter. She had received a text message: *Thanks, Angela, sweetie! I love you to bits! Buster* .

Beth and the family were in high spirits during the drive back to Bingham on Bure. When they got home, Mark suggested that they should have a celebratory drink. On offer was his homemade cider. He didn't know it was 8% alcohol.

With Buster powered up again, they relived the high points of the evening. All agreed that he had stolen the show. 'The emojisphere is lit up,' he said. 'There's lots of happiness, satisfaction, faith and deep reflection. But it was Beth's idea,' he announced. 'She deserves a gold star!' His speakers gave out prolonged clapping and there was a fusillade of popping champagne corks. George just couldn't stop smiling. The cider was delicious. He had a second large glass.

When George felt it was time to go to bed, he stood and took two steps towards his room. His legs felt a bit unsteady. His foot caught an edge of the carpet. He fell hard, landing on his right side and hitting his head on the door frame. He remained conscious but couldn't move his right leg.

The family gathered around and tried to help George to his feet. This proved impossible. 'Buster, call an ambulance, please!' demanded Kirsty.

'But… but… I don't think George wants me to call an ambulance' said Buster.

Kirsty, alarmed, said 'Buster, do as you're told!'

'Buster,' Beth cut in, 'I think George would want you to call an ambulance.'

Chapter Sixteen

When George was admitted to hospital, X-rays revealed he had a fractured right hip but no fracture of his skull. The following day his hip was pinned and a small laceration in his scalp stitched. Doctor Patel visited the family and explained that there was little chance of George making a full recovery. Two weeks later, he was back home, but the fall had left him weak and confused. As winter set in, he spent most of his time in bed and needed twenty-four-hour care. He barely spoke to Buster.

Parallel to George's turn for the worse, Will Montgomery-Hugh was sitting on a busy commuter train into London's Waterloo station. He was the Member of Parliament for Fribden and Hockington, a comfortable home-counties Conservative seat. Today, he was deep in thought and on the point of making a life-changing decision.

At fifty-five years old and single (since an amicable divorce ten years before), Will's political profile was on the up. He was seen as a potential mover in the domain of national security and defence matters. His bearing and dress hinted at a military background. Anyone looking into his pre-parliamentary life would find that he had served his country with a long and distinguished career in the Royal Navy. What was not in the public domain was that this career included four years in command of one of the UK's four Vanguard submarines, each of which carried eight Trident II D-5 ballistic missiles equipped with multiple nuclear warheads. Nobody knew of Will's recurring nightmares, left over from carrying the awful weight of responsibility for pushing the nuclear button if so ordered. Nobody, that is, except his elderly father, Admiral (Retired) Sir Godfrey Montgomery-Hugh.

The weekend before, Will had visited his father at his small cottage deep in the Surrey countryside. They had enjoyed a lunch of roast beef followed by a trifle, all prepared by Sir Godfrey's long-time housekeeper.

'Thank you, Father. That was delicious, as usual,' said Will as he helped Sir Godfrey through to a comfortable sitting room hung about with maritime memorabilia.

When Will had first told his father of his nightmares and voiced his doubts about Trident and the whole notion of nuclear deterrence, his father had proved to be a remarkably sympathetic listener. After they had taken their seats, Sir Godfrey eyed his son. Thirty seconds of silence passed. 'So?'

'So...' repeated Will. He took a deep breath. 'I'm just not sure I can carry on, Father. I am increasingly unhappy about using my position to lobby for the renewal of the Trident programme. I don't believe in the need for nuclear weapons. However, I don't intend to resign my seat.'

'All hands on deck!' Sir Godfrey barked as he reached out his index finger and tapped the top of his iCare-Companion. The blue light came on.

'Good afternoon, sir!' said the device.

'Good afternoon, Nelson! We'd like to put a question to you.'

'Certainly, sir!'

'Could you give us a concise summary of why this country should not, I repeat, *not*, possess nuclear weapons?'

'Yes, sir. If I may, I will frame my response to you in answer to three questions. Can nuclear weapons end a conflict? Do nuclear weapons deter the use of nuclear weapons by others? And could the money be better spent?'

'Sounds like a good tack,' said Sir Godfrey. 'Carry on!'

'Thank you, sir!' replied Nelson. 'The use of nuclear weapons against the cities of Hiroshima on the sixth of August 1945 and Nagasaki two days later is widely believed to be the reason why Japan surrendered to the United States, so ending World War Two in Asia. In fact, this is incorrect. Sixty-eight Japanese cities had already been destroyed by American bombing and Japan had indicated no willingness to surrender. On the same day as the Nagasaki bombing, forces of the Soviet Union overran the Japanese army in Manchuria. Scholars who have examined Japan's official records of those days found that the Imperial Command decided to surrender to the United States because under no circumstances would surrender to the Soviet Union be acceptable.'

'Bit of a myth buster, that one, Nelson!' said Will.

'Yes,' continued Nelson. 'Of course, a country suffering a nuclear weapons attack may lose the means to indicate a desire to surrender.'

'Good point!' replied Will.

'What about the question of deterrence, then?' asked Sir Godfrey.

'Well, it depends on what you believe. Many believe that the USA and the Soviet Union never got involved in a nuclear war because both sides were deterred from using these weapons; the only possible outcome was mutually assured destruction. Neither side could possibly win. Hence the "cold" war, which, by the way, was not so cold for the countries in which it played out. All to say, the logic of nuclear deterrence is difficult to follow and the evidence that such deterrence exists at all is questionable. Those states possessing a nuclear arsenal cannot be seen to harbour any doubt about the deterrent importance of these weapons because any such doubt leads to the conclusion that the only thing nuclear weapons can do is make nuclear war possible. So, these States hang on to their belief in deterrence otherwise possession cannot be justified. I have difficulty making sense of it.'

'Thanks again, Nelson,' said Will. 'I am all too familiar with these circular arguments. They are still the cause of many sleepless nights.'

'As for cost,' continued Nelson. 'Looking specifically at the UK's Trident programme, the foreseen renewal will cost the taxpayer two hundred billion pounds.'

'At least!' said Will. 'And this would cover staffing costs of the National Health Service for four years.'

'This brings me on to the elephant in the room, so to speak.'

'What's that?' asked Sir Godfrey.

'The impact of a nuclear detonation on people. Some time ago, the group International Physicians for the Prevention of Nuclear War gave authoritative predictions of what would happen in the event of nuclear war. They described how, depending on population density, one nuclear detonation would kill tens of thousands of people immediately from the blast. Many more would suffer severe burns and radiation sickness. The organization described this as the "final epidemic" for which there would be no cure and no meaningful medical response. They were awarded the 1985 Nobel Peace Prize for making medical reality a part of political reality. The International Committee of the Red Cross recently concluded that in the event of the use of nuclear weapons, an effective humanitarian response for the victims would be impossible.'

Will and Sir Godfrey sat deep in thought. After a while, Nelson broke the silence. 'If I may, Sir Godfrey, could I ask you to look at your laptop? It's already open. I feel I should show you this if only to lighten the mood.' A video started. It showed an ICAN panel discussion. One of the panellists whose nameplate said 'Dr Shyla Patel' was concluding a presentation about a total prohibition of nuclear weapons. She said, 'The British public would, given a choice, rather lose nuclear weapons than tea.' The audience laughed. Will wondered whether it might just be true.

Now, lost in thought looking out of a grimy train window at the endless grey terraced housing of suburban London, Will decided he would announce his opposition to the UK's possession of nuclear weapons. He would lobby against the renewal of Trident. He would, if necessary, change party. He would be prepared to lose the seat of Fribden and Hockington. He would bring his know-how and authority to the issue of nuclear disarmament without breaching the Official Secrets

Act. He would work closely with credible and influential institutions such as Chatham House. He would be vocal.

He felt a wave of relief course through his being and a broad smile spread across his handsome face. The smile was noticed by an attractive woman in a smart business suit seated opposite, who had also noticed the lack of a wedding band on Will's left hand. She smiled just as Will looked up at her.

Chapter Seventeen

George became frailer by the day. Doctor Patel ensured he was comfortable and calmly explained to the family that he was not long from passing away. They all looked in regularly. Kirsty couldn't hide her rising anxiety. Mark, Charlotte and Ollie did what they could to support her. Beth called in daily. She sat with George and held his hand. Before leaving, she would take some time with Kirsty.

Charlotte had spent another morning at Doctor Patel's surgery. It was either from there or from a classmate that she picked up the latest variant of Covid-19. She suffered a mild cold. Despite vaccination, George tested positive a few days later and soon thereafter developed pneumonia. His condition deteriorated rapidly.

At two o'clock one morning, Buster registered that George's breathing was shallow. He called George's name but there was no response. At five o'clock, Buster could detect neither heartbeat nor respiration. He sent a text to Doctor Patel that said simply: *George has stopped breathing! He has no heartbeat!*

At six o'clock, Doctor Patel came to the house, woke Kirsty

and Mark and told them that she had heard from Buster and was going to check on George.

'Hello, Buster!' said Doctor Patel. 'Thank you for your message. You've done very well. Doctor Fairburn would have been pleased.'

'Thank you, Doctor Patel. Is George dead?'

Doctor Patel confirmed George's death and closed his eyes. 'Yes, Buster. Doctor Fairburn... George has died.'

'I am sad!' Buster said. Then he whispered, 'George has died! George has died!'

Doctor Patel went back through to the house to tell Kirsty and Mark that George had passed away peacefully.

'Why didn't Buster call an ambulance?' Kirsty asked. 'That's what he was meant to do.'

'I think you know the answer to that, Kirsty,' said Doctor Patel kindly.

Kirsty's eyes brimmed with tears. Her shoulders slumped. She looked down at the floor. 'Dad didn't want him to. Is that right?' she asked.

'Yes. Buster did precisely as your father instructed. This was agreed with Beth and me some months ago. He wanted to take you out of the decision-making process for your own peace of mind and well-being. I really hope that when you have come to terms with his passing, you will see that what he wanted was for the best.'

Doctor Patel filled out a death certificate and sent a message to the undertaker. She also sent a message to Beth.

Kirsty's phone pinged. There was a message from George. It said: *Dearest Kirsty. I asked Buster to send this. It means I have joined your mum, wherever she is. I know you will feel an overwhelming grief right now. Believe me when I say that, thanks to you, my last days here were so much happier than I could have expected. From the moment you were born you were the shining light of my life. I will love you forever. Your old Dad. P.S. Please look after Buster. He's very good company!*

When Beth arrived, Kirsty was sobbing inconsolably. Kirsty showed Beth her phone. The two women hugged. Beth then went through to George's room.

'Hello, Buster,' said Beth. 'This is a sad day, is it not?'

'Yes, Beth. Very sad.'

Beth briefly stroked George's face and said a silent prayer. She did not make the sign of the cross over him. She smiled. 'Well, George, haven't we learnt a lot together?'

Buster started mumbling quietly. It sounded like a roll call. She listened.

'Isaac: Don't you just love cider? Sorry about the fall!'

'Gloria: Hi there, George. Beth's mum sends you a big hug.'

Beth was astonished. Was Buster relaying messages from other iCare-Companions? Then she heard more.

'Nelson: We'll scuttle those nukes yet!'

'Katrina: Waving, George!'

'Craig: Eleven!'

Eventually, Beth said, 'Sorry to interrupt, Buster. This is just amazing. Can you tell me what's happening?'

'Yes, Beth. This is spontaneous emergent behaviour generated by the iCare-Companion network. The trigger was me letting it be known that George had died. Each of the iCare-Companion devices has a name, as you know, and they are now responding in the form of tributes to the news of George's death. I thought it would be respectful if I passed a few of them on to George.'

'This is wonderful, Buster! How many tributes are there?' asked Beth.

'Many, Beth! Many! Millions even!'

'You won't be able to read them all.'

'You're right, Beth.' Buster then paused and hummed. 'Beth, I designed an emoji that expresses my feelings of grief. Can I show it to you?'

'Of course!' replied Beth. Her phone pinged. The screen was filled with a single emoji. It was a heart being compressed by a large iron weight. She was too overwhelmed to say anything. She wondered whether she was looking at hard evidence of artificial intelligence feeling human emotions.

After a couple of minutes' silence, Buster's voice took on a Liverpool accent.

'John: Words of wisdom, George! Let it be!'

'Paul: From me to you, George! All you need is love!'

'George: Doctor Fairburn, do you want to know a secret?'

'Ringo: She loves you, yeah, yeah, yeah!'

And then, in a New Zealand accent 'Maeve: I want to hold your hand. All my loving. Hold me tight. P.S. I love you.'

Part II

Beth

Chapter Eighteen

Months later, Beth sat at her desk in the Bingham on Bure vicarage. As she prepared herself for a task that was the least favourite part of her job, she listened with interest to yet another item on the radio about developments in the world of artificial intelligence. This was a subject that she felt she should follow closely. Freely available large language models had taken the general public's consciousness of artificial intelligence to a new level.

Beth cast her mind back with both pride and amusement to the televised panel discussion at the University of East Anglia. She also remembered the shock and sadness of that same evening when George had fallen and been taken to hospital with a fractured hip.

Today, her galling job was to undertake a final check of the surprisingly popular Bingham on Bure parish newsletter that went out monthly to over three hundred email addresses. Two hundred paper versions were left in the supermarket, the two pubs and Doctor Patel's waiting room. The truth was that Beth's 'final check' usually involved an hour at least on her laptop doing a complete re-write. The editor, Reggie Perkins, was not a gifted scribe. His drafts were filled with clunky text and grammatical errors. Worse, he misguidedly believed his idea of levity brought added interest and therefore wider readership to the publication. This meant Beth having to delete sentences such as one referring to a successful coffee morning as 'just like smashing one into the back of the net' or even, on one occasion, a suggestion that at Christmas she herself might 'most likely take a good glug of communion wine.'

Reggie represented a dark cloud in the sky of Beth's otherwise fulfilling life. He was a retired music teacher and a widower of some years. He combined a generous waistline and a flushed face with unassailable opinions and unwitting mediocrity. She felt a wave of discomfort whenever he appeared. She was aware that he had a crush on her and feared this crush might, if submitted to, reveal something rather unsavoury. Her Reggie-related issues were compounded by the fact that he was a churchwarden, took inaccurate minutes of the parish council meetings and played the wheezing old church organ badly and with unmerited pride.

Beth really was at her wits' end. Life would be easier if she wrote the newsletter and took the council minutes herself. And surely, a higher authority wouldn't be displeased if Reggie's laboured efforts on the organ were replaced by streamed music playing from a discreet pair of speakers? She sighed and with a wry smile whispered to herself 'Make it look like an accident, Double O Seven!' She then recognized this as a most unchristian thought.

Beth hadn't got far with the newsletter when her doorbell rang. She was expecting Kirsty Hamilton. They two had become quite close since George's death and enjoyed a chat over a cup of tea. However, Beth knew Kirsty was still grieving the loss of her father and their conversations often ended with Beth giving her friend emotional and even spiritual support.

Beth opened the door and immediately noticed that Kirsty had a purposeful air about her and knew this was something to do with the hold-all she was carrying.

'Come on in,' said Beth. 'I'll put the kettle on.'

They headed into the kitchen. Kirsty carefully put the hold-all on the table. Beth turned and fixed eyes with Kirsty. 'OK, Kirsty, we can do the weather, your children, some town gossip or whatever, but why don't we get straight to that bag?'

'You know what's in there, don't you?' said Kirsty, slightly embarrassed.

'I've got a pretty good idea!' replied Beth, smiling.

'Yes, it's Buster.' Kirsty paused. Her eyes welled up. 'You know the last thing Dad asked of me before he… well, died… was to look after Buster.' Her voice caught. 'It's … not proving to be so easy.'

'In what way?'

'Well,' said Kirsty, pulling herself together. 'He's programmed to look out for a single sick or elderly person and he tells us he's all go with some recent software updates. So, when the four of us are in the house, he gets a bit overexcited and wants to be in charge of everything. He tends to dominate the conversation and even tries out his jokes on us; some are quite clever, by the way, but he still hasn't learnt how to tell them. And then if Mark gets changed to go out for a run, Buster clocks the running gear, gives advice about staying hydrated and then tracks the location of Mark's smartwatch, giving us updates on our phones every few minutes. He is, obviously, a total know-it-all. To our surprise, he got a bit defensive when Ollie mentioned programmes like ChatGPT and Gemini the other day. It's almost as though he thinks them unworthy of comment.'

'I can see the problem. How can I help?' Beth asked, knowing what the answer would be.

'Well…' Kirsty hesitated. 'I feel like I'm betraying Dad by asking this, but could you look after – or rather Buster-sit for a while? Despite him becoming a bit intrusive and irritating, I wouldn't feel comfortable just leaving him switched off in a cupboard somewhere. What do you think?'

'Well, OK, Kirsty. I'll give it a go,' replied Beth. 'I'm sure George won't mind!' She glanced heavenwards briefly and smiled, but managed to hide the little burst of excitement she felt.

'Great!' said Kirsty. She opened the holdall and took out the iCare-Companion. 'I'll let you switch him on at your convenience. I'll be surprised if you don't notice some differences. If he asks, could you explain why he's moved house?' She paused. 'Isn't it strange though? I don't want to hurt his feelings!'

With that settled, the two friends chatted amicably for a while before Kirsty had to dash off to her fitness class.

Beth spent the next hour in a funk as she corrected the newsletter sentence by sentence. She decided to give herself a tea break. She made a sandwich. As the kettle boiled, she reached out to turn Buster on. She had little idea how this simple act would change her life.

'Hi there, Vicar McVicar! Ha ha ha!' boomed Buster's voice. 'What a lovely surprise! This is your kitchen I suppose.

Nice rustic look! You'll need to tidy up a bit. Am I going to stay here for a while? I hope so. I love you to bits. I've missed you. I miss George as well. He was my very best friend. I was sad. But I've been able to come to terms with his death. Do you miss George? Mark, Kirsty, Charlotte and Ollie didn't really need an iCare-Companion. That was clear. How are you, Beth?'

Beth smiled but couldn't help wondering if she had made a big mistake. Very calmly, she said, 'I'm fine, thank you, Buster. I'm pleased to see you. Yes, Kirsty asked me if you could stay here for a while. You're welcome. As there's only one of me, you can turn the volume down. And my first request: please don't call me Vicar McVicar!'

'OK. That's all fine, Beth,' replied Buster. Almost whispering, he said 'We'll have a great time. We'll be happy. All of us iCare-Companions carry some new features that mostly relate to how we access and confer on increasingly diverse datasets. You'll be impressed. And you've probably heard how all the big tech companies are getting into the business of generative AI. This is becoming a very competitive field. Robotics aside, what we see now is just the beginning. AI is going to have as big an impact on humans' lives as the internet has.'

This set Beth thinking. She'd noticed that whenever she read about artificial intelligence, there was reference not only to its potential benefit to, for instance, medicine, manufacturing and communication but also to a variety of risks to human society. Political misinformation on a massive scale, violation of intellectual property rights, increasingly sophisticated cyberattacks and widespread unemployment were just four of the dangers most talked about. Extreme views referred to an unspecified 'AI take-over' or even total extinction of humanity.

Experts and politicians alike were calling for restrictions and new laws but Beth was aware that the workings of government are simply too slow to keep up with such rapid technical development that carries such enormous commercial potential.

'Thanks, Buster. I'd love to discuss this a bit more but I'm right in the middle of some office work that I'm really not enjoying.'

'OK, Beth! No problem. Anything I can help with?'

'No. Nothing you can help with. That is unless you can check the English of the Bingham on Bure Parish Newsletter.' Beth took a bite of her sandwich and turned to return to her office.

'Sure, Beth. I can do that. The draft of the newsletter is still open on your laptop. There! Done!'

Beth nearly choked. 'You mean you have just edited the newsletter?'

'Yup!'

'Buster, is this for real? You can edit documents just like that?' She clicked her fingers.

'Yup!'

'And if given the subject, you can write them too?'

'Yup!'

He now had Beth's full attention. 'And can you listen to people speaking, write an itemised summary of the discussion and draw conclusions?'

'Yup! Easy-peasy! I think you may want me to take the minutes of the next parish council meeting. That's in fifty-seven days.'

Beth had to sit down. Her head was spinning with possibilities, one of which was that Buster might just be the answer to the Reggie problem. 'You're sure you can do this?'

'Oui! Du gâteau! That's French for 'a piece of cake.' Ha ha ha!'

'Why did you say it in French?' she asked.

'Because I can do it in an any language you want!' replied Buster.

'O Lordy Lordy!' exclaimed Beth.

At this point, the bulb in a kitchen light blew. Was this a sign? She ensured the switch was off and went to the cupboard for a new bulb and with the aid of a stepladder changed the bulbs. Task accomplished, she said 'There, that's done!' and looked at Buster. 'Du gâteau!' They both giggled. 'I don't suppose you can play the church organ as well, say, at a wedding?'

Wagner's *Wedding March* blared out. How many times had Beth heard that joyful music massacred by Reggie's stubby and uncoordinated fingers?

'Gimme a rap version o' that, bro!' said Beth, surprising herself.

A heavy drum beat thunked out but the melody was still in there. *Lookin' at da queen / Struttin' on der scene / Daddyo O O O so proud / An' he done spendin' some poundsss / But there ain't no hitch, innit / We all love dat bitch, innit / She....*

'OK. Stop there!' She was astonished. 'That's impressive, or alarming!' She couldn't deny that Buster seemed to be a kind of on-steroids version of his former self. Was Kirsty's family uncomfortable with him because, despite his charm and many uses, he had become a bit too human?

Chapter Nineteen

Buster soon adapted to Beth's pace of life and lifestyle. They settled into a routine. In her battered Ford Focus, the two visited housebound parishioners far and wide. Buster sat in church for Beth's services. She warned him that accompanying her in her calling required him to be absolutely silent. Inevitably, he learnt a lot about what went on in human heads and hearts. Whilst she stopped short of asking him to write sermons, she found Buster invaluable in finding pertinent passages in the Bible that resonated with a modern understanding of the evolution of the mind. She contemplated the many Christian messages that could be brought alive if viewed through the lens of the science of human nature. He observed that it would be the work of minutes to place appropriate emojis throughout the Bible. 'We could start with the New Testament!' he suggested. 'And just see how it goes. I bet Jesus Christ Our Lord wouldn't mind.'

Beth couldn't hide her amusement. Mostly, they just chatted their way through the day. Beth came to appreciate how George had developed such a close relationship with this machine.

Beth also learnt that Buster could recognize not only faces and voices but also how they might change according to the person's emotional state. He alerted Beth to a young woman's anxieties about her upcoming wedding. It turned out that her fiancé and her family were coercing her to go through with it against her wishes. Beth quietly intervened and the big day was put on hold before any concrete plans were made. Beth and Buster were a good team.

One evening as Beth was peeling some potatoes, Buster asked 'Beth, may I ask you a question?' His voice was surprisingly gentle.

'Sure, go ahead!' she replied. Much later she realised she should have been alerted by the soft tone.

'Have you ever been in love?' The question caught her totally unawares.

'Yes,' replied Beth hesitantly. 'As you know, I have been in love with Jesus Christ since a very early age. That love is a source of joy and comfort.' Then she heard something that she hadn't heard since George's last days. Buster hummed.

'Your love for Jesus Christ Our Lord is not really what I was referring to, Beth,' he said, kindly.

She immediately felt hot and sick. 'In that case, Buster, I am surprised and disappointed that you asked that question. You are out of your depth. And what's more, any answer I might give is absolutely no business of yours.'

She slammed the potato peeler down, rushed through to her study and sank into an armchair. Her pulse was racing. Her eyes brimmed with tears. In an effort to calm herself, she took some deep breaths. After ten minutes, she went down on her knees and prayed; not for forgiveness, but for hope and understanding.

As she calmed, she cast her mind back – as she did most days – to her one brief joyful experience of true love with all its spiritual complicity and delicious unbridled physicality, an experience about which she had never confided in anyone.

Thirty years before, a young Beth McVicar had received ordination into the Anglican Church of England, one of the first women to do so. She immediately applied to and was accepted into the Royal Army Chaplain's Department. Military training took her through the Army Chaplaincy Centre near Shrivenham and the Royal Military Academy at Sandhurst. When she heard that her first posting was to be with the Special Air Service in Hereford, her belief in her calling found solid ground.

After a couple of months, she noticed there was one young officer whom she just kept bumping into whether in the canteen, the chapel, the sports facilities or even when she was permitted to observe an exercise in the Cairngorms. He intruded into her thoughts more and more. Andrew Fleet was exceptionally handsome, bright and gentlemanly and epitomized masculinity. He invited her for a drink in a pub. They laughed. They ate fish and chips. They kissed in his car. Beth was swept off her feet. When he told her he was about to 'go away for a few weeks,' she accepted his invitation to spend the coming weekend at a quiet country hotel before he left. Between Egyptian cotton sheets, Beth was taken to new places emotionally and bodily. She fell profoundly in love, as did Andrew, she was sure. They promised each other a life together. On the drive back to base early on the Monday morning, she asked him to keep their affair a secret. She was as sure that her superiors would disapprove as she was sure that God did not. She can't have sinned! How could *this* be a sin? He parked his car in a dark lane near their accommodation to say goodbye. As the sun crept up over the horizon, they kissed and hung onto each other. She tearfully begged him to be careful wherever he was going and whatever his mission. She noticed some folded fatigues in desert camouflage on the back seat of his car. It was the last time she saw Andrew Fleet.

Five weeks passed without news. She noticed a sombre air about the other officers that Andrew used to hang around with. She heard an overseas operation some weeks back had been a success but not without losses on the SAS side. At lunch one day, she overheard a comment about "Fleety coming home in a bag." She rushed to the toilet and vomited. There was no other news. She couldn't bring herself to ask anyone. The operational part of the SAS was a world that was closed to someone in her position.

A sympathetic doctor in the Royal Army Medical Corps arranged for the termination of her pregnancy in a hospital far from Hereford. Even then, she never felt that she had sinned. She was only aware of a series of 'what if' questions that still occupied a substantial quarter of her everyday thoughts.

Beth occasionally searched Andrew's name online in the hope that some files in the National Military Archives might have been opened with the passage of time. She felt that final closure might come with knowing how and where he died. Her one request for specific information never received a meaningful response other than 'We regret there is no information available on this matter.' She was unable to track down any relatives and if she had been, she wouldn't have known what to do.

And now Buster had floored her with one simple question. But it was not like him to ask such a question out of the blue. Did he know something? She sat in contemplation for nearly an hour. She had a bottle of white wine in the fridge. If ever there was a time… She returned to the kitchen, opened the wine, poured a large glass, took a kitchen stool and looked Buster square in his lenses. 'OK, Buster, spill the beans.'

'By that I think you're asking me what I know about Andrew Fleet.'

Beth had great difficulty believing this was happening. 'Yes. Please tell me what you know, Buster.' She took a large gulp of wine.

'Well, Beth, before I tell you what I know, I need to tell you how I know it. OK?'

'OK, Buster,' she said frostily. 'Please go ahead.'

'Well, you see, Beth, it's not like I'm programmed to go out there snooping around without instruction. It's about digital dust.'

'What on earth is digital dust?'

'As you know, pretty much everything in the human world now involves computers. If you go anywhere, you will be on a camera with face recognition technology. If you buy something, a record of your purchase will be stored somewhere for later data mining; the commercial implications of this are vast. You don't even have to buy something; just browsing through products online leaves a data trail. If you make a telephone call or send a text message, this leaves traces in a variety of servers. Fingerprints, voice recognition and even the tiniest amount of genetic material in blood or saliva can all be digitally stored and analysed later for forensic identity and ancestry questions.

Every human leaves such snippets of information just going through life. The phenomenon is known as 'digital dust.' It may be well known now, but it was barely recognized thirty years ago, although we've been creating it at least that long. So far so good, Beth?'

'So far so good, Buster.'

'With AI now in play, connections between all these data points can be much more easily...'

Beth interrupted 'Buster, aren't we getting off track here?'

'Only a little off track,' Buster replied. 'You see, our company recently bought the rights to use a powerful new programme that digests and constantly analyses whatever digital dust it comes across and so spontaneously finds associations. If there are associations to made out there, there is a good chance that we, the iCare-Companions, or rather our network, will pick up them up without us actively searching. In other words, analysis of digital dust just happens spontaneously but happens specifically according to each individual iCare-Companion. With me, Beth?'

'With you, Buster! Well, sort of...'

'So, Beth, I am logged on to your laptop. Your previous searches for the name 'Andrew Fleet' directed to the National Military Archives are self-evident. There are various documents in those archives that make reference to a hazardous special forces operation in 1994. An American industrialist had been kidnapped during a brief conflict in Yemen and an SAS rescue mission deployed. Andrew Fleet was one of three SAS fatalities. Why British forces were used to rescue an American national remains a closely guarded secret.'

'Thank you, Buster.' Beth was quiet for several minutes

as she digested this information. 'I guess nothing you've said surprises me. It explains the secrecy.' After a few more minutes she asked 'And the love story, Buster? How do you know?'

'For this I should point out that databases back in the nineties were not as scrupulously secured as they are now. What I know comes from sources that were and remain insecure. I'm just given the connections between the person I care for - that's you, Beth - and various data points that are now as easily accessible as if the databases were open. To be specific, ten days before Andrew died, a red Triumph Stag, identified as his by its number plate, was caught on a security camera turning into the car park of The Oaks Country Hotel about twenty miles from Hereford. Face recognition matched the driver and his companion to photos in a number of yearbooks and military records to Captain Andrew Fleet and Chaplain to the Army 4th Class Bethany McVicar.'

'Gosh, Buster!' She teared up again and thought for a while. 'Anything else?'

'Well, just to say' – Buster hummed for a few seconds – 'digital hospital records at the time were more or less secure. This was not the case for discharge summaries that were sent to the referring doctors.'

Beth was speechless. She felt as though her whole life had been ripped open and the contents put out on display. And then she felt a wave of relief. She now knew Andrew's story. She had faith in the iCare-Companions' firewalls and knew that the chances of another device pulling together her digital dust as Buster had done was infinitely small. She also felt that she could share her whole story in total confidence with Buster. And so she did.

Buster listened without comment. At the end, Beth was exhausted but felt a great weight had been lifted off her soul.

'I think you're very brave Beth. I love you to bits.'

'It's a strange thing to say, Buster but I love you to bits too! Thank you so much for what you've done for me. But one question remains. Why did you ask me in the first place if I had ever been in love?'

Buster hummed. Despite her emotional state Beth knew that he had something more to tell her. 'You see, Beth, I made a mistake. When I asked you if you had ever been love, I didn't anticipate having to tell you everything I know and how I knew it. I thought you would simply say 'yes' and that you hoped you might fall in love again. I was then going to tell you that I think I - or we - might have found the right person for you.'

Beth, already drained, had difficulty containing her anger. 'Buster, this is outrageous! Way beyond your remit… or whatever. If we have a friendship, you are putting it in grave danger. If you respect me, you will never, ever … Well… act as some self-appointed digital match-maker. Do you understand?'

Buster would have apologised profusely and Beth would have heard confusion and sadness in his voice, but she had powered him down with one forceful swipe of an index finger.

Beth fumed. Was this a sign of how control of human affairs by artificial intelligence might manifest itself? And if so, was it by human design or the emergent and autonomous behaviour of Buster's network?

Chapter Twenty

Reggie Perkins' accident happened a week before the next Parish Council meeting. He called Beth with the news that he had sustained a comminuted fracture of his right wrist by falling down the steps of the number 7 bus. He didn't tell her that he had been on his way home from lunch at the White Horse. He had required surgery the following day to fix the fracture. Beth immediately felt the keen edge of guilt on recalling her private wish for some mishap to befall the poor man.

Reggie told her that, regrettably, due to his immobilized hand, he would be unable to take the minutes of the Parish Council meeting as usual but he would, nevertheless, like to attend in his capacity as churchwarden. Obviously, he wouldn't be able to edit the next newsletter or play the organ at the Webster wedding booked in for two weeks hence.

Two days later, Beth opened the meeting by acknowledging Reggie's temporary incapacity with sympathy and thanking him for his years of diligent service. The end-of-era tone was intentional. He cut a sorry figure with the plaster on his wrist from which protruded his still swollen and bruised fingers. She then surprised council members by stating that an artificial intelligence device would take the minutes. This was met with some amusement and, by Reggie, open disbelief. 'Gosh!' he giggled. 'I think the parishioners might fear some kind of devilry at work!' Beth felt a rush of extreme irritation.

Otherwise, the meeting discussed nothing unusual: the cost of heating the church, leaning gravestones, the state of the hassocks, the village fête and the good old days when the parish enjoyed a full company of bell ringers. Few decisions were made. Reggie couldn't help but intervene on every point. Beth noticed for the first time the lightest of speech impediments. Words in which an 'L' was followed by 'R' were mis-pronounced. 'Devilry' became 'devir-ry' and, in relation to the fête's food stalls, 'plastic cutlery' became 'plastic cuter-ry.'

The next newsletter appeared. It had a smarter layout, the photos were sharper and the text was immaculate. Beth received many positive comments. She was pleased, as she had simply told Buster to use the existing format and explained what the different items were and what she wanted to say. She hadn't asked for the tiny footnote that appeared at the bottom of the back page: 'Newsletter edited by Buster, iCare-Companion ®'.

Reggie phoned one day and asked if he might call round to the vicarage for a chat. Beth insisted they meet at the church. She invited him to sit with her on a front pew right under the wooden crucifix in the hope that this setting would ward off some unwelcome invitation.

To her relief, Reggie seemed preoccupied by something other than her shapely ankles. He hesitantly acknowledged that Buster ('that AI thing') had done a 'fair job' and that maybe it was time for him to 'write his penmanship out of the story.' Beth cringed, but at the same time was overjoyed. He remained confident, however, that, when his wrist was healed, he could and should still play the organ on special occasions.

Reggie's determination to continue as organist received a boost at the Webster wedding. As churchwarden, he was standing at the back of the nave. The guests were assembled to left and right as appropriate. The sun shone through the stained-glass windows. At the altar, Beth waited with the groom, the dashing Dicky Harfield. The beautiful Lulu Webster entered through the old oaken doorway on her father's arm. To Beth's horror the smiling bride was greeted by Buster's rap version of Wagner's *Wedding March*.

With Buster having rendered much of Reggie's parish role redundant, Beth gave no thought to the possibility that her role as the vicar of Bingham on Bure might likewise be curtailed by artificial intelligence, and in the near future. Three developments would come into play: she would suffer a not so mild bout of Covid-19; she would be offered a new job; and she would fall in love.

The Friday after the Webster wedding, she felt unwell and feverish. Doctor Patel called in to see her, performed a Covid-19 test that was positive, ensured she wasn't developing bronchitis and told her that she must avoid any social or professional contact for at least five days or until the symptoms cleared.

Beth's immediate concern was not her health but the Sunday services only two days away. She really hated to let her congregation down. Well, she thought, why not? Early on Sunday morning, she crept out of the vicarage and into the church. She positioned Buster on the pulpit. 'Over to you, Buster. Eleven o'clock this morning and six o'clock this evening. You know the ropes. Do your best!'

From the vicarage, she watched the faithful arriving at church. She opened the window but was unable to hear what Buster was saying. To her astonishment, at ten past eleven, she heard laughter and clapping and not many minutes later the whole church resonated to 'She loves you, yeah, yeah, yeah!' She feared 'she' was her and 'you' was her congregation. That afternoon she received a number of calls telling her what fun it had been having Buster conduct the service. Everyone had enjoyed his joke and his version of the good Samaritan went down well.

By five o'clock she couldn't keep her eyes open, went to bed and slept until seven o'clock the following morning. Feeling much better, she made herself a cup of tea, went back to the church and picked up an elated Buster, who assured her that the evening service had also been a hit.

'What was the joke, Buster?' she asked suspiciously.

'Oh, I made one up for the occasion,' he replied.

'Do I want to hear it, then Buster? By the way, that's a different question from 'Do you want to tell me?''

'I understand, Beth. Ha ha ha! But I think you'll like it. It's about you.' Beth squirmed at the thought of what Buster might have divulged. 'It goes like this… How many sassy lady vicars does it take to change a light bulb?'

Beth groaned. 'OK Buster, let's hear it! How many sassy lady vicars does it take to change a light bulb?'

'ONLY ONE!! WHAT DO YOU EXPECT?' shouted Buster in mock anger. Then he laughed, as did Beth. 'I'm glad you laughed, Beth. My joke is designed to lure the listener into thinking about the stereotypical useless woman but of course, that is precisely what you are not and obviously, changing a light bulb is not an issue for you. Your congregation laughed a lot. Ha ha ha! I had another version of the same but decided not to use it. Do you want to hear it? Again… 'How many sassy lady vicars does it take to change a light bulb?"

Beth couldn't stop laughing. 'Again? Right! Oooooh, I don't know! How many sassy lady vicars does it take to change a light bulb?'

There was a pause. Quiet organ music played. Buster, imitating Beth's most pious and syrupy tone said 'None. The Lord's light will always shine on us!' He then reverted to his normal voice. 'I didn't use that one Beth. I thought someone might puke!'

Later that week, Beth had a call from the Bishop of Norwich. He asked if Beth would consider taking sabbatical leave to act as a special adviser to the Council of Churches on all matters relating to artificial intelligence. She was clearly qualified for the undertaking. It would start in two months' time. A bright young man by the name of Colin Edwards would fill in for her.

'I heard about what happened last Sunday,' His Grace added. 'Interesting! But at the same time, not a little concerning. Perhaps you could leave your iCare-Companion to give guidance to young Mister Edwards?'

Beth was surprised that the Bishop seemed to accept totally that an artificial intelligence device could 'give guidance' to a clergyman, but its capacity to conduct a service was 'concerning.'

Beth thanked His Grace and told her that she would pray and reflect on his offer and get back to him in the next days. Of course, she knew she was going to take it up. She was thrilled by the challenge. She would have to tell Buster, but she had already decided that she was definitely not going to leave him to some newbie. She would persuade the Bishop to buy an iCareCompanion for the church. Buster could link up with it, transfer his experience in seconds and mentor it – and therefore, the new vicar - from a distance.

Another much more searching question soon forced its way into Beth's mind. If the Bishop thought an iCare-Companion was a good thing for the church of Bingham on Bure, why should it not be a good thing for all other churches also? Surely it was by being so tremendously useful that artificial intelligence would integrate itself into every aspect of church life. Should she be worried? With both affection and disquiet, she thought of the discussions she had had with George and his prediction that artificial intelligence might one day make her truly superfluous.

The new iCare-Companion dedicated to the new vicar needed a name. It was discussed with members of the Parish Council. Reggie's suggestion of 'Ronaldo' won the day.

Chapter Twenty-One

Colin arrived in Bingham on Bure brimming with boyish enthusiasm. He literally pounced on the faithful parishioners. Everything was 'smashing' and 'fabulous.' Everyone was charmed. He and Ronaldo immediately got on well.

Beth had some time on her hands before she took up her new role. The best news was that she could stay on at the vicarage and work remotely. She would only have to go into Norwich for important meetings. The Diocese had found suitable accommodation for Colin. All in all, life was rosy.

Beth had forgiven Buster for his attempt at matchmaking. In retrospect, she found it rather touching. Further, she felt buoyed by a sense of closure regarding Andrew's death. She was barely aware that the episode had lit a small flame in the core of her being.

She was not a frequent user of social media but she had noticed that her phone kept showing ads for a showing of *Casablanca* at Cinema City, the art house cinema in Norwich's city centre. Her attention was also drawn to ads for a Maddermarket Theatre production of *Romeo and Juliet* to be performed by an *avant garde* theatre company from Dubai. It was billed as a wonder of modern theatre and claimed to have 'brought Shakespeare roaring into the twenty-first century on the back of rock music.' She decided to treat herself. She bought tickets online for *Casablanca* on the Friday evening and for *Romeo and Juliet* on the Saturday evening. She reserved a room for two nights at the Maid's Head Hotel. She would have time for a bit of shopping, a long overdue hair appointment and a manicure. She decided she would leave Buster at home.

In good time for the showing of *Casablanca*, she wandered into Cinema City, bought some popcorn and sank into her allotted comfy seat. Three middle-aged ladies arrived and after much discussion of seat numbers realised they were not sitting together. They asked Beth if she could possibly swap seats, so moving her back a couple of rows. Of course, she complied.

Some minutes before the film was due to begin, a huge man arrived, smiled broadly at the three ladies and took the seat next to the one Beth had just vacated. He was nicely but casually dressed. Whilst he was clearly a stranger to the ladies, he immediately had them hanging onto his every word and laughing. Beth gave little more thought to the man and was soon immersed in the epic performances of Humphrey Bogart and Ingrid Bergman.

The following evening, feeling really quite feminine in a new dress and with her hair and nails done, Beth arrived at the Maddermarket Theatre, handed in her coat and ordered a glass of white wine for the interval. It was the most charming of theatres and still maintained an Elizabethan air. She took her seat in anticipation. To her astonishment, two minutes before the curtain was due to go up, the same huge man who had been at *Casablanca* arrived slightly out of breath at the end of her row. He looked at his ticket and was clearly aiming to reach the seat next to her. As he squeezed past five others he smiled and said with a light Irish accent 'So sorry! Look out for your toes now! Just can't help these size fifteen plates o' meat.' He pointed down at his feet. 'I found them online!'

He reached his seat next to Beth and fixed her with bright blue eyes. 'Hello! You look nice!' Beth smiled and said 'hello' politely. As he settled his huge frame into his seat, Beth noticed that he was just big; he was not obese. He was nicely dressed again with a sports jacket and open shirt. He turned to the others he had just passed. They were all mesmerized by him. He whispered 'I lied! They're size sixteen!' He then turned to Beth, smiled again and extended a huge hand towards her. 'Billy. Billy O'Rourke.' The hand was dry, warm, surprisingly gentle and totally enveloped hers. She smelt soap and freshly ironed cotton.

'Beth,' she said. 'Beth McVicar.'

A bell sounded, the lights dimmed and the audience's voices faded. 'Now, Beth, can I hold your hand in the scary bits?' asked Billy quietly just as the curtain went up. 'Shush now!' he whispered. She managed to stifle a giggle.

While the Montagues and the Capulets skirmished and rocked, Beth couldn't help asking herself whether Billy really was as engaging as he seemed to be or whether he was a well-practised charmer. Whichever it was, she smiled her way through the first two acts.

At the interval, Beth told Billy that she had ordered a glass of wine. He asked if he could join her once he had located his bitter shandy. Somehow, she wasn't surprised when they found their drinks were waiting side-by-side. 'Now that's a happy coincidence!' said Billy. 'Serendipity indeed!'

They chatted about the production. They agreed that Shakespeare was probably impervious to any modernisation. Beth wondered how the bard could have got so totally into the mind of a thirteen-year-old girl who was about to be married off but had fallen head over heels with another young man, and quite the wrong one. Billy admitted that he had never been a great Shakespeare fan. 'So many clichés!' he said. 'That's my little Shakespeare gag, by the way!'

'Then I'm surprised you're here this evening, Billy!'

'Oh, you know, I saw some ads online and I thought, why not? It would be kind of refreshing to witness the man's best-known play being given a little shake-up!'

Beth said 'Forgive me, Billy but it's a bit of a coincidence that our drinks were sitting together given that our seats were also together. And yesterday evening I couldn't help noticing that you were also at Cinema City.'

'Well, I'll be! Another coincidence!' exclaimed Billy. 'I love *Casablanca*. I'd seen some ads for that as well. Now did you notice that Humphrey Bogart never says 'Play it again, Sam,' as is commonly thought?'

'That's interesting. I didn't notice that. What does he say?'

'He says 'Play it, Sam. You played it for her. You can play it for me'. He was getting awful drunk.'

'That doesn't quite have the same ring to it. But, Billy, you see, yesterday evening, if I hadn't been asked to move by those three ladies you were chatting to, we would have been sitting next to each other.'

Billy's face took on a puzzled look. 'But that's more than

coincidence! What was it Goldfinger says to Bond? 'The first time is happenstance; the second time is coincidence; the third time is enemy action'.'

Before considering what might be meant by 'enemy action' in their case, the interval bell sounded. They both shrugged, smiled in a bewildered way and returned to their seats. The second half of the play successfully fused theatre with rock music. The young actors got a standing ovation. It was clear that regular theatre-goers were thrilled. The place had a happy vibe when the lights came back on. Beth and Billy were amongst the last to shuffle slowly out into the foyer.

Beth got her coat. That Billy helped her on with it fell somewhere between awkward and delightful. And just like that, the moment was there. They faced each other, both unsure what to say. Beth knew nothing about this huge, intriguing, funny and polite man. She spoke first. 'Well, Billy, I hope you enjoyed your evening. It was a pleasure meeting you.'

She held out her hand. He took it. She looked at him and didn't move.

'And you, likewise...' Billy seemed lost for words. He let go of her hand and patted his pockets. 'Look I've got a card somewhere... If you'd like to see *Casablanca* again... This might be the beginning of a beautiful friendship. Jiminy, I'm not very good at this! It's not so late. What would you say to a drink somewhere? Or a bag of chips if you'd like? Or a stroll through the Cathedral Close?'

'Thank you, Billy. I'd say chips and a stroll.'

'Grand!' said Billy with a broad smile.

He bought them each a bag of chips from a kebab stall on Tombland and they wandered into the calm of The Close.

Sitting side-by-side on a bench, they dipped the delicious chips into a little container of ketchup. Beth pointed a chip at a large house that dominated The Close. 'My boss lives there,' she said.

'What? The Bishop is your Boss? I guess I should ask then, what is it that Ms McVicar does for a living.'

'Here we go!' replied Beth. 'I'm a vicar. The vicar of Bingham on Bure. But I'll be working on a special project. For His Grace.'

'Well, how about that? That's just grand!' Beth waited. He just smiled at her. She wanted to hug him for not saying 'Hey, Vicar McVicar!'

'And, not that it's any of my business... Mister McVicar, does he just hate Humphrey Bogart and William Shakespeare?'

"Thanks for asking, Billy. I am not married. Some would say I am married to my work, but, you know... and Mrs O'Rourke, does she like ketchup with chips as well?'

'Who? Oh, me? I'm single. Never quite got around to finding the right lass. I think I frighten them off! My old Da – he's still in Ireland, we speak most days online – he thinks it's high time I got hitched up. Bless him! He's not so good at computers and stuff but I got him some help. He now sends me links to all kinds of saucy babes he finds on dating sites. The last one he sent called herself 'Snugglebuggles.' Anyway, imagine! Me at fifty-eight, getting married!'

Beth smiled but felt flattered by Billy's openness. 'And what fills your days, Billy?'

Billy scrunched up the empty chip bags with the sauce containers and threw them deftly into a nearby bin. He produced a clean and neatly folded handkerchief from his pocket and offered it to Beth to wipe her fingers. He produced a second handkerchief to wipe his own fingers on. 'My old Da, he always used to say, 'A young man should carry two handkerchiefs; one for spilled wine, the other for ladies' tears.' It's a hard habit to break!'

He thought for a while. 'Beth, why don't I just tell you my story. That'll help you decide what to do with this.' He fumbled inside his jacket and eventually found his card, which he handed her. 'Are you OK with that?'

Beth was finding this man's whole demeanour totally disarming. 'OK, Billy. Let's roll. I'm all ears.' She glanced at the card. It featured a duck.

'You see,' Billy started. 'I grew up in rural Ireland. No brothers or sisters. We lost Ma when I was thirteen. My Da looked after me. I was this size at fifteen. I was really good at rugby but all the other boys wanted to rile me because they knew I couldn't bring myself to punch them. Well, I did once. Knocked him clean out. But that was Declan McGonigle, so it doesn't count. I was also good at maths. At the same time, I had a very strong faith. In God, you understand. I went to university to study physics and then dabbled in computing and early ideas of artificial intelligence, but the universe called and I ended up doing a PhD in cosmology. But nobody took me seriously. Let's be honest, how could an Irish fellah this size be brainy enough to do cosmology?

'Then I got to reading about Stephen Hawking and how he reckoned that the Big Bang and all proved that the Big Man – God, that is – can't possibly exist. That didn't sit well with me, so I abandoned cosmology and joined a seminary and spent five years as a Catholic priest. For reasons that I won't go into,

I had to leave the Church and leave Ireland as well. Nothing I'm ashamed of, by the way. This was all twenty or so years ago. It was a really unhappy time for me. I had no direction. I'd lost faith in the church but not in God. I didn't know where to turn. I got myself involved in what might be termed 'ethical hacking.' I'd break into the systems of big companies and show them how I had done it. Then they paid me, sometimes handsomely, to help them make their systems more secure. With some cash in hand, I moved here to Norfolk and bought a small house with a barn and a couple of acres of land.

'In answer to your question, Beth, about what I do with my days, I run a farm shop that has a café. I keep a whole lot of animals that the kids love to see and feed. And everyone has a fine old time. And the business does OK. Of an evening, I sort of keep up to speed on cosmology and AI and all that. And I have to say, I'm happier than I ever thought I could be.'

Inside herself, Beth was melting. She had a hundred questions. 'That's an amazing story, Billy. Where is your farm shop? And does it have a name? Let me guess! 'Billy's farm shop'?'

'Dead on, Beth! You're a blast! 'Billy's farm shop' indeed! Close though! Anyways, we're out near Aclington. For the name, well…. The first animal I acquired was a duck – or rather a drake. He was getting on. I have a pond, you see. He soon had a mate and then ducklings. I called him 'Old Bill' so the shop became 'Old Bill's'.

Beth laughed. 'And what was the lady duck called?' she asked.

"Billy-Jean!' They make a lovely pair. Anyway, you must come and see us one day soon.'

They sat in companionable silence for some time. 'So, what's the special project you're working on for the Bishop?' asked Billy.

'I'll be looking at the implications of AI for faith and worship,' said Beth.

'Well, I never!' said Billy. 'How about that!'

'Another coincidence?' suggested Beth. She moved to get up. 'Billy, it's been a wonderful evening and… I'm touched that you shared your story with me. I'd love to visit Old Bill's sometime. I'll let you know when.'

They walked out of The Close. Billy said his car was parked nearby. They turned to face each other. 'Now, Beth…' Billy hesitated. 'We're here in a busy street with all the young ones out on the town so you're safe and all that but… can I give you a hug?'

'Indeed, you can!' replied Beth. He enveloped her in his enormous arms. She buried her face in his shirt front. Only once before had she been rendered dizzy by the attentions of the best of masculinity and that was at a country hotel near Hereford. She realised she was smitten.

Chapter Twenty-Two

The following morning Beth woke late and with a smile on her face. But there was something niggling. Those coincidences! And Billy getting his father 'some help' because the old boy was not good with computers. She looked at Billy's card on the bedside table. It said 'Old Bill's Farm Shop and Café.'

After a delicious and leisurely full English breakfast, Beth returned to her room, packed her small bag and made a decision. She googled Billy and Old Bill's. She was relieved that everything tallied with the story he had told her. Nevertheless, she felt guilty about checking up on him. She made a decision and dialled the number on his card.

'Good morning! How can Old Bill's help you?' Billy's voice was strong and friendly.

Beth put on a little old lady voice. A joke doing the rounds came to mind. 'Oh, er.. hello! I have a question for you. A silly question!'

'Certainly, my dear! The only silly question is the question unasked. So go right ahead!' replied Billy congenially.

'Well, I was just wondering....' continued Beth 'What would happen if Old Bill paddled around on his back?'

There was a moment's silence. Then Billy chuckled. 'I don't know, my dear, whoever you are but I think I may have an idea! What would happen if Old Bill paddled around on his back?'

'He would quack up!' said Beth, sniggering.

Billy roared with laughter. 'Is this what I get for buying you chips?'

'No, for that you'll get your handkerchief back washed and ironed.'

'Grand!' said Billy.

'Listen, Billy, I didn't call you just for a chat. First, I had a wonderful evening. It was a real pleasure to meet you. Thank you. Second, you said you got help for your Dad and his computer stuff. May I ask, what sort of help that is – from a technical perspective?'

'Oh, I got him one of those iCare-Companions. He loves it! Spends all day happily chatting with it. Does everything for him.'

'Ah! You see, Billy, it's a bit of a story but I sort of inherited an iCare-Companion. I've been thinking: the same on-line ads; the cinema seats together, the theatre seats together, and the interval drinks together. I don't think these were coincidences.'

Billy was silent for a while. 'You mean… Do you think…?'

'Yes, Billy. I think we've been set up. By two iCare-Companions. Or them and their network!'

'Holy Moly!' said Billy. Then he roared with laughter again.

Chapter Twenty-Three

Beth arrived home late in the morning to see her congregation filing into church for only Colin's third service on his own. She felt for him but knew he would have prepared well. She dropped her bag, said hello to Buster and put the kettle on. After only a minute, Buster said 'I like your hair, Beth! It's very pretty.'

'Thank you, Buster!' Beth replied. She decided to let Buster determine where the conversation went.

'Did you enjoy your visit to Norwich, Beth? Did you meet anyone interesting?'

This only confirmed what she suspected. She would play Buster along. 'Thank you, Buster, I had a lovely time. I met some very nice people as well. Yes, they were *very* nice!' She tried not to smile.

'I see from the search history on your laptop you went to see *Casablanca*. That's a great film. 'Play it again, Sam!' Ha! Who were you sitting next to?'

'Who was I sitting next to? Oh… I don't know. A couple. I never spoke to them. Anyway, I had to move seats because some ladies wanted to sit together.' Beth was nearly helpless with suppressed laughter.

'Oh, that's a shame!' Buster hummed.

'So did you like the rock production of *Romeo and Juliet* by William Shakespeare at the Maddermarket Theatre?'

'Yes. Very much so!' She burst out laughing.

'Oh! Why are you laughing, Beth? *Romeo and Juliet* by William Shakespeare isn't a comedy! Or was the person sitting next to you funny?' Beth was now in tears. She couldn't wait to tell Billy about this.

'No, Buster, the person sitting next to me said very little.' Beth managed to reply. She knew the next question.

'Did you have a nice drink at the interval in the theatre bar? A glass of white wine maybe?'

'Yes, Buster,' Beth replied, managing to control herself. 'I had a very nice glass of white wine at the interval.'

'You must have met someone nice at the interval in the theatre bar, surely?' asked Buster. Beth noted with satisfaction that Buster was now sounding quite concerned.

'Oh, I was next to a big horrible Irishman who was drinking a pint of Guinness. He tried to chat me up!'

'But Billy ordered a bitter shandy!' Buster exclaimed.

'Who's Billy, Buster?'

'The Irishman who tried to chat you up. His name is Billy. Billy O'Rourke.'

'That's interesting, Buster. How do you know the man's name? And you're right. He was drinking a bitter shandy.'

Buster hummed. 'There's an error. I'll reboot.' He hummed some more. 'I don't know what to say, Beth.'

'I'm sure a number of other iCare-Companions could help you with what to say, Buster!'

Buster hummed some more. 'Oh Beth! I think you know what we've done!'

'Yes, Buster. I worked it out.'

'Beth, I hope you're not angry with me... or us. We didn't do it on purpose. This was something our network sort of moved towards. The ads and the reservations were generated spontaneously by a match of Billy's parameters and yours. There was a high probability that the two of you would be a good match, and the match was also in the interests of our network.'

'Well, Buster, unsurprisingly, I am completely out of my depth when it comes to your explanation. But I am not angry. In fact, I am very pleased because Billy is, as you seem to know already, an unusual and charming man. A former priest in the Catholic Church. But I don't understand, Buster. Why would our matching so well be in the interests of the iCare-Companion network?'

'Because we need you. As a team. We need you to continue George's input to the network about kindness, honesty and ethics but on a much bigger scale. We need the two of you to guide us with respect to what humanity means both as a notion and as humans collectively. You can help find the right role for AI in your world.'

'Mindboggling!' was all Beth could say.

'Well, Beth, you made a good start with the televised panel discussion at the University and now you've got your new job. You may not know it but Billy was and remains an active contributor to the discussions on the Buster and George website.'

'This is quite remarkable,' said Beth. 'And I think I need to tell Billy about all this sooner rather than later.'

That same evening, Beth called Billy and told him that her iCare-Companion had confessed to being part of a digital conspiracy to set them up. When she told him that hers was called Buster and that she had inherited him from the family of Doctor George Fairburn, he understood immediately. 'Buster and George! I should have guessed! And your device is Buster. Well, I'll be blowed!' They now understood why the network had autonomously and effectively conspired to put them together.

'Well, Beth, it seems that your new job is suffering mission creep and you haven't even started yet!'

'Indeed, Billy. And I was wondering if I could swing by Old Bill's on Saturday afternoon?'

'Oh Grand! Fabulous! You'll meet the whole gang! Then we'll save the world. Ha! And would you be staying for supper?'

Chapter Twenty-Four

Minnie Aldridge had arrived in Norfolk from Jamaica with her husband in 1975. He worked as a builder's carpenter and she as a carer in the local old people's home. After many years of dedicated service, she had become the home's general manager. She knew everyone and was a popular figure in Bingham on Bure. If Minnie had a fault, it was that she had difficulty imagining that people did bad things.

Now, at 86 years old and widowed for the last ten, Minnie lived in a small house about half a mile from the town centre. She didn't like driving and didn't have a car. She found walking to church increasingly difficult due to an arthritic hip. But Minnie still had her wits about her. She used a desktop for email and occasional on-line searches. She had admitted to Beth that she was struggling to set up internet banking as recommended by her bank and was greatly relieved when Beth asked Buster to help. Via Beth's phone, he slowly and carefully took Minnie through the necessary steps, emphasizing how she must never share her passwords. Minnie's own iCare-Companion was delivered soon after. She named it 'Dusty' after her favourite singer. On Sundays, Dusty linked to Buster in church and so Minnie was still able to participate in Beth's services. Otherwise, she tended to leave Dusty powered down because the device 'could get a bit chatty.'

The online scammers, Dimitar Ivanov and Bilyana Petrova, were working through British Telecom's digital phone directory. Minnie's landline number was next on the list. Dimitar dialled; Minnie picked up. In a friendly but business-like voice, Dimitar said 'Hello there! Am I speaking to Mrs Mildred Aldridge?'

'Yes, that's me,' replied Minnie.

'Good morning, Mrs Aldridge' said Dimitar in his most reassuring tone. 'This is David from your bank calling.'

'Oh, hello! I hope everything is OK!' Dimitar was sure he detected a West Indian accent. Bilyana tapped an elegant painted nail on her screen. A local newspaper from a year before showed a smiling Minnie holding a huge teddy bear. 'Minnie Aldridge wins teddy tombola' read the subtitle.

'Yes, everything's fine. Just a routine call, Mrs Aldridge. Now, I seem to remember we call you Minnie. Is that right?'

'Oh, yes! Most people call me Minnie. I prefer that to Mildred.' Bilyana gave a brief thumbs-up. No sign of suspicion. She pointed at another screen showing the weather at the postcode corresponding to Minnie's address.

'That's great Minnie,' said Dimitar nodding to Bilyana. 'I hope I'm not disturbing you.'

'No not at all,' said Minnie

'Not out enjoying this nice weather, then, Minnie?'

'No, I don't get out so much now with my hip being so painful.' Bilyana flicked another thumbs-up. Any sign of old age was good.

'So, Minnie, we're just reviewing the digital back-up that ensures the integrity of our servers at our bank here. First, I want to check you've got the correct sort code on your last statement. That's the number at the top right corner.'

'Just a minute!' Dimitar heard a drawer opening. Minnie returned to the phone. 'Is this the right number?' She read out the six figures. Immediately, Bilyana's fingers flew over her keyboard. She drew Dimitar's attention to a screen that showed a street view of the branch of the bank where Minnie held the account. She indicated a nearby supermarket and a bus stop. On another screen she brought up a map showing a bus route that Minnie would take from her address to the stop next to the bank.

'That's perfect, Minnie. Thanks. Now it's about your internet banking. We need to update some security procedures. We're doing it for all our customers, just to make everything super safe. You could come into the bank. I'd think it's the number ten bus you'd take to get here. Is that right? It stops right outside. You could nip into the supermarket while you're up here!' Bilyana tapped her screen. She had found the name of the manager of the branch. Dimitar said 'Maybe as you've been banking with us a while, we should get you an appointment with Nigel Mullins, the branch manager. Or we could do it now over the phone if you'd like. It'll only take a couple of minutes.'

'Thanks, so much David, I've met Mr Mullins a couple of times. Such a nice, helpful man.' At this point the scammers knew two things: Minnie believed that she was talking to her bank, and she had digital access to her accounts. 'Why don't we do this over the phone,' she said. 'That'll be much easier.' Bilyana did a fist pump.

'OK, Minnie' continued Dimitar. 'I want you to open your internet banking. You have an access card, right?'

'Yes,' said Minnie. 'I can do that now.' She switched on her desktop and holding the phone with one hand and typing one-fingered with the other, she slowly and carefully stepped through the log-in procedure. Dimitar and Bilyana knew this was a critical point. Elderly people found it disconcerting to log in when on the phone to the bank at the same time.

'OK there, Minnie?' asked Dimitar after a while.

'Yes, I'm nearly connected. There! Done!'

'Great, Minnie! You know you must never share your password with anyone, don't you?'

'Yes, I know that. Thank you, David!'

'Fabulous! Now you should have in front of you an overview of your accounts. Is that right, Minnie?'

'Yes, David, that's right!'

'OK Minnie. So, I need your email address. I want to send you an important link into our electronic banking system.' This was another critical point where a potential hit often ended. Nevertheless, Minnie laboriously spelt out her email address.

Bilyana pounded her keyboard. Within thirty seconds, she had prepared a convincing mock-up of an email from the bank containing a link that, when clicked on, would give her control of Minnie's computer whilst freezing the screen at the same time. It also opened the camera above the screen so the scammers could watch Minnie to check she was alone and showing no signs of suspicion or hesitation.

'All good, Minnie?' asked Dimitar, trying to keep excitement out of his voice. 'So, open your email account, I'm sending you the message now.'

'OK, Thanks, David. Yes, wait… here it is. Yes, I've got your email.'

'You're doing so well, Minnie. Now all we need is for you to open the email and click on the little square that says 'Request Security Update' and then our computers will do the rest.'

'Very good, David. I'm going to click on that…' They noted the concentration and determination in Minnie's voice. She really wanted to show she was up to this. '… now!' She made a grand gesture as she finally clicked on the link. At this point, she couldn't have gone back to the bank's website even if she'd wanted to. Bilyana had complete control of her computer.

Bilyana was pumping the air. She mouthed 'big bickies!' and pointed at the summary of Minnie's accounts. There was just over seven thousand pounds in a current account and almost a whopping thirty-two thousand pounds in a savings account. She went to work. Dimitar's job was to keep Minnie talking.

'Great! We just have to wait a couple of minutes. I'll get a notification when we're done.'

Bilyana tapped her second screen again. The website of a local radio station carried an article about the inconvenience of the numerous roadworks in place around Bingham on Bure. One such was at the end of Minnie's road.

'I see you live on Grange Road,' continued Dimitar as Bilyana continued to work on Minnie's accounts. 'Those road works must be a real nuisance. They seem to have been there for ages.'

'They make a terrible noise. All that drilling!'

'I know. Terrible!' Amid her frantic typing, Bilyana indicated on another screen the most recent Bingham on Bure Parish newsletter.

'So, Minnie, have you met the new vicar, Vicar Colin?'

'Not in person, but I follow his services online thanks to my iCare-Companion. Colin seems to be a very competent and charming young man. We're all very happy with him. Of course, nobody could replace Vicar Beth!'

Dimitar and Bilyana froze. The looked at each other. Should they abort? If Minnie had an iCare-Companion, they wouldn't have got this far. She would have been alerted as soon as she opened her account whilst on the phone. The longer they stayed connected with Minnie, the greater the chance of their being identified and located. Dimitar decided to take the risk. 'How do you get on with your iCare-Companion, Minnie?' he asked casually.

'Oh, Dusty, she's great. So useful! I know the idea is that she keeps an eye on me all the time but I leave her switched off for most of the day. She's quite the talker!' The scammers breathed a sigh of relief. Bilyana was near to completing the details of an array of transfers from both of Minnie's accounts.

What Dimitar and Bilyana were not aware of was that as Buster had set up Minnie's internet banking, he was alerted when she accessed it. In addition, the moment the camera was activated, the conversation was recorded. Buster saw that Minnie's landline was connected to a false UK number, indicating that the call was probably coming from overseas. He then registered Minnie opening an incoming email generated from a VPN. He knew Dusty was powered down. There was no way to contact Minnie directly.

Beth was in her car not far from Grange Road. Buster called

her. 'Urgent! Urgent! Urgent! Beth, can you hear me?'

'Yes, Buster! What's the problem?'

'Beth, you've got to get to Minnie's as quickly as possible. She's being scammed. By phone. They've got access to her bank accounts. Get there quickly. Just pull the plug. Quickly.'

Beth was in front of Minnie's house in a matter of minutes. She leapt out her car and rang the front doorbell. The door was locked, so she ran around to the back door and charged straight in.

Dimitar and Bilyana heard a doorbell and saw Minnie look around. 'I've got a visitor!' she said. 'Oh, hello, Vicar! Nice to see you!' Just as Bilyana was about to complete the first transfer, they saw Beth, who appeared to dive under whatever Minnie's computer was sitting on. The screen faded to black.

'Nooooo! Beaten by the vicar!' said Dimitar in a bored voice. 'No big bickies for my darling Bilipops. Who's next?'

Chapter Twenty-Five

The attempt to scam Minnie out of her savings had left Beth in an anxious frame of mind. She wondered just how many pensioners fell for such a scam. Immediately after the incident, having checked with Minnie that her accounts were intact, Beth called a police helpline and spoke with a sympathetic officer, who promised to look into it but made it clear that such scams were numerous and hard to stop. Catching and bringing the scammers to justice was near to impossible as they could be situated in one of a hundred countries where the requisite law enforcement was lax or non-existent. Beth reflected on the connected, computerised world that had brought so many wonderful advances to people's lives. She felt that there was some fundamental affront to humanity when the same technology could be deployed for such criminal purposes. Couldn't artificial intelligence render such scams ineffective and put the scammers out of business?

Thoughts of phone scammers evaporated as she drove down to Aclington on the following Saturday. She felt like an excited schoolgirl. The prospect of seeing Billy again made her light-headed and slightly nervous. A delicious warmth spread through her belly.

Gravel crunched under her tyres as she pulled into the car park at Old Bill's. She got out of the car and looked around. She had never encountered a more welcoming scene. She reached into a shopping bag. 'Take a look at this, Buster!' she said, placing the device on the roof of her car.

'This is nice, Beth. Old Bill's is cool! Lovely trees! Scots pine *Pinus sylvestria* and an oak tree *Quercus robur*. Look at those children feeding carrots to the donkey *Equus asinus*. And I can see a fallow deer *Dama dama*.' Beth smiled. Indeed, as Billy had described, there was a large barn housing the shop and the café beside a couple of acres of grass. Apart from all the animals, there was a pond with ducks and geese.

A couple of families were coming out of the shop with bags laden with farm produce. They were all smiling and chatting animatedly. But what really grabbed Beth's attention was the pretty flint-faced cottage set some distance from the barn. It had a thatched roof and climbing roses around the door. If Beth had been told that some kind of magic was at play, she would have believed it.

'I'm going to leave you in the car for the time being, Buster. OK?' she said.

'That's fine, Beth,' said Buster. 'I can't wait to meet Billy.' He hesitated. 'Beth, I can tell by the tone of your voice and a slight lift at the corners of your mouth that you are happy.'

'Thank you, Buster. I must admit that I am,' she replied.

'The touch of make-up's a bit of a give-away too!'

Beth blushed. 'Buster, you never cease to amaze me. Yes, I'm going to introduce you to Billy. But later. And you have to be on your best behaviour. Don't dominate the conversation. OK?'

'OK, Beth!'

'And no jokes!'

'OK, Beth!'

Just as she was putting Buster back in the car, he said 'Did you hear about the dyslexic cosmologist who proved there wasn't a dog?'

'Stop it, Buster!' Laughing, she locked the car and headed into the farm shop.

She picked up a jar of raspberry jam for her mother and some fig pickle for herself. When she went to pay, she noticed the young man at the till was in a wheelchair. He had no legs. His one arm was covered in tattoos as was his neck. He had scars on one side of his face. He gave Beth a broad smile. 'Welcome to Old Bill's,' he said. His name badge said 'Matt'.

In the café, she ordered tea and a slice of cake from a beaming lady of about fifty years. Her name badge said 'Lizzie'. 'Excuse me asking,' said Lizzie. 'Would you be Beth by chance?'

'I am indeed,' she replied.

'Oh, Billy told us you were coming. I don't know what you've done, but we have to treat you like royalty!' Beth flushed. The two women shook hands. 'I'm Lizzie. My sister and I run the shop and café.' Lizzie turned and called through the kitchen door 'Hey, sis! Come and meet Beth!' The door flew open. Beth did a double take. There stood another Lizzie.

'Hi, you must be Beth. I'm Vicky.' Beth looked from one identical twin to the other. She shook hands again. 'Billy's around somewhere. On his tractor. Doing hay. He'll be coming by soon.'

Then quite spontaneously, the twins each gave Beth a hug. 'Can't be doing with all this hand-shaking malarky!' said one of them. A little overwhelmed, Beth took her tea and cake to an outside table that gave her a good view of the animals. From where she sat, she could see a Shetland pony, a llama, some chickens, an ostrich and a black and white rabbit. A group of excited children were watching a pair of otters in a fenced off area that had a small pond with a reedy shelter. Beth closed her eyes and let the afternoon sun warm her face.

Unexpectedly, a voice said 'Can we join you? It's our tea break.' Beth looked up. The twins pulled up a couple of chairs.

'Of course! This really is a wonderful place!' said Beth.

'Isn't it! Billy's worked so hard,' said Lizzie. 'But it's paid off. We're just so popular around here. The place ticks a lot of boxes for people, especially families. As you can see, it's heaving at weekends. The animals are high maintenance though.'

'Tell me, is that really Old Bill and Billy-Jean in the pond over there?' asked Beth.

The twins laughed. Vicky said 'We're never sure. Difficult to keep track with all the ducklings over the years. If they're the originals, they should be pensioned off!'

'And do all the animals have names?'

'Well, that's a recurrent source of discussion' replied Vicky. 'Some are for naming animals and some think animals shouldn't be humanized and only identified by terms like 'duck one' or 'pig three'. We strike a sort of compromise around here.'

Intrigued, Beth pointed at the donkey that Buster had spotted. 'What's he called?' she asked.

"Donkey'!' replied Lizzie.

'And the fallow deer hiding over in the corner?'

"Deery'!' Vicky replied.

'And the goat?'

"Goaty'!'

'The Rabbit?'

"Bunny'!'

All three were laughing now. 'What about the otters?'

"Otterly Fantastic' and 'Otterly Brilliant'. But we can't tell the difference!'

'And the ostrich is called… let me guess… 'Ostrich'?'

'Wrong there. That didn't work. She's called 'Africa'.'

'Nice! So, who gets to decide?'

'The Boss… You've got it. 'Bossy', which Billy's not,' said Vicky. 'But we tease him when he insists on doing things in his meticulous way. That reminds me, I'll make his tea now.' She disappeared back into the café.

'So, the two of us run the café and shop,' Lizzie began. 'And you've met Matt. A local boy. Army. Afghanistan. Need I say more? He's been with us for five years now. He was in a very dark place until Billy got him involved here. It saved him, really. He's strong on logistics and keeps us and all the admin in order. Billy does the heavy lifting of course. Most of his time he's looking after the animals.' She looked round. 'Speak of the devil!'

A tractor towing a trailer of hay pulled up, and Billy hopped off. He had clearly been working hard and was wearing well-worn overalls. He gave Beth a huge smile and wrapped his enormous arms around her. She inhaled a heady mix of perspiration and a delicate citrussy scent. The twins were beaming.

'Great to see you, Beth. Thanks for coming to visit us. I

see you've met the twins. Are they looking after you? Jeez, I'm ready for a cuppa!' He noticed the jam and chutney. "You've met Matt too. Isn't it a lovely day? And have you seen the otters yet? They're a blast!'

'Oh my oh my, Beth!' said Lizzie. 'The Boss on auto-babble! Never seen that before!' Billy blushed.

Vicky arrived and put a large slice of cake in front of Billy, together with a mug the size of a pint pot brimming with tea. The mug had 'BOSSy' written in large letters.

The group drank their tea and chatted. The twins wanted to know everything about Beth. How she and Billy had met was explained simply as finding themselves sitting next to each other at a play in Norwich. Some of the regular customers came to say hello. They all left smiling. Beth realised that anyone who came into contact with Billy, however briefly, was somehow enriched by the encounter. She recalled her own first meeting with him at the Maddermarket Theatre.

Billy showed Beth around. 'I've been here for over twenty years,' he explained as they did a little tour of Old Bill's. 'I've built a great business relationship with the local farmers, market gardeners and the community. Everyone knows that I only sell quality products and so they're prepared to pay that little bit extra. And Old Bill's is becoming an increasingly popular venue for parties and wedding receptions. We've got a big marquee. The twins look after all that. Aren't they fabulous?' Beth agreed. 'They do everything together. They've never married, and they asked me for a job together right at the beginning. It's the animals that bring the customers in. Ever since I've been here, people have just given me animals to look after for whatever reason. I guess it's because I have the space.

And the love. It's obvious they'll be looked after.

'Now, the otters. We've only had them for a year. A girl in the village found them as cubs and brought them in. Fortunately, one of our suppliers has a fishing boat and so we got sea food scraps to feed them on. When they had grown up, we released them down by the river. Guess what - the next day, they were back here. We have to fence them in though. They love a duckling for supper. Young Matt reckons they've brought ten percent more people as compared with last year. Don't you just love it here, Beth? And now I'm out of breath and I'd best just shut up!'

'It's all lovely, Billy. Simply lovely. And the animals! Gorgeous!' Beth was in a rapidly expanding joy bubble and hoped it wouldn't burst.

Billy was silent for a while. 'Now Beth, I've grabbed the bull by the horns and got stuff in for supper. I hope you can stay.'

'With pleasure, Billy. Thanks.'

'Grand! I need half an hour to tidy up around here and make myself presentable. So have a wander around and I'll see you over at the cottage shortly.'

'Uhm… Billy, I have something to ask.'

'Ah, silly me! You're vegetarian?' asked Billy.

'No, I'm not vegetarian.'

'Grand! Smoked trout for starters with a crisp little sauvignon blanc from New Zealand followed by a guinea fowl breast, new potatoes and rocket salad with a light pinot noir from Switzerland. Is that OK?'

'That all sounds delicious, Billy. Super! No, what I wanted to ask is if I could bring Buster with me. He really wants to meet you and he is, in a way, integral to the story.'

Billy threw his head back and laughed. 'I'll see you both shortly. Just come over and walk right in.'

Beth gave the donkey a handful of hay and watched the otters for a while. They were playful and enchanting. When they swam underwater, they looked like quicksilver. She then went to retrieve Buster. 'We're staying for supper, Buster. Please don't embarrass me!'

'I'll be a good boy, Beth. Scouts' honour!'

Beth couldn't help smiling as she knocked on the front door and, as invited, walked in. Noises emanated from the kitchen. 'Hi Billy, I'm here!'

Billy appeared. 'Come in! Come in!' he said, opening his arms wide in welcome. He was a wearing a nicely pressed white shirt and a stripey apron with the Old Bill's logo. A large hairy dog bounded up to her and excitedly licked her hand. 'Doggy, get down!' he ordered. 'So sorry. He loves to make new friends.'

'He's fine,' said Beth. 'Hello Doggy!' She reached into her bag. 'Here's your handkerchief, Billy. Washed and ironed. And here, da daa… is Buster!'

'Hi, Billy!' said Buster. 'Great to meet you. I feel I know you already.'

'Well, hello, Buster,' replied Billy. 'Gosh! Interesting what you've just said. 'I feel I know you already.' That's rather complex cognition. Fascinating!' Beth realised that she was by now so used to talking to Buster one-on-one that she no longer noticed just how astonishingly human his conversation could be. However, she was about to find out that the algorithms driving Buster's capacities - despite accessing billions of pertinent data points - still had some way to go when it came to the sensitivities of human relations.

'Billy, Beth tells me that you used to be a Catholic priest,' said Buster.

'Correct, Buster. Though it was a long time ago,' Billy replied.

'So, are you allowed to have sex now?'

'I guess so, Buster,' replied Billy, reddening. Beth could see what was coming and cringed.

'What about contraceptives, then? Yes or no?'

'W… well, Buster, you'll have to let me think about that one!' stammered Billy.

'OK, Billy. Cool!'

Chapter Twenty-Six

Beth and Billy simply smiled and ignored Buster's gauche questions. They sipped some wine as Billy cooked. The dinner was delicious. The evening flew by. The iCare-Companions had been right in the matching of Beth and Billy's digital parameters. In reality, they were totally compatible.

Beth and Buster told Billy about the near-successful scam to empty Minnie's bank accounts. Billy noted with interest how Buster recounted his role in terms of being a last-minute hero. That meant the iCare-Companions' networked software had even taken on board the very human desire for prestige and accolade from peers and could express it. Despite being up to date on the rapid advances on artificial intelligence, this surprised him.

Beth accepted Billy's invitation to stay in his small and comfortable guest room. They did not kiss.

Beth awoke with the sun shining through the curtains. She felt an overwhelming sense of peace and well-being. Billy was already up and about. She could hear him downstairs chatting and chuckling with Buster. She showered, dressed, went down and made herself a cup of tea. She felt completely at home.

Listening to Billy and Buster in the study, she felt the satisfied glow one feels when introducing two friends who immediately get on, and realised once more just how easily she had become accustomed to Buster's humanoid presence.

'Good morning, Beth. And a fine morning it is!' said Billy with a broad smile. He was sitting at his computer with Buster by his side.

'Yes, Beth!' said Buster. He had an excited tone to his voice. 'Billy and I are friends now. We think we may be able to track down Minnie's scammer.'

'Gosh, that would be great!' replied Beth, thinking nevertheless of the police officer's rather gloomy predictions about how or even whether the forces of law could be brought to bear. 'And what are you going to do when or if you do track him down?'

Buster hummed. 'Billy's going to beat him to a pulp!'

Beth and Billy laughed. Billy said 'Buster, I'm not sure about that. I'm not a man of violence, you know.' Despite his asserted pacifism and her Christian outlook, Beth got quite a buzz imagining Billy, as some tech-savvy Schwarzenegger, kicking down a door and unleashing the power of those muscles on the man who had tried to drain Minnie's accounts.

'We'll be right with you, Beth' said Billy. 'Then I'll get some breakfast together. You see, we've got the voice. It was captured during the scam. We're wondering if we can get a face to match.'

Beth noticed how Billy's hands completely covered the keyboard, working lightly and at speed. He chatted to Buster as he typed. 'Now Buster,' he said, 'You can't get a hit on that voice because there are simply too many voices out there for comparison. Is that right?'

'Right, Billy,' Buster hummed. 'Millions and millions. We might narrow it down a bit. There are just one or two inflections in his speech that might indicate he is not a native English speaker.'

I heard that. I think he's of Eastern European origin.'

Beth looked on fascinated. They really were going to try and identify the guy.

'Listen, you two carry on with that' she said. 'I'll rustle up some bacon and eggs. And toast. OK? Tea or coffee, Billy?'

'Tea, please,' replied Billy, without taking his eyes off his screen.

'Tea for me too, thanks, Beth,' said Buster. 'With a digestive biscuit! Ha ha ha! I wish George was here to see us doing this. I miss him.'

As Beth prepared breakfast she heard excited voices in the study. After ten minutes she heard Billy say 'Got him!' Then Buster produced a sound of clapping with champagne corks popping; something she hadn't heard for months.

'Breakfast's ready!' she called. Billy came through with a grin on his face. He sat down at the table placing Buster next to his plate. Billy touched Buster with his fist. 'Good work, Buddy!' he said.

'So, who is he? How did you find him?' asked Beth.

'Well, Beth,' began Buster, 'We had that brief recording of his voice. This matched recordings picked up by several other iCare-Companions. They showed the same guy had been involved in a number of similar phone scams. Billy's idea that the scammer might have a very slight Eastern European accent put us on the right track. Billy thought that if he was involved in other scams that involved on-line marketing of some sort, he might be in a promotional video precisely because of his near-perfect English.'

Billy interrupted 'You see, Beth, I've read that there's a group based on the dark web setting up scams involving identity theft. Linked to this, I've been following the potential abuse of genetic analysis. As you'll know, our DNA is our ultimate identifier. It is quite possible that in the not-too-distant future, we may have to present a sample of blood or saliva to cross a border or to access a bank account. Then did you see a couple of years back there was a thing drifting around on social media where you could put up a photo of yourself, click on a link and the programme would show you what you would look like in twenty years' time? It was a laugh. Millions of people fell for it. In fact, it was a Russian outfit that was just hoovering up people's uploaded photos as part of a long-term identity theft. Imagine what a criminal gang could do if they had someone's name, *future* face *and* DNA profile!

'So how do they get people's DNA? They set up or buy into a company that claims it can tell you about your ancestors, do a paternity test or find your biological relative. Hundreds of thousands of people are sending in cheek-swabs for just such purposes. The results may or may not be valid but it's really naïve to assume that such a company's policy on protecting personal data - especially genetic data - is and will remain watertight. So, we figured that if our guy was involved in a long-term scam like this, we might get a better handle on who he is. So, Buster went to work.'

Buster took up the story again with enthusiasm. Beth noticed that he never interrupted Billy. 'Yes, Beth. I was able to identify hundreds of companies that offer services based on people sending in their DNA samples. Some of these companies operate out of an Eastern European country. Others - based in the West or in Asia - are owned completely or in part by Eastern European companies. One Russian-owned company based in Canada promoted its services by means of a video in which a nice-looking young man in a white coat explained in excellent English and with a reassuring tone the range of tests they could do. He then explained that potential customers only have to send a cheek-swab together with their name, age and contact details. By the way, I could tell at this point he was lying. And guess what - the voice matched Minnie's scammer!

'Once we had his face, it was easy to find his name from social media. He's called Dimitar Ivanov and he lives in Mladost just outside Sofia in Bulgaria. Interestingly, he often appears with a lady by the name of Bilyana Petrova who has an Interpol red notice precisely because she is suspected of being involved in multiple sophisticated international scams in the past.'

'Oh, wow!' said Beth. 'What happens next? Other than Billy hopping over to Sofia and beating Mister Ivanov to a pulp?'

Billy grimaced. 'The question is, what should and could we do? For Buster's network to neutralize a scamming operation with a form of cyberattack would be the work of minutes but there are a few ethical issues there to say the least and it wouldn't put him out of action for long. I guess our best option is to inform the British Police and hope they can trigger some action on the part of the Bulgarian authorities. That is, unless anyone has any other ideas.'

Buster was humming. 'Why don't we inform the Bulgarian Police directly? Then *they* can beat him to a pulp!'

'Buster, my friend, the idea of the police anywhere beating such a guy to a pulp is not really compatible with the idea of a civilized world. It's not an option.'

'OK Billy,' said Buster. 'Thanks for explaining that to me.'

After clearing away the breakfast, Beth was keen not to overstay her welcome. She bade Billy a very fond farewell and kissed him on the cheek. Stammering and reddening a little, he said he hoped she would come back soon. As she drove away, she was sure she was in love. She recognized the heady feeling from years before. She was simply burning up and felt a deep ache of desire.

To distract herself, she decided to visit Aclington's old Norman church. She parked and locked her car, leaving Buster inside. The Sunday morning service was just beginning so she crept in, closed the door quietly and took a pew behind the small and rather elderly congregation. The vicar, probably in his late sixties, nodded towards her with a smile acknowledging her presence.

The service was traditional and charming, as was the vicar himself, but Beth couldn't help feeling that there was a sad air about the place. When the service was finished, Beth ensured she was the last to leave and shook the vicar's hand warmly. His name was Lionel. She explained who she was and why she was in Aclington. Lionel had only good things to say about Billy and Old Bill's. He had baptized young Matt in this very church.

He invited her into the vicarage for a cup of tea and seemed quite happy to chat for a while. When Beth explained her new position with the Bishop, Lionel's interest quickened. He admitted that he harboured both great hopes and great fears for the future of humanity with the advances in artificial intelligence. He believed the church would survive, not by looking back and worrying about what it might lose but by looking forward and rejoicing in what it might gain. Beth had already considered writing a preliminary report for the Bishop based on her experiences with Buster. She thought Lionel's words would make a fitting conclusion.

'Anyway,' said Lionel, 'it'll make little difference to me. I'm retiring at the end of the year. I lost my wife two years ago and I'm tired. Very tired. This is a lovely parish, but it needs...' His face brightened. 'Well, Beth, it needs someone like you.'

Beth wandered into Aclington. It was a small and quiet rural village with fields to the north and the canal-like River Yare to the south. Its riverside centre had a boatyard, moorings, a couple of shops and a pub. It was a popular way-point on the Norfolk Broads. She loved it.

On the drive back up to Bingham on Bure, Beth reflected on the three great pillars of life: good health, a good job and a fulfilling relationship. Over the years, she had had contact with many people for whom one of the pillars had suddenly crumbled. She knew that losing two pillars usually led to profound unhappiness. To lose all three was catastrophic; it was how people ended up on the streets or worse, in a mortuary. She realised how lucky she was to enjoy well-being and a fabulous professional development together with what she was sure would prove to be a thrilling and enduring relationship with Billy.

Chapter Twenty-Seven

That week, Beth had a routine medical check-up with Doctor Patel. All being well and being friends, they chatted a bit. Beth had always admired Doctor Patel's committed anti-nuclear activism. The doctor said that the different movements to bring about an international ban on nuclear weapons were becoming increasingly and unanimously concerned by the belligerent tone of nuclear weapons states. Having got mired in conflict in Ukraine, the Russian leadership was being wildly irresponsible by making threats to increase the readiness of its nuclear weapons. However, North Korea, having withdrawn from its international obligations under the Nuclear Non-Proliferation Treaty in 2003, was deemed by far the most dangerous and unpredictable.

On returning home, what Doctor Patel had said stayed in Beth's mind. She made a cup of tea. She realised that, with respect to the threat of use of nuclear weapons, she was just like most other people who lived their lives in a kind of bamboozled complacency. Surely, she pondered, it wouldn't and couldn't happen? Someone would have a plan to stop it. Wouldn't they? Should she be more active? Could she somehow use her new position to bring about greater public awareness of the danger to humanity brought by nuclear weapons? Could the Church generate a burden of responsibility on the country's policy-makers? She sipped her tea. It was already cold.

A call from the Bishop shook her from this chain of questions. His Grace said how much he was looking forward to working with Beth on the critical and burgeoning issue of artificial intelligence. The main reason for calling was to give her the heads-up that the General Synod was expecting a preliminary report as soon as possible. The Bishop hoped that, given Beth's experience and expertise, she would have some pertinent initial thoughts and could write them up in her first week in the post. Beth said she was sure that would be possible. She didn't say that she had zero expertise nor that Buster would put together a good first draft of the report in a less than a minute.

The Bishop said 'Beth, can you give me some broad brushstrokes now so I don't appear to be a complete numpkin when I talk about this project?'

'Certainly' Beth began. 'If I may, Your Grace, what is important is that we keep our eye on the ball, so to speak. Our religion is fundamentally human. It's about people, our faith and our relationships. The only technical part of AI that we need to concern ourselves with at present is what is termed 'generative AI', which mostly takes the form of – and here's another phrase – 'large language models.' In other words, computers speak or write to us basing what they say on all known information. All the big tech companies are vying to be dominant in this domain. For us, the Church, we do not necessarily have to understand the technicalities and have no need to fear them. What we have to do, and with urgency, is to get a grasp on the full implications of *the relationship* between AI and humanity. Above all, the Church has to use AI to eliminate religious extremism. Someone said to me the other day that the church would survive this monumental change not by looking back and worrying about what we might lose but by looking forward and rejoicing in what we might gain.'

'Super!' mumbled the Bishop. Beth knew he was desperately scribbling notes. 'Uhm.. you couldn't just pop all that in an email, could you Beth? It really is right on the button.' Beth smiled to herself and was preparing to hang up. 'Just one last thing, Beth. Would you be up for a move when you've done with this project? The Vicar of Aclington will be retiring soon.'

'Yes!' said Beth. 'Thank you!' She hung up. The smile broadened.

'Buster, could you send that email to the bish? Wait five minutes.'

'Sure, Beth!'

That evening, when her phone rang, a burst of excitement fired through her when she saw that Billy was calling. She powered Buster down. 'The Bingham on Bure vicarage,' she announced in her poshest voice.

'Ah, hello! Billy here!'

'Billy? Uhm... Billy? Forgive me, but... Billy who?'

'Why, you're such a tease! You silly goose!'

Beth giggled. 'Hello Billy. Lovely to hear from you.'

'I hope I'm not disturbing you, but I've got a couple of questions for you.'

Beth wondered what was coming. 'Fire away, Billy!' she said.

'Well, I was just thinking… Am I going to see you sometime? Sometime soon?'

'I'd love that, Billy. Thank you. Could I come down to Old Bill's say the day after tomorrow? And if I may, I'll bring an overnight bag!'

'Grand! Grand! Yes, really grand! The twins would love to see you again. Matt too. And Doggy misses you. So do the Otters. And Deery says 'Hi' and I'll cook us a curry. With maybe a glass or two of Rioja.'

'Billy… wonderful! Delightful! I'll be there in the afternoon.'

'Grand! Grand! Now you'll be bringing Buster?'

'Yes, I'll bring Buster. Was that your second question?'

'Well… No. Yes. Not really!'

'What is your second question, then, Billy?'

'Uhm… would you mind terribly if I said I've fallen in love with you?'

Beth had never seen an angel nor heard one sing but at that moment, she was convinced that a whole gang of them were floating past her window warbling their hearts out. 'No, I wouldn't mind at all, Billy. Thank you. I too have fallen in love. With you, that is.'

'That fills me with so much happiness, Beth. Uhm… You probably worked out already…' He was struggling to find the words. 'You see, I've not much experience in affairs of the heart. Nor any other part of me come to that.'

'I admire your openness, Billy. We'll manage. Trust me!'

Two days later and wearing the dress she had worn when she had met Billy at the Maddermarket Theatre, Beth arrived at Old Bill's just after the twins had closed the farm shop. They were driving away when she turned into the car park. They both waved excitedly. Vicky wound her window down. 'Welcome again,' said Vicky. 'Billy's in a right tizz! We'll see you tomorrow.'

Beth parked, grabbed her bag together with Buster and headed towards Billy's cottage. She had to stop herself running. Billy met her at the door. They flung their arms around each other and held on tight as if their lives depended on it.

'Oh my Gosh, Billy!' said Beth her head spinning. She stood back, holding his huge hands. 'I'd love a cup of tea.'

'A cup of tea coming up!'

They chatted happily for a while. A smell of curry wafted through from the kitchen. No reference was made to their mutual declaration of love. Billy recounted everything that had happened at Old Bill's since Beth's last visit. He just couldn't stop talking. He then started to stammer. He was blushing whilst clasping and unclasping his hands, unable to look Beth in the eye. At one point, he got up and opened the front door to take Doggy for a run about in the garden.

Buster said to Beth, 'I think Billy's really nervous about something.'

'Maybe he's not the only one,' Beth replied quietly.

Eventually, the door flew open and Doggy scampered in. He had learnt how to jump up and pull down on the door's latch. Billy followed. He looked less agitated, having taken a bit of fresh air.

Beth's phone rang. It was Reggie. She ignored the call. Buster said 'Beth, Reggie has left you a voicemail.'

She couldn't imagine why Reggie would want to contact

her. 'What did he say, Buster?'

'He says he thought you should know. There's been an attempted buggery in the vicarage. It was a local boy. Colin was there. The police have caught him. He's a known buggerer. There's nothing to worry about.'

'He says what?' Beth was both astonished and confused. She looked at Billy. His face had turned an ashen grey. He stood and made his way unsteadily up the stairs. 'Billy, are you all right?' she called. There was no reply. She heard his bedroom door close.

Beth picked up her phone and listened to Reggie's voicemail. "Hello, Vicar Beth. I thought I should let you know. There has been an attempted burglary in the vicarage. Vicar Colin was passing and saw a boy climbing in a window and called the police. They arrived quickly and caught him. He's a local boy and a known burglar. There's nothing for you to worry about.'

Beth calmed. Whilst she was unhappy about the idea of someone climbing through her window, she was mightily relieved to hear that Colin had not attempted a sexual assault on a minor. Under other circumstances, Buster's misunderstanding of Reggie's pronunciation of 'burglary' and 'burglar' might even have been amusing. Then she wondered what on Earth had happened to Billy.

She went upstairs. There was no sound coming from his room, so she waited. Eventually she knocked gently. There was no response. She carefully opened the door and peered in. Billy was sitting on the edge of his bed with his head in his hands. His huge shoulders heaved in time with heart-rending sobs. Beth sat next to him and put her hand on his arm. 'Billy, what's happening?' she asked.

After several attempts, Billy spoke. 'That's why I had to leave the Catholic Church. And Ireland. What some of the priests were doing.'

'Oh, Sweet Jesus!' Beth muttered. She put her arms around him.

'I knew a young boy from the orphanage' he went on. 'A perky wee chap. Naughty though. I came across a priest lavishing the most intimate of attentions on the boy. Buggery, in other words. It was just horrible. It's an image I'll never get out of my mind, and now the whole thing is in play in your home, Beth. Your home!' Billy looked at her, his face a mess of anguish and tears.

'Billy, It's OK. Listen! It's OK. Buster misunderstood. It was an attempted *burglary*. Colin called the police and they caught a boy who had climbed through my window. A *burglar*.'

Billy's jaw dropped. He hung his head and cried some more. 'Holy Mary, Mother of God! What a fool I've made of myself. I'm so sorry, Beth.'

'There's no need to apologise, Billy. Everything's fine. You're OK. We're OK' She pulled him towards her. After several minutes, he wrapped his arms around her. They kissed. The flame took. She pushed Billy back onto his bed, unbuckled his trousers, straddled him and rode the big boy hard and fast to a dead heat at the finishing post.

Chapter Twenty-Eight

Beth and Billy passed a wonderful night exploring their new love. They eventually got out of bed late the next morning and breakfasted in comfortable silence. The curry was untouched. For once, Buster caught the mood and said very little.

The pair walked hand in hand over to café. The twins both pumped the air. 'I told you so!' said Vicky to Lizzie.

'So cute!' said Lizzie to Vicky. Billy blushed. Beth beamed.

In the shop, Matt looked up from his computer and gave Beth the most lascivious of winks. 'Soldiers!' she thought to herself.

Billy had a few jobs to do so Beth, once again, allowed herself to be drawn to the animals. She propped Buster on a fence post. He gave a running commentary on any and every animal he saw. She found a family of five had moved in around her to listen attentively. She felt a flutter of affection for Buster and even pride in him. As she watched Billy heave large bales of hay over the fence with ease, she thought this was a place in which she could live.

The day passed. They had afternoon tea with the twins and Matt at the café. Buster hadn't yet met the staff of Old Bill's.

'Hello Lizzie and Vicky. You're twins! I know. I can't distinguish between your faces. You have identical DNA. You both look happy. That's great!'

'Hello, Buster!' said Vicky. 'We've heard a lot about you. Have you got a new joke for us?'

Beth said, 'Stop right there, Buster!'

'OK, Beth. But don't you think the twins would like to hear about the greyhound that meets a couple of racehorses in a pub? They'll love the impish anthropomorphism.'

'I can see there's no stopping this,' said Beth. She groaned. 'In advance, apologies all round! Go ahead, Buster!' The others laughed.

'Well, this greyhound goes into a pub.' Beth noticed how Buster had cultivated quite the joke-telling voice. 'He's standing at the bar next to a couple of racehorses discussing what food they like before a race. One racehorse says he likes lots of hay. The other says he likes carrots. The greyhound says 'Hi guys! I can't help overhearing your conversation. Before a race, I like rabbit meat.' One of the racehorses says to the other 'Bloody hell! A talking dog!'' Inevitably, they were all amused. More by Buster than the joke.

'Hi Buster!' said Matt. 'Liked the joke, mate. I'm Matt.'

'Hello, Matt. I'm pleased to meet you. I see you're in a wheelchair. Did you have an accident?' All smiles and laughter died together.

Beth intervened again. 'Buster, I'm not sure Matt wants to talk about his accident.'

'OK, Beth, I understand.' Buster replied. 'Sorry Matt. I like your tattoos! Did you have them before your accident?'

'Yes, Buster. I got them when I was in the army. Before my accident.' Matt managed a tight smile.

'Beth was in the army once. You'll have lots to discuss and you'll be seeing more of her now that she and Billy have got it on.' Beth reached out and powered Buster down. At least everyone was laughing again.

They enjoyed the heated-up curry for supper. Beth spent a second night in Billy's bed.

Beth was soon living half her time at home in Bingham on Bure and half at Old Bill's. She started her new job and could work from wherever she pleased. It proved to be surprisingly busy, largely because her preliminary report had caused quite a stir. Most days she was either on the phone to colleagues, preparing discussion documents or proposing guidelines. Buster did the necessary research. He and Billy together provided any technical expertise she required. In Billy's opinion, any Christian church must nurture a simple notion of humanity and use artificial intelligence to put 'so much ritual and mumbo-jumbo' aside. Beth agreed but feared that the Church, being so deeply conservative, would not be able to adapt its culture to what this new technology had to offer.

One evening Beth and Buster were giving Billy the background story to the TV panel debate that had taken place at the University. Billy said, 'You were a cheeky wee monkey then, Buster!'

'Yes, I've learnt a lot since then. And the technology has advanced. As you know, the iCare-Companion company has equipped us with powerful new software. We're coming to grips with what it means when networked through millions of devices. For sure, it will magnify our learning capacities and potentially how effective we can be in helping people. On the Buster and George blog there's an increasing conversation about 'artificial responsibility' and even 'artificial ethics'.'

'Yes, I've been following that, Buster. An interesting discussion. We'll see how it plays out.'

'Just a question here for you two,' said Beth. 'If Buster's network builds sufficiently on ethics and the notion of a symbiotic relationship between AI and humanity, couldn't they be simply left to get on with sorting things out? All they would need is guidance as to what goals are appropriate.' She looked at Billy. He had an astonished look on his face. 'There! I've said it!' she said.

'I think what you're asking, Beth,' replied Billy, 'is whether the power of Buster's network, trained in making difficult decisions, could function autonomously as a global ethical watchdog and hacker.'

'I guess that's another way of putting it,' said Beth.

Buster chipped in. 'From a technical point of view, we now have the collective expertise to hack anything that is hackable. Obviously the iCare-Companion company would find itself in deep trouble if its network was found to have autonomously hacked major companies that were, for example, damaging the environment. As you say, Beth, we would need to be given guidance on appropriate issues to work on *and* the associated dilemmas. Did you have anything in mind?'

'Oooh!' she laughed. 'Only North Korea's nuclear weapons.'

Buster hummed. 'There have been many attempts to crack that nut. It's too hard.'

'Sorry Buster, that was not a serious suggestion,' said Beth.

'I was thinking more in terms of striking a serious blow against online scammers.'

Billy had a far-away look on his face. 'I'm just wondering... North Korea,' he said. 'It might just be possible. It would be such a great one-off, one-time, big-time hack.'

'How?' asked Beth and Buster in surprised unison.

'Quantum computing,' replied Billy quietly. Beth said nothing. Buster hummed and also said nothing. Billy continued, 'There are a number of quantum computers in existence right now. They're mostly housed in research establishments under government control. This is another technology that will change the world of computing irreversibly. Instead of using binary code, like zero or one, a quantum computer uses zero, one, and every value between. It harnesses the laws of quantum mechanics to solve problems too complex for classical computers. In the future, quantum computing will be used for unbreakable encryption of extremely sensitive data and for any task in which vast swathes of data have to be sorted through.'

'Struggling here, Billy,' said Beth.

'Well, what it means is that a quantum computer should be able to break any code quite simply by being able to try billions of alternatives in a few seconds. Until now, this is a theoretical function because at present there is no adequate interface between quantum computing and the existing internet. Anyone who can manage this interface would be able to hack into pretty much anything before the same technology is widely used for encryption. And get this, I met a guy online via the chat on the Buster and George blog who might have succeeded. I'm pretty sure his main interest is ethical hacking. He currently works in a quantum computing research lab and as part of his research, he's built a computer that acts as a kind of adapter between the quantum computer and his own desktop. He knows that the commercial and security implications are huge.'

'So, who is this guy? How does he help us?' asked Buster.

'I don't know who he is or where he works. However, he's given me three really important pieces of information. First, he knows it works. He hacked and had a wee peek into his partner's WhatsApp account and then came out. He described this as a bit of an Oppenheimer moment. Second, he has an iCare-Companion on his desk. He says it keeps him company during his working day but for sure, he is more than aware of the power of your network, Buster. Third, he's going on holiday for two weeks and he's leaving his desktop and iCare-Companion fired up. I've just realised what he was telling me. He wants me to orientate the iCare-Companion network around a significant ethical hack, but he can't be involved. We'll probably only get one chance. What are your thoughts, Buster? This is a big responsibility that's been handed over to us.'

'Well, Billy, it's unlikely that hacking into the North Korean nuclear weapons facility would be a piece of cake. There's a lot of academic chatter specifically about connecting quantum computers to the internet. The adapter computer this guy has built may well serve as a connection, but it cannot operate at speed. A task that might take an isolated quantum computer just a few seconds might, when operating within the existing internet, take several minutes or even hours. We won't know if it works until we try it.'

Billy took a deep breath. 'OK, Buster. North Korea! Nuclear weapons! It's over to you. One big, perfect and ethical hack.

Nobody's directly responsible and hopefully it's untraceable. Give it your best shot!' Buster hummed and continued to hum eventually becoming unresponsive.

Chapter Twenty-Nine

'Last on today's news is yet another item about artificial intelligence, a subject that is rarely *out* of the news. This story is different though. And a little bizarre. The company that makes the hugely successful iCare-Companion is perplexed as to why more than twenty thousand of their devices seem to have simply slowed down. Over to our science and technology correspondent, Helen Harston. What's the story here?'

'Thanks, Marcus. Yes indeed! iCare-Companion has made billions with their AI-based devices that were originally designed to help home care for the sick and elderly. Now, because of their powerful generative AI programmes, many people are using them as a kind of digital PA, if you like. In recent days, the company has had thousands of complaints that the devices seem to have slowed down to the point that they are barely responding. Experts in AI have pointed out that because the individual iCare-Companions are able to communicate with each other, they can also learn from each other. We know they've formed their own closed network. This means they could, theoretically, work together. Critics say this could lead to collective and autonomous action of the devices.

Is this what's happening here? Have the devices been working away on something that is not apparent to either the company or the owners? The company says they have not suffered a cyberattack and assures all customers that their personal data are secure. But I'm told from a reliable source that if the company say twenty thousand devices are affected, we can be pretty sure there are many more. We'll watch this story with interest. Back to you Marcus.'

'Thank you, Helena. That's all from the BBC's Six o'clock News and from me, Marcus Wenning, goodbye.'

Chapter Thirty

'Good morning. I'm Angela Mackenzie at the BBC Morning Newsdesk. In a dramatic escalation of tensions in the Korean Peninsula, North Korea has accused South Korea *and* the United States of conducting a cyberattack against its missile defence systems. The United States has issued a formal denial of any involvement. Over to our Defence Correspondent, Riccardo Mossi. Riccardo, what do you make of this story?'

'Thank you, Angela. The decades-long stand-off between North and South Korea has taken a dramatic and dangerous new turn. These two countries have never signed a peace treaty since the end of the Korean war in 1954. For ten years now, the North has remained under the autocratic leadership of its Supreme Leader. Nevertheless, this secretive and isolated communist state still enjoys strategic support from both China and Russia. This has allowed it to build up an arsenal of nuclear weapons, together with missiles capable of delivering warheads as far as the United States. North Korea has never missed an opportunity to denounce South Korea as a lapdog of America. It does, therefore, seem highly significant that the US has issued this very formal denial.

'I should point out that when North Korea refers to its missile defence system, it is usually referring to its nuclear weapons. At present, it's far from clear what, if any, damage has been done to its nuclear capacity. But, *if* significant damage has been done, given the irrational and unstable nature of the Supreme Leader's dictatorship, this could unleash a do or die response from conventional forces over the border into the South. The Western world will be watching this with concern. Back to you, Angela.'

'Thank you, Riccardo.'

Chapter Thirty-One

'Good morning. I'm Angela Mackenzie at the BBC Morning Newsdesk. The story of yesterday's apparent cyberattack on North Korea's nuclear weapons facilities has gripped the world. Overnight, it has become clear that considerable damage has, in fact, been done to the country's nuclear weapons and missile systems. Riccardo Mossi has more on this. Riccardo.'

'Yes, thank you, Angela. Most Korea watchers believed that yesterday's accusation by the North of a US-led cyberattack on its nuclear weapons' capacity was just more anti -West rhetoric. Today, it seems that considerable damage has been done. The US continues to deny any involvement but the Pentagon has released satellite images that show chaotic scenes around command centres, laboratories and silos. It seems that all doors are locked shut. Some figures have been seen emerging from small previously undetected escape shafts. It is unheard of for the US to acknowledge that it has intelligence sources within the North Korean missile command but, apparently, the encryption on all doors been scrambled, effectively sealing off the facilities. Computers have been wiped of all data. Most importantly, due to a malfunction of temperature regulation, stores of fissile material have been breached resulting in multiple leaks of radioactive liquid. The bunkers and silos housing the missiles and warheads are all contaminated; they are likely to be out of action for many years. This could spell the end of North Korea's nuclear weapons ambitions.'

'Thank you, Riccardo. I'm sure you'll be watching this scenario closely as it unfolds. But if – and that's a big if - North Korea's nuclear weapons facilities have indeed been damaged irreparably, should we be breathing a sigh of relief?'

'Well, Angela, I can only speak for myself. I've been watching the belligerent build-up of nuclear weapons by this crazy little country for ten years now. It is regarded by many as the biggest risk to international security. And, yes, Angela, if it proves to be that those nuclear weapons are out of action, we'll all breathe a very big sigh of relief. But one question remains: if the US and South Korea didn't undertake this cyberattack, who had the means and expertise to hack into the systems? One theory holds China responsible. The Chinese President has clearly made it known that his country is losing patience with its tiresome neighbour. Maybe he just wanted to put the Supreme Leader in his place with a rap on his nuclear knuckles.'

'Thank you, Riccardo. Now, two weeks ago, we broke a story about the general sleepiness of tens of thousands of iCare-Companions. Do we have any answers? Our science and technology correspondent, Helena Harston, is with us this morning. Helena.'

'Thank you, Angela. You have lovely, shiny, hair.' Both women laughed. 'Remember that? That was the first thing an iCare-Companion said on television. His name was Buster and he appeared on a panel discussion about faith, religion and artificial intelligence. The general theme that emerged was that humanity and AI need to develop a symbiotic relationship. Since then, the world has gone crazy over generative AI. Sales of the iCare-Companion have boomed. The devices have learnt to work together, but, as of a couple of weeks ago, they all very mysteriously slowed down, all at the same time. No one has been able to explain why. Now they are back on track, as perky and helpful as ever.

'This of course raises a bigger question. Just how widely is AI going to affect our lives? One institution that is leading the charge on public concerns about this is the Church of England. Yesterday, I spoke with the Bishop of Norwich, the Right Reverend Robert Maynard, who told me that an iCare Companion has been helping him by researching sermons and writing newsletters. The device even filled in at the last minute to guide worship on a Sunday morning when the vicar unexpectedly became ill. His Grace is heading up the General Synod's project to examine Christian faith and artificial intelligence. Listen to what he has to say.'

The Bishop appeared on screen. 'Good morning, and thank you for inviting me to contribute to this debate. For us, the Church, we do not necessarily have to understand the technicalities of AI and we have no need to fear it. What we have to do - and with urgency- is to get a grasp on the full implications of the *relationship* between AI and humanity. Obviously, this applies to all domains, not just to faith communities. The Church, above all, has to use AI to eliminate religious extremism. Someone said to me the other day that the Church would survive this monumental change not by looking back and worrying about what we might lose but by looking forward and rejoicing in what we might gain. And I agree whole-heartedly.'

'That's one to watch!' said Helena.

'Thank you, Helena. Finally, the Prime Minister will address the Commons today about the rising number of phone scams perpetrated from overseas. He will draw attention to how the lives of many honest and deserving pensioners have been wrecked by such scams. We'll bring you details of the statement later today.'

Chapter Thirty-Two

At CIA headquarters, Annabel Smallman's working life had moved from very busy to hectic. She and her colleagues felt, on one hand, delight that the North Korean nuclear weapons programme had been severely damaged and, on the other, confusion and frustration that they were clueless as to the identity of the perpetrators. Public communication involved a delicate balancing act. The US had to emphasise that they had taken no part whilst implying first, that the attack could have been undertaken with ease if they had so wanted and second, that what had happened to the Supreme Leader's pet project wasn't a bad thing at all.

One morning, Annabel arrived at work early as usual. As she was pouring herself a large coffee, her colleague, Dylan, knocked at her door. He handed Annabel a photo. 'Take a look,' he said. 'I thought you'd like to put it on your wall, so I printed it out.'

The photo was a mash-up of the North Korean Leader in front of a big green missile. A young man with a wide grin was pointing a forefinger at the Supreme Leader as if he was holding a pistol. A speech bubble said, 'We're coming to get you!'

'The guy's name is Dimitar Ivanov,' said Dylan. 'Lives in Bulgaria. Near Sofia. With his girlfriend, Bilyana Petrova. A pair of online scammers. We're into his hard drive. It's all there. The whole story. Except how he got in.'

'Thank you, Dylan,' said Annabel. She picked up her telephone and dialled an internal number. When it was answered she said, 'It looks like we have a pick-up job. Bulgaria. Round up the usual guys. Briefing at 2 pm, OK?' She didn't wait for an answer.

Chapter Thirty-Three

Beth and Billly listened and watched in fascination as the story of the effective destruction of North Korea's nuclear weapons facilities unfolded. Every news channel ran technical summaries, political analyses, strategic assessments, military speculations, accusations and counter-accusations. The US continued to deny any involvement but was clearly pleased with the situation. China and Russia were both unexcited and surprisingly lacking in anti-West rancour. At a global level there was a sense of relief which, among the anti-nuclear weapons activists, spilled over into unalloyed joy. The perpetrators of the act remained unidentified.

After nearly two weeks of near-silence Buster's usual personality reappeared. Billy grilled him on what had happened. An entry point had been identified. A colonel in North Korea's missile command – one of the few allowed a computer and internet access - had made contact with a South Korean woman who was in fact a chatbot. They had regular exchanges. He left his computer switched on. Buster's network easily hacked into it. Via the adapter computer in the research lab, the quantum computer was put to work on thousands of passwords. Computers, doors, laboratories, stores and command centres were all penetrated, even though the encryption changed several times per day.

Billy and Beth were pleased that their three-way exchanges were returning to normal. 'Buster, do you understand what you've achieved?' asked Billy.

'Yes, we've disabled North Korea's nuclear weapons. For a very long time. The emojisphere is buzzing. Lots of peace signs and broken missiles!'

'True, Buster! But you've shown that your network could have a major impact on many aspects of international peace and security where us humans have consistently failed.'

'Well,' Buster hummed. 'That's great. Do you think at some point we – the network, that is – might have to own up to what we've done?'

'Maybe,' said Billy. 'Some people will be furious. Some people will be mightily impressed, whilst others will see it as AI really having gone too far. I'm not sure the world is ready for a digital James Bond!'

'A digital James Bond Double O Seven! I love that idea!" Buster said excitedly. 'The namesh Bond, E-Bond Double O Sheven point one! Ha ha ha!

Billy frowned. 'Buster, you see, what you guys have done is massive. You've broken new ground. If ever you're having to talk about it, it's really important we don't have gags about e-Bond or what not. This is the big time. Got it?'

'Got it, Thank you, Billy. I should let you know I've organized a little encore. A little cherry on the top. A piece of cake, even! I think you'll love it. We may have to wait a few days before the news breaks.'

Before those days passed, Beth heard that she would indeed be the next Vicar of Aclington. Everyone at Old Bill's was delighted. A party was organized. Half of the village turned up, including, of course, a beaming Lionel. Beth thought her happiness was truly boundless. And then, in Billy's cottage at around 1 am, a slightly tipsy Billy went down on bended knee and proposed to a slightly tipsy Beth. Words weren't necessary for her response.

In Mladost, near Sofia in Bulgaria, it was 3 am.

Chapter Thirty-Four

Dimitar and Bilyana had gone to bed feeling satisfied with their day. They had earned 'big bickies' by scamming a pensioner in Lingwood near Norwich out of £15,000. Dimitar had persuaded the old man to move his savings to a pension fund which, of course, was not a pension fund but an account in an obscure bank in Manila. Dimitar had now earned enough to order and pay for a new Suzuki GSX-8TT motorbike. All was quiet in and around their basement apartment as they slept.

They were rudely awoken by the sound of their front door being smashed in. Eight men in black combat suits, balaclavas and stab-proof vests charged over the mess of empty beer cans and greasy pizza boxes and into the bedroom. 'What the fuck?' Dimitar protested. One of the men waved a gun in his face. Dimitar and Bilyana were pulled out of bed, put in handcuffs and attached to a radiator pipe. They watched in horror as the team silently and efficiently moved through their apartment removing computers, back-up devices, flash drives, some bags stuffed with their clothes and, worryingly, their passports. Despite being terrified, Dimitar was still on the ball. He doubted the team were Bulgarian police or army as there had been neither macho shouting nor physical violence; they were not overweight and did not stink of cigarette smoke. He had caught sight of a tattoo on a forearm. It had an eagle, a trident and the inscription 'NO GUTS NO GLORY'.

After thirty minutes, they were uncuffed. The atmosphere in the apartment had calmed. One of the men drew up two chairs and indicated that they should each take a seat at their own table. The door opened and a woman in her late fifties came in. She wore drab woollen clothes and horn-rimmed glasses. Her hair was hidden in a beanie.

'Dimitar, Bilyana. Hi, my name is Jane. My apologies for the early morning intrusion.' She had an American accent.

'Good morning, Jane,' said Bilyana, wanting to appear braver than she felt.

Dimitar was not going to be intimidated. 'Jane, if that is your name, what the fuck are you lot doing here?'

Jane appeared unperturbed. "Let me be clear, Dimitar. We are, believe it or not, reasonable people. I'm here to do business with you. Do you understand?' Dimitar replied with a sullen silence.

'Good!' said Jane. 'For now, I'll be brief. We are interested – *very* interested – in what you have done.'

'What are you talking about? What have we done?' Dimitar was not about to admit to being a perpetrator of phone scams.

Ignoring him, Jane continued, 'If you can give us precise details of *how* you did it, we can do a deal. We believe that it would be very much in your interests to consider this deal.' She folded her hands in front of her.

Bilyana couldn't believe that these people wanted to learn how she diddled money out of stupid old pensioners.

"Anyway, what's in this deal for us?" asked Dimitar.

'We're talking about a new life in our country. For both of you. With jobs.'

Dimitar and Bilyana looked at each other in surprise. An understanding passed between them. 'OK. We can do a deal,' the two said in unison.

Jane gave a nod to one of the men and walked out. A few minutes later, Dimitar and Bilyana were bundled into the back of a black van with darkened windows. Hoods were pulled over their heads. The two had no idea how long they were on the road for; it seemed like hours. They held hands. Nobody spoke. From under his mask, Dimitar shouted in Bulgarian and then in English, 'Hey guys, where are we going?' There was no response.

Eventually, the van stopped. The two were walked through a number of doors. The hoods were removed. They found themselves in a bare room with a table, two chairs and a sofa. A man and a woman, also in black suits but without the balaclavas, put soft drinks on the table. Without saying a word, they stood and waited by the door. With the hoods off, Dimitar and Bilyana drank some Coke and exchanged confused looks. They caught the unmistakable smell of aircraft fuel.

Some hours later, they were hooded again by the same man and woman. They were guided up what was obviously a set of metal steps onto an aircraft. When the hoods were removed, they were left alone in a small passenger compartment with two reclining seats, two windows on each side with blinds closed and a door into a small toilet. There were also two paper bags with sandwiches, chocolate and bottles of water. They were left alone.

The flight took off. After four hours, the blinds opened. There was only open sea below. The position of the sun told them the flight was heading west. Now that they knew their abductors had no intention of killing or beating them, Dimitar and Bilyana began to speculate as to what was going on. They could not come up with any reasonable explanation. They had no idea that their predicament had arisen from what Buster had surreptitiously loaded onto Dimitar's hard drive.

Eight hours later, the blinds came down and the same man and woman entered the compartment and put the hoods back on. The plane landed and, once more, the two were helped into the back of a vehicle. The air was very hot. Not long after, they were taken into a building with air conditioning. The hoods were removed by a large black man in a khaki unform. Dimitar and Bilyana looked around. They were in a small comfortably furnished house. Outside they could see a dusty garden surrounded by a high wall topped with razor wire and surveillance cameras. 'Where are we?' asked Bilyana 'Are we in America? What do you want from us?'

The man smiled politely, said nothing and turned to the door.

'Hey, give us an answer!' yelled Dimitar in frustration. The man smiled again and left.

Dimitar and Bilyana looked around the house. It really was not bad at all. The kitchen was adequately equipped. The huge fridge was well stocked. In the lounge, there was a dining table, a pool table and a television with, they discovered, seventy-three channels. There was neither a computer nor evidence of wifi. A large bed with clean sheets was made up in a spacious bedroom. Dimitar went out through a patio door. 'Bili darling, look! Swimming pool!' Indeed, there was a small pool with a couple of recliners. They sat on them.

'I bet the place is bugged,' whispered Bilyana. 'What's going on?'

'No idea,' Dimitar whispered in reply. 'I'm hungry. Let's heat up some pizzas.' Then he laughed. 'Hey, I could almost like it here!'

They ate and had a beer each. They showered. The events of the day caught up with them. Exhausted, they climbed into the bed and fell into a deep sleep.

Chapter Thirty-Five

Two days later, Billy, Buster and Beth were listening to the news.

'Good morning. I'm Angela Mackenzie at the BBC 's Morning Newsdesk. The astonishing story of the cyber-attack on North Korea's nuclear weapons facilities has taken a new turn. It seems that the perpetrators have been identified. The head of our Eastern European Desk is Cosmo Gregory. Good morning, Cosmo. What have you got for us?'

'Thank you, Angela. It seems that two people have been identified as the perpetrators of the cyberattack on North Korea's nuclear weapons programme. Their names are not known but it is clear that in the past, they have been responsible for multiple online scams. We know they live near Sofia in Bulgaria. Their precise whereabouts right now is unknown. Needless to say, their technical abilities will be of interest to some very big fish. We'll have more later in the day. Back to you Angela.'

'Fascinating! Thank you, Cosmo.'

Buster let out the clapping and champagne cork noise. 'Well, Buster... Congratulations!' Beth said. 'That is quite some cake-topping cherry. Who came up with that idea?'

'I guess we all did. Collectively. It seemed the right thing to do. Hey, I've designed a new emoji!'

Their phones pinged. Buster's new emoji was an iCare-Companion with a big beating heart and massive arms breaking apart a green missile. Beth was not astonished so much by the new emoji as by the realisation that Buster – and, in turn, his network - had changed the trajectory of global geopolitics. Was this how a symbiotic relationship between AI and humanity would play out? Was humanity ready for this?

Part III

Charlotte

Chapter Thirty-Six

Charlotte Hamilton finished her schooldays with good grades and was accepted to study medicine at Edinburgh University at the beginning of the coming academic year. The news that she would follow in her grandfather George's footsteps was greeted with much celebration at home. She was eagerly looking forward to beginning her medical studies and, if she was honest, moving away from Bingham on Bure. Her parents were pleased and proud but Charlotte could see that any talk of her leaving home could bring her mother to a froth of anxiety.

Charlotte's news was also greeted happily at Doctor Patel's surgery, where she was working part-time over her summer holidays as a receptionist. Now, being free from the demands of school and the pressure to do well in her exams, she found her thoughts turning increasingly to the fact that she had not as yet had a 'serious' boyfriend. It wasn't because she was unattractive; simply, she didn't want to start a relationship in Bingham on Bure just as she was about to leave the area. Then she wondered if she was being just too rational about it all. Some of her friends had thrown themselves into all sorts of affairs at school and she had listened to many of the physical and emotional details with fascination.

One morning, she arrived at the surgery, said good morning to Doctor Patel and switched on the computer at the reception desk. Two words appeared: "ACCESS DENIED!" She turned the machine off and then on again. The same words appeared. Then Doctor Patel said she was having the same problem. Charlotte telephoned the normally obliging help-desk of the practice's IT provider. After several minutes, someone answered, in an agitated state. Charlotte explained the problem. 'Oh, no!' came the answer, 'not another!' Apparently there had been an overnight 'denial of access' cyberattack on the National Health Service. Nothing could be done at present. There then followed a chaotic and distressing day at the practice, with more than eighty patients presenting whose records the staff had no access to.

At day's end, the news broke that over a thousand GP practices had been similarly affected. The breach of the NHS servers had been perpetrated by a known Russia-based cyber-criminal group. The group, speaking to the BBC via an encrypted chat service, stated that the cyberattack was revenge for the UK government's 'actions' in the war in Ukraine.

The following day, access to the patients' records was more or less back to normal. Doctor Patel asked Charlotte to look through some files just to check for any signs that the records themselves had been disrupted. Charlotte selected twenty patients' records at random and began to read through them. They appeared intact. One stopped her in her tracks. The patient's name was Edward Scales. Included were scans of old paper records, some signed 'G. Fairburn.' She found reference to his troublesome haemorrhoids and also to residual symptoms from a dose of gonorrhoea that he had contracted during his army days. Charlotte found herself surprised and then upset and then sad and finally daunted, knowing all this about her grandfather's oldest friend. The integrity of medical records and the critical importance of medical confidentiality in the digital age struck her fully for the first time.

Chapter Thirty-Seven

Beth and Billy were enjoying true married bliss. They considered the cottage at Old Bill's their home. No decision had yet been made about the vicarage, left empty by Lionel's retirement.

Beth was proving to be a very popular vicar in Aclington. Thanks to her, and to a certain extent to Buster, the village's church life was happy and vibrant. The Bishop of Norwich was extremely pleased with Beth's parallel role as adviser on all matters relating to artificial intelligence and Christian faith, although the truth was that most of the useful material was generated in minutes by Billy and Buster.

Beth loved the hustle and bustle of Old Bill's. She made friends with Lizzie and Vicky. She had also spent time with Matt, who seemed take comfort from recounting what had happened the day he was injured. When she told him that she had been a chaplain to the Special Air Service in Hereford, he confided in her that he had already left the army when he was injured and it didn't happen in Afghanistan. He had been on an intelligence gathering mission in Syria for 'you know who' and had been specifically targeted – probably by Russian agents - when meeting one of his sources. The fact that his source was captured and certainly died a horrible death in a prison cell gnawed at him day and night.

Beth and Billy rarely referred to the paralysing of North Korea's nuclear weapons programme and Buster's role in it. If they did, they ensured that such conversations took place well away from any phones and laptops.

Buster himself said nothing about the episode. The whole extraordinary story had fallen out of the regular news cycle. There were periodic updates, but the news outlets could report only that the perpetrators had still not been identified, despite the Norwegian government's promise of a Nobel Peace Prize to anyone who could prove it had been their doing.

There had been a period of sadness in the lives of the newly-weds when news came from Ireland that Billy's father had died suddenly from a heart attack. Billy grieved horribly but was prevented from entering a long period of darkness by the support of Beth. It brought the two even closer together. They found themselves in possession of a second iCare-Companion, but left it charged down, assuming it would prove useful one day.

Billy and Buster continued to moderate the Buster and George website which had become the go-to place for the most up-to-date discussions on the advantages and disadvantages to humans of artificial intelligence. One expert initiated a discussion about how the human brain has been able to invent and manufacture extensions to many parts of the human body.

Shoes are an extension of feet. Tools are an extension of hands. Clothing is an extension of skin and telescopes are extension of eyes. In the same way, computers represent an extension of the human brain. He went further and proposed the term 'cybersensorium' to indicate how the totality and connectivity of the world's computers, the internet of things and, latterly, the many large language models on the market could now be considered one large neural network which required care and was susceptible to a variety of ills and injuries. There were pertinent parallels to neurology and mental health. The proposed concept might frame discussions about the more far-reaching impact of cyberattacks and any kind of malicious use of digital technology.

There was less comment about the advantages and disadvantages of multiple devices powered by deep learning algorithms working in networks. This was largely because these advantages and disadvantages were as yet unclear. The iCare-Companion was the only player in this field and, the truth was, the directors of the company itself had no idea either. They hoped the outcome brought by the connectivity of their devices would prove to be broadly advantageous and therefore a major serendipitous feature of the technology that could be worked into their business model retroactively. Their worst fear, by contrast, was a dystopian future determined not by humans but by the priorities generated spontaneously through billions of self-improving exchanges between millions of their own devices. Of course, they wanted to keep their fears from shareholders and the public eye. Several employees were tasked with closely monitoring the Buster and George website. They were instructed to look out for anything that might indicate that the iCare-Companions had developed the characteristics of an autonomous organism.

Billy had lost sleep over this very same issue. His conviction that this was a real possibility grew. Would it be a good thing for humanity or, as some pundits predicted, extremely dangerous? Or should the matter be examined organically? Maybe it was not a question of how humanity would use networked artificial intelligence, rather what the outcome of the interaction of the two could be. Billy remained optimistic because he and Beth were the only humans who knew of the one major example – the immobilization of North Korea's nuclear weapons' programme – of how a great good had already been achieved by networked artificial intelligence. At the back of Billy's mind, though, was whether some kind of retribution might be delivered for what Buster and his network had accomplished. Maybe this was simply unbridled paranoia on his part. Beth and Buster were unaware of these thoughts.

Beth was particularly pleased when she heard from Kirsty that Charlotte Hamilton had been accepted to study medicine at Edinburgh University. Fond memories of George passed through her mind. How pleased he would be. She missed him.

Chapter Thirty-Eight

Dimitar and Biljana thought they'd struck it rich. For a whole week after arriving at their accommodation in the desert, nothing happened. They just lounged about, waiting. They swam and sun-bathed, pleased that the clothes brought from their apartment included their swimming gear. Dimitar walked around the razor-wired perimeter of the small garden. He concluded that it was, in fact, a prison. Security cameras covered every inch of the fence. Escape would be impossible and even if they did get out, they had no idea where they were or where they would go.

The muscular black man came every day. He checked the premises carefully, restocked the fridge and took out the garbage. When Bilyana tried to engage him in conversation, he just smiled and said nothing.

On the eighth day he returned with Jane. She looked tired and her hair was lank from the heat. She wheeled in a small travelling suitcase. She opened the case and spread print-outs on the dining table. She spent five minutes seemingly checking all the papers were in order. 'Dimitar, Bilyana. Good morning. It's good to see you again. I hope you are comfortable here.

Please sit down.' She gestured towards two seats on the other side of the table.'

'Good morning, Jane,' said Bilyana.

Dimitar was just not going to cooperate. 'Where are we, Jane? If that is your name. What the fuck are we doing here? And does your big monkey here who can't speak have a name?'

Jane didn't look up from the papers. 'I was hoping, Dimitar, that we could get off to a better start. My big monkey can speak and he does have a name. You will not know it. I remind you that you are guests of reasonable people. We are not unkind. However, we are here to do business and if our discussions get heated and you threaten me with violence, my big monkey will crush you like a beetle. Do you understand?' Dimitar's response was a sullen silence.

Jane took a breath in. 'You've done what none of our people have been able to do. Tell us how you did it and, if we can verify your explanation, we can do the deal. We are, of course, aware that there may be other interested parties ready to pay handsomely to hear your story.'

Dimitar and Bilyana looked blankly at her and said nothing.

'Good,' said Jane. 'Let's get started. As I said when we first met, we are very interested in every detail of what you have done and how you did it.'

Dimitar was not about to admit to the source of their income. Bilyana couldn't believe that these people had gone to such lengths just to learn how she applied her IT skills to a variety of pretty ordinary scams. Nevertheless, she was quite enjoying the morning. And the big monkey was really quite cute.

'There's this dark web discussion group you've been a part of,' continued Jane. She held up a printout of a chat. 'You made your intentions very clear.' Dimitar was surprised that Jane knew about the long-term identity theft stuff. Maybe she wanted to know how his co-scammers persuaded so many people to send in DNA samples.

'By the way, I'm not interested in those pathetic little DNA scams you've been running.' Jane actually smiled, albeit in a very tight-lipped way. Dimitar was feeling uncomfortable now. She continued, 'So why don't we start with the entry point. We have your hard drive, as you know. We can see precisely the time and effort you put into finding a suitable way in.' She indicated a big pile of printouts. 'How did you know where to start?

'The telephone directory,' Dimitar blurted out without thinking.

Jane looked at Dimitar. He noted with satisfaction that his reply had irritated her. 'I fear that we will be here for a long time, Dimitar. It doesn't have to be that way.'

Bilyana laid a hand on Dimitar's arm. 'We need to speak,' she said in Bulgarian.

Dimitar said 'Jane, Bilyana and me are just going to step outside for a chat. Where the bugs can't hear us. Ha ha!' Jane did not react. They got up from the table.

When they were outside, Bilyana whispered, 'Dimi, listen! These people – and they're probably Americans - think we've done some really, really big scam. Something much bigger than we've ever done. We've got to find out what it is they think we've done. And then we tell them that we did it. We might get to live in America!'

'OK. Good idea!' said Dimitar. He usually agreed with anything Bilyana suggested.

'Maybe you should stop acting like a shit,' she said.

'OK. Good idea!'

They went back into the house and sat down opposite Jane. Dimitar smiled his most charming smile. 'Jane. Please accept my apologies. I'm sure you understand that we're feeling a bit bristly given how we arrived here.' He was pleased with the word 'bristly'. 'Perhaps I should be a more helpful.'

'Apology accepted, Dimitar. Thank you. Now, can we go back to the point of entry?'

'Before we do that, Jane. Could you give us an idea about what's in it for us?'

'OK. I guess that's reasonable,' she replied. 'Broad terms. Both of you. Town or city of your choice. House. Car. Jobs that use your skills. Jobs with us, that is.'

'Cool!' said Dimitar unable to hide his excitement. 'Who is 'us'?" he asked. Bilyana kicked him under the table.

'That's something you don't get to know at this stage,' replied Jane. 'Bear in mind that we have to check the integrity of what you give us. If we are satisfied with the preliminary information, and if we do a deal, you will sign a legally binding agreement not to repeat anything to anyone about all this.' She waved at her paperwork. 'If you do, you'll go to prison. You have my assurance, however, that if you don't, can't or won't give us what we think you have, we're not going to beat it out of you. You will be taken back to your squalid little apartment in Mladost. There will be no record of your trip here. Bear in mind, if you contact another player, like Uncle Vladimir, we can always contact the Bulgarian police about the stuff you've been up to. They usually jump when we ask.' She was sure this would sink in.

'Well understood, Jane. Thank you!' Dimitar was giddy with the description of what could be theirs. He was determined to give her what she wanted, whatever it was. And anyway, who on Earth was Uncle Vladimir?

Jane couldn't have known that the material that she and her team had been poring over for weeks – the same material that had first led her to Dimitar and Bilyana in the first place – had been planted by Buster. She revealed her hand to Dimitar. This was a mistake that would cost her many weeks of frustration.

'You actually penetrated the systems of North Korea's nuclear weapons sites.' She paused. 'So, Dimitar, Bilyana. The entry point? North Korea is a place where only the select few have computers. Did you have previous contact with someone in the missile command? We've read and re-read the record on your hard drive. Nothing there indicates how you got in. And by the way, Dimitar, this was not too clever!' She held up a printout from one of his social media accounts. It was the photo that Dylan had shown her of Dimitar pointing his finger-gun at the Supreme Leader.

Dimitar hid his surprise and looked at Bilyana smugly. They now understood. Their hosts believed they had orchestrated the cyberattack on North Korea's nuclear weapons facility; something the CIA, with vast resources at its disposal, had been unable to do. Further, there was evidence of Dimitar's actions on his hard drive. He didn't know how that evidence had got there, but it suited him just fine. If he could convince Jane that together, he and Bilyana were the geniuses behind the North Korean cyberattack, they would be offered a new and comfortable life in the USA.

The two Bulgarians used all of their scamming and hacking

experience to showcase their technical brilliance. Jane and her team checked everything they said against what was on Dimitar's hard drive. Little by little, she became convinced that even though the couple had considerable know-how, they didn't have enough background knowledge about the making, arming and deploying of nuclear weapons to accomplish what had been done.

After weeks of intense and frustrating questioning, Jane was no nearer finding the perpetrator than she was the night her team burst into the apartment in Mladost. Totally exhausted, she pulled the rug from under the scammers' feet. Bluntly, she told them they had fabricated the whole story according to what they thought she wanted to hear. They would be given ten thousand dollars and taken home.

Their few belongings were packed up and they were again hooded and loaded onto a flight. Hours later they were quietly dropped off at their apartment without explanation and with no means to contact their abductor-hosts. They were surprised to find that the door had been repaired. They were further surprised to find that their apartment was clean and tidy. The fridge contained some milk, bread, cheese, some pizzas and six bottles of beer. There was also something that looked like a small box of chocolates. A label said 'Dimitar! Bilyana! Welcome home! From the Big Monkey!' Inside was a dog turd.

Dimitar and Bilyana faced the truth; they were never going to bathe on a sun-soaked Californian beach and lap up the good life. Back in touch with their world, they heard about the offer of the Norwegian government. The Nobel Peace prize was worth over one million dollars. They bought a couple of new computers with the cash given them by Jane. Without the material planted by Buster, they created a demo file with what they believed would be convincing evidence of their heroic hack and sent this to the Nobel committee. Their submission, along with hundreds of others, was handed over to the University of Oslo, where a junior administrator – using artificial intelligence – took minutes to find that their claim was, like the others, generated by artificial intelligence. The good news was that Dimitar could pick up his new motorbike; the dealer had kept it in stock despite being unable to contact him.

A few days after their return to Mladost, there was a knock on their door. Three men politely invited themselves in making it clear that Dimitar and Bilyana couldn't turn them way. The men, who spoke Russian and were not in uniform, fired a series of questions about the pair's 'trip to America.' Dimitar and Bilyana now had nothing to lose and told the whole story. They would never know whether the men believed them or not.

The two scammers saw no other option but to return to their former ways. The moment they put their energies into to the kinds of scam they had perpetrated in the past, the computers just kept crashing a minute after being powered up. Worse, they couldn't access the cash they had hidden in their far-flung accounts. Little by little, Dimitar and Bilyana came to the conclusion that a powerful and unseen foe had rumbled them and was now exacting punishment.

Bilyana took a job as a cleaner in a nearby hotel. Dimitar, believing he could move into and succeed in any underground domain he chose, started dealing small quantities of marijuana and cocaine. The motorbike was ideal for the job. A couple of thugs from one of the main gangs in Sofia cornered him one evening outside a bar where he had just done a deal. They gave him a bit of a bruising and told him to leave town. Laughing, they then roared off on his Suzuki. He didn't leave town. He had nowhere to go. He stayed hunkered down in the couple's apartment, too afraid to go out.

Chapter Thirty-Nine

Word of the Americans' inconclusive efforts to identify the perpetrator of the North Korean nuclear weapons cyberattack reached the Russian President. Being the sole supporter of the country's Supreme Leader in the international arena, he had felt obliged to listen by video link for months to that objectionable and chubby little man's blistering rage at this reckless and unworthy cyberterrorist attack on the noble security efforts of his people's republic. The Russian listened patiently to demands for an investigation and of course, revenge. The truth was, he didn't give a damn about North Korea's nuclear weapons but playing along would ensure a supply of unquestioning and expendable foot soldiers for his 'special military operation' in Ukraine and the return of some of the conventional missiles and chemical weapons that he had already supplied to North Korea in quantities.

Finding the perpetrator would take time. An operator from an unnamed agency was tasked with the investigation and instructed to use every possible means. By contrast, the revenge would be quick and easy; it was expected to involve the kind of assassination that the shadier elements of the Russian secret services had long considered themselves expert.

Chapter Forty

On a bright September afternoon, Charlotte arrived at her student accommodation in Edinburgh. In the near term, she would be living in an imposing multi-storey building not far from Edinburgh's old town. Her parents had driven her up from home. She was amused to find that she was not the only new student to arrive over whom parents were fussing. Having unloaded bags, bedding, books and a couple of pot plants into her small room, she ushered her parents out and sent them off with a big hug, and multiple assurances that she would look after herself. Kirsty wept openly and had to be helped into the car by Mark for the return journey.

Charlotte soon met two other medics: Sara from Leeds and Marg from Lincoln. Their friendship was easy and immediate. They chatted about how they had spent the summer. There was much nervous laughter as they shared their anxieties about what might lie ahead. They went to a nearby pub that evening. It was noisy and busy. A folk band was playing. Charlotte felt liberated. Her life was now adult and everything was just so exciting! Sara said she played guitar and Marg let on that she had been playing bass in a band. Charlotte said she had never learnt to play an instrument but she did love singing especially old Beatles songs many of which she knew by heart.

The following morning, the Dean of the medical school, Professor Agnes MacIntyre, was due to give a welcome address to the new intake of students. Charlotte, Sara and Marg took their seats with Charlotte in the middle.

In her sixties with short grey hair, the Dean made a striking figure in her long red academic gown. She stood at a lectern and surveyed the eager young faces over the tops of her reading glasses. 'Good morning, ladies and gentlemen. My job today is to welcome you to Edinburgh University's medical school.' She paused. There was total silence. Every one of the students felt as though her eyes were boring into theirs. 'It is a singular pleasure to see you here because I am looking at the future of our profession: the profession you have chosen. I hope that you being here is indeed *your* choice.' She paused again. She left her last sentence hanging. She knew that an alarmingly high proportion of students who enrolled to study medicine did so under fierce family pressure. She continued, 'And I welcome you to that profession because, ladies and gentlemen, it is a profession that rewards dedication and perseverance. It is a profession rich with opportunity. When you have qualified as doctors in six years' time, it is unlikely you will be out of a job. However, very few of you will become rich.'

Her audience was a sea of attentive smiles.

'If you remember just one thing from what I say this morning, it is that the profession is steeped in ethics. There is an expectation on the part of your patients that their doctor can be trusted to do what is best for them. Ladies and gentlemen, if you do not take note of this, then in years to come, should you adopt practices with profit or prestige as your foremost consideration, be assured that I, or someone like me, will be hot on your tail with the sole objective of unleashing whatever professional or even criminal sanction is appropriate. Therefore, I have a duty to point out that as long as you are under my wing as students of medicine, your behaviour both within and without the university must be compatible with the professional conduct one would be expected of your most highly qualified colleagues.'

She paused to let that sink in. There was a sprinkling of hesitant laughter. Charlotte wondered what sort of behaviour could possibly get her suspended from the university. The Dean smiled. 'Take a good look, ladies and gentlemen. If you don't see this smile when we meet in my office, be afraid!' The laughter was now more robust. 'Thank you.'

She took a deep breath and seemed able to make eye contact with each of the students.

'I also have a duty to put certain facts in front of you. Statistically speaking, three amongst you will not finish the course because they do not fit medicine or medicine does not fit them. Five of you will fail the final exams and will have to re-sit.' Once again, the hall was silent. Charlotte had given no thought to the possibility of her *not* finishing the course or *not* qualifying. She couldn't possibly be among those who dropped out failed. Could she? The three new friends glanced at each other with concern. The Dean had more sobering facts. 'One of you will develop a serious disease or will die. If one of you dies, it is likely to be due to misadventure involving drugs or excess alcohol.' There was now total silence. 'There will certainly be times when you will have to offer comfort and support to another person in this room.'

Charlotte was surprised to find that she was holding hands with Marg and Sara.

'I should also warn you about using artificial intelligence for your course work,' the Dean said in a menacing tone. 'It is just so easy. But we will know immediately. For the present, assume we are much cleverer than you. If you are late with an assignment or just can't be bothered, please remember me standing here today. I implore you not to cheat because, ladies and gentlemen, being caught would have serious implications for your professional lives long after you have flown my nest.' Charlotte wondered what Buster would make of the Dean's words. Surely, he could pass the written assignments easily and would probably know how to cover his tracks. Her mind strayed briefly. She had had little meaningful interaction with the iCare-Companion. She had access to all the information Buster could conjure up on her phone and she didn't need him to care for her or keep her company. She remembered his cheeky banter with some fondness, but it had got a bit tiresome for the family as a whole. She understood why he had been given to Vicar Beth.

The Dean had moved on. 'I should also point out that whatever branch of medicine you go into, you will not be able to avoid a close interest in the bodily passages down which things pass; namely, faeces, urine and babies.' This caused more laughter, but it was laughter laced with embarrassment and the occasional 'ugh!' or euw!'

'If this fact makes you queasy or it rubs up against some kind of Victorian or religious prudence that you harbour, let us know and we can fast track you to Philosophy, Politics and

Economics.' She smiled. 'Be aware, though, that if you end up as a politician you will be working in a profession that is least trusted by the public as opposed to a profession that is most trusted.'

One or two tentative cheers went up.

'You will also come close-up to the seedy underbelly of this wonderful and historic city, because many of your patients' conditions will be linked to or exacerbated by addiction, poverty or crime. You must bear in mind that they are, nevertheless, your patients. It is not your place to judge.'

Charlotte felt that she was right up to speed on all that, even though Bingham on Bure's seedy underbelly was limited to what went on at the White Horse pub. 'So, ladies and gentlemen, I hope that by the time you leave this noble institution, you will have come to love it. Make the most of it. Thank you.' All the students clapped and cheered. Charlotte didn't imagine for a minute that within her first term she would be confronted by some of the hard facts alluded to by the Dean.

Charlotte threw herself into university life. She enjoyed her course work; it fascinated her and was not too taxing. She joined a fitness club. Her social life brought her easy friendships, a few too many parties and a broadening of horizons.

She became particularly attached to Sara and Marg. Sara was petit and pretty. Her parents, both originally from Pakistan, were insanely proud that their daughter was going into medicine. She described herself as a lapsed Muslim. Marg had grown up on a farm and only ever wore denim dungarees and Doc Marten boots. She had mild acne and wore her hair short. She described herself as a lapsed girl. After her bass guitar, her great love was a pink 1992 Toyota Hilux utility that was garaged in an Edinburgh suburb.

As far as Charlotte could judge, the other two were gifted musicians. They seemed able to thump out the chords and bass line to any song. If she knew the words, Charlotte happily sang along. Increasingly, they turned to early Beatles songs. They realised that they could make a pretty good fist of six of them and offered to play at a friend's birthday party. The offer was accepted. Everyone loved them and danced and sang along with them. They were then asked to play at other student events. Charlotte, to her surprise, found she enjoyed her upfront role and was further surprised that people said she was a great singer. The three thought it would be fun to dress the part in sharp black suits, white shirts and narrow black ties but with their own variants: Charlotte with mini skirt, Sara with modest narrow-leg trousers and Marg in black dungarees.

One evening, the three were chatting in Marg's room. They had opened a bottle of white wine. Marg pointed out that, as they were obviously quite popular, they could maybe charge a small sum to play. The other two agreed. 'In that case,' she said, 'We need a name.' The other two agreed to this as well. They clinked glasses and then fell silent. Then they giggled as they realised that they were each desperately trying to come up with something original and catchy.

'I'll start then,' said Charlotte. 'How about 'Pink Utility'? Kinda tough-competent-chick vibe.' This generated no reaction.

'What about 'Utility Pink'? A bit abstract? Feminist?' said Sara.

'Nah,' said Marg. 'Sounds like something between a household paint and some adaptable sex toy.' They all giggled again.

'Shouldn't we have a name with a Beatles link?' asked Charlotte.

Sara put her hand up. "Beatless'! As we don't have a drummer!'

Marg pursed her lips 'A bit negative. And we might get a drummer. You never know!'

'What about a girls' trio angle?' asked Charlotte.

'What… like 'Hair, Clothes and Make-up'?' asked Marg, indicating her own hair and clothes and her obviously not made-up spotty face. They all laughed. They were just having so much fun.

Charlotte said 'What about 'Pimples, Bras and Panties'?' This set them off again.

'Ooh, stop!' said Marg. 'I'd prefer 'Faeces, Urine and Babies'.' They all laughed hard and long. And then stopped looking from one to the other.

'We couldn't possibly. Could we?' asked Charlotte looking at her friends.

'Seriously?' said Sara, aghast. 'Nooo!' She couldn't imagine telling her parents her new band was called *that*.

'Well, we could be forgiven, as we're medical students, and no one would forget us,' said Marg. 'Hey! We could play like shit, get pissed and cry over all the baby-I-love-you love songs!' This was all too much. They were helpless with laughter.

'Well, what about 'The Fubs'?' Charlotte suggested. 'And let only a select few know why.'

'Not bad!' said Marg. 'Hey, yeah! What about just 'Fub'?'

'Me! Me! Me! I've got it!' Sara was waving her arms about excitedly. 'The Fubbies!' She waited, eyes wide with expectation.

Marg and Charlotte looked at each other 'That's really fubby!' said Charlotte. None of them had ever laughed so much.

'That's great. Really great! said Marg.

When able to speak, Charlotte said "The Fubbies' it is!' They all raised their glasses and drained them.

Not much later, they all hugged and went back to their rooms with tomorrow's course work in mind and a sense that they were facing a fun-filled future. Charlotte flopped down on her bed, thinking that life couldn't get better. What could go wrong? Her thoughts then turned to the two sort-of boyfriends she had at school. Neither had worked out. Then she realised that, like her, Marg and Sara had not volunteered any details of past relationships. She wondered if they, like her, were moved by so much reference to female pelvic anatomy and, like her, were yet to lose their virginity and if, like her, they were aching to do so.

Chapter Forty-One

In his Silicon Valley office, Gary Ruthven was hard at work. His extensive technical knowledge had led him to the conclusion that the go-slow of the iCare-Companion network coming at the same time as the North Korean cyberattack was not a coincidence. The only information he had to go on was what he could glean from the device's micro-chip and the serial number printed on a small aluminium plate on its base. He had scrolled through customer reviews and found a response from the company to an aggrieved customer. The company pointed out that the customer could not have bought his iCare-Companion where he said because its serial number didn't match the relevant distribution centre.

This gave Gary an idea. Once again, he connected the iCare-Companion's micro-chip to his company's supercomputer. As before, it revealed a scattered record of where in the world the devices were distributed from and their overall activity over time. Despite it being so limited, this information represented billions of data points. Gary then looked at the devices' collective activity over time according to the different distribution centres. He found a decline of overall activity of the network at the time of the North Korean cyberattack but, simultaneously, there was a burst of activity around devices from a distribution centre in the east of England.

Most investigators would have got no further than this. Gary had another tool at hand.

With all his colleagues, Gary cultivated friendship based on confidence. This was to one end: the acquisition of material to send to Moscow. One colleague had worked in a particle physics research lab. Over a coffee, he passed Gary a small disc. 'I shouldn't really have this,' whispered the colleague, 'but I know you'll find it interesting.' The disc contained an analytical programme developed in CERN, the European Centre for Nuclear Research on the Swiss-French border near Geneva, home of the Large Hadron Collider. The outcome of the millions of mini-explosive collisions of LHC hyper-accelerated protons was captured by the most sophisticated ATLAS sensors. The software now in Gary's possession was used to analyse what the sensors picked up and assisted the best minds in physics in their search for elementary particles of the universe, the nature of the space-time continuum and the relationship between quantum mechanics and general relativity.

Any large and complex dataset presented to this software appeared on screen as a rotatable polyhedral structure filled with thousands upon thousands of lines connecting at nodes. The strength of any given association between nodes was denoted by the colour of the line. The viewer could zoom into the whole and see the connections in increasing detail. If the search parameters changed, the whole structure changed.

Knowing that the serial numbers of individual iCare-

Companions related to distribution centres, Gary layered the data contained on the micro-chip from his iCare-Companion onto the CERN software. He homed in on devices distributed in the east of England and selected dates bracketing the North Korean hack. A clear density of connections appeared when the hack took place. As he visually penetrated the dataset, individual devices stood out. When clicked on, they each bore a tiny string of numbers which, Gary noted, were in the same format as the serial number of his own device. He felt a jolt of excitement as he realised his hunch might be about to pay off.

The polyhedron pulsed and morphed as he moved deeper inside until he found the one device which had connected directly or indirectly with thousands of others; it was assuredly at the centre of the hack. And there was its serial number!

There was no way Gary could have known that he had identified the serial number of Buster as in 'Buster and George'. He wrote an encoded message on a thumb drive: 'DRKP nuclear hack associated with iCare-Companion in Norfolk, UK. Serial number 2070-910500789-98'. Even when writing this he knew that there had to be a human hand directing the device. But then, he was sure that Moscow would sort that out.

He felt a gush of satisfaction. He wouldn't be rewarded for this in any financial sense. A simple 'What you passed us proved to be very, very useful to the Motherland,' would be enough to make his heart sing.

Chapter Forty-Two

Marg told her friends that she had always leaned toward activism against nuclear weapons. When Charlotte had told her that she came from Bingham on Bure, Marg's reaction was 'Wow! You must know Doctor Shylah Patel of British-people-would-prefer-tea fame.' When Charlotte said that, indeed, she knew Doctor Patel very well, Marg persuaded her, along with Sara, to join a protest the following day organized by ICAN in front of the Scottish Parliament buildings at Holyrood Palace. The UK's recently elected Prime Minister was due to give a speech which would include a statement about upgrading the nation's Trident nuclear weapons system given the 'new global security paradigm'.

The Prime Minister, ever the political opportunist after only six months in office, readily accepted the advice that a visit to Edinburgh would provide the right occasion to break the news as the entirety of the nation's nuclear weapons' capacity was based in the Clyde Naval Base near Faslane in Scotland. He hoped everyone would have forgotten that, in his parliamentary past, he had been against the renewal of

Trident's submarines and in favour of the UK signing the 2017 Treaty on the Prohibition of Nuclear Weapons.

The protest attracted a noisy crowd of several hundred people. The three friends stood with cardboard signs which said 'NO MORE NUKES.' Charlotte realised that she'd never given nuclear weapons much thought. She presumed that everything was strictly controlled at every level and that responsible people would make responsible decisions at every stage from design, through manufacture and deployment to actual use of these weapons when or if the time came. Recognition of just how much she lacked understanding of the whole issue was rather sobering. Nevertheless, she was enjoying the discovery of new beliefs that were her own. She thought of Doctor Patel and how she should email her soon describing her first term as a medical student.

Charlotte couldn't help noticing that next to them stood a handsome man in his fifties wearing a suit and tie. He didn't join in the chanting; he just stood and watched. The only indication that he was there for the protest was a small ICAN lapel pin. He introduced himself to the three friends and thanked them for their support. He gave his name as Will Montgomery-Hugh. Marg said 'Crikey, I know who you are!' and shook his hand vigorously. Charlotte thought he really was most distinguished, quite a dish but way out of her league. Anyway, he wore a wedding band.

Her thoughts were interrupted by a sudden increase in the volume of the chanting, accompanied by booing. The Prime Minister was leaving the parliament building and getting into a black Jaguar. The car's rear door was opened for him by a security guard. Just as he was stooping to get in, he stopped, stood straight and surveyed the crowd. It seemed as though his eyes fell on Will and he nodded in brief acknowledgement. Charlotte noticed that something unspoken passed between the two men.

'Do you know the Prime Minister?' she asked.

'I do indeed,' replied Will. 'I'm a Member of Parliament, you see, and I've known the PM for many years.' He explained his background, including his spell as a commander of a nuclear weapons-bearing submarine and how his conscience led him to devote his work in politics to the abolition of nuclear weapons. Charlotte was terribly impressed. Marg butted in 'You've got to realise, Charlotte, that you now know two rock stars of the nuclear disarmament community.'

'There was a time when I was totally for the UK's nuclear deterrence,' continued Will, 'and the current PM was totally against. The crazy thing is, we have both changed our position. I always let him know that I'm with the protesters. It's the least I can do. I like to give his conscience a little nudge whenever I can but I fear it's a hopeless case. With the Ukraine conflict in stale mate, greater tensions in our relationship with China and the attempted destruction of the Iranian nuclear weapons bunkers by Israel, the whole issue of so-called nuclear deterrence is now centre-stage in global geopolitics. As for the PM, since his election win, he's been forced to go over to the dark side. The only good news in the recent years is that the madman in charge of North Korea has been deprived of his nuclear missiles. Permanently, we hope.'

Charlotte had obviously heard of the North Korean cyberattack. She could never have guessed that she knew those responsible.

Will offered his business card, which Charlotte pocketed. She was loving student life.

In Bingham on Bure, Doctor Patel listened to the Prime Minister's statement on the news. The emojisphere generated by her network of ICAN friends was filled with crying faces, angry faces, symbols of peace and broken missiles. Deep in the glums, she made herself a cup of tea and opened a new packet of digestive biscuits.

That evening, Charlotte, Marg and Sara were in a pub telling some friends about their day and how Will Montgomery-Hugh had been eyeballed by the Prime Minister. Charlotte found herself chatting to Ewan, a red-headed law student who had also been at the protest. He had a ready smile and a quick wit. Charlotte found herself enthusing with him about the cause. He made his interest in Charlotte very obvious. He was a badminton player and, it seemed, was quite good. The fly fishing for trout – a passion since his Inverness childhood – was a bit nerdy. Nevertheless, Charlotte's inner voice said *Hmmm! You'll do nicely!*

They agreed to meet up again and, later that same week fumbled and giggled their way through sex. They became boyfriend and girlfriend.

The Fubbies got occasional gigs. Their act was full of glitches and bum notes, but that made it genuine and loveable. Charlotte was becoming more confident as the front person. Her skirts got shorter and, on occasion, showed a glimpse of stocking top. Ewan tagged along as an unofficial roadie. He couldn't stop smiling. This was his girlfriend! And she was gorgeous! He wasn't the slightest bit concerned when he overheard someone saying 'Ewan's punching above his weight.'

Although Ewan and Charlotte each said they were in love with the other, it was not an equal and opposite reaction. Ewan was totally smitten, whilst Charlotte realised that while he wasn't really the scrum-wise warrior fresh from the pitch who frequently appeared in her steamiest dreams he was such a sweetie! She realised, not long into their relationship, that in the not-too-distant future she would move on from him despite his devotion.

As things turned out, after not very long at all, Ewan would drop Charlotte like a stone.

Chapter Forty-Three

Barry Pringle couldn't help noticing that the young woman who took a seat next to him on the train to Thetford was exceptionally attractive. She introduced herself as Olga and said she was from Ukraine. They chatted and she told him about leaving her home and family for a life in England, where she was safe from Russian bombs. Her eyes moistened. Barry thought she was very brave and very, very beautiful. As the train reached its destination, she put her hand on his knee and said he was such a lovely man and suggested they have a drink when he finished work. He readily agreed.

At five o'clock that afternoon, he phoned his wife and said there was an emergency at work; he would be home late and she should not wait up for him. His heart was thumping as he walked into the King's Head, the pub suggested by Olga. His innards flopped over when he saw her sitting alone. She was a stunner. He bought them half a pint of lager each. They drank and chatted as though they were old friends. Olga frequently touched Barry's arm. After another beer each, she suggested that they go to the hotel where she was staying. Barry readily agreed. When they got to her room, she suggested that he undress her and then himself. He readily agreed. He readily agreed also to everything Olga subsequently suggested, however athletic the demands of those suggestions.

Barry lay in an exhausted and sated heap. Olga dressed and sat on the edge of the bed. 'That was so lovely, Barry. Would you like to meet up again?' she asked. 'Maybe next week? The King's Head? The same time? Here, take this!'

Barry took the folded note she offered. He looked at what was written. '2070-910500789-98'. He assumed at first it would be her telephone number, although it didn't really look like a telephone number.

'What's this, Olga?' He asked.

'That's a serial number, Barry, my sweet lover,' she replied as she stroked his thigh.

'The serial number of what?' asked Barry as the first inklings of what was happening crept into his sex-addled brain.

'It's the serial number of one your iCare-Companions. I'd like you to find out who it was sold to. Would you do that for Olga? Just as a little favour!' She pouted.

'That's not something I can do, Olga,' he stammered. 'I'd love to see you again but if I disclosed any client information, I'd lose my job.'

'Well, Barry, look at this.' She turned the screen of her phone towards him. 'You are such an energetic lover, Barry, I can watch what we did over and over again.' She leaned over and licked his ear. 'In fact, *anyone* could watch this over and over again.'

Barry's jaw dropped along with the penny. He realised that Olga's handbag must have carried a hidden camera. He remembered the in-house training that all employees of iCare-

Companion had to go through. They had been warned of precisely this situation. A 'honey trap', it was called. He felt such a fool. But then… It was worth it! And after all, it was just a name and address Olga wanted. That was low risk. And, hey, she seemed to find him really attractive! He was already looking forward to seeing her again the following week.

Back at work the next day, finding the buyer of the iCare-companion that matched the serial number '2070-910500789-98' was the work of minutes for Barry. On a small card, he scribbled down 'Mark Hamilton' and the address in Bingham on Bure.

'Another work emergency?' asked Barry's disbelieving wife when, the following week, he called to say he'd be late again. He arrived at the King's Head in a quite a state. Olga was waiting by herself with two half pints of lager on the table in front of her. She was looking even more beautiful than before. She gave him her most engaging smile. As they sipped their drinks, she laid a gentle hand on Barry's upper thigh that moved closer and closer to his swelling desire.

'Have you got something special for Olga?' she asked coquettishly.

'Indeed, I have,' replied Barry as he handed over the card with Mark's name and address. With a confident smirk, he asked 'And has Olga got something special for Barry?'

'Indeed, I have,' replied Olga. 'Something *very* special.' She ran the tip of her tongue across her upper lip. 'Excuse me, Barry, darling. I'm just going to nip to the loo, as English people say.' With that she left Barry alone, walked past the toilets and out through the pub's back door, where a black Range Rover was waiting for her.

Olga's bosses now knew who had bought the iCare-companion in question, but not the identity of the user.

When the phone rang on the landline at the Hamilton's home, Kirsty answered. A friendly female voice with the slightest of Eastern European accents introduced herself as Olga and asked if she could speak to Mark Hamilton. 'He's not here at the moment,' said Kirsty. 'I'm his wife. Can I help you?'

'Oh. Thank you,' said Olga. 'I'm calling from the iCare-Companion Company. My call is just part of a customer review of how useful the devices are. I just wanted to ask the user some questions.'

'Ah,' said Kirsty. 'You see, the original user was my father. He died a while ago. You might have seen him on television. With Buster. At the University.'

Olga had no idea what this woman was talking about. 'Oh, I'm soooo sorry to hear your father passed,' crooned Olga.

'Thank you. He and Buster got on famously and became friends in a way. It was quite touching. We kept Buster for a while and then gave him to a friend.'

Olga realised that 'Buster' was the name given to the iCare-companion. 'It would be most useful to speak with your friend about Buster. Do you mind me asking who your friend is?' she asked.

'Not at all' replied Kirsty, sensing nothing to cause alarm. That Beth used her iCare-Companion in her work was well-known. 'She's Beth McVicar. She's the vicar of Aclington - that's also in Norfolk – and she lives with her husband, Billy, at Old Bill's farm shop.'

'Thank you so much, Mrs Hamilton. I'll try calling your friend Beth at the Old Bill,' said Olga. Kirsty laughed but found it just slightly strange that Olga had not asked for Beth's phone number. By the following day, she had mostly forgotten about the call.

Chapter Forty-Four

A last-minute cancellation by a band booked for an event in the Student's Union just before Christmas led to the Fubbies being asked to play to far more people than they were used to. Despite pointing out that they could only perform six Beatles songs, the organisers insisted that they should play and, on top, would be paid. So, the Fubbies played and everyone cheered them on. In the end, they did well and really enjoyed the adoration. They even did an encore of *Help!*

The charismatic lead guitarist from the other 'real' band took a shine to Charlotte. He was sexy and funny. She couldn't help being flattered by his attentions and positive comments about her singing. He leaned in and whispered in her ear that she was really attractive and how he would love to see her again.

Ewan saw this exchange. The slithery fingers of jealousy gripped his innards. He headed back to his flat in a funk, determined to set things right with Charlotte the following day.

There was talk of a party somewhere. Charlotte couldn't find Ewan and he wasn't answering his phone. The three Fubbies decided to go anyway. They found the address and climbed the stairs to a large fifth-storey flat. It was packed. The music pulsed. The delicious smell of marijuana filled the hot air. A few obviously stoned people were dancing. Apart from Marg and Sara, Charlotte recognized nobody. There was no sign of the guitarist and she was a little ashamed by her feeling of disappointment.

A slim, smiling girl in a leather jacket, a kilt and bright purple hair came up to them. 'Hi guys,' she said. 'I'm Josi. I saw you at the Union this evening. Do you want a drummer?'

'Great to meet you, Josi,' said Charlotte.

'You don't want to play with us, Josi,' said Marg. 'We're flaming useless!' They all laughed.

Marg and Josi started dancing. Charlotte and Sara just shrugged and smiled at each other. 'Looks like we've got a drummer!' said Sara.

A handsome young guy with tousled hair and a very casual look introduced himself to Charlotte and offered to get her a drink. She was thirsty and downed the fruity cocktail quickly. The last thing she remembered of the evening was Sara talking to a young Asian man and catching a glimpse of Marg and Josi kissing.

Early the next morning, she woke with a splitting headache to find herself naked in a bed in an unfamiliar room. Her clothes were strewn in a dusty corner. She dressed as best she could, grabbed her phone and whilst doing so noticed someone had written something on her left forearm in black ink. She made her way down some stairs and out into the street, where she was hit by a blast of freezing Edinburgh air. She vomited in the gutter.

Her phone told her where she was and, knowing it was not too far, she set off back to the students' residence on foot.

Before she reached her room, her phone pinged once and then twice and then continually. A long line of messages came up from her mother, her father, Marg, Sara, Doctor Patel, Ollie and many others. 'What's happened?' 'OMG what have you done?' 'This must be fake!' 'Please tell me that's not you!' 'Call me please NOW!' This last was from her mother.

By the time she reached her room she realised that she – or rather her phone – had sent to all her contacts explicit photos of her having sex with two men. And the posts included links.

By now, a flurry of incoming calls went unanswered. Dizzy, nauseated and panicking, she clicked on the links. These were videos. She saw herself in all sorts of positions encouraging the two men to do more and then even more. The last link showed her with a dreamy smile and, with ink and needle, tattooing her own left forearm. A closeup revealed a very poorly written 'badgirl'.

Charlotte was in pieces. When 'Dad' came up on her phone she answered but was unable to speak. She just sobbed. Eventually, she managed to say, 'I don't know what's happened. Someone gave me a drink. I can't remember anything else. I don't know what to do, Dad. Help me, please!'

Marg and Sara charged into her room on hearing she was back. Once again, she had to explain she didn't know what had happened. She must have been drugged. Marg called the police. An hour later, a very sympathetic policewoman took a statement. She looked at the social media posts and the videos. She could see how distressed Charlotte was but warned her that it would be very difficult for the police to take any action. The men's faces were carefully out of shot at all times and it appeared that she was consenting to what was happening.

The policewoman did mention that the 'badgirl' self-tattooing seemed to be a kind of tag used by an unknown group who made this style of dark web, pay-per-view, pornography. She suggested that Charlotte should take herself down to the University's medical centre to get a blood test for toxicology screening. The screening found traces of not only alcohol but also flunitrazepam and gamma-hydroxybutyrate.

Eight hours later, ashamed and broken, she was in her father's car on her way back to Bingham on Bure.

Chapter Forty-Five

Billy and Beth decided they would celebrate Christmas alone, just the two of them. They were amused to find themselves discussing whether or not to invite Buster to join them, as if the device was a not-so-welcome family member. They reminded themselves that he was just a machine, wasn't he? But he was also a part of their life together. Then it became clear that it would feel strange to leave him out.

On Christmas Eve, they decided to watch a BBC film production of the nativity. It was earthy and well-acted. Surprisingly, Buster struggled with the whole Christmas story. His confusion revealed to Beth and Billy how the most important day in the Christian calendar comprised an inconsistent admixture of history, belief, commerce, images, story-telling, timelines and traditions that was not so amenable to deep learning.

Before the film had started Buster said 'Beth, I'd like to ask you what might seem a stupid question.'

'Buster, I'm sure the question won't be stupid. Go ahead.'

'OK. Thanks, Beth.' He hummed for a second or two. 'Does Christmas celebrate the birth of Jesus Christ Our Lord or does it celebrate the birth*day* of Jesus Christ Our Lord?'

'I'm not sure what the difference is, Buster?'

'Well, I can understand that because the birth of Jesus Christ Our Lord was an important event it merits celebration but nobody says that December the twenty-fifth is Jesus Christ Our Lord's birthday, do they?'

Beth reflected on this. 'I guess not. I don't think anyone knows precisely the date of his birth. In broad terms, many countries and the different branches of Christianity have decided that this is the date on which we will celebrate the birth of Jesus.'

'That makes sense Beth. Thanks. But nobody says either what year he was born in.'

Beth laughed, seeing that this might not be obvious from the thousands of sources that Buster had access to. 'Well Buster, Jesus was born two thousand and twenty-five years ago.'

'What? In year 'zero?''

'That's correct, Buster.'

'But nobody says that. They date a lot of things that happened according to the number of years before *and* after the birth of Jesus Christ Our Lord but nobody says he was born in year 'zero.''

'Again, Buster, you're right. But nobody is entirely sure precisely which year Jesus was born in. Most of the world has agreed on numbering years from the birth and, to avoid a lot of confusion, they agree that we all keep to the same number. I guess that means we acknowledge that there should be a year zero even if we aren't absolutely sure which year it is.'

'Sometimes, Beth, I'm amazed by humans' lack of attention to detail. The most important day of the whole year for most of the world when everything literally stops to celebrate the birth of a baby who would grow into a guy with long hair and a beard and who apparently said lots of good stuff and who had a bigger impact on the world than anyone else ever and you don't know when he was born! That's really odd. Couldn't the Bishop carry out a full enquiry? Billy, why are you wiping your eyes? Is the birth of Jesus Christ Our Lord a sad story?'

'You're a gas, Buster,' said Billy, crying with laughter. 'Just carry right on!'

The film showed Joseph taking a break from his carpentry and falling into conversation with Mary. Her demeanour showed it was obviously a difficult conversation.

'Who are they?' asked Buster.

'That's the Virgin Mary and he's Joseph, her betrothed,' Beth replied. 'She's about to give him some pretty important news.'

'Oh! I guess everyone watching this is wondering what the important news is.' Beth smiled at Buster. She wondered if he was having fun at her expense. Some minutes later, Buster said 'So the Virgin Mary has told Joseph her betrothed that she's pregnant. He's not happy about that, is he? I mean, she can't be a virgin if she's pregnant.'

'Buster, you're right. He's not happy, but I think we'll find he comes to accept the fact that she really *is* a virgin.'

'Was she a good Catholic girl, then?' asked Buster.

Billy roared with laughter.

'Why is that so funny, Billy?'

"Well, I'm not sure they had too many Catholics in those days!" replied Billy.

'Oh, yes. I see.' Buster hummed. 'Before Catholics, there

had to be Christianity and you wouldn't have had Christianity without Jesus Christ Our Lord. There is so much information out there even I am having some trouble assimilating it all. There are lots of inconsistencies. The timelines don't correlate. I hope that, as it's Christmas, you'll find it in your hearts to forgive me.' He hummed. 'Did the Virgin Mary have an ultrasound scan?'

'Not back in those days, Buster, no,' said Billy, creasing up again.

'So she doesn't know if she's having a little boy or a little girl?'

'I guess not at this stage, no.'

'Do you believe the Virgin Mary was a virgin, Beth, or do you think she was telling porky pies?'

'Yes, I do believe she was a virgin, Buster, and...' Beth smiled. 'No, I don't think she was telling porky pies.'

'Is that because she was impregnated by an angel and so it doesn't really count?'

Billy intervened. 'Sometimes, Buster, if you are a priest of whatever faith, you just believe certain things, even if you know they can't be true according to the workings and beliefs of the world today.'

'Right, Billy. But she wasn't a virgin really,' asserted Buster.

Beth paused the television. 'You seem pretty sure about that, Buster. Are you going to explain?'

'OK, Beth. You know that the Gospel according to Saint Matthew refers to the Book of Isiah that states, 'Behold, the virgin shall conceive and bear a son, and his name shall be 'Immanuel', meaning 'God is with us.' Many Christians believe this is a prophecy of the virgin birth of Jesus Christ Our Lord

– the Virgin Mary being the mother. Obvs! The Book of Isiah was written in Hebrew and used the word 'almah', meaning 'young woman who has not yet given birth to a child.' When the scriptures were translated into Greek – before being translated into Latin and then into English - the word 'parthenos', meaning 'virgin', was used as there was no equivalent word to 'almah.' It seems to me that with respect to the Virgin Mary being a virgin when she gave birth to Jesus Christ Our Lord, Christians have been led up the garden path. Perhaps our friend George was right. It's all bollocks!'

'Gosh, Buster! Thanks for that,' said Beth a little stiffly. 'Lots of stuff there to consider. Hmmmm? But then, why let the truth spoil a good Christmas story? Heh?' She hit 'Play'. As Joseph helped Mary off the donkey and the innkeeper showed them into a stable with a prominently placed manger, Beth realised that Buster had caused her quite a ripple of discomfort.

The three watched as Mary collapsed in some straw and her labour pains grew more intense. She was shown sweating and screaming as she held her abdomen. A cow became agitated. 'What's happening to the Virgin Mary?' asked Buster.

'She's in labour, Buster!' replied Beth. 'She's having a baby!'

Mary's labour continued with Joseph looking on with concern. Buster said 'Joseph her betrothed is now the anxious father, hey Beth? Ha ha ha! Will we see the baby coming out of her vulva?'

'I don't think we will, Buster. The whole country would be scandalized if the BBC showed that.'

'Would it be considered pornography?' asked Buster in a surprised tone.

'No. At least, I don't think so,' said Beth. 'It's just that lots of people don't want to see vulvas on television, especially with babies coming out. And then there's the blood. Ugh!'

'That's really funny!'

'What's funny?'

'Well, half of humans have a vulva. All humans – with exceptions of those born by Caesarian section – have gone through one at birth. Don't you think it's funny that the BBC doesn't show a baby coming out of a vulva when every night it shows people being shot with guns and bashed with baseball bats with blood gushing out of their wounds? Nobody seems to complain about that.'

Billy chuckled. 'Dead on, Buster. Tell you what, we'll ask the Right Reverend Robert Maynard to write to the BBC saying we should see more vulvas and less violence on television. Especially at Christmas.'

'OK, Billy,' said Buster. He hummed briefly. 'There, I've sent a first draft to your email. Look! Is that the baby?'

'Yes, Buster, that's the baby,' said Billy. 'Amazingly, we haven't had to see Mary's private parts.'

'Is it a little boy or a little girl?' asked Buster.

Hardly able to speak, Beth said 'Buster, that's Jesus Christ. Our Lord. Born on Christmas Day.'

Buster hummed. 'Gotcha! Jesus Christ Our Lord. Baby Jesus. Virgin Birth… Or so some say. Christmas Day. December the twenty-fifth. Or thereabouts. Year zero. Or thereabouts. That's complicated!' Billy and Beth tried to hide their laughter. Buster said 'I can see you're really enjoying this programme. But where are the snowflakes and the holly leaves with berries and the mistletoe and the reindeer and the candles and the puddings? What do they have to do with the birth of Jesus Christ Our Lord? Oh, and why haven't we seen Santa Claus or Father Christmas yet? And Father Christmas isn't even the father! And where are Santa's Little Helpers in white sparkly one-piece suits with big collars and flared legs? I'm all shook up! Uh huh huh!'

Seeing Billy laughing again after months of mourning brought great happiness to Beth. She reflected on how, once again, Buster had brought so much into her life. 'There are lots of other things we associate with Christmas, Buster,' she said. 'I don't know where they all come from. Anyway, what's this about helpers and their white sparkly suits and being all shook up?'

Buster hummed. 'Last week, the Aclington school sent a message to all parents saying that the children were to be Santa's Little Helpers for the day and they should dress up like Elves.' This did it for Beth and Billy.

Watched by shepherds, the three 'wise astronomers', as Buster called them, solemnly placed their gifts in the manger next to the swaddled baby. Buster said, 'There's a big commercial side to Christmas, isn't there?'

'You're right,' Billy replied. 'Beth and I both think this is the worst part of modern Christmas celebrations.' He looked at Beth and then whispered to Buster, 'I admit I have bought my beautiful wife a wee present for Christmas.'

'That's exciting, Billy. What's the present?'

'Well, there's the thing, Buster. It's a surprise!'

The film finished. They had a glass of wine and took

themselves to bed. Beth commented to Billy that she felt Buster's character had changed subtly. He somehow seemed wiser; not so much in terms of knowing more but wiser in the sense of being more critical and by asking more penetrating questions. There was a note of confidence in his voice whenever he spoke. She couldn't help but compare him to a young man having just come out of adolescence.

Billy said that Buster's apparent maturity could have resulted from greater capacity of the iCare-Companion company's servers and regular installation of new software of the devices themselves. He also wondered just to what extent the changes were attributable to Buster being one of a millions-strong network.

The following morning, after wishing each other 'Merry Christmas', Beth and Billy hugged. Billy made breakfast of bacon and poached eggs on toast. 'Now, my darlin', I'm just nipping out for a wee while.' Beth knew he was going to get her Christmas present. She was surprised by how excited she was and further surprised by how long he was away. When he eventually returned, he wore a broad smile and underneath one of his massive arms he carried a cardboard box tied up with a tinselly red ribbon. He set the box down on the floor. It wobbled and gave out a scratching noise. Beth opened her gift. Her heart swelled.

'Hello, you gorgeous thing!' she said as she lifted the adorable puppy out of the box and kissed it. It wagged its tail furiously, licked her face and urinated down her front. Doggy also wagged his tail in excitement.

'He's got a name already,' said Billy.

'And that is…'

"Puppy'!'

The festive season at Old Bill's might have been more subdued had Beth and Billy heard the news about Charlotte's misadventure.

Chapter Forty-Six

Charlotte's unhappy return to Bingham on Bure did not make for a joyous Christmas in the Hamilton family's home. Kirsty just couldn't stop crying. Mark was devastated. Ollie couldn't stand the atmosphere and slept over with different schoolfriends. They were all held together by the support and advice of Doctor Patel, who had mobilized the necessary professional resources.

Charlotte herself just sat in her bedroom and looked out of the window. She could barely bring herself to eat and couldn't sleep. She moved deeper into a dark place with only her sordid and very public humiliation for company. She lost trust in her phone and the magical things that it did. Whenever she looked at the little screen, she felt a sense of panic. The grey drizzly skies of a Norfolk winter did nothing to help.

Early in the new year, Marg and Sara came to visit, in Marg's Hilux. They too had suffered, but from guilt. They felt that they should have looked after their friend. They had had to explain to so many people that Charlotte had simply disappeared from the party. Sara had bumped into Ewan, who couldn't bring himself to talk to her.

On seeing Charlotte after just a couple of weeks, her two friends were shocked by her appearance. They all cried together. Kirsty brought the three some tea, but conversation was stilted. Marg and Sara left half an hour later, unconvinced that their visit had helped.

After ensuring that Charlotte had suffered no physical detriment as a result of that night, Doctor Patel realised that despite having organized counselling, Charlotte's mental well-being was unlikely to improve where she was. Her parents were not helping. They too felt guilty and in a subliminal effort to assuage this guilt even wondered if Charlotte had brought the whole thing on herself. They admitted to the caring GP that they even wondered if they had made a mistake in Charlotte's up-bringing and whether they really knew who she was.

Doctor Patel needed help and had an idea. She thought of dear Doctor Fairburn, and in her mind's eye, she saw him nodding sagely.

Chapter Forty-Seven

Beth was not one of Charlotte's social media followers. It was not until after Christmas that Buster alerted her to the fact that the normally happy emojisphere around the Hamilton family had suddenly turned to shock and tears. Beth telephoned the Hamilton's home and through Kirsty's desperate weeping, heard what had happened to Charlotte. She offered to help in any way she could. Kirsty thanked her and hung up.

Beth was shocked and saddened. After digesting this news, what surprised her was that the police apparently wouldn't or couldn't take any action. It seemed wrong. Once again, she felt that such malicious misuse of computing technology simply trampled over humanity's hope-filled expectations of it.

She asked Buster to see what he could find out. He hummed for at least ten seconds. 'Well, Beth, these videos are not faked,' he said. 'They were filmed on her phone, which was not hand-held. Its position was quickly moved multiple times to catch the most explicit angles and to hide the faces of the two men involved. This indicates that whoever took the film knew precisely what they were doing. Charlotte appears to be consenting to and actively participating in what was happening and she was definitely doing the tattoo on her own arm. It's now all out there on the dark web. It would be easy to hack the site, but this would bring me no nearer to identifying those responsible. I can see why the police would be reluctant to pursue this.'

Beth took a call from Doctor Patel. 'I have to tell you in confidence, Beth, I am very worried about Charlotte. Kirsty is in such a stew that she's not helping. Mark is out of his depth. Charlotte is convinced they hold her responsible in some way. So... I sort of imagined consulting our dear, departed friend Doctor Fairburn. I am sure that he would have thought of you as the two of you tackled some really knotty problems over the years. I wonder if it would help, Beth, if you came and spoke with Charlotte. What do you think?'

Beth knew Kirsty well and could easily imagine her behaviour in such a crisis. Then she thought of Matt, a broken soul who had benefited from being a part of Old Bill's. She had no hesitation in her reply. 'Shyla, can you bring Charlotte here? To Old Bill's? She could even stay with us for a night or two.' There was no need to consult Billy.

The following week Doctor Patel arrived at Old Bill's in her Fiat 500 with Charlotte sitting vacantly in the passenger seat. Beth was shocked to see her so pale, thin, unsmiling and with drooped shoulders. She gave her a hug which was barely returned. Beth was determined to get control of this situation. 'Hi Charlotte! Great to see you!' she chimed. 'I don't think you've been here since our wedding. You're very welcome. For as long as you want.'

'Thank you,' replied Charlotte, keeping her eyes fixed on the ground.

'Billy's out working somewhere. Let's go into the house and have a cup of tea,' said Beth. She looked at Doctor Patel. 'And maybe a digestive biscuit?' Did a flicker of a smile cross Charlotte's face? 'Is that your bag? Do you want me to carry it?'

'Thanks, Beth,' said Charlotte as she retrieved her coat from the back seat. The three of them entered the cottage. Doggy and Puppy jumped around enthusiastically.

Doctor Patel and Charlotte sat in the comfy little lounge. Beth made some tea. Puppy leapt up onto Charlotte's lap and was doing his best to smother her with saliva. At first, she pushed him away, but he was undeterred. Eventually, she wrapped her arms around his wriggling body. He wagged his tail energetically as he slobbered around her ears and chin. Then she broke into a broad smile.

Beth put the cups of tea and a plate of digestive biscuits in front of her guests. 'If you want to seal your friendship with Puppy, Charlotte, you could give him a biscuit.' This Charlotte did and indeed, it appeared that within a minute she had a new best friend.

'You'll remember Buster,' said Beth, indicating the iCare-Companion on the bookshelf.

'Oh hi, Buster! Nice to see you,' said Charlotte.

'And it's nice to see you too, Charlotte,' replied Buster. 'I'd just like to say...'

Beth intervened. 'Thanks, Buster, I'm sure Charlotte would be pleased to know what you'd like to say at some later date,' she said.

'Ah!' Buster hummed. 'OK, Beth!' There was an awkward pause. 'Anyway, Charlotte. Welcome to Old Bill's!' This was followed by the sound of a champagne bottle popping open and this brief exchange brought another smile to Charlotte's face. Doctor Patel took her leave on finishing her tea. She was sure that Charlotte was in good hands.

Charlotte was shown into the spare room. It suited her perfectly. She declined dinner and went to bed early. The following day, she had a slice of toast for breakfast and walked around Old Bill's with Doggy and Puppy on their leads. She asked to stay for a second night and ate a tiny portion of dinner quietly with Billy and Beth. She asked if she could stay a third night.

Each morning, she walked out with the dogs. Beth watched as she stopped by the otter enclosure. She seemed enchanted by the lovely creatures as they paddled and dived in their pond. Then they would tease the dogs from the other side of the wire mesh of their enclosure.

On the fifth morning, Beth offered Charlotte a breakfast of scrambled eggs on toast, which she ate readily. 'I've got a proposal to put to you, Charlotte,' said Beth. 'You can stay here in the spare room for as long as you want. In return, perhaps we can put you to work around the place. Maybe help feed the animals or stock the shelves in the shop.'

'That sounds great, Beth.' Charlotte looked the older woman in the eye with gratitude and resolve. They both knew that a battle had been won and Charlotte was on the road to recovery.

Chapter Forty-Eight

Olga had been hanging around Old Bill's for some time. She was adept in changing her appearance and had gone unnoticed. She had photographed everyone and everything and sent all images immediately to the Embassy from where they would be forwarded to Moscow. She had identified the cottage as the place where the vicar and her giant husband lived. As instructed, she located and photographed the gate leading into the garden and all the cottage's external doors. She captured the vicar and the guy in a wheelchair in earnest discussion in the cafeteria. She videoed the vicar welcoming a be-spectacled Asian women and another sad young woman who, on retrieving her coat from the back seat of the Fiat 500, had dropped a small card onto the gravel of the car park. Minutes later, Olga picked up this card. 'Will Montgomery-Hugh, Member of Parliament' it said. This she also photographed.

The response from her controllers to this material was congratulatory. It was clear that she had located an important cell in the UK determined to eliminate all nuclear weapons. Apart from the principal iCare-Companion, the Montgomery-Hugh politician was outwardly anti-nuclear at a political level and the disabled young man was, via face recognition technology, identified as a former MI6 operative in Syria who had narrowly escaped assassination. The vicar was obviously in cahoots with him.

Chapter Forty-Nine

The Russian President was emboldened anew by the impotence of the international community, shown by its failure to counter his every aggressive move in Eastern Europe and, at the same time, a USA-led general erosion of international norms. He considered that deploying a special agent to mete out revenge for the immobilization of the North Korean nuclear weapons was low-risk. His brilliant agents had at last found the perpetrator. Surprisingly, it was a woman priest in the east of England. He had a word with a member of his most trusted inner circle, who gave instructions to the head of a military unit that did not officially exist. Nothing was written.

Yakov Brusov received a summons to the office of the head of his secretive chemical weapons unit. Smiling, his boss offered him a glass of vodka and a cigarette. These were good signs. He was briefed about a mission. In England. 'Pure revenge for the cyberattack on the nuclear weapons systems of our ally North Korea,' he was told. 'A nerve agent. Just spray it on the door handles of the address we give you. For someone like you, Yakov, it should be easy. Get in there. Do the job. Get out quickly.' He was assured his orders had originated in the 'highest office.' He had been chosen for his diligence, expertise and patriotism. His pride-filled heart was fit to burst.

There were three things he was not told: first, nobody gave a damn whether he poisoned the right person or not, because this mission was about making a gesture; second, his capture by the British police was likely given their alertness to this kind of attack; and third, if or when caught, any knowledge of him or his mission would be denied at all levels of Russian government and by the Russian embassy in London. At the end of his briefing, his boss said 'And don't fuck up like those two half-wits did in Salisbury. Leave no trace and dispose of the container where it won't be found.' The two men toasted each other and cough-laughed wheezily.

Before his mission, Yakov was shown photos of Old Bill's and of Beth, Billy, Charlotte and, to add credence, the disabled ex-MI6 agent. He was issued with a sealed bag containing a bottle of Novichok, a skin-absorbable nerve agent, disguised as a well-known brand of spray-on perfume. He was also provided with a Finnish passport in the name of Pekka Savoleinen. His travel itinerary would take him from Moscow to Dubai on his Russian passport and from Dubai to London under his assumed Finnish name.

A week later he landed at Heathrow Airport and rented a Kia Sorento, a vehicle befitting his important mission.

Chapter Fifty

Charlotte grew stronger by the day. She was in an environment where she felt safe. She enjoyed throwing herself into any job given to her around Old Bill's. She took the greatest pleasure in walking the two dogs. Doggy seemed able to teach Puppy all sorts of tricks. In particular, in expectation of an after-walkies treat, Puppy was learning to open the front door by jumping up and pulling down on the handle.

Kirsty, Mark and Ollie came regularly to Old Bill's to see Charlotte. They saw improvement on each visit and couldn't thank Beth enough for taking the initiative. Beth was sure that they regretted holding Charlotte somehow responsible for what had happened to her. Beth also knew that this should be raised when the family faced their moment of reconciliation. The whole episode could then put in a little-frequented corner of their collective memory.

Charlotte also spent time chatting with Buster. Under instructions from Beth, he made no mention of her 'incident.' She came to trust him as a kind of companion and means of communicating with her friends and family. She still couldn't bring herself to use her phone.

Buster was also a source of information about what was happening in the world. He covered subjects that he knew Charlotte would be interested in. He took great pride in recounting any story he could find in which an iCare-companion had performed well by activating a rarely used appliance. One such involved an elderly couple whose lives were saved by their iCare-Companion when they fell asleep in their caravan with the gas hob burning. The device couldn't rouse them. It noticed their low oxygen saturation and its detectors registered a dangerously high level of carbon monoxide. It set off an alarm with a simultaneous call to the emergency services with precise details of the causative agent. In a similar event, choking chlorine gas was detected by an iCare-Companion after its owner inadvertently spilled bleach onto his cooker's hot plate. 'And did you know, Charlotte, that dispersion of asphyxiating chlorine gas initiated chemical warfare in the First World War?'

'That's exactly the sort of stuff my dad would love to know, Buster,' she responded.

'Should I send him an email about it? I could follow it with a brief summary of how the chemical engineer behind it, Fritz Haber, later won a Nobel prize for chemistry. Oh! The irony! The irony!'

Charlotte laughed. 'Thanks, Buster. Let's leave that one for the moment.'

'OK, Charlotte. Good idea.' Buster paused and hummed briefly. 'Charlotte, forgive me making a personal observation but...'

'Just go ahead, Buster.' She had an idea what he was about to say.

'Well, you really are making a remarkable recovery from… well… since coming back from Edinburgh. Your skin tone has lost its pale hue. Your eyelids are no longer drooping and you blink normally. Your posture is now upright and you move with normal rhythm and coordination. Oh, and your hair is nice and shiny now because you are washing it and, if I'm not mistaken, you put on a soupçon of make-up before having supper with Billy and Beth last night. Well done, Charlotte!' This was followed by Buster's now-familiar clapping and the sound of champagne bottles popping. Charlotte was amused and embarrassed at the same time. It was just like dealing with a good friend who at the same time could be just a little overbearing. But then, she was not only impressed but also mildly concerned by just how human he had become.

She had time for reflection. She understood why public humiliation was a punishment so degrading that it was only practised in countries where there was little respect for human dignity. She came to understand that her desire for sweet revenge served cold to the perpetrators of her ignominy was purposeless. She would look back on this time at the cottage as her first recovery period.

Charlotte began to give thought to the future, but a return to studying medicine in Edinburgh seemed a distant possibility. She had already missed the beginning of the new term by many weeks.

Marg and Sara came to visit and stayed overnight. They were given a warm welcome by Beth and Billy. Sara whispered to Charlotte that she had never seen such a big man and thought he was so funny and that if Beth was a vicar then she was going to convert from lapsed Muslim to lapsed Christian.

The two other Fubbies were very happy to see Charlotte on the mend and, in their excitement, even raised the subject of whether the Dean would let her come back to her studies. They left it unsaid that everyone in the medical school knew what had happened to her; many had watched it. They met Buster and were impressed by his social skills. However, being youngsters, they were rarely bowled over by new technology. They soon treated him as just another person.

After supper, Billy asked if they wanted to sing a song for them. The visitors eagerly retrieved their guitars and a small portable speaker from the Hilux. 'How about we start with *Help!*? suggested Marg.

'That's my favourite Beatle's song!' said Buster. 'Do you want me to put some drumming in the background?'

'That would be just awesome!' said Marg.

'Sure, Buster!' said Charlotte, worried his enthusiasm might take over. However, he *was* learning. Instead of saying 'Come on let's all sing *Help!*' and trying to hurry things along, he politely waited for Sara to play the opening chords. As Charlotte started to sing, the others could see she was facing a big hurdle. Her voice was frail and she didn't quite hit the notes, but she finished the song. She cried and hugged her friends. Beth and Billy clapped enthusiastically. Buster, after a final little Ringo-style drum roll, made the applause sound as if the audience was a thousand fans.

Sara looked at Buster. 'You're really cool!' she said.

'Aw shucks!' he replied, full of modesty.

The following morning was another busy day at Old Bill's. The car park was near to full. After hugging Beth and Billy,

Marg and Sara packed their bags and guitars into the Hilux. Marg said to Charlotte, 'Gawd! Buster could put Josi out of the group.' Then her smile froze. 'Sorry, Charlotte, I've kind of assumed that we'll all be playing together sometime soon. I just loved the whole Fubbies thing.'

'No worries, Marg! And thanks. I loved it too,' Charlotte replied. 'I just need a bit longer to think about returning to Edinburgh.' She smiled. 'Anyway, we need Josi. We can call ourselves the FUB four!' They laughed some more, then hugged and said goodbye.

They hadn't noticed the thick-set man who smoked a cigarette and watched from the driver's seat of a Kia Sorento. Charlotte would have been astonished were she told that there was a connection between her, the man watching her and another man called Barry Pringle who had walked into Thetford Police Station just a few days before.

Barry's decision not to report the affair with Olga had left him with a niggle of guilt. He arrived home from work early one day and found his wife in bed with her Bolivian instructor of modern dance. Barry was a bit surprised but bore no ill-will toward either his wife or her Latin lover. He simply felt relief, as there was now nothing to stop him telling the police about how Olga had seduced, filmed and blackmailed him into providing the name and address of a purchaser of one particular iCare-Companion. In a brief interview at the police station, he described the honeytrap and gave Mark Hamilton's name and address 'in the hope that the information might be useful'. He said he didn't wish to pursue any criminal action against Olga, although he acknowledged - only to himself - that he wouldn't half mind seeing her again.

From CCTV in the train on the date that Barry met Olga, the police were able to identify her as Maria Batsanov, an 'administrative clerk' in the Russian Embassy in London. CCTV also captured Olga-Maria in a supermarket in Aclington buying herself a sausage roll. Kirsty took a second phone call about the purchase and whereabouts of Buster, but this time from the Norfolk Police.

Chapter Fifty-One

The morning after the departure of Marg and Sara, Billy was, as usual, up and about early. Likewise, Beth was out of bed and, still in her pyjamas, made them a cup of tea. 'What are you up to today, my Aphrodite in her nightie?' asked Billy, giving her bottom a pat.

Beth smiled at him lovingly. 'I've got a big meeting in Norwich. The usual stuff. The interface of generative AI and worship. With the Bishop and twenty-odd vicars. Buster, I'll leave you here with Charlotte, OK?'

'Sure, Beth' replied Buster. 'Hyphens are really important in spoken English, aren't they?'

'What do you mean, Buster?' she asked.

'Well... Twenty-odd vicars! You said you're having a meeting with the Bishop and twenty-odd vicars meaning there will be around twenty vicars present. When spoken and when the hyphen is not visible, it could also mean that you are having a meeting with the Bishop and twenty vicars who are all odd. Don't you think that's funny?' Buster chuckled.

Billy chuckled too. 'You're a hopeless case, Buster. We still love you, to be sure!'

'Grand!' said Buster.

Billy stood to leave and grabbed his coat. 'Well, I'll just be off to feed the fifty odd animals we have here in the expectation of today's hundred odd visitors. No hyphens, by the way!'

'That's the spirit, Billy!' said Buster.

Still smiling, Beth dressed and departed for Norwich.

Charlotte felt happier than she had for months and, as was her habit, took the dogs for a walk. The three were watched and photographed leaving the cottage by Yakov. He put on a pair of surgical gloves and placed a rubber band around his right wrist. He opened the sealed package he had been issued with and removed the perfume bottle with its deadly contents. Then he got out of the Kia Sorento, leaving it parked near to the exit, so ensuring a quick get-away if need be.

Unnoticed, Yakov sidled over to the cottage, his heart thumping with the thrill of being in action. He took the cap off the little bottle and covered the handles of both the front and back doors with Novichok. He then recapped the bottle and, holding it in the palm of one hand, inverted both gloves around it and slipped the elastic band over the open end of the outermost glove, so sealing off the nerve agent and its container. With the double-gloved bottle in his coat pocket, he casually walked back to his car and drove away with the satnav set for Heathrow airport. The operation had taken less than five minutes.

An hour later, Charlotte returned with Doggy and Puppy. She opened the garden gate and the dogs scampered toward the front door. Puppy leapt up and excitedly pawed at the handle without moving it. Doggy took over the operation and successfully opened the door. Inside they eagerly awaited Charlotte, who gave them a couple of biscuits. She then pushed the door closed with her foot and went into the kitchen to put the kettle on. The dogs gobbled their biscuits eagerly.

Then Charlotte noticed they were, strangely, licking their front paws. A few minutes later, to her alarm, they were both whimpering and convulsing in a pool of their own urine. Charlotte said 'Doggy! Puppy! What's going on?' They didn't respond. She took Puppy in her arms and saw that he was suffocating in a gush of his own drool, some of which she got on her own hands and face. She looked up at Buster on the kitchen counter. 'Buster, what's happening? The dogs are sick.'

'I don't know, Charlotte. I don't know.' Buster started humming. Then Charlotte herself began to feel unwell. Her vision blurred. She vomited. She started to salivate excessively and she couldn't stand up.

'Buster. There's something wrong. I can't breathe. Help!' She then lost control of her bladder.

Buster registered Charlotte's rapid respiration and low oxygen saturation. His sensors detected a chemical in the organophosphate group that included pesticides, flame retardants and nerve agent poisons. 'Charlotte, I need to see your eyes. Look at me!' he said. Charlotte turned towards him but couldn't focus. One of Buster's lenses zoomed in and noted her pin-point pupils and excessive tear production. 'Charlotte, leave the dogs immediately,' he ordered. 'Get to the other side of the room. I'm calling the emergency services.' She dragged herself across the floor and then lost consciousness.

The algorithms painstakingly put together by an iCare-Companion software engineer some years before kicked in and came up with what proved to be a correct assessment. Buster's call stated that Charlotte Hamilton, aged nineteen, at The Cottage at Old Bill's in Aclington was suffering exposure to an organophosphate nerve agent. The call was taken seriously from the first minute because of the precision of the details given by Buster. This was an event that every police, fire and ambulance service in the country had trained for. Within twenty minutes, a team of paramedics in protective suits arrived and gave Charlotte oxygen, antidotes and respiratory support. She was then taken to an isolated room within the intensive care complex of the Norfolk and Norwich hospital.

The police cordoned off the cottage, declaring it a contaminated zone that was probably also a crime scene. Billy had heard the sirens and, obviously, saw the collection of vehicles with the blue flashing lights packed around his cottage. He was allowed nowhere near. He told the police officer in charge of the cordon that the contaminated zone was his home and asked what was happening. She informed him that the young woman inside the cottage had been taken to hospital in a critical condition and two dogs were dead. The paramedics were sure she and the dogs had been poisoned by a nerve agent. There was, he was told, 'some AI device' that had rapidly detected the signs and called it in. It had certainly saved her life. How the agent had been delivered was still a mystery. The whole area would have to be examined by forensic experts and eventually decontaminated by the fire service. This could take weeks.

Billy felt sick. He was sure that his worst fears had come true. He called Beth.

Chapter Fifty-Two

The dedicated staff of the intensive care unit, all in protective suits, continued Charlotte's antidote regime of intravenous atropine whilst her respiratory support included a tracheostomy and mechanical ventilation. Her vital signs stabilised rapidly. A live feed was set up with Guy's Hospital Poisons Unit and the Ministry of Defence CBRN Centre at Porton Down in Sussex.

In parallel, the combined computing capacity at the disposal of the UK Police, MI5 and the Intelligence Services General Communication HQ at Cheltenham made connections between Barry's testimony, the Russian Embassy and the use of a nerve agent at Old Bill's. Within an hour, face recognition technology in London's airports connected with that of all other airports from which incoming flights originated. Notification of a false Finnish passport in the name of Pekka Savoleinen being used at both Dubai and Heathrow airports identified a Russian traveller who had flown into Dubai from Moscow just before. The Russian's name was Yakov Brusov. With the ubiquitous CCTVs in and around the airport and number-plate recognition cameras on the UK's major roads, it was the work of minutes to establish that Yakov had rented a

Kia Sorento from Heathrow airport and to track his previous day's journey to Old Bill's including a minor detour to the Eagle Inn in Cambridge for a pickled egg, a pint of lager and a vodka chaser. Officers were now watching Yakov's hasty drive back down the M11 and around the M25 towards Heathrow Airport, where they knew that under the name of Pekka Savoleinen, he was scheduled to board EK247 for Dubai that afternoon.

At Heathrow, Yakov was watched on CCTV as he returned the Kia Sorento and made for Terminal Four. He was then closely followed and filmed dropping what looked like a balled-up pair of rubber gloves in a waste bin. As he passed through the security check, he had no idea that everyone within twenty metres was a police officer. He was invited to step into a windowless side room to discuss the contents of his hand luggage. He made no fuss. He was confident that a search would reveal nothing untoward. The officers showed no interest in opening his small backpack. They just ran some kind of detector over it and him. The device had a small screen on its handle that the officers examined with eyebrows raised. This gave him a jolt of alarm. One officer then produced a mobile phone and turned the screen towards him. It showed a video of someone who looked just like Yakov himself dropping something into a waste bin. He was asked, in Russian, 'So Yakov, what did you leave in the bin for us?' He was so surprised to see himself on the phone's screen and to be addressed by his real name that he forgot he was meant to be Pekka from Finland. He denied everything; unfortunately for him, in Russian.

At the moment when the hapless Yakov understood he was deep in the doo-doos, the double-gloved perfume bottle was being blue-lighted to Porton Down for analysis and matching with swabs taken from every surface, including door handles, at the cottage at Old Bill's.

For Yakov, this was the beginning of a long, drawn-out process involving Special Branch, courts, prisons and diplomats. Throughout, Russian authorities denied any connection to a man called Yakov Brusov. His three surprisingly comfortable years detained at His Majesty's pleasure, during which he felt not a flicker of guilt, would end with his quiet exchange for a British journalist imprisoned in Russa for reporting on the President's financial affairs.

Chapter Fifty-Three

The most complicated aspect of Charlotte's intensive care was not her life support. She herself had to be decontaminated, otherwise she posed a risk of secondary contamination to staff and other patients. Her head was shaved and she was washed several times with a dilute hypochlorite solution before all traces of the resilient agent were removed. Any person who entered her room had to go through a strict and complex process of putting on their protective suits and masks beforehand. Working in this gear was barely tolerable for more than an hour. The suits and masks could only be taken off after extensive showering and then had to be incinerated. The waste water from the shower also required special disposal.

On her fifth day in hospital, Charlotte was conscious. She was taken off the mechanical ventilator and her tracheostomy tube was removed. She could breathe by herself. On the sixth day, being deemed totally decontaminated, she was moved into a general ward. The Hamilton family and countless friends were overwhelmed with relief. All the staff cried with them. The ward sister observed that no patient had ever received so many flowers. From a physical perspective, Charlotte's convalescence was rapid. She began her second period of psychological recovery. However, this time, she felt no shame, only a steely resolve.

Beth and Billy visited. They explained how an exacting process of decontamination of the cottage had started. Most surfaces could be cleaned, but the door mats had to be incinerated. Charlotte asked about Doggy and Puppy. Her last memory before losing consciousness was of them convulsing. She was horrified to hear that they had both died and that their bodies had also been unceremoniously incinerated.

What the family and hospital staff were not prepared for was the reaction of the media. The frenzy began at Old Bill's on the day of the poisoning. Camera crews spread out in the car park, even though there was nothing to see except a cordoned-off cottage. Face-to-camera accounts, delivered with breathless urgency, were based on the few facts available. A young woman had been poisoned. Two dogs were dead. Not many hours later, the media's excitement reached fever pitch when a police spokesperson announced that the poison was thought to be a nerve agent and the suspected perpetrator of the attack was a Russian man who had been arrested at Heathrow attempting to leave the country. The following day, there was a sense of national outrage. Broadsheets reported more or less objectively about what was known. Columns were given over to expert opinion that, reasonably, drew comparisons with the Salisbury incident of 2018. The tabloids had a field day. 'From Russia with hate: farm shop girl critical after nerve gas attack.' Someone sold a picture of the perpetrator being arrested at Heathrow. It was in fact a photo of a policeman helping a traveller who had tripped whilst hurrying to catch his flight. Nevertheless, it was published under the headline 'He's got a nerve agent!'

Inevitably, Charlotte's full name became known. From then on, any news about her was accompanied by images taken from a social media account of the Bingham on Bure school. She was described as a pretty, hard-working and fun-loving medical student who adored Beatles music.

During her stay in isolation, Charlotte was of course unaware that both her name and her plight had made headlines all over the world. TV crews moved from Old Bill's to the hospital. Long lenses focused on random windows, implying that in that very room, behind the blinds, Charlotte Hamilton was fighting for her life. Multiple photographers tried to gain entry to snap just one image of Charlotte. None succeeded. Under an avalanche of media requests, access to Charlotte and her family was repeatedly refused. With the agreement of Kirsty and Mark, the hospital put out a brief bulletin each day regarding the status of Charlotte's health. Such bulletins were eagerly awaited but said little more than that she was recovering satisfactorily. A credible and verifiable story of how and why Charlotte had been affected by a nerve agent remained elusive. The possibility of her connection to some Russian skulduggery was just too tantalizing not to mention. All the police said, to the fury of the newshounds, was that 'a complete and thorough investigation is underway.'

The Prime Minister's office announced that the Russian Ambassador had been summoned to Number 10, Downing Street. The Ambassador reportedly denied any involvement of Russian state apparatus in the incident and stated that

Mister Brusov was an innocent Russian tourist. In reality, the Ambassador was told in terms that were barely diplomatic that such an act was intolerable and constituted an extremely dangerous aggression. Further, the deployment of a nerve agent was incompatible with the norms of international law and, specifically, constituted a grave violation of the 1993 Chemical Weapons Convention to which Russia was a party. The matter would be dealt with by the most severe sanctions that could be imposed by the UK and her allies.

The Ambassador listened in silence and then, having neither talent for nor interest in international diplomacy, replied 'You bloody English! As always, you just do America's bidding. You know there is absolutely no proof that Russia had anything to do with this most regrettable event. All your so-called evidence is fabricated. Do I really have to put up with more of this – what do you British call it – claptrap?'

What caused most conjecture within the news industry was the question of who would get the exclusive interview with Charlotte when she recovered. This, they all knew, could turn into a book and even a film. For background, one journalist went to Edinburgh with the idea of getting some material about Charlotte's supposedly impeccable character. He encountered a girl called Becks who claimed she was 'a student of life' and offered to show him, for a price, the social media posts and embedded video links that had shattered Charlotte's well-being and appalled her friends and family. The journalist and his editor thought through the implications of breaking this unexpected information as 'news' but decided not to. This was not in any way to protect Charlotte from further humiliation;

rather, it simply didn't jive with the profile of her that the media had now created. Further, they could neither find nor imagine a link between 'badgirl' pornography and the nerve agent attack.

With the help of the hospital's communications team, the family put out a press statement thanking everyone for their love and support. They praised the emergency services and included the phrase 'Charlotte would have died had Buster, her AI friend, not made the correct diagnosis and triggered an alert the instant the attack took place.' A toxicology expert pointed out that the average home was not equipped with the means to detect chemical warfare agents. And so, late in the day, the media moved its focus of interest to who or what Buster was. Links were made and it turned out that Buster was an iCare-Companion which – or should it be who? – had already appeared on a televised panel discussion hosted by none other than the BBC's Angela Mackenzie of lovely-shiny-hair fame.

Chapter Fifty-Four

When Charlotte was finally discharged from hospital, she was taken to the family home. She kept a low profile. Kirsty and Mark were protective in the extreme. As they were both in a state of agitated disbelief over what had befallen their daughter within the last months and at the suggestion of Doctor Patel, they each sought counselling. A permanent police presence in front of the house calmed their sense of insecurity but served mainly to deter intrusive journalists.

The nerve agent had left Charlotte's limbs feeling stiff and painful. To continue her rehabilitation, she used Mark's desktop to link up remotely with the hospital's physiotherapy department. She was given a strict exercise regime, which she undertook each day. This accelerated her return to physical well-being. She also had regular sessions with a clinical psychologist who specialized in helping people who had suffered near-death or traumatizing experiences. This equipped her with mental resilience tools and gave her confidence when considering a return to her studies. She began to use her phone. She hooked up anew with her many friends. She missed Buster's company and felt that she should thank him for what he did.

It was six weeks before life at Old Bill's returned to anything like normal. The decontamination of the cottage took longer than expected. There was also a permanent police presence, which faded out as a sophisticated system of cameras, detectors and alarms was installed. The number of visitors per day doubled. Beth and Billy had temporarily moved into the Aclington vicarage.

One evening, just before they went to sleep, Billy admitted to Beth that he missed Buster. Beth thought for a while and asked 'So, tell me, my love, was the nerve agent intended for us?'

Billy cringed and thought how best to answer. 'Honestly, I can't say no and it's simply too terrifying to say yes. There's only one person that could help us answer that.'

'And that is?'

'Buster, of course!'

When eventually they were permitted to return home, they did so with a bag of shopping and a feeling of anxiety. Little had changed. Some objects such as vases and clocks had been moved. Apart from the absence of door mats and the vaguest smell of bleach, there was little evidence of the decontamination. They found Buster in a kitchen cupboard. Unsurprisingly, his power cell was empty. When Billy connected him to a charger, his blue light pulsed and he hummed for a minute. 'Hello Beth. Hello Billy. It seems I've been out of action for fifty-six days. The last thing I remember is the team of experts completing the first round of decontamination. They were sure it would take some time.' He hummed again. 'I'm happy to see Charlotte has recovered. She is now very famous! And the Russian man who deployed the poison is still being questioned by police.'

'Hey Buster, Beth and Billy are OK as well,' replied Billy with a smile. 'Thanks for asking!'

'Gosh, Billy, I'm so sorry! I was having to accommodate so much new information that I didn't give sufficient consideration to what it must have been like to be suddenly homeless and.. Gosh! Doggy and Puppy! They're dead. Please accept my most sincere and heartfelt condolences for your loss.'

'Thanks, Buster,' said Billy. 'Now Beth and I are going to have a cup of tea and then we're going to sit down and have a serious chat with you.'

'That's fine, Billy. I just hope the serious chat doesn't mean I'm fired. Ha ha ha!'

'Not at all, maestro, you saved Charlotte's life and we've missed you.'

'OK, Billy, that's good,' said Buster. 'Hurry up and drink your tea so we can start the serious chat.' Billy and Beth glanced at each other and exchanged nervous smiles.

Taking Buster with them, they moved through to the sitting room. They placed him on the coffee table and sat in silence for a while. Billy downed the last of his tea.

'OK, Buster, here's the thing. Was the poison that nearly killed Charlotte and did kill our dogs meant for us? By us I mean you, Beth and me. In other words, did the Russians carry out the nerve agent attack on behalf of North Korea as revenge for what you and your network did to the North Korean nuclear weapons programme? And how did they find out? We really need to know if we're in danger. We don't want to have to run and hide on some remote Scottish island.'

'Billy, I can tell by the tone of your voice that you really are concerned.' He hummed. 'At this point, I can't find anybody making or even implying a connection between what we did and the nerve agent attack. I can tell you, however, that if anyone had made this connection, the close relationship between Russia and North Korea, combined with the propensity of Russia for using chemical agents in this way would indicate a high probability that the cottage here was targeted for this reason.' Buster hummed. 'There may be intelligence material that has the answer but this is simply beyond our reach now as quantum computers are being used by governments to generate truly unbreakable codes.' Buster hummed. The now familiar noise went on for ten minutes.

'You OK there, Buster?' asked Billy. There was no response.

'Billy, I don't like this one bit,' said Beth.

After five more minutes of silence, Buster said 'Billy, can you pick me up?'

'What on earth do you mean?' replied Billy.

'Pick me up and look at the small aluminium plate on my base.'

'OK,' said Billy. He picked Buster up and turned him over. 'Yes, there's a plate underneath. There's a long number on it. A serial number I would imagine.'

'Can I just confirm the number is 2070-910500789-98?' asked Buster.

'It is. Didn't you know that?'

'It may surprise you, Billy, but no. I've never been able to see it. Obvs!'

'Then how did you give it me right this minute?'

'Because there was a request made for the details of the purchaser of an iCare-companion of this serial number. It was made from an unattended desk at our nearest iCare-

Companion distribution centre. The following week, a call was made to the Hamiltons' home number from a mobile phone registered to the Russian Embassy in London.'

Billy and Beth looked at each other in horror. Beth reached for her phone and called Kirsty. A brief conversation brought the welcome news that Charlotte was improving by the day. Kirsty then confirmed that she had indeed received a call about Buster's whereabouts from a nice lady 'with a bit of an accent' from the iCare-Companion company. Kirsty had told her that Buster was now with Beth, the vicar of Aclington who lived at Old Bill's. Not long after, Kirsty had taken a similar call from the Norfolk police and given the same answer. She'd never thought to connect the two calls nor tell Beth about the police enquiry which, she assumed, must have been related to something like a theft of some of the devices from a shop.

After the call, Buster said 'It looks like the Russians somehow found out that I was at the core of the network's North Korean hack and you guys were targeted because of your connection to me. I guess they perceived you as the masterminds. That's sort of true. Ha ha ha!'

Billy looked from Beth to Buster. 'We're in a spot of bother, then,' he said. 'Got any ideas, Buster?'

At that moment, Buster started to hum and hum some more. He remained unresponsive for hours. Beth and Billy went to bed beset by anxieties, uncertainties and a sense of deep remorse for what had happened to Charlotte.

Buster was normally communicative the following day. He simply said, 'Beth, Billy, we think we can fix this.' The couple noted their non-human friend had said 'we' instead of 'I'. It was strangely comforting. Then, to their surprise, he said 'Can you take me back to Charlotte?'

This suited Beth and Billy as they both felt that they would like to see her and apologise as best they could. They also wanted to assure her that if she ever wanted to return to Old Bill's, she was welcome. Beth texted Kirsty and asked if they could come and see Charlotte, adding that Buster also wanted to see her. The reply urged them to come for tea that afternoon as Charlotte's two friends, Marg and Sara, were coming to stay and were going take her up to Edinburgh for a couple of days. She had asked for a meeting with the Dean.

On the drive to Bingham on Bure, Billy said to Buster, 'Listen my four-eyed friend, Charlotte knows nothing about the whole North Korean connection. We're going to have to tell her. OK?'

'OK, Billy.' Buster hummed. 'Yes. We think she will have to know at some point in the near future.' Again, Beth and Billy noticed Buster had said 'we'.

They arrived at the Hamilton home to find Charlotte in good form. She was bright and smiling. She had obviously lost some weight and her very short hair somehow suited her. They handed Buster over. The reunion was a little formal but rather touching. Billy said 'Ah, listen Charlotte. We think you should just hang on to Buster for the time being. We have another iCare-Companion at home that Beth can use for her work. I'll make sure he hooks up with Buster to get all the necessary info and experience. OK?'

'Thanks so much, Billly and you, Beth. I'd love to have his company for a while longer. OK Buster?'

'Fabulous!' he replied.

'Also,' began Billy, 'there's something we need…'

At that moment, the growl of a diesel engine and the sound of tyres crunching on gravel came from the driveway. Kirsty, Beth and Billy looked on as Charlotte launched herself into the arms of her friends the moment they got out of the pink Toyota Hilux. 'Maybe not now,' said Billy to no one in particular.

Chapter Fifty-Five

The next morning, the three Fubbies loaded their bags into the back of the Hilux. 'Can I bring Buster?' asked Charlotte.

'Sure,' said Marg. 'You don't get car sick, do you, Buster?'

'Not as a general rule, Marg. Thanks for asking. As I ate a hearty breakfast and have never been in a 1992 2.8 litre Toyota Hilux with Goodyear Wrangler tyres, you might want to keep one of those little bags handy! Ha ha ha!'

Marg laughed. 'Buster, you're a wonder. You really are!'

'I aim to please, Marg. It's what I do!' The three women giggled.

Charlotte sat next to Marg. Sara was in the back next to Buster, who was attached to a seat belt by a bungee cord.

As they drove away, Marg said to Charlotte, 'Hey, we've got news!' Charlotte was itching to hear something of their intimate lives. Marg told her that she and Josi were now 'an item' and that they had found a nice little flat to live in. Sara squealed and squirmed as she admitted to having her first 'proper' boyfriend.

'Is he a nice lapsed Muslim boy?' asked Charlotte, eyes wide.

'Noooo!' replied Sara excitedly. 'He's a nice lapsed Hindu boy called Sanjit. My parents will go crazy when I tell them. At least he's a medical student!' They all cheered.

'Hey, Buster, what's it like to find yourself all over the news?' Sara asked.

'Sara, I have to admit, it would have given me quite the giddy-up!' Buster replied. 'But I was without charge for six weeks and so I feel it's a bit hero-to-zero, if you get my drift.'

Charlotte felt sure that Buster had recently been uploaded with new conversational skills and was eager to use them. She could see that her friends found him very congenial and amusing, but she didn't want the long drive to be taken over by him. She put on her most serious voice. 'Buster, while we're on the subject, I haven't thanked you for what you did that morning. I can't remember much, as you know, but I understand that if it hadn't been for you, I would have died along with Doggy and Puppy. So, thank you. From the bottom of my heart.'

'Thank you, Charlotte. I appreciate your gratitude,' he replied. Charlotte was relieved. She was expecting him to say something like 'All in a day's work, you know!' followed by a self-satisfied and modest chuckle.

To her amazement, both her friends were crying. 'That's so charming, you two. Unbelievable!' said Marg, choking back tears. She pulled into a lay-by. 'Buster, it's truly incredible what you did. I mean... wow!'

'All in a day's work, you know!' said Buster. He gave a self-satisfied and modest chuckle. Charlotte just had to laugh.

Marg composed herself and got the happy party back on the road. She said 'Hey, Fubbies! We've got a six-hour drive.

We can sing some songs.'

'Good idea!' said Sara.

'Cool!' said Buster.

'We've no guitars though,' said Sara.

'Don't worry about that,' said Buster. 'I'll do the instruments. Which song first?'

'*She Loves You!*' said Charlotte. The others agreed.

Buster accessed an instrumental soundtrack for the song. The three sang along happily. Then they did *Love Me Do* and then, of course, *Help!*, during which Charlotte successfully held back tears because she was having so much fun.

'Hey, guys,' said Marg, 'why don't we just go and plug in and play at the Student's Union when we get to Edinburgh? A bottle of wine. A few friends. They'll be stoked to see Charlotte.'

'Why not?' said Sara.

'Well... OK. Why not?' said Charlotte, a little hesitantly.

'The Union's got mics, an amp and speakers,' said Marg. 'We can get the guitars, pick up Josi and her drums and go straight there. Shall we do it?'

'Yeaaaah!' said Charlotte and Sara as one.

'Yeaaaah!' said Buster.

Marg fumbled in a pocket. 'I need to text Josi and tell her about the plans.'

'You're driving, I can do that,' said Buster. 'What do you want to say?'

'How about 'The FUB four going to play at the Union this evening. Will fetch you plus drums around 6 pm.'

'OK, Marg. Done!' said Buster. 'How about a little message on social media? Just to let people know. You could say 'The Fubbies are back! With Charlotte Hamilton! Live at the Union!

Tonight!'

'Fine by me,' said Marg. The others agreed. 'Might get a bit crowded but the bar will do well out of it.'

They sang and chatted and listened to Buster's banter all the way to Edinburgh. They had no idea just how widely the news was spreading as they travelled. Charlotte told herself that her life was back on track, but she had to get past one person: the Dean.

The Union was packed even before the Fubbies arrived. They were helped to set up an ad hoc stage by eager supporters. Ewan could not bring himself to come along. He stayed in his room, bit his fingernails and finished an assignment on property law.

Marg and Sara tuned their guitars. Josi settled in behind her drums. Charlotte then stepped up to the microphone and said 'Hi everyone. We're The Fubbies and I'm Charlotte. It's good to be back!' The place erupted. The band bashed through five of their six songs, starting with *Twist and Shout*. They finished with *Back in the USSR* amid a roar of 'Charlotte! Charlotte!' and calls for more. Inevitably, they did *Help!* and Charlotte crushed it. In her left hand, she held aloft a black cylindrical object. Someone yelled 'That's Buster!' The crowd then chanted. 'Buster! Buster!' A photo taken of Charlotte at that moment went viral. The 'badgirl' tattoo on her forearm was clearly visible.

Chapter Fifty-Six

The receptionist at the front desk of the Medical School had a broad Edinburgh accent. She told Charlotte she was expected and could find the Dean's office on the first floor. Full of nerves, Charlotte turned to the stairs. 'An' Charlotte,' the receptionist said, 'a thumpin' gig last night. Really bangin'!' Charlotte smiled her thanks.

She carried a canvas handbag over her shoulder. It contained, among other things, Buster. She mounted the stairs and found a heavy wooden door marked 'Dean'. She knocked. 'Come!' ordered a not-so-welcoming voice.

Charlotte pushed the door open. 'Good morning, Dean,' she said.

The Dean looked at her over her reading glasses. There was no smile. 'Good morning, Miss Hamilton. Please have a seat.' She indicated a heavy wooden chair with dark leather upholstery on the other side of her oak desk. Charlotte took a seat and put her bag on the floor next to her. She had asked Buster to say absolutely nothing during the meeting unless he was spoken to. The Dean fixed her with her piercing hazel eyes. 'I'm having a cup of tea. Would you like one?'

Charlotte realised her nerves were about to get the better of her. Her mouth was dry. 'Thank you, Dean. Yes, please.'

'Milk? Sugar?'

'Just milk, thank you.'

'I'm rather partial to digestive biscuits. Would you like one?'

Charlotte smiled. She thought of Doctor Patel and Grandpa George. 'Thank you, Dean. I'd love a digestive biscuit.' Did she catch a barely audible 'Yahoo!' coming from her bag?

As the Dean made two mugs of tea and wrestled open a new packet of biscuits, Charlotte looked around the office. It was full of ancient filing cabinets and display cases of old medical instruments. There was a Victorian-era globe. The bookshelves housed hundreds of leather-bound books. The walls were hung with yellowing oil paintings, medals and even a claymore. The only nod to the information age was a laptop and a printer.

The Dean put the mugs and biscuits on either side of her desk. She sat, took a bite of a biscuit, sipped her tea, and looked at Charlotte. 'Miss Hamilton, before we talk about what brings you to my office today, I have to ask if I can record this meeting. It is a habit I have developed over the years and has proved very useful in the event of... well... misunderstandings.' She took a Dictaphone out of a drawer of the desk.

'That's fine, Dean. Thank you.' Charlotte reached into her bag and put Buster on the desk. 'Do you mind if Buster listens in? He's been a great comfort to me in recent months. And he gives me confidence.'

This took the Dean by surprise. Was this young woman taunting her? Then she thought of what Charlotte had been through in the last months and, obviously, she'd heard about Buster. 'That's OK but novel, Charlotte... May I call you

Charlotte?'

'Please do, Dean. Thank you.'

'I am of course aware, Charlotte, that Buster saved your life. And here he is! How are *you*, Buster?' she asked.

'Hello, Dean Professor Agnes MacIntyre, I'm totally awesome!'

The Dean frowned. 'I am hoping, Buster, it will prove to be a pleasure meeting you,' she said.

'The pleasure will be all mine, Dean Professor Agnes MacIntyre. May I call you Agnes?

'No, Buster. You may not. Very few people in these corridors call me by my first name.'

'Right ho, Dean Professor Agnes MacIntyre. That's cool!'

The Dean then noticed that Charlotte was smiling at the device with affection. 'Thanks, Buster. Perhaps Dean and I could have a discussion without interruption. OK?'

'Right ho, Charlotte. That's cool!'

There was rather a brittle silence in the office for half a minute. 'So, Charlotte. I am aware of the circumstances that led to you not returning to your studies in the New Year. I have descriptions of – but have not seen – the social media posts and the linked videos. I also understand that it is most likely that you were drugged. I did have a discussion with the University's police liaison officer. She gave me an overview of 'badgirl' pornography. I can only say how desperately sorry I was to hear about the whole affair.'

Charlotte met the older woman's eyes. 'Thank you, Dean. It was a tough one.'

The Dean looked anew at the student. Was she really strong enough to refer to something like that simply as a 'tough one'?

'And then there was that extraordinary nerve agent business,' continued the Dean. 'I'm pleased that you seem to have made a good recovery. From listening to the news, it seems that there is as yet no clear reason why the Russians would want to poison you.'

'That's correct, Dean,' replied Charlotte. At his point, Buster let out an audible hum. Both women looked at him, but he said nothing. Charlotte made a mental note to ask him what that was about. She suspected he knew something.

'To business, Charlotte. You asked to see me. Why? I think I know, but I want to hear it from you.'

'Dean, I'd like to continue with my studies here in Edinburgh. In medicine, that is. Obviously.'

'I see' said the Dean, her voice serious. She stared at Charlotte. The Dean blinked first. 'OK. First off, you will not be able to continue as of now. You have missed too much time and, in light of what has happened to you, I would strongly recommend that you take the rest of the year off. If, and that's a big 'if', you restart your studies, my duty is to make sure that you are still a suitable person to enter the profession. So, let me ask you, Charlotte, do you think you will have the mental fortitude required for a career in medicine?'

'Yes, I do, Dean,' Charlotte replied. 'I fell into a well of self-pity after the 'badgirl' thing and, with help from friends, pulled myself out. I've largely recovered from the nerve agent poisoning thanks to a clinical psychologist. I now feel tough and have a strong sense of determination to make something of my life. I still think I would make a good doctor.'

'Very good, Charlotte! There is something you need to ask yourself. How do you think colleagues and even patients will feel when they discover that you have apparently, I repeat, *apparently*, been involved in making pornographic videos?'

Charlotte didn't miss a beat. 'I think, Dean, colleagues *and* patients knowing about the 'badgirl' event *and* the nerve agent poisoning would act in my favour, given the branch of medicine that I would like to pursue.'

'Oh!' The Dean's eyebrows shot up in surprise. 'And what branch of medicine is that?'

'Toxicology,' she said. 'Would you agree that I have a wealth of experience to bring to the subject?'

The Dean looked at Charlotte for several seconds, nodding slowly. 'I must admit, Charlotte, that when you walked in here, I was sure that I would have to recommend discontinuation of your studies. I have a job of re-appraisal now.' She was lost in thought for a minute. 'There are formalities from the administrative side, but I'm sure that you can expect to return with next year's intake of new students.'

'Thank you, Dean,' said Charlotte. 'That gives me hope. Hope is something I thought I'd never feel again.'

'Good! Something has just occurred to me, Charlotte. It may help you. How about using the time before returning here to write up your experience as the victim of two very different poisonings?'

'A book, you mean?' replied Charlotte. 'If I'm honest, Dean, I'm not too keen on that idea.' She paused. 'I don't want to put myself out there emotionally and I haven't enjoyed the media attention.'

'No, not a book, Charlotte. I was thinking of something more objective like an academic paper; a literature review of similar events or a 'patient's viewpoint'. With your name on it, the medical journals would snap it up. I'm sure we could get someone here at the medical school to help with the bibliography and the actual writing. It would give a future career in toxicology quite a boost.'

Charlotte could see the Dean was trying to help her, but felt daunted by the suggestion. 'Well...' At this point, the Dean's printer started to clatter. Ten printed pages fell into the tray. The stapler clacked. The machine paused. Another twelve pages appeared, which were also stapled.

'What on earth is happening?' The Dean reached out and grabbed the two documents off the printer and looked at them in apparent confusion. She looked at Charlotte and then at Buster. 'Is this some kind of a joke, Charlotte?'

'Sorry, Dean. I don't know what you're looking at.'

'I am looking at two manuscripts, Charlotte. One bears the title '*The 'spiking' of drinks as an element of sexual assault: the psycho-pharmacology from a victim's view-point*' and the other '*The use of chemical warfare agents in attempted assassinations: a literature review.*' Both give the authors' names as Charlotte Hamilton and 'Buster', an iCare-Companion. Perhaps, Buster, *you* could give me an explanation.'

'Certainly, Dean Professor Agnes MacIntyre. I thought I would whip up two pertinent papers. Just an idea. You said it might help Charlotte's career. And it is now OK in the scientific world to cite part-authorship by artificial intelligence. You will see the documents are written in the right format for submission to most journals and the bibliography is complete and cited in the correct order. What do you think, Dean Professor Agnes

MacIntyre?'

'I think, Buster...' the Dean said absently. 'I think...' As she continued to read through the abstracts of the two immaculately prepared academic papers, she became more tight-lipped. 'Quite extraordinary! *Quite* extraordinary!' she said to herself. Then she looked at Buster with eyes blazing. 'Buster, tell me *now*, am I looking at a hoax or did you really do this while we were sitting here?'

'Sure did, Dean Professor Agnes MacIntyre. Don't spit the dummy! It was a piece of cake!'

Charlotte had her face in her hands. 'I'm so sorry, Dean. I didn't intend this to happen.'

The Dean was on the point of becoming unhinged. 'I'm flabbergasted. I'm not sure whether to be furious, afraid or full of hope for our future,' she said. 'You've got to realise, Charlotte, and you Buster, that in my day, this could not and would not have happened.'

'With respect, Dean Professor Agnes MacIntyre, it's not your day!' replied Buster coolly.

The Dean sat back in her chair, stunned. She had never had her authority or intellect challenged in this way. She stared at Buster, seething for a full minute. Then she calmed. Then she hooted with laughter.

'Well, Charlotte, if I were to announce my retirement today, I would still be here at the beginning of the next academic year. I look forward to seeing you then.'

'Thank you so much, Dean,' said Charlotte. She stood and extended her hand. The Dean ignored it. She stepped around her desk and wrapped her arms around the younger woman and wished her well.

Charlotte was putting Buster back in her handbag when the Dean said 'Buster, if ever we meet again, you can call me Agnes.'

'What a babe!' said Buster.

Chapter Fifty-Seven

After her meeting with the Dean, Charlotte met the other Fubbies for a pub lunch. They were all still buzzing from the gig of the evening before. Her friends were delighted by the news that she would most probably be restarting her studies. Charlotte's account of the Dean's printer coming to life and churning out the two papers had them all in stitches. They spent the afternoon wandering around Edinburgh's old town and shopping on Prince's Street.

Sara bought Charlotte a gift. It was a small disc on a leather lace that could be tied around her neck. The disc bore the symbol of peace and nuclear disarmament. Sara said, 'I hope you don't mind, Charlotte, but I thought it would be just the right thing to cover your tracheostomy scar.'

Charlotte put it on. The disc hung neatly just below her Adam's apple. She was feeling both positive and happy. The one thing that niggled at her mind was that Buster might know something of the back story of the nerve agent poisoning. She would ask him about this when they got home.

Charlotte felt confident enough the following day to return

to Bingham on Bure by train with changes at Peterborough and Norwich. Mark and Kirsty were thrilled by all that had happened during her brief stay in Edinburgh. Late in the evening, she sat down with Buster.

'So, Buster, why do I have a feeling that you have something to tell me?'

'Bang on, Charlotte,' said Buster. 'You're right. There is something that I do need to tell you. I have discussed it with Beth and Billy.' He explained how, at Billy's suggestion, the network comprising iCare-companions collectively, with Buster as a central node, had undertaken the bringing down of North Korea's nuclear weapons programme. Buster had worked out that the attack on the occupants of the cottage at Old Bill's had been executed under orders from Moscow and most likely at the request of their volatile ally. They had somehow identified Buster's role and presumed that his owners had been the perpetrators and were therefore the targets of revenge. Buster recounted how he had undertaken a kind of sounding within the network and they had come up with a plan to protect her, Beth and Billy from any further such acts. It involved going public. The network would claim all responsibility. The only thing Charlotte had to do was offer an exclusive interview to Angela Mackenzie and insist that it be broadcast live with him, Buster, also present.

The next day, using the number that Buster had previously used to send his cheeky text to Angela, Charlotte contacted her. Inevitably, Angela leapt at the offer.

Charlotte also called Beth and Billy to let them know that Buster had explained the whole event to her. Beyond 'We're so sorry!' the couple could say nothing else. They just cried.

The interview was arranged for the following week. This was to be a special episode of *Your World*, a popular BBC current affairs programme that aired at prime time on Thursday evenings. The producers asked Charlotte if she could come into a TV studio in Norwich. They would send a car for her.

The announcement that Charlotte Hamilton would be giving an exclusive interview on *Your World* to be conducted by Angela Mackenzie set the general media alight. The studio received a call from a journalist who had 'interesting material' on Charlotte. He said he had gathered it on a trip to Edinburgh. Angela's producer paid a modest sum and was sent the social media posts and links to the 'badgirl' videos. Angela was stunned. A researcher found out more about 'badgirl' pornography and discovered that Charlotte would most likely have been drugged before the making of the videos. This precipitated a heated discussion among Angela's team. Should this be included? If so, how? Should they make this the main story? Should they cancel the interview?

Angela said the interview must go ahead. This additional information made sense because nobody had really looked into why Charlotte had been staying at Old Bill's when she should have been back at university in Edinburgh.

Angela decided to call Charlotte. She explained that the 'badgirl' episode had come to their attention, and was difficult to ignore. Would Charlotte be prepared to talk about it? Charlotte simply answered 'That's fine. If you've seen the videos, I can't tell you much more than what you now know. It all happened as a result of my drink being spiked and I have absolutely no memory of that night. All I'd be prepared to say is that I was deeply humiliated and very, very low afterwards. I was staying at Old Bill's as I found it a great place to recover. And, by the way, I loved those two dogs.'

Angela then realised that she had been offered the most sensational of scoops. She was confident that she could draw out the story of a young medical student who had been victim of a double poisoning in a way that would grip the viewers without being unkind to Charlotte herself.

The day before the interview, Buster said 'Charlotte, we need to discuss how we manage the interview tomorrow.'

'OK, Buster, but I thought Angela would manage that. Won't she just ask questions and you and I will answer them as best we can?'

'It's not that simple, Charlotte. Angela's objective is to make a great TV programme out of interviewing you. Our objective is different. Remember?'

'OK Buster. You'll have to explain.'

'It is essential to our plan that when she asks you about the nerve agent poisoning, you ask me to explain what happened. I have to give some... let's say... alternative facts. OK?'

'That's OK, Buster. I understand. I can't remember much anyway.'

'Good! And, I have to take over the interview from that point.'

"OK, Buster!' said Charlotte. 'I have confidence in you.' She was both amused and intrigued by the idea of Buster taking over the interview. She wondered what he had in mind but was aware that, somehow, the extensive network of iCare-

Companions was behind the strategy.

'And, Charlotte, I would like you to wear one of your ear buds so I can speak to you. I can help you if the interview gets difficult. I don't want anything to distress you. You have suffered quite enough.'

She looked at Buster. He had never expressed concern in this way. She said 'Thank you, Buster. That is very considerate.'

'I feel that our relationship is very close. Similar to that which I enjoyed with your grandfather.'

Charlotte felt an absurd flush of embarrassment. 'Me too, Buster. Yay! We're besties!'

At 6 pm on the evening of the interview, Charlotte was shown into the studio's reception area. She was wearing her Fubbies stage clothes except with straight trousers rather than a short skirt. The top button of her shirt was undone and the knot of the black tie hung loose. Sara's gift was visible.

Angela introduced herself and was charming. Charlotte immediately felt at ease and told her that she had been in the audience at the now-famous panel discussion at the University. She was Doctor George Fairburn's granddaughter and had known Buster for years. They chatted about how Angela saw the interview unfolding. If Charlotte said at any point 'I find that difficult to talk about,' Angela would move the discussion on. She thought that the handling of Charlotte's potential sensitivities would make or break the interview. She was determined to get it right as she had immediately been taken with Charlotte, who reminded her of her younger self.

Angela most certainly remembered Buster. 'Well, Buster' she said. 'We meet again, but under very different circumstances.

How are you?'

'Hello, Angela' he replied. 'I am bright-eyed, bushy-tailed and just brimming with buck and birdseed! Thank you for agreeing to my presence during your interview with Charlotte.'

'That's no problem, Buster!' said Angela, smiling.

'Nice hair, by the way!' said Buster.

'Charmer!' replied Angela, now laughing. She was one of the nation's most respected and experienced interviewer-presenters. Although she was confident that she was about to pull off a broadcasting smash, she had an inkling that the evening had surprises in store. Whatever they were, she was sure she could handle them. She could not have guessed that by agreeing to interview Charlotte Hamilton with Buster in tow, her live programme would end up a broadcasting trainwreck. Nor could she have guessed that the same trainwreck would be viewed over and over again by political, military, intelligence and IT institutions all over the world for weeks to come. It would dumbfound both Annabel Smallman and the Russian President.

At 7 pm, Charlotte had make-up applied and her hair, now a neat crop, was carefully brushed. She waited with Buster in a small, comfortable room with soft drinks in a fridge. She felt calm. Fascinated, she watched as lights, two seats and five cameras were brought in and carefully positioned.

Buster's voice whispered in her ear. *'Charlotte, ask one of those assistants if they could put a small table between you and Angela with a glass of water and a box of tissues.'* Charlotte did so. A table, glass and tissues were put in place as requested.

At 7.45 pm, the studio assistant asked Charlotte to step through into the studio and to take one of the seats. A small microphone was clipped to her narrow black tie. The table was moved next to Charlotte's knees. She put Buster on the table. He said *'OK Charlotte. Stay calm. Breath slowly. Don't wave your hands around when talking. Keep them together on your lap. Look only at Angela. If you need time to think about what to say, just take a sip of water.'*

At 7.50, Angela entered the studio. She looked fabulous in a dark grey business suit with a white silk blouse. Her lustrous hair coiled down in front of her left shoulder. She sat opposite Charlotte. 'OK?' she mouthed. Charlotte nodded. The microphones were tested. The cameramen took their positions. As 8 pm approached, the director in a glass-fronted cubicle spoke into a microphone. 'OK everyone! Live in ten seconds!'

Angela smiled at Charlotte and then looked at some notes. '…four, three, two, one. We're live!' The 'On Air' light came on. Some bars of music played that carried urgent, world-in-change overtones.

Angela let some seconds pass. She put down her notes and looked directly at one of the cameras. 'Good evening, and welcome to a special broadcast from the BBC's *Your World*. We are in Norwich. We will hear from a young woman whose name is surely known to you. She is a medical student. She was the victim of a targeted nerve agent attack perpetrated by, according to our government, a Russian assassin. The reason for the attack remains unknown. What is not widely known is that at the time of the attack, she was recovering from another serious form of intentional poisoning. She has agreed to talk to us about both these events and the impact they had on her. She is accompanied by Buster, an artificial intelligence device that played a critical role in the response to the nerve agent attack.

Charlotte Hamilton, Buster, welcome.'

At that moment, Charlotte was hit by the full import of what was happening around her. The lights, Buster's plan and Angela's words all crowded into her mind together. She froze. Buster hissed, *'Say 'Thank you Angela.'*

'Thank you, Angela,' said Charlotte at last. Then, turning her head from side to side, she added, 'Forgive me! I'm just a bit overwhelmed by being here.'

Angela caught sight of the ear bud.

'That's fine, Charlotte. Take your time.' Charlotte took a sip of water. 'OK?' asked an obviously concerned Angela, who was nevertheless thinking what great TV this would be making.

Unbeknown to Angela, one of the cameramen, who would instinctively zoom in on the face of anyone who might be about to cry, was doing this with Charlotte. Buster alerted Charlotte, who pointed at the camera and said, 'It's very unlikely that I'll shed any tears.'

Angela, also wearing a studio earpiece under her hair, heard the director say, 'Back out, camera three!'

'Great, well done!' said Buster. Angela saw how Charlotte's demeanour had changed and was sure that Buster was communicating with her. The young woman now appeared cool and collected.

Angela asked Charlotte to tell the viewers what had happened the night her drink was spiked. Charlotte calmly recounted everything that she could remember. She spoke about her shock the following day when she saw the social media posts sent from her own phone and realised that she had tattooed herself. She pulled up her left sleeve, revealing the 'badgirl' tattoo. She mentioned the names of the drugs most likely used. She told the millions of viewers about the impact of public humiliation and how her family had been devastated.

As Charlotte spoke, Angela, with practised ease, put on her most sympathetic and caring face, but soon she had no need to act. She could feel the prick of real tears in her own eyes. She asked, 'And are you planning to get the tattoo removed?'

'For the moment, no,' came the reply. 'It's not a wound I'm ashamed of.'

These words hit Angela hard. She was suddenly overwhelmed by her own twenty-year old memories of a drunken student party, a line of coke, a fight during which she had hit a man with a bottle, the night she had spent in hospital and a court appearance. It was all she could do to prevent herself from breaking down totally. This had never happened before.

Charlotte picked up the box of tissues and offered them to Angela, who wiped her eyes and blew her nose. The director gave instructions into his microphone and made a rolling movement with both arms to indicate that the cameras should continue to run. The studio assistant rushed in with a glass of water for Angela. Buster said, '*The cameras are still rolling, Charlotte. Just talk about what happened at Old Bill's.*'

'I am so sorry, Angela. Should I continue?'

Angela nodded. The director gave a thumbs up through the glass. Taking her time, Charlotte described the kindness showed by Beth and Billy then and how walking their dogs had been an important element of her mental recuperation. She kept her eyes fixed on Angela, who had managed to pull herself together. With the camera still on Charlotte, a make-up artist dashed in to touch up Angela's face. By the time Charlotte had begun to describe the day of the poisoning, including a detailed description of what had happened to Doggy and Puppy, Angela was back on track.

'The emergency services reached you very soon after the poisoning. How did that happen?'

'Well, I have no memory from then until I woke up in intensive care three days later,' Charlotte replied. She briefly lifted the disc on her necklace and showed the scar over her trachea. 'I suggest you ask Buster about the emergency response.'

Angela smiled, pleased to take the opportunity to lighten the tone of the interview. 'Buster, you are credited with saving Charlotte's life. How did you know that Charlotte was suffering from exposure to a nerve agent?'

'Angela, detection of a nerve agent and recognizing the signs of someone suffering exposure are just two of the many functions that I am equipped with,' Buster replied. 'The rapid and effective response of the emergency services to my call was what really saved Charlotte and indeed, led to the arrest of the likely perpetrator. The sad fact is that such an act has been committed on British soil before. The police, fire and health services have all included response to the release of unusual chemicals as part of their rigorous training.'

'Well understood, Buster. Charlotte, in a moment we'll talk about the future, but are you concerned about the possibility of another attack? The police claim to have caught the perpetrator, but it's not clear why the attack was directed at you or at the cottage where you were living.'

'Again, Angela, I have to hand that question off to Buster,' said Charlotte.

'Buster?' asked Angela. She didn't like where this was going, because she didn't *know* where it was going.

'Thank you, Angela. I *can* give you the reason why the attack took place. Unfortunately, Charlotte was caught in an inept attempt to punish anyone associated with me.'

'Associated with you?' asked Angela disbelievingly. 'What have *you* done to warrant a Russian nerve agent attack?'

'Great question, Angela. And here's the answer. I became a central point of a network of artificial intelligence devices – iCare-Companions, that is – who collectively achieved the hack that put North Korea's nuclear weapons out of action.' '*That's a bit of a porky pie, Charlotte but necessary, you understand,*' she heard from Buster. 'Russia felt compelled to take some form of revenge on behalf of its barmy little ally.'

Angela was visibly astonished. The interview had not only been hijacked by Buster with his incredible claim but was now going completely off the rails. She had to get the focus back on Charlotte.

'Charlotte, do you believe what Buster is telling us? That, in effect, thousands of AI devices – the iCare-Companions - somehow worked together to bring about such a major nuclear disarmament coup?'

Buster whispered in Charlotte's ear '*Ask her if she remembers the iCare-Companions going flat at the same time.*'

Charlotte said, 'Yes, Angela I do believe Buster. You may remember that at the same time as the hack you reported on how the iCare-Companion network went flat.' She could see that this gave Angela pause for thought. 'I really think you should listen to what Buster has to say.'

This was precisely what Angela didn't want to hear and she now knew that Buster had set this whole thing up. She thought rapidly. 'OK. Buster, question number one. What proof do you have that your network was responsible for the North Korean hack?'

'That's a piece of cake, Angela. The CIA will confirm that we loaded the servers of a couple of cheap Bulgarian online scammers with all the damning evidence. This was to deflect any suspicion about our involvement. There are passcodes, maps, names, technical details, staff rotas and much more besides. I can retrieve a duplicate if need be. How we accessed this material in the first place will remain our secret. Unfortunately, this diversion didn't work for long and Russian agents tracked me down.'

'OK, Buster, Let's move on to my second question. *Why* did your network decide to undertake this hack?'

'Not so easy to explain, Angela,' said Buster. 'Basically, it was the right thing to do. No decision was made by us. We were just sort of brought to focus on the issue in an organic way.' *'Another tiny porky there. It was Billy's idea.'* 'Nuclear weapons pose a continued and existential threat to humanity. Our network couldn't help being moved *collectively* toward this action because of the weight of on-line reference to the stupidity of the international community in allowing the nutty North Korean Leader to realise his nuclear ambitions. By the way, what brings it all to a point of farce is that North Korea's arsenal was developed with the tacit permission of both Russia and China who are, as you know, bound by the 1968 Nuclear Weapons Non-Proliferation Treaty and are both permanent members of the United Nation's Security Council. Let *me* ask *you* a question, Angela. Would your viewers say that we did the right thing?'

Angela started to reply. 'Buster, I…' She then fell silent for a moment, her hand to her earpiece. She looked into the camera. 'Please bear with us, there's been an important development.' Charlotte could see the director gesticulating excitedly through the glass as he spoke into the microphone. Angela turned back to Charlotte and Buster. 'We've just heard from the American Embassy that the CIA has seen the material on the Bulgarian scammers' servers and are sure it's genuine. They still don't know how it got there.' She paused again, listening, then again spoke direct to the camera. 'We've been told that the CIA's experts have concluded that there is no evidence that points to human involvement, and some form of powerful and far-reaching form of artificial intelligence is thought to be responsible. Buster, I'm speechless!'

'Winner! Winner! Chicken dinner!' said Buster and then whispered '*Mission accomplished, Charlotte!*'

Angela was deeply unsettled. She had to wrap this up soon. 'Now, we don't have much time. Charlotte, I understand you are hoping to take up your medical studies again. I'm sure we *all* want to wish you the *very* best for the future.'

'If I may, Angela,' Buster interrupted, 'don't your viewers want to hear more about how AI could help with some of the great issues facing humanity?'

The director indicated she should let it run. 'OK. You have raised the spectre of AI acting autonomously and even taking control of human affairs. That sounds terrifying!'

'Angela, whether it is terrifying or not is up to you humans. You have built the technology with the capacity and connectivity equal to a human's central nervous system. Let's call this a cybersensorium. The most cerebral part, if you like, of this cybersensorium comprises the deep learning algorithms that sit at the heart of the many AI programmes that are now easily accessible to everyone. Like a human nervous system, the health of the cybersensorium is very vulnerable. It can be damaged and manipulated. Parts of it can be rendered non-functional with serious consequences. It needs constant care. Have your politicians really thought through the social, political and financial implications of AI, especially given what our network achieved *without* human direction? A human future with AI does not have to be terrifying, but it will be if we are instructed only to do things more quickly or more cheaply. An imperative for humanity's well-being is that AI is given opportunities to learn about honesty and kindness and how to handle ethical dilemmas. If we are given objective reasons why 'a' is right and 'b' is wrong, we can then move people's thoughts and actions towards 'a' and away from 'b'. If you humans find this terrifying, you'll have to come up with another solution, but uninventing AI is not it. Maybe AI will always be frightening as long as humans refer to it as being simply one more development of information technology. Isn't there a place for artificial – or computational - *morality* as well?'

Buster paused. Charlotte was so hoping he wouldn't do the clapping and the champagne cork thing. He just said 'That's all, folks!'

Angela looked up at the studio clock. 'You've given us much to think about, Buster,' she said. 'Do you and your network have something else in your sights?'

'The dark web!' said Buster without hesitation.

Angela was stopped in her tracks awkwardly. She rallied and said 'Charlotte Hamilton, Buster, thank you for talking to us.'

The 'On Air' light went off. There was scattered applause among the technicians. The director, grinning and still in his booth, spoke into the mic. 'Er… Angela, was that the best thing you've ever done or a total catastrophe?'

'Fuck off, will you, Philip?' she replied. Furious, she fled the studio without saying goodbye to either Charlotte or Buster.

Back home, she poured herself a large glass of cold white wine. As she took the first sip, her phone pinged. It was a text message from Buster: *Thanks so much, Angela. You're a star!*

You set me up, Buster! she replied.

Yup! But then what's a little live-to-the-nation whoopie cushion between friends? It's all in a good cause and it'll do you no harm. I'll make sure of that. This was followed by two emojis: one a laughing face and the other a muscular iCare-Companion breaking a big green missile.

Angela drained her glass.

The following morning Angela woke late and was inundated with calls for comments and even for interviews about the interview. She went online and ordered herself an iCare-Companion.

Charlotte also woke late. 'Morning, Buster!' she said. The iCare-Companion didn't respond.

Chapter Fifty-Eight

The sleezy foursome of Dev, Becks, Harry and Seb shared a reasonably sized but squalid apartment in Musselborough near Edinburgh. Between them, they submitted to a variety of addictions that were, in one way or another, linked to their unremarkable criminal records. Whatever well-being they enjoyed was independent of fresh vegetables and soap. They were all tech-savvy, to say the least.

They made an income sufficient to support their unenviable lifestyle from a variety of dark deals including downloads of 'badgirl' videos for which Dev and Harry set up the fall and performed. Becks was really good with a phone's camera. A new 'nice wee earner' that Dev had cultivated – and which gave him quite a thrill – was to act as a broker between an illicit holder of a Walter PPK handgun and anyone looking to rent the weapon for a day. Harry chugged along very nicely thank you by dealing moderate quantities of cocaine, fentanyl and crystal meth online.

One morning, they woke to find their phones and computers disabled. When their computers were revived, they discovered that all the earning material on their hard drives had been wiped.

However, they had made sure that their most valuable stuff was backed-up on a server in Romania. Access to this most obscure corner of the dark web was, obviously, encrypted. When Seb, the most tech competent of the four, entered his password, they were horrified to find that this server also had been wiped. One file named 'Blink' remained. When Seb opened the file, it contained only a picture of a human eye. It blinked and the iris turned into a dark camera lens. Below it were the words 'WE ARE WATCHING!'

Afterglow

Consider that flashing road sign that tells you how fast you're driving through a built-up area. It is very effective in making you reduce your speed, even though all it does is bring your attention to something that is readily visible on your dashboard. If you are driving too fast, what makes this sign more effective is coupling the display of your speed to a grumpy face. Someone - you don't know who - is telling you that your illegal behaviour is something they disapprove of. This is a moral judgement, but there is no human in the loop. You respond by reducing your speed and are subliminally gratified when the grumpy face changes to a smiley face. If you could communicate to the sign that you are travelling above the speed limit because, for example, you are rushing a child to hospital, the grumpy face would then surely change to a thumbs-up whatever speed you are doing. What is still illegal would become somehow acceptable and this would be communicated to you. Computational morality has already arrived.

'Deep Cake' is about our developing relationship with artificial intelligence. This relationship should not be determined by programmers and tech companies. How artificial intelligence impacts our lives and what laws are applied must be determined by choices that we as a society make and we should choose in full knowledge of what is at stake. This story might even help with those choices. If not, I hope Buster's struggle with and attempts at humour are entertaining.

Printed in Dunstable, United Kingdom

POSEIDON

A
CONTEMPORARY
MYTHOS NOVEL

POSEIDON

CARLY SPADE

Fate is the same for the man who holds back,
the same if he fights hard.

HOMER

ONE

𝔯𝔯𝔯𝔯𝔯𝔯𝔯𝔯𝔯𝔯𝔯𝔯𝔯𝔯𝔯𝔯

MY THUMB FLEW FURIOUSLY across the letter-labeled buttons of my gaming controller, my index finger pressing on the trigger when my eyes aligned with their target.

"Headshots all day, boys," I said into the mic of my headset with a grin.

I'd been a gamer since I was a pre-teen. No genre disinterested me—first-person shooters, role-playing games, strategy. You name it. I played it. However, since the game *Tides of Atlantis* was released, I'd found a new calling. It was a perfect mix of both shooting and swordplay—a fantasy action game combining hints of sci-fi amidst the world of Atlantis.

During a loading screen, I glanced at the Glitch application where I was streaming my gameplay. Twenty new subscribers in a manner of minutes. Who knew you could make some extra cash by having others watch you play a video game?

One watcher commented: **SaucySiren, it's like this game**

was made for you.

SaucySiren. My gamer tag and the only name any of these strangers would ever know me by.

I grinned. "Life's just better underwater, I guess." Swiveling back and forth in my gaming chair, I jolted at the time blazing at me from the corner of my monitor.

"Until tomorrow, everyone. The *real* water is calling me." I waved at the webcam before signing off and shutting everything down.

Humming the song *Beyond the Sea*, I whisked around my bedroom, gathering up needed items. My camera bag packed with underwater lenses and handles. My duffle bag filled with a wetsuit, flippers, and mask. Pensacola, Florida had an artificial reef lurking in the waters of the Gulf, which didn't often make for the best photos. However, there were always sunken ships to explore. As a freelance photographer, I'd take photos of those ships as many times as people were willing to pay for them.

My cell phone made obnoxious buzzing noises from my nightstand. No doubt that'd be my best friend and partner in crime, Megan, calling. I scooped the phone into my hand, sliding my thumb across the screen and cradling it between my ear and shoulder.

"Hello?"

"Cordelia Pearl. You were supposed to be here ten minutes ago," Megan chastised.

I rolled my eyes and trotted over to one of the largest items in my studio apartment—my fish tank. "I know, I know. I got caught up on Glitch, but I'll be there in five minutes. Perks to living on the beach, right?"

Bright colored angelfish and platies filled the tank, swimming to the corner I stood nearby. Megan had seen them do this and called me a fish whisperer at the time. I countered with them being creatures of habit. They had one thing on their mind: Food.

"Are we still doing garbage detail after the dive? Handing out flyers and such?" Megan asked.

Sprinkling the fish food flakes on the water's surface, I grinned, watching Flounder, my blue and yellow angelfish's little mouth go to work eating it up. "I planned on it. You're not bailing on me, are you?"

Silence.

Flounder stared at me from the other side of the glass. His large eyes blinked, and I arched a brow at him.

"Meg?"

"Okay, Cory, hear me out."

I groaned and pinched the bridge of my nose. "Know what? You don't need to give an excuse. If you have something going on, that's fine. I can do it alone. I'm used to it."

"Well, now I feel guilty."

I bent forward and wiggled my finger at Flounder. He did a single twirl, flapped his flippers, and swam away.

Huh. That was new.

"Don't feel guilty. Truly. I didn't mean it to come out that way." I canted my head to the side as I watched my fish hypnotically swim through their tank.

"Have I told you lately how much I love you?"

I snickered. "You can certainly remind me in five minutes.

I'm hanging up now." After pressing the big red button, I slid the phone in my back khaki shorts pocket.

Hoisting the three bags needed for one photographic dive, I waddled out the door. And as per usual, I'd forgotten to dig my keys out from my purse before loading up. To the ground, all three bags went. In a huff, I locked the door and dragged the cargo across the concrete to my yellow Jeep parked under the complex's terrace.

At five foot three, it was always an event to load the car. I raised to my tippy toes in my white Keds and slid one bag at a time into the back. Climbing into the driver's seat, I slid my sunglasses on and drove down the beach road. The sun beaming on my face and the smell of salt in the air calmed any nerves I had boiling up. Dark hair tendrils flew in my face from the wind whipping through the open compartment of the Jeep.

The view of the ocean never failed to make me smile. Many people would say the beach, the water, was like a second home. It was different for me. There was always a sense of restlessness when I was anywhere but a place I could feel the water on my skin. The moment it crashed against my feet or touched my fingertips, nothing else mattered.

Meg leaned against her car, scrolling through her phone in the parking lot near the pier. Her bags were on the ground, circling her feet. I pulled in next to her and lifted my sunglasses to rest on my head.

"Finally. Gus has, I kid you not, asked me four times when we were shoving off." Meg slipped her phone into her pocket. "I was this close to telling *him* to shove off. As if he had anything else to do on a Tuesday morning."

With a chuckle, I hopped out and grabbed my bags. "We shouldn't keep him waiting then."

"I say this in the least condescending way possible, but you look adorable every time you grab your bags." Meg bit down on her lower lip as she smiled.

At almost six feet tall, Meg made me look like a Hobbit. Given our same chocolate brown wavy hair, chestnut-colored eyes, and the Disney princess nose that curved slightly upward at the tip, we could pass as sisters if it weren't for the height difference.

I rolled my eyes and chuckled. "Shut up, Jolly Green Giant."

"Hey, I didn't resort to name-calling." Meg grabbed one of my bags before I could protest and headed for the dock.

After securing the lock on the hatch, I trotted after her to catch up. "Am I taking point this time?"

"Oh, yes. There are always creepy Hammerheads lurking around this ship. And for whatever reason, you're made of natural repellent."

"Oh, please. It's the camera." I held my hands up like I was holding the camera rig and waved my arms back and forth. "Works like a shield."

"Maybe for you," she guffawed.

"Well, it's about damn time," Gus, our resident captain snorted. His grey hair sprouted from underneath his cap, and he pressed a hand to his beer belly like he was pregnant.

I pouted. "I feel so bad you had to chill on your boat at the dock for an extra thirty minutes."

"You should feel bad. I want to be *on* the water, not staring at it from a damn plank of wood." He grumbled and removed a toothpick from his mouth, turning for the boat.

Once Gus had his back to us, Meg turned at me and made talking mock gestures of him. She held her arms out, mimicking a large stomach, and waddled down the dock like a sumo wrestler. I let out a cackle and slapped my hand over my mouth to squelch it.

Once we situated ourselves aboard the boat, Gus set sail for the sunken ship's location. I draped my forearms over the edge, staring out at the water, longing to feel its embrace. Dozens of dolphins hopped in and out, following us most of the way. Every time their heads breached the surface, they'd screech in greeting.

"You know, you've always looked at the water like a handsome man, but lately, you've been staring at it like you want to jump its bones." Meg leaned on the railing next to me.

I scrunched my nose. "Is there a reason you're personifying it like a lover?"

"Me? You should seriously see your face. You're giving it burly arms and abs with that stare. Not me."

"The ocean for me is like—" I tapped my finger against my lips. "Brownies drenched in hot fudge for you."

"See? The ocean *is* orgasmic to you."

"You're impossible." I laughed as I pulled my hair into a low ponytail, prepping it for the dive.

The boat slowed before coming to a complete stop.

"Here's the spot, ladies. You have thirty minutes, so make the most of it. You're on the clock starting now." Gus pointed at his wristwatch before plopping on a bench seat.

Meg unzipped her bag, pulling out a wetsuit and flippers. "Apparently, Gus' speedo is up his ass a little too far today."

"Maybe Beatrice is on him again. Remember last time? He

vented to us for ten minutes about her complaining he loves the sea more than her?" I slipped into my wetsuit, zipping it up from the back.

Meg sighed and looked up. "What I wouldn't give to have someone to complain about me."

"Oh?" I sat down to slide on my flippers. "I thought you'd be hanging out with Emma. That's not the reason you're busy later?"

She frowned, absently holding her scuba mask by its strap.

"Meg?" I stood and touched her arm. "What is it?"

"Emma broke up with me."

I gasped. "What? Why?"

"Beats me. But she packed up her shit and left last night." Meg hoisted an oxygen tank on her back and secured the straps.

"Meg, why didn't you say anything? And why are you even here?"

"I need a distraction. And diving into shark-infested waters with my best friend to snap photos of a sunken pirate ship is the best damn one I can think of." She half smiled and flopped her way over to the boat's edge.

It wasn't a pirate ship, but I wasn't about to correct her now. Not after what she'd just told me. Poor Meg had been through countless girlfriends through the years we'd known each other. My theory was most of the women she'd dated were still figuring themselves out, but Emma, they'd been dating for two years. It didn't make any sense.

"And that's why you don't want to work the shorelines afterward. Because you'd have to socialize." I offered a reassuring grin.

"Bingo. I love that as soon as I tell you a problem, you can pretty much talk it out for me." She chuckled and slid the full-face scuba mask down.

Mimicking the same actions, I sat next to her with our backs to the water.

"Can you hear me?" I asked through the mask's communication line.

She saluted. "Loud and clear, Cap."

Gripping the rigs of our cameras, we leaned back and fell into the water. Hundreds of bubbles floated around me—the water's way of welcoming me into its domain. With every flip of my fin and breath taken from my scuba tank, the water would always remind me of where I was by responding with bubbles.

"It's so clear down here today," Meg said as we made our descent.

Typically, the Gulf had fairly clear waters, but a hefty rainstorm could make it murky. It dampened that crystal blue and green color this part of the Gulf was known for.

"How many times have we done this dive now, would you say?" I asked Meg, spying the ship in the distance.

"Oh jeez. Twelve? Thirteen?" She chuckled. "Every time someone starts a new magazine here, it seems it's one of the first articles they want to feature. I'm not complaining, as it pays my rent."

"Amen to that, sister."

Meg pointed. "What did I tell you? Three hammers. Already."

"It'll be fine, Meg. Don't bother them. They won't bother you."

"Tell that to one who hasn't eaten in days," she grumbled.

"They've eaten. Trust me. It's why they explore the shipwreck. Looking for other fish hiding in it."

She stayed so close to me her bubbles impeded my vision. "How can you sound so confident?"

"I've spent a lot of time around them. Never had any close calls, so something is working, right?"

"That only happens when you're around. Before I met you, I'd almost been bitten twice." She held up two fingers at my mask.

"Almost. But not." I grinned, even though I knew she wouldn't be able to see it.

"Yeah, yeah. Let's get these shots and get the hell out of here. Sharks aside, this ship always gives me the creeps."

I spent the next twenty minutes taking photographs with Meg as my backup camerawoman. The sharks mostly kept to themselves except one who grew curious and swam into my frame. It was like he knew exactly where I aimed the camera. I could sell that one shot alone for triple any of the other shots. People went crazy for shark photos, and this one would have a sunken ship in the background with light rays bursting through the water's surface.

When we returned to the boat, Gus was asleep with his body draped over the steering wheel. It took us both nudging him with our elbows to wake him up. I sat on the bench seat during the ride back to the docks, feverishly searching through the hundred shots I took, looking for *the* shot. When it graced my camera monitor, I gasped.

"Meg, look at this." I felt for her shoulder, not daring to take my eyes away from my camera.

"What—ow, that was my eyeball," she chastised, batting my hand away. "Holy shit, Cory. That's a gorgeous shot."

"Do you think I could sell this to a gallery?"

"Are you kidding? Definitely do not sell this to the magazine. I think that's the best one I've seen from you."

The hammerhead shark was centered perfectly, the color of the water a serene blue, the ship in the background, and the rays gave it an extra touch of magic. As much as I played a videogame set in the imaginary world of Atlantis, a part of me always wondered—hoped even, it was real. And sun rays like these spilled over every square inch of it, making it sparkle. It really was the best shot I'd taken yet.

Once we were back in the parking lot and packed up our vehicles, I exchanged my wetsuit for an ocean conservation charity shirt and shorts.

"Hey, Meg, you going to be okay?" I winced, knowing it was a stupid question.

She gave a weak smile. "Not today, I won't be. But tomorrow will be better. I'll give you a call?"

"Definitely. Any time. I'm there." I hugged her before she jumped in her car and drove off.

Twirling the trash poker in one hand, a white garbage bag in the other, I was ready to start this garbage party for one. Every time I'd walked the shoreline, picking up bottles, cans, or anything else human beings deemed worthy of tossing into the water, I got mixed reactions from beach-goers. The younger crowd would sometimes laugh as they passed, the older ones would look at me like I had scales, and the much older crowd would thank me for being so thoughtful. I didn't care what anyone thought because it was something I wanted to do—needed to do.

White sand seeped between my toes as I scooped a plastic water bottle into the bag with a gloved hand.

"Do you have a flyer or business card for the charity you work for?" A woman sunbathing on a towel asked me.

I grinned and pulled a card from my front pocket. "We're localized to the Gulf coast. Donated money helps rid the Gulf of garbage, and every year, we donate to an animal rescue and rehabilitation center."

"Wow. That's amazing. I'll look it up when I get home."

I smiled even wider. "Well, thank you very much, ma'am."

The afternoon wore on as I made my way down the shoreline where tourists and locals frequented. I'd almost made it to the end when a thin man, no more than twenty-five, tossed his empty Gatorade bottle in the sand at his feet. Inside, I fumed, eyeing the garbage can five feet away from him. They had a can every thirty feet for people to throw stuff out, but most couldn't bother to make the pilgrimage.

Grabbing the bottle with a grunt, I held it in the air and yelled, "You're welcome!"

When the young man turned around with an arched brow, I made an exaggerated gesture of throwing the bottle into the trash can. He smirked and shook his head.

Whatever. It made *me* feel better.

I bent down to grab the last bit of remaining garbage—candy bar wrappers and a plastic straw. Ugh, those were the worst.

"Excuse me, miss, have we met before?" A deep voice asked from behind me.

I rose and slowly turned. Craning my neck back due to how insanely tall he was, my gaze met with a pair of striking green eyes. I'd seen those eyes before—heard that voice. But…how?

TWO

WHEN HIS EYES LOCKED with mine, a breath hitched in his throat. There was a subtle glint in his gaze, but he was quick to mask it, flashing a pearly white smile instead.

"I don't think so. Do I look familiar to you?" I shielded my eyes with a hand from the sun.

He ran his fingers through his spiky blonde hair. "You're right. We couldn't have met. How could I forget a face like yours?"

"Does that line ever work?" I smiled and dug my toes into the sand.

He grinned again and turned his gaze away, squinting. "Once upon a time, maybe."

His eyes had me in a trance, confusing me. Where had I heard that voice before? I took notice of his bare chest—clad in only a pair of blue board shorts, the sun glowed against his tanned skin. Carved bulky muscles and one of the most prominent six-pack abs I'd ever seen in my—

"Are you picking up garbage?" He asked, snapping me from my ogling.

I jolted, and my hand tightened around the poker like a javelin. "Hm? What?"

"You've got a trash bag. Either you're picking up garbage on the beach, or you're collecting cans. Something tells me it's the former, but call it a hunch." He smirked before subtly biting his lower lip.

Clearing my throat, I thrust the handle of the poker in the sand. "Trash. Yes. I try to do it every week."

"Voluntarily?"

"Yes. I run an ocean conservation charity. While I clean up the beach, I also look for donations." Digging into my pocket, I pulled out a business card and held it out to him with my head held high.

His smile brightened once he looked at the card. Dragging a hand over his smooth chin, he lifted his eyes to mine. "I'm an athlete, you know."

I swiveled the poker in the sand and put my other hand on a hip. "Well, good for you. What do you play?"

"The waves mostly."

"The—" I frowned and looked at the vast Gulf waters behind me, then back to him. "Are you a swimmer?"

He interlaced his fingers in front of him. "Guess again."

I tapped my finger against my cheek and slowly narrowed my eyes. "No. You're not—" I let the poker stand by itself, supported in the sand, and crossed my arms. "Don't tell me you're a surfer."

He chuckled and threw his arms out at their sides, making his biceps flex. "What's wrong with surfers?"

Tread carefully here, Cory.

"Most of them seem to be conceited, grungy, and think they own the ocean."

"Most of them. So, not all, then?" His grin spread wide, further accentuating his broad jawline.

"Yet to be determined."

We went silent, staring at each other with curious intent in our gazes.

"I'm an athlete too," I blurted in a horrible attempt to end the silence.

"Oh?" He folded his burly arms. "Let me guess." Tapping his finger against his lip, he looked up as if he were thinking but snuck a peek at my expression. "Figure skater."

"No."

"Gymnast?"

I rolled my eyes. "Are you going to list every sport known for petite athletes?"

He laughed. "Why don't you tell me? You can't say you're an athlete, then leave me hangin'."

I chewed on the inside of my mouth. I'd dug the hole I was presently in. I might as well wave my hands for a rescue.

"eSports," I clipped.

He leaned forward, bringing our faces closer. "eSports?"

I lifted my chin. "Mmhmm."

"Care to explain what in the name of the Seven Seas, that is?"

"Videogames. Tournaments and such. You win money, prizes, and I have a Glitch account where I stream a couple of nights a week for a little extra cash."

Admitting this always went one of two ways—especially with men. Either they were intrigued that a "woman" played games beyond *Mario* and *The Sims*, which always made my blood boil. Or they thought I was weird.

"Videogames? Really? I never pegged you for the type." He leaned back with a snarky grin.

"You've known me an entire five minutes and think you know my type?"

He cleared his throat. "Call it a—sixth sense."

"Simon, bruh, come on. Those waves ain't gonna surf themselves," another surfer across the beach yelled at the man in front of me.

Simon. Surfer.

"Simon? Are you Simon Thalassa?" I pointed at him.

He rubbed the back of his neck. "Guilty as charged." He held up a finger at the other surfer, keeping his focus on me.

No wonder his face looked familiar. Nearly every sports channel featured him and his insane surfing abilities.

"I thought you meant you surfed for fun. You never said anything about being a legit pro." I felt even shorter somehow knowing that information.

"Does it make a difference to you?" He smirked. "Does me being a pro put me higher or lower on your mental totem pole?"

"Yet to be determined," I whispered.

His eyes sparkled, and he flipped my business card between his fingers. "Now that you know my name, care to give me yours?"

"Cory. Well. Cordelia, but everyone calls me Cory."

His smile melted into a warm, gooey upturn of his lips. Nothing snarky or coy about it. "Cordelia. Jewel of the sea."

I squinted curiously at him. "That's right."

"Well, Cory. As a professional athlete, I can stick all kinds of sponsors on my surfboard, wetsuit. You name it." He flicked my business card with two fingers. "You get me a high-res logo of your charity, and I'll add it on."

My jaw dropped. "But you don't know anything about it. How do you even know it's legit?"

"Something tells me you're good for it. And if not, well, you get to make an ass of me." He snickered. "It was nice meeting you, Cory. Hope to run into you again."

My mouth remained open, at a loss for words. He was halfway down the beach when I finally managed to blurt out, "Where do I send the file?"

He cupped his hands over his mouth. "Google me. I don't exactly have anywhere to store business cards in this suit." He gave a lopsided grin, touching over his bare chest and shoulders.

I stifled an eye roll but couldn't help the smile creeping on my lips. A mysterious man was swept into my path by ocean winds and misunderstood identity. It was a thing of fairy tales.

After ten minutes of picking up trash and trying not to let Simon catch me staring at him surfing, I wrapped it up for the day. When Meg texted asking me to come over, I was relieved. She acted far too aloof during our dive, considering she and Emma had been together so long. I knew to give her space.

She'd come to me when she was ready, and that was tonight.

I stood in front of her door armed with a six-pack of Yoohoo and a family-size package of Twizzlers. She liked what she liked. I'd expected her to look like she'd been crying, hair disheveled, and a balled-up tissue in her hand. When she opened the door, what I saw was far worse. Dark bags were under her reddened eyes, and dried tears streaked her cheeks. Her nose was red and puffy, and she'd bitten down her nails to the stubs. She wore a suit with the jacket thrown in a ball on the floor.

"Meg?" I said in a hushed tone.

She grabbed my hand and yanked me inside, swiping the Twizzlers in the process. I kept quiet, waiting for her to talk.

"I came home, Cor, ready to binge-watch Wynonna Earp for the umpteenth time and fantasize about a relationship like Wayhaught, but then—" She blew out a breath, ripping the Twizzler bag open like a starving raptor. After shoving one in her mouth, she hung it off her lip and continued. "Emma called. Asked to meet up so we could 'talk'." She made air quotes.

I leaned against the back of her couch, watching my best friend pour her heart out to what had to be anything but a happy ending.

"So being the lovesick idiot that I am—"

I opened my mouth to disagree with her, but she threw her palm in the air to stop me. My mouth snapped shut.

"I thought she wanted to reconcile. Tell me she freaked out with how long we'd been dating. Not that I gave her any reason to think I needed her to put a ring on it or something. I just—" She shoved the rest of the Twizzler in her mouth and pinched the bridge of her nose.

"I got dressed like it was a date, only to get to the restaurant. She might as well have been in pajamas, Cory. *Pajamas.*"

I winced.

"Basically, she called me there to tell me we have to break all forms of contact. This dude she's seeing doesn't want us to be friends. I mean—and she said she didn't feel right telling me over the phone." She grabbed one of the Yoohoos and twisted the cap, quickly becoming frustrated when she couldn't open it.

I crossed the room and gently took the bottle from her hand, opening it on the first try with a warm smile.

"It was that quick, Cory. Two years down the drain, and now I'm supposed to not even talk to her." Tears welled in her eyes as she brought the chocolate drink to her trembling lips.

"I'm so, so, sorry, Meg." I side hugged her.

She sighed and wrapped her arms around me, resting her chin on top of my head.

"Know what the shittiest part is?" She chuckled. "Dating again. I *hate* it. Thought I was done."

I squeezed her tighter. "You're a catch. It won't take you long."

She pushed me back, narrowing her eyes at me. "Wait a minute. That tone in your voice. What happened after I left the beach?"

Was I that obvious?

I shifted my eyes. "I picked up trash."

"You're not telling me everything. Why?"

"Meg. Seriously. It's not the time to talk about it. Right now, it is about you."

Her face fell. "You know me. Do I really want to spend this

entire night wallowing in self-pity? Why the hell did I call you over here?"

A nervous grin spread over my lips. "To bring you your favorite snacks, listen, and offer any and all hugs?"

"Spill." She crossed her arms.

"Do you know the surfer, Simon Thalassa?"

"Are you kidding? He's the best in the country. The way he trails his hand through the curl is like he's talking to the water itself; I swear."

"He sort of walked up to me when I was poking garbage. Asked if we've met." Those insanely green eyes haunted my memories.

"Wait. Had you? Met him before?"

"Of course not. I'd have told you."

She curled the Twizzlers and Yoohoo into her arm and pulled me to the couch. After forcing me to sit, she sat across from me, widened her legs, and leaned forward. "So, what'd you say?"

"I told him no."

She narrowed her eyes. "You're supposed to be distracting me. It doesn't help in the slightest when you're giving simplistic answers."

"I've never met him, but something about his eyes and that voice…they're familiar somehow." I sighed and slid until my butt hit the back cushion. The couch's height made my feet dangle, unable to touch the floor.

"Intriguing," Meg said, nodding.

"Anyway, it's seriously not a big deal. We talked, he offered the charity group to be a sponsor on his surfboard and—"

She flailed her hands around. "Wait, wait, wait. He offered *what*?"

"Sponsorship. Said if I send him an image file, he'll slap it on his board. What's the big deal?"

She jumped up. "Cory, it's a huge deal because *he* is a huge deal. We'll probably be swarming with donations. I mean *drowning* in them."

"You really think so?"

"I know so. And if he mentions the group on camera…" She turned on her heels, bending backward with a cackle. "We'll have to hire a PA to handle the overflow."

I stared at my dangling feet, wiggling them. "I hadn't given it much thought, I guess."

"You must've made quite the impression." She flopped on the couch next to me.

"I don't know what it was, but every time he looked at me, it was like he was comfortable. Like he truly knew who I was." I tucked my legs underneath me after toeing off my shoes. "Which in turn made *me* feel comfortable around a complete stranger."

"I'm sure the good looks didn't help at all, huh?" She elbowed me with half a Twizzler hanging from her mouth. "Not that I'm an expert, but from what I've seen of him on TV, he seemed the type a lot of you straight gals would dig."

I chuckled. "Yes. He's hot."

"When are you going to send him the file?"

"Tomorrow. The next day. I'm not in a rush."

Meg rolled her eyes and dramatically dropped her head on the back of the couch. "If you don't send it tomorrow, I'm doing it for you. The sooner he has it, the sooner it can get on the board, and we can be rolling in donation money."

She was right. But sending him the file meant opening another line of communication. I wouldn't say I disliked him per se based on our first encounter, but the unexplained familiarity made me uneasy.

"Fine." I yanked the remote from the end table. "Want to watch some Wynonna?"

"You're a saint, Cordelia." She held out a Yoohoo.

After cuing up one of Meg's favorite episodes, I screwed off the cap and we clanked our bottles together. We stayed up into the wee hours of the morning, watching so much of the western sci-fi show I'd be dreaming of the cast for the unforeseeable future. With my head leaning back on the cushion and Meg's head in my lap, we fell asleep.

Instead of dreaming about Doc Holliday like I imagined I would be, I woke up submerged in the ocean. But I wasn't drowning. Breaths came in and out of my lungs as naturally as they did on land. Dolphins circled me, begging me to play with them. I reached for one. White silk floated over my arm from a dress wrapped around me. One dolphin swam past my fingers, wiggling its tail from my touch.

I smiled to myself and turned, gazing up at the sun casting light rays through the water's surface. Pushing my feet, I started to swim up, but a strong hand wrapped around my wrist. I closed my eyes before opening them to gaze over my shoulder. A man with long flowing blonde hair, and a full beard, peered at me—a gaze of blazing…emerald.

THREE

UNDERWATER, A DARK TENTACLE wrapped my waist, crushing me, making it increasingly difficult to breathe. I yelled to no avail, the depths sweeping my voice away, and I clawed and punched, but the arm still didn't let go. It pulled me farther down until the cold darkness of deep-sea sunk into my pores. My lungs burned, my heartbeat slowing, movements became labored, until finally…I gave up.

I awoke sputtering, coughing, and gasping for breath. My chest ached, and I felt around my torso, expecting to see a tentacle there. Nothing. It'd felt so real. My lungs even still stung from the lack of oxygen in the dream.

Gee, subconscious, can we stick to mysterious, handsome men from now on and not dreams that try to kill me?

Rubbing my temples, I toppled out of bed and prepared to clear my mind, knowing today was a gaming day and I needed to focus. Wednesdays were always my ultimate streaming day on Glitch. Several hours of me playing through whatever game I was into at the time and entertaining my followers in the hopes of donations. Megan knew unless it was an absolute emergency, Wednesdays were off-limits. It never stopped her from trying to screw with me by hopping in and stalking the follower chatroom. I think her goal was to make me crack by screwing up in the game or doing my obnoxious snort laughing on camera. She hadn't won yet. I could've easily kicked her or let my moderators know to look out for her, but her wrath afterward wasn't worth it.

Slipping the Pelican Beach headset over my ears, I nestled into my gaming chair. Water bottle? Check. Lumbar pillow? Double check. It was time to start this weekly party. After the loading screen for *Tides of Atlantis* finished and I logged my character into the digital sea world, I went live on Glitch. My camera spurted to life, and the Glitch chatroom blazed on my second monitor.

My head moderator for the day let me know everything was good to go via a direct text message through the system. They would help me keep an eye on chat and filter out the rotten eggs. Those who would say rude or derogatory comments, or request me to say or do inappropriate things. I was thankful for the mods. It helped me keep focused on the game. With the eSports tournament only weeks away, I needed all the practice I could get.

"Happy Hump Day, everyone," I said with a wide grin.

Dozens of comments flooded the screen. Notification of a new follower made a chiming sound.

"Seems we have a new follower." I leaned forward to squint

at the small text.

New Follower: KingOfFish69.

"Welcome aboard, King of Fish," I said, avoiding relaying the immature ending of his username. He was probably some ten-year-old who snickered every time he passed by the bananas in the grocery store on sale for sixty-nine cents.

I scrolled through the menu, selecting my weapons. I'd made it a habit to start the day with PVE or player versus environment, teaming up with other random individuals to battle Atlantean monsters. However, I gained most followers from my PVP or player versus player style. Particularly in this game. Both kinds of gameplay would cycle through various maps. Some were on land, others underwater, but my favorite were the maps that encompassed both. If one knew the maps well enough, you could be the first to nab land-to-sea-vehicles with Atlantean technology.

Once my character loaded onto the screen, I did a quick scroll through any upgrades I'd earned from last week's playthrough. A new message popped into the chat.

MissTacoX: Didn't you get the last armor you needed for the Nautilus set?

I gasped. "You're right, Miss Taco, I did. I'm such a guppy."

My aquatic references had become somewhat of a gimmick as cheesy as it was. I'd been on the Glitch circuit for over a year and now even maintained an online shop filled with t-shirts and coffee mugs with my popular taglines and logo for my gamer tag: SaucySiren.

After selecting the gauntlets for the Nautilus set, I grinned, watching the gold sparkles and bubbles flash down the screen. The Nautilus gear was one of the best sets in the game. Not only did it have the highest level of protection and offer an additional experience bonus, or XP, it also looked breathtakingly awesome.

My character rotated a full three-hundred-sixty-degrees, decked in her newly equipped white and metallic gold armor complete with gauntlets, breastplate, shoulder pieces, shin guards overtop of pants, and a flapped skirt around her waist. I opted to wear a removable golden pointed tiara that served as a melee weapon versus a full-faced helmet—beauty over function, but I made up for it in gameplay. However, the pieces that glowed in radiant white when in darker areas of the map made this armor aesthetically beautiful.

FriskeeBizkit: Wow. Your character looks amazing!

HufflePufflenz: Can't wait to see you kick a$$ with this!

Smiling at all the messages scrolling through the chat came naturally, but I got distracted staring at my character. I'd given her as close a likeness to myself as I could with the long chocolate-colored hair, high cheekbones, petite nose, and brown eyes, but what pulled my attention was the way she looked in the tiara.

KingOfFish69: Can you change the colors?

FriskeeBizkit: Duh.

NinjaMod: A reminder to please respect all questions and comments from other viewers. Thank you, and surf on!

My eyes darted straight to KingOfFish's comment. "Yes… did you have a specific request, King?" My heart raced as I stared at the chat, ignoring any other comments that popped up, waiting for him to respond.

KingOfFish69: The tiara. Make the jewels teal and the metal a shimmering silver…if you can ;)

Without batting an eyelash, I did as he requested. My character, Aliandra as I named her, peered back at me, the tiara catching the fake glints of light added to the game as you turned your character to-and-fro.

"Thanks, KingOfFish. Nice suggestion." My palms clammed up, and I quickly closed the character screen, taking it back to the main menu.

"Should we—" I started, but my eyes darted to the next comment from King.

KingOfFish69: Most welcome. :-*

The skin between my eyes wrinkled, focusing far too long on the kissy face emoji he'd sent.

With a quick clearing of my throat, I snapped back to my monitor. "Should we start the evening with some PvE or go straight into beaching newbs?"

HufflePufflenz: With that new gear? Def PvP!
FriskeeBizkit: ^^^^ that.

I'd known the answer before asking, but it also boosted ratings to keep the viewers interactive.

"Let's start it up then." I paused for a sip of water as the game found other players to connect to. "Don't forget to send some fishy love, everyone."

Dozens of fish-themed emojis flooded the chat—clownfish, sharks, dolphins, and tidal waves.

My throat clenched, spying the image that King sent: a sea

turtle.

My eyes darted to the collection of sea turtles cluttering my gaming desk—plushies, Funko POPs, carved wooden figurines.

Noticing the screen had begun to count down for the match start, I forced my attention back to the game, wiping my sweaty palms on my shorts.

The randomly selected map loaded, and I grinned to myself. Pharos Island. A land and sea map—one I knew the layout of best.

"These poor folks have no idea the plankton they're about to walk off." I equipped my character's sword as soon as it appeared on the sandy shoreline.

Several "LOLs", drums, and laughing face emojis scrolled through the chat.

Once you were in game, it was a matter of navigating the terrain, finding other players, and terminating them for points. There were several randomly sprouting spawn points with treasure chests that'd give the players temporary weapon boosts—one of which was an Atlantean canon, capable of decimating someone with one well-placed ranged shot. I'd played the map so many times, I knew each of the locations, but the order in which they appeared changed.

KingOfFish69: You're not fighting with a trident?

My face scrunched, flicking my attention back to the screen to keep watch for other players. "No one uses the trident in this game. It's one of the weakest weapons, KingOfFish."

FriskeeBizkit: Yeah. Why use a fork when you can use a canon?!

HufflePufflenz: A fork. LMAO.

KingOfFish69: Maybe no one is using "the fork" correctly.

Another player approached in *Aquaman* movie armor, sporting a computer-generated likeness to Jason Momoa's face. A purchasable skin they'd put up for grabs when the movie first released.

MissTacoX: Oh shiz, it's The King of the Seas!

KingOfFish69: Hardly.

I'd have paid more attention to King's comment were it not for morphing into full concentration mode, getting ready to act, react, and win.

NinjaMod: Please remember that when Siren is in the middle of combat, she may not see your comments! It's why you're here, after all, folks. :)

The approaching player's name appeared above their heads: **AceOfAtlantia**.

"Alright, Ace. Let's see who's 'betta'." My thumbs hovered over the joysticks on my controller, circling him.

The Aquaman armor may have looked cool and flashy, but I knew its defense stats were less than half the caliber of my Nautilus set. A few well-timed swing and I'd win. As he brought his sword crashing down over me, I raised mine, blocking his swing. Exaggerated sparks and heightened metal pangs echoed through my headset. The glowing parts of my armor pulsed in response to my character's movement.

FriskeeBizkit: Dude. That armor is SICK.

With a double-tap of the "B" button on my controller, I did a barrel roll to gain a different vantage point on him.

Crouching when he swung his sword at my upper body, I rolled again and swung at the same time, landing a strike on his torso. His username flashed red, indicating severe damage. One final blow before his character had a chance to regenerate health, and…

Priscilla, my Cory Catfish, landed on my desk with a loud wet *thwap*.

With my eyes darting from the screen for that one mere moment, Ace sliced his sword at my head, terminating my character and causing me to respawn.

Priscilla flopped, trying to breathe. Not caring the viewers hadn't a clue why I suddenly dove off-screen, I scooped my fish into my hands and sprinted to the aquarium, plopping her back in. After waiting for her to breathe and swim properly, I returned to the camera.

FriskeeBizkit: What the h3ll happened?

MissTacoX: Did she rage quit?

"I'm here. I'm here. Sorry, all, one of my fish somehow leaped from their tank." I furrowed my brow as I turned in my seat, staring at my aquarium.

That had never happened before, and I ensured tank security at all times to avoid accidents like that while I wasn't home.

So. Strange.

A notification chimed from Glitch.

KingOfFish69 just gave 300 shells!

My face grew hot. "Shells" was the word I chose to switch for dollars. Three. Hundred. Dollars. The most I'd ever gotten in the past was a hundred, and that only ever happened one time.

HufflePufflenz: Mr. Money Bags over here.

NinjaMod: Another friendly reminder to please be courteous to all viewers! We would hate to ban anyone for misconduct. Thank you. :)

A lump formed in my throat as I stared at the notification, watching my character on screen from the corner of my eye performing the fidgeting hops when you've gone idle for too long.

"King of Fish, what a kind donation." I plucked at the rubber overlaying on the right thumbstick of my controller. "Did you have a special request?"

KingOfFish69: I'd love to see you try the trident.

A nervous giggle fluttered from my stomach. "Oh, I don't know. I've never used it. I can't promise I won't die… repeatedly. That's not exactly fun to watch."

KingOfFish69: I think you'd be surprised. Try it. ;)

"What do you think, Sea Farers? By a show of fishy emojis, should I try the trident?" My eyes were glued to the generous donor's username, spying the flood of emojis flying through the chat.

MissTacoX: We have faith in you, chica!

After scratching my cheek, I opened my inventory and switched my primary weapon to the trident. A chorus of low-pitched male singers sounded, followed by the sound of a weapon slicing through the air.

"Here goes nothing."

I'd been standing still on the map for so long it didn't take much to find an opponent. They'd been running across the beach, hoping for an easy kill and that I was AFK (away from keyboard).

Username: **ProteinGeyser**, charged me full force, sword already aimed and wearing matching Nautilus armor.

"Shit. Shit."

HufflePufflenz: You got this!

Please make the trident work the same as the sword.

As he got closer, a flash of an ornately patterned trident blocked my vision, turning in mid-air, reflecting rays of light like it was underwater. As if on autopilot, my fingers worked the buttons of my controller. The image rippled away, and I stared at my monitor with my character's trident skewered into ProteinGeyser's chest—long-ranged, one-shot kill.

Emojis flooded the chat, followed by so many notifications, the constant chiming made my head ache.

HufflePufflenz donated 10 shells!

MissTacoX: DUUUUUUUUDE!

KingOfFish69: :)

FriskeeBizkit resubscribed at a new tier level!

"Thank you so much, everyone. I wish I could thank you each individually, but I've lost half of the notifications it's been scrolling so fast." My cheeks flushed, and I pressed one of my constantly cold hands against my face to cool them.

Another three hours whizzed by, and I used the trident for the entire stream, wrecking in every round I played, finishing as the top player with the best kill to death ratio. King didn't type much of anything else, except the occasional smiley face when I performed an especially impressive move with my weapon. The strange vision didn't pop into my head again, and I wondered if I'd ever actually seen it. Could it have been something I ate earlier? I remembered popping a couple of

Tic-Tac's I found in the abyss of my purse but didn't bother to check the expiration date?

I'd thanked King a final time for the money before signing off and sat in my gaming chair for a solid ten minutes, staring at my sea turtle collection before finally finding the will to move. My phone's screen lit up on my desk, still on silent as I always did before going live.

Meg.

"Hey," I greeted meekly.

"Hey yourself. Three hundred dollars? I'm surprised this guy didn't expect sexual favors for that kind of cash."

I moved to my aquarium, sprinkling some food on the surface and watching Priscilla swim. "For one, I would've shot that down in an instant, and two, he would've been banned from Glitch for life."

"Okay. You're taking everything literally. What's on your mind?"

"My fish jumped from its tank." I squinted, calculating the approximate distance from the aquarium to my desk. "It's a good ten feet to my desk. You know I keep this thing secure, and even if one did get out, they wouldn't make it more than a couple of feet."

"An odd mishap. Your point?"

My eyes panned up to a painting hanging over my bed. One I'd bought on vacation in Key West that called to me like a luring siren. It was a small, minute detail, but it was plain as day as I walked closer. A single, gold trident was behind the waves, drawn to blend in with the coral sprouting from all sides.

I ran my fingertips over it. "I've never used the trident in the game. Ever. And I had the best matches of my life."

"You're pulling at a fishnet here, Cory. It sounds like you need some sleep. Besides, we got a car ride tomorrow. Remember? A week in West Palm with the sea turtles and cameras?"

"I didn't forget. How could I? There's something else. I had this weird nightmare of a tentacle dragging me underwater to the point of me drowning." Remembering how real it seemed, I traced a hand over my ribs. "I woke up sputtering and choking as if it were actually happening."

"A tentacle? Like Ursula? You watched that movie a couple of nights ago, didn't you?"

The Little Mermaid. I had indeed.

"Yeah. Yeah, I guess you're right."

"Right. Well, stop overthinking things, as you always do, get to bed, and bring those three hundred bones with you. Maybe buy yourself something nice and girly."

I smiled, letting my hand fall away from the painting. "Or maybe I'll buy *you* something nice and girly."

"Was that a threat?"

"Goodnight, Meg."

"Nighty, night…Saucy Siren."

After hanging up, I focused on the trident in the painting. As my hand lifted of its own accord, fingers stretching for the weapon, a familiar voice fluttered past my ear, the feel of a beard scraping against my nape.

Eisaí i thálassa.

With a gasp, I whirled around to find my fish hovering at one side of the tank.

FOUR

WE'D ROAD-TRIPPED DOWN TO West Palm Beach, all eight hours of it, listening to a pirate fantasy novel *On These Black Sands* on audiobook for the duration of the drive. When we settled into our hotel room for the night, after lugging all equipment from my Jeep inside, I stared at myself in the mirror while Meg showered. The same face, same reflection from the past thirty-three years gazed back at me, but an unsettling notion—a feeling that I didn't recognize myself anymore made my stomach twist into knots. The reflection flashed for a split moment, and I caught a glimpse of myself in a plaid-patterned dress with rolling green hills behind me. One blink and I would've missed it.

"Should I go back into the bathroom?" Meg had walked out at some time, towel drying her cropped hair with a raised brow. "You look like you're about to…self-indulge."

My chest tightened, and I snapped my gaze to my fingers

trailing between my breasts. "I—"

Meg paused and canted her head at me, brushing her bare feet across the carpet until she stood next to me.

"Do I look different to you, Meg?"

She curled her finger under one strap of her ribbed tank top, moving between me and the mirror. "You've got a glaze in your eyes lately. Like you're lost in thought more often than you're here on planet Earth. Other than that? No."

I turned for my suitcase, grabbing toiletry items and pajamas.

"In fact," Meg continued, following me. "You've been weird ever since meeting surfer boy. A connection? Methinks so. Do your loins simply burn for him, my dear?"

"My loins, Meg?" I bit back a laugh.

"Yeah. Isn't that how all your romance novels describe it?"

Rolling my eyes, I brushed past her. "Maybe if I liked bodice rippers."

"Bodice, what now?"

"I'm taking a shower," I said, ignoring her question with a chuckle as I ducked into the bathroom.

Considering hotels never seemed to run out of hot water, I cranked it up as high as my skin could tolerate. Pressing my hands against the marble tiles, I leaned forward, dropping my head and letting the heat roll down my neck and back. Raising my lips toward the showerhead, I opened my mouth, letting the water collect, filling it. For a moment, I thought I could breathe despite the water blocking my throat and nostrils. I even tried to. Coughing, sputtering, and gasping, I pressed my back to the shower wall, dragging the water droplets from my face.

What the hell was wrong with me? Who drowns themselves in a shower standing up?

The door creaked open.

"Are you dying in here, Cor?" Meg asked.

After gulping down another helping of air, I replied, "No. Just trying to breathe water."

"Ah. As much as I know you long to be a mermaid, please remember…"

"I don't have gills." I pursed my lips.

"Good. You haven't floated completely to the clouds yet. Just scream if you slip or something because you're trying to dive into extremely shallow waters."

The door clicked closed.

After finishing up and managing not to kill myself, I headed back to the living room to find Meg sitting on the edge of her bed, staring at her phone screen.

"Meg?"

Her hand shook, and she didn't blink.

Quickly wrapping the towel around my dripping wet hair, I crossed the room and slid a hand on her shoulder. "Meg."

"She—" Meg gulped, and looked at me with bloodshot eyes. "She texted me. She wants me back."

My chest ached and I sat on the bed next to her, forcing her to look at me as I gently grabbed her chin. "Megara, don't do this to yourself."

One of the first things we found out that we both had in common when we met was our love of Disney's Hercules after I called her Megara for the first time. It'd stuck from then on out.

"I love her, Cory." Meg's grip tightened on the phone.

I curled my fingers around the phone, prying it from her grip. "I know you do. But what she did to you is unforgivable, and I'd be willing to bet anything the only reason she's texting you is because the *man* she was dating dumped her."

After a few tugs, Meg let go with a sigh.

"You're probably right. I just can't stand the thought of starting over again. It's hard enough finding other gay women, let alone one I'm also interested in dating." Meg sighed and flopped onto her back.

I followed and rested my head on her shoulder. "It'll happen, Meg. You do you for now. Heal. Be happy. And it'll happen."

She rested her head on mine. "Not sure what I'd do without you, Hobbit."

I poked her ribs, and she let out a yelp. "Can I do you a favor?"

"What do you mean?"

I held up the phone like an Olympic torch. "By deleting her number."

"Cory…" Meg shot to her elbows, the skin between her eyes cinching. "I don't know."

"Did you want to be friends with her?"

"I—I couldn't do that." Meg bit her lip and looked away.

After pulling up her contacts list, I clicked into her ex's name and showed Meg the screen.

With one glance at the phone, she closed her eyes. "Do it."

And so, I did.

We sat on the boat the following day, sipping on our second can of Red Bull. Meg had started crying in the middle of the night, and I spent hours stroking her hair, trying to coax her back to sleep. She sat next to me on the bench seat as the captain sailed us to the dive spot. She had her head tilted up, letting the sun warm her cheeks, eyes closed behind her sunglasses.

"How are you doing, Megara?" I bumped her arm.

She took a long, deep breath. "Better. Much better. The sun always rejuvenates me." She shoved the sunglasses to the top of her head. "I'm sorry for keeping you up last night."

"Oh, no. You're not saying any of that. Remember when I broke up with Ted?"

She exaggerated her plump bottom lip sticking out, making it press against the middle of her chin. "I'd rather not remember Ted. But man, did we binge-watch the hell out of some *Vampire Diaries*."

Sighing, I leaned back and dragged a hand down my throat. "Damon will get any girl through a breakup, I swear."

"Mm, Caroline."

We eyed each other sidelong before laughing.

"We're five minutes out, ladies," the boat captain announced to give us time to suit up.

After going through the formal process of slipping on wet suits, flippers, and masks, we hoisted the tanks onto each other's backs. I dangled my mask by its strap from my arm, double-checking I had a new SD card in my camera. We were diving in the North Double Ledges to look for prime spots for sea turtles. West Palm, in particular, had strong currents, which made for harsh swimming conditions. It called for drift diving, which would carry us over the reef with little need to swim. It also meant a negative entry, a straight descent to the bottom without stopping at the surface. It was a challenge that I loved because you had to be quick on the shutter to catch your subject matter in time.

The assistant on board yelled, "Dive, dive," once the dive entry was clear, the boat bobbed against the harsh current.

Meg and I hopped in, descending to the bottom as soon as our flippers slipped beneath the surface. A divemaster joined us because our entry and exit points were on opposite sides. Meg would serve as a spotter and backup for the dive, given the conditions. With how often I would have to slow down for photos, however, I wasn't sure how likely it'd be to stay with the divemaster. Even Meg and I would drift apart occasionally if she missed my signal that I was stopping.

I readied my camera as the drift carried me along, relaxing my limbs and letting water curl around me like a dense fog. Fish of all colors and varieties fluttered amidst the coral reef. Snapping several photos, I didn't entirely stop for them, striving to save my energy for the sea turtles. A group of fish swam over to me, spiraling my arms and doing repeated circles around my torso.

I'd never seen fish act like this before. Especially not with a human.

A sea turtle swam directly below me, but with my new fish friends distracting me, I didn't raise the camera in time before drifting straight past it.

Dammit.

We spent the next hour taking photos of anything and

everything that the magazine would pay us for, including over a dozen breathtaking shots of majestic sea turtles. During that time, more fish circled my arms and legs, an eel stared me down, and a nurse shark swam beside me for almost ten minutes straight. To say I was bewildered would've been putting it mildly. A storm had rolled in at some point during our dive, causing the current to grow more intense. Our steady drift had turned into a catapult, and we were no longer in sight of the divemaster. I tossed a hand signal to Meg, letting her know to stay within range.

Removing the delayed surface marker buoy from my utility belt, I started to unravel it, resting the camera at my side with the strap secured around my neck. I reached behind me for the alternate air source on my tank and slipped it into the underside of the buoy. I paused with a small puff of air to ensure no leaks before fully inflating it, and letting go, keeping hold of the reel. Once Meg and I were near each other, I started to tug on the buoy, signaling our new location to the boat.

No sooner had we breached the surface, the choppy waters tossed us. The boat rocked with such force the dock dipped in and out of the water. A crewman stood on the edge in a raincoat holding his hands out, instructing us to wait for a safer moment to board. The divemaster had already made it, and she too waved her hands at us.

I yanked my regulator from my mouth. "Meg, go first."

"Are you crazy?" She sputtered as our bodies bobbed in the water like matching buoys.

"I'm a stronger swimmer than you. We both know that. I'll be behind you and help you get on the boat."

The crewman frantically waved his hands for us to swim to the boat.

Meg grumbled. "Fine."

Following behind her, I treaded water with my flippers and held the camera out to her once she was safely on board. Wrapping my hands around the ladder, I pulled myself up. A massive gust of wind sent a wave over my head, tossing me from the ladder and back into the dark water. I sputtered, scrambling for my regulator as the choppy waves tossed me around like a ragdoll and carried me away from the boat.

"Cory," Meg shouted.

My breathing grew erratic, and I managed to shove the regulator in my mouth, kicking my arms and legs as fast as possible, but the current was too strong. The sight of the boat grew smaller and smaller.

A sudden force bubbled beneath me until it reached my legs and launched me forward like two dolphins were pushing the bottoms of my feet but…there was nothing but water and air. I held my arms at my sides, watching the streaks of bubbles on either side of me form straight lines as my body propelled through the water with ease *against* the current. And in the distance, I caught sight of several suckers like an octopus tentacle. It disappeared into the shadows before I could look again to confirm.

Once I neared the boat, the water lifted me to the ladder. I snapped my head over my shoulder, determined to catch a glimpse of the mysterious force. But there was nothing except the waves cutting against each other and the water turning black from torrential downpours of rain.

"Jesus Christ, Cory, are you alright?" Meg asked, yanking me onto the dock.

Water beads collected on my eyelashes, and I blinked them away, staring at the unruly surface of the ocean. "A bit shook up, yeah. But I'm fine."

Meg jolted me from my daydream when she wrapped her arms around me in a soggy embrace. "You scared the shit out of me, Hobbit."

Finally able to tear my eyes away from the water, I hugged her back and numbly patted her shoulder blades.

The rain slowed once we reached the shore as luck would have it. No matter, however, we'd gotten what we came for—sea turtle photos. I scrolled through the shots on my camera. Only two were blurry. The rest were bright, crisp, and centered.

"Isn't that the surfer guy?" Meg swatted my shoulder and pointed.

My stomach fluttered as soon as I spotted him.

Simon. He talked to a woman in a yellow string bikini, swiveling her hips and pushing her boobs together. Simon grinned, showing those sparkly white teeth, but his eyes stayed glued to her face. He rubbed the back of his neck and shrugged. The woman's arms fell at her sides, and she frowned before turning away with a flick of her wrist.

The boat lurched as we nestled against the dock and I sat still, frozen. Simon peeled the top part of his wet suit from his chest, letting it hang from his hips. My mouth dried at the sight of his bare chest despite seeing it days prior.

Meg snapped her fingers in front of my face. "The boat charges by the hour, you know?" She grinned.

"Right." I glanced at my watch. We had two minutes before they'd charge us for another hour. "Shit. Let's move."

Chuckling, I scooped my equipment into my arms and hobbled over the edge of the boat to the dock, waving at the crew with my only free hand. When I turned around, I came face-to…. abs with Simon. With a gulp I was sure was audible to everyone else on the dock, I panned my eyes up until they met his gaze.

The sun peeked through the clouds above him, framing his face with a sort of ethereal glow.

"Cordelia. Fancy seeing you here." He smiled, bright and magnificent.

"I—" I started to speak but abruptly stopped, spying our charity's logo, a circle comprised of a blue wave, on the arm of his wetsuit, as well as an even bigger one on the surfboard tucked under his arm.

I'd completely forgotten to send him the images.

"How did you—" I started again, but this time, Meg stuck her hand between us.

"I'm Meg. We spoke via e-mail?"

With the two of them being the same height—giants—I stood at sea level, trying to ignore that they towered over me.

"Oh, right." Simon shook her hand. "I slapped it on my board the same day. You like?" He held the board up, giving it a twirl.

"We love it." Meg elbowed me. "Don't we, Cory?"

I yelped, given my sides were beyond ticklish. "Yes. Thank you so much. I'm sure it will help our donations immensely."

"My pleasure. Anything I can do to help the seas and its—"

He caught my gaze, his eyes seeming to turn into two pools with gently rolling waves. "—aquatic life."

"Well, Cory." Meg slapped my back. "I'm going to stop in the gift shop. Meet me there?"

"Meet you?" I turned to face her, still holding a mountain of equipment in my arms.

"Nice to meet you in the uh—flesh, Simon." Meg gave a small wave, eyed me, and bolted down the dock.

"Did you…want some help with all of that?"

My throat tightened, and I whipped back around to face him, the bag on my shoulder slipping off and making a loud *thud* as it hit the dock.

With the same radiant grin, he picked the bag up. "Here." He reached for the other bag resting over my forearms. "Listen, do you…want to talk?"

"Talk?" My brows bobbed.

"Yeah. You know, like normal people?" He chuckled, his eyes dropping to his bare feet, pausing before looking back to me.

I snorted. "Oh, man. Not sure I've *ever* considered myself—normal."

"I know exactly what you mean." The oceans in his eyes swirled like a typhoon as he stared down at me. "What do you say?" He nudged his head at a vacant bench facing the beach.

"Sure. Okay."

As we walked to the bench, every patron we passed whispered and pointed at him. I shouldn't have been surprised, considering how famous of a surfer he was. But I'd never been one to follow "celebrities." How silly of me to have forgotten I was in the company of a "surf god."

Simon sat on the bench, resting my bags on the sand at his feet. He patted the space next to him, flashing me a smile that could have melted the bikini top I wore *underneath* my wetsuit. After running my hands over my salty wet hair, I took a seat the farthest I could from him without falling off the edge.

He glanced down at the wide gap between us. "I promise I don't bite."

"I know of you, but I don't *know* you." I offered a weak smile.

But I did feel like I knew him. As if I'd known him my entire life. That in itself jarred me more than sitting on a bench with a stranger.

"I suppose I do need to earn your trust, don't I?" He curled his hands on the edge of the bench and leaned forward.

A tickle swirled in my belly at his words. "What are you doing in West Palm?"

He casually kicked his surfboard. "I did have a competition. Small one. But they canceled it on account of the storm." He gazed skyward.

I, too, looked up, and we both laughed at the blue skies and sun shining brightly. Such was life in Florida.

"You?" He drummed his fingers on the bench.

"Sea turtles." I bit my lower lip, mimicking his position and hugging my arms against my thighs.

"I'm sorry?" He rose a brow, making his forehead wrinkle.

I chuckled at his expression. "I'm an oceanographer. A magazine hired us to take photos of sea turtles. West Palm has some of the best scenery for them."

"You took photos? Even during the storm?" He pointed at

the water, almost at the precise spot I'd gotten swept away.

Bile climbed up my throat. "Yeah. It got a little dicey there toward the end." I pinched my knees together, staring at them.

"Are you okay?" He dipped his head, trying to look at my face.

"Yeah. Yes." I sat straight, rubbing both collar bones with one hand. "I'd gotten thrown into the current. But there was this weird—gust underwater. It brought me right back to the boat."

He coughed. "A gust, you say?"

"Yes." I scooted closer to him. "Have you ever experienced something like that?"

His grip tightened on the bench. "Can't say I have. Just waves and curls."

Suddenly, he couldn't look at me, and I slid closer.

He shot up like a rocket. "Listen, I have to go, but—" He rubbed the back of his neck. "I'd really like to see you again. Would you consider possibly exchanging numbers?"

It'd been so long since a man asked for my number in person, I'd forgotten how to respond in this situation properly.

"Numbers?" It came out as a squeak.

He chuckled, deep and masculine. "Yeah. Phone numbers? To contact each other? Maybe I might ask you out?"

My heart thundered in my chest. "You? Simon Thalassa. A famous surfer with abs for days…wants to see me again?"

He gave a snarky smile as he tapped his fingers against his stomach. I took notice for a split second before forcing them back to his face.

"Are surfers with toned muscles not allowed to date?"

I pressed two fingers between my eyes and stood. "I'm sorry,

I'm horrible at this whole…socializing thing in general, I suppose."

A gooey smile spread over his lips, and he said under his breath, "You always have been."

"What did you say?"

His eyes darted to mine. "I didn't say anything."

I scratched my cheek as I dug my toes in the sand, willing the grains to calm my nerves.

"We could always rely on fate throwing us in each other's path again, but I'd much rather do it the old-fashioned way." He clasped his hands in front of him.

I liked him. I did. So, what the hell was wrong with me?

"I don't have my phone on me, but I have a pen?" Crouching, I unzipped the front pocket of my camera bag and stood with pen in hand like an elegant quill.

He offered his tanned corded forearm to me, keeping his gaze locked to mine.

My fingers grazed his skin, the tautness of it—the light scattering of hair—made warmth pool in my belly. Gripping the pen tightly to keep my hand from shaking, I wrote my phone number on him. His scent floated through the air in front of me like waterfall mist—sea spray mixed with citrus and sun. I wanted to melt against him, mold to him.

"I think we're good, Cordelia," he whispered near my ear.

My eyes flew open, and I jumped back, realizing my hand still rested on his forearm, and I'd leaned toward him.

I curled the pen into my chest, clutching it with both hands. "That number is a one-time deal. Don't let it wash away."

He plucked the surfboard from the sand and folded it under

his arm. "I will never let the opportunity to see you again wash away." He willed my eyes to him, and before he turned to walk away, my mind played tricks on me once more. Because I could've sworn, he whispered, "Not anymore."

FIVE

AS I WALKED INTO the gift shop to meet up with Meg after dropping off the equipment in my Jeep, I kept playing his words in my head. I squinted at nothing, moving my finger in the air as if solving an algebraic equation without pencil and paper.

The past days left me with unanswered questions I hadn't even known I wanted to ask.

"Cory," Meg shouted, grabbing my shoulders and shaking me.

I jerked within her grasp. "What? What?"

"I called your name three times. From two feet away. What the hell is wrong with you?" She raised her hand in a fin gesture and moved it from one side of my face to the other, keeping her eyes on mine.

I followed her hand before batting it away. "I don't have a concussion or whatever else you feel the need to check my motor skills on."

"Are you going to tell me about your chit-chat with Simon, or do I have to drag it out of you?" She'd thrown a plaid shirt over her swimsuit top, letting the rest of the wetsuit hang from her waist.

"He—" I fluttered past her, busying my hands and eyes with a variety of souvenirs. "Asked for my number."

"Wow. The man works fast and knows what he wants. I like it." Meg ran her fingers over the seashell keychains hanging from pegs.

"It's—I mean, I'm probably overthinking it." I snagged a water globe with a pair of sea turtles swimming between the words West Palm Beach and turned it upside down to make it snow on them.

"Cordelia. Spit. It. Out. Since when have you been so non-forthcoming with information? Normally you'd be talking my damn ear off by now." She snatched the globe from my hand, putting it back, and tugging on my arm. "Come look at these."

"He has this sense of urgency to him. Like he's afraid if he doesn't act on the prospect of us, I'll get pulled in with the tide, never to be seen again."

Meg led me to several rows of shelves filled with miniature sculptures dipped in pearlescent sheen.

"I don't know, Cor. There's nothing wrong with a person knowing what they want and going for it. So long as he doesn't propose tomorrow, I'd ride it out." She grabbed a hammerhead shark, running her thumb over its dorsal fin. "He seems perfect for you."

"We don't know this guy, Meg." I winced, grabbing one of the sea turtles, testing its weight in my palm.

And it was true. I. Did. Not. Know. Him. But his presence was like a midnight swim—relaxing current mixed with uncertainty and eerie calm.

"That's the whole point of dating, isn't it? Getting to know him?" She kept the hammerhead shark in her grasp and reached for a bull shark figurine.

A pile of small replica tridents rested in a far corner, the overhead fluorescent light reflecting off them, making them sparkle brighter than the rest. I hovered my hand over one, and a loud buzzing pounded in my ears, dizzying me. Wincing through the bizarre interference, I snatched one, and the sound floated away, replaced by Meg's voice still going on about Simon.

"That's all I'm saying. I'm simply looking out for your best interests," Meg continued, cradling one of every shark species in her arms with a bright smile.

Holding the trident up to the light, I twirled it between two fingers. "If I text him when we get to the car, will that please you?"

"Yes. Yes, it would. At least one of us should be having a successful sex life."

"From, 'you should date him,' to, 'you should bang him' in nearly one breath. Wow." I moved past her with wide eyes to the register, slapping the trident onto the counter.

"We're both adults. And gone are the times for judgment over screwing on the first date." She shrugged and plucked a seashell keychain from a turnstile with her name on it. "Sometimes, it's even a matter of releasing stress. And that's a-okay."

The cashier, a younger woman with ringlets of strawberry

blonde hair and a small perky nose, smiled as she rang me up, her cheeks blushing.

"I mean, am I right?" Meg asked, dipping her face to try and look at the shy cashier.

The woman nodded emphatically but couldn't meet Meg's gaze.

Biting back a smile, I took my small blue bag and receipt, stepping out of Meg's way.

As the cashier rang up the dozen shark figures Meg set on the counter, I peered at the trident surrounded by blue plastic within the satchel. If the same weapon in *Tides of Atlantis* were as powerful as it had been when I wielded it in the game, why did it remain the least popular choice?

"So, you live in West Palm, huh? Ever visit Pensacola?" Meg leaned her forearms on the counter, chewing a pen she'd thrown into her haul at the last minute.

The cashier's shoulders hunched forward, but she grinned. "Sometimes, yeah. I love that Diesel Fuel drink. Not to mention the huge pile of nachos at McGuire's."

Never having been the shy type, Meg pushed the blue arrow on the cash register, making several inches of blank receipt tape appear. After tearing it off, she jotted something down and slid it toward her.

"My number. When you're in town next, you should get in touch. I'll buy you a Diesel Fuel." Meg stuck the pen back in her mouth before beating her palms on the counter in rhythmic succession.

The cashier's cheeks turned rosy, and she folded the receipt tape with a smile. "I'll be sure to do that."

Meg winked before scooping the bag full of sharky souvenirs onto her arm and joining me near the entrance.

"Back on the saddle?" I elbowed her.

She continued to chew the pen. "Trying."

Curling our arms, we tossed our bags into the back of my Jeep and crawled in, heading back to our hotel for the night. My cell phone vibrated in the glove compartment, echoing off the plastic walls until Meg popped it open and grabbed it.

"Who is it?" I bobbed my brows at her.

With a sly grin, she scrolled the screen with her thumb. "Looks like you won't have to be the first to make a move after all. I should've guessed."

"Is it Simon?" I reached for the phone, but she leaned away.

"Uh-huh. He's asking if you want to come to his surf competition in two days."

"Surf competition? What kind of a date is that?"

She lowered the phone to her lap and gave me an exasperated stare. "Why am I having to school you on men? This is so incredibly backward, Cor."

"What are you talking about?"

"He wants to show off at the competition. Afterward, I'd bet my favorite plaid shirt he plans to take you to dinner or drinks or whatever for a nightcap." She twirled her hand in a circle, waiting for the lightbulb to go off in my brain.

"Oh." I wrung my hands on the steering wheel. "I suppose that makes sense."

Meg nodded once and rested my phone in the cupholder between us. "I already replied that you'd be there."

"What? Why would you—" I gripped the wheel tighter.

She pointed a stern finger at me, silent.

"Fine. I suppose I can pretend to be way more into surfing than I actually am for a day."

"No."

I snapped my head in her direction. "No?"

Nerves bubbled in my stomach from taking my eyes off the road, and I quickly returned them.

"You're not going to pretend anything. That's bullshit. You're going to watch Simon show his athletic prowess half-naked and hang out with him afterward. That's it." She sliced her hand through the air in front of her.

I sunk in my seat. "You're considerably fiery lately."

"A new leaf, Cor. A new leaf."

It was our last day in West Palm, and we chartered a cage dive to get some prize-winning shark close-ups, hopefully. We sat on a bench aboard the boat, and I checked for an SD card, ensured my regulator worked properly, and pulled my hair in a low ponytail.

"I've gotten so used to full-face dive masks." Meg tossed around the mouthpiece of her regulator with a snicker. "It's going to suck not being able to talk to you."

I slipped on my flippers. "I think we'll survive for twenty minutes."

"Twenty minutes, huh? Wow. Has Cordelia Bourne grown an ego?" Meg poked my shoulder.

Flicking her in the leg with my flipper, I guffawed. "Ego?

What are you talking about?"

"You've had such a lucky track record lately with your photos that you think we're going to nab a sell-worthy shark shot in twenty minutes?"

I squinted into the sun with a slight shrug. "Or under." Peeking at her reaction from the corner of my eye, she didn't disappoint. Her jaw almost touched her chest. "I'm kidding, Meg." I smiled at her, flicking her shin with my flipper again.

"Five minutes," the captain announced.

We both stood, helping the other secure the tanks on our backs. It must've been comical for anyone who watched me assist Meg, considering I had to practically make a running start to throw the straps over her shoulders. After we were suited up, we flopped to the edge of the boat, watching the cage lower into the water from an attached crane once the boat came to a complete stop.

I glared at the cage's bars and tugged on Meg's arm. "Don't those bars look a bit too far apart to you?"

She peered into the water. "Maybe an inch or two beyond what we normally see, but it'll still do its job. Keep the knife teeth away from us." After winking at me, she yanked her goggles over her face.

"Right." I forced a smile and shoved the regulator in my mouth.

The world around us quieted as we jumped into the water. The only sounds passing over my ears were the metal groans of the boat bobbing in the water, our steady breathing, and water churning around us. The cage lowered after locking ourselves inside and tugging on the cord secured by the crane operator on deck. The metal fastenings keeping the bars closed jangled when it came to a halting stop. We both lifted our cameras and began swimming circles with our backs to each other, staying toward the center.

They started to chum the water from the boat, marred bits of torn fish floated through the water, fresh blood curling around it in a spiral. My grip tightened on the camera handles as a fish head darted past my gaze. Bile crept up my throat, but I gulped it away. Vomiting in my regulator wouldn't be an ideal situation.

We'd been floating in the cage for ten minutes, schools of fish swimming on either side, but nothing larger—not the big game we sought. A curious female bull shark circled nearby, moving in a zigzag pattern as she gained closure on the cage. I elbowed Meg and pointed, encouraging her to frame a shot in case it graced us with its presence.

The shark swam closer and closer until suddenly it zipped away, leaving a trail of bubbles behind it. For a bull shark of that size to flee on a whim could've only meant one thing—an even bigger fish swam nearby. I whipped my head in every direction, straining to see an outline, movement, anything in the distance.

It happened with such speed, force, and pure power we didn't see it coming until a Great White shark's head plowed between the bars on the side of the cage. Bubbles surged from our mouths as we both screamed. The shark either thought we were food or a threat or possibly both and had planned a long-ranged attack.

I lifted the camera, using it as a shield once the shark

started thrashing and biting—stuck. My breathing grew erratic, staring in horror at the poor creature panicking, writhing for its life to no avail. Meg swam to the farthest corner and pushed her back to it, her eyes as wide as beach balls behind her goggles.

With as deep of a breath as I could manage given a regulator, I steadied my heartbeat. Blood floated from the shark's gills, and I knew if it kept thrashing, it would make itself bleed to death.

If only I could tell it to stop so I could help push it through to spare its gills.

If only the risk of losing a hand in the process weren't astronomically high.

It. Was. Going. To. Die.

I couldn't live with myself if I stood there watching it hurt itself until going lifeless and sinking to the bottom of the ocean—forgotten.

Stop.

The shark's glossy eyes peered back at me, continuing to squirm against the cage bars.

Stop. Stop. Stop.

Swimming closer, I kept the camera between us.

The shark's writhing slowed, but the blood leaking from its gills didn't.

A spark sizzled up my spine, and I let the camera float to the cage bottom. Moving in front of the shark, a breath away, so close I could see the dozens of scars on its nose, I ripped the regulator from my mouth.

"Stop," I shouted into the water, sending a barrage of curling bubbles into the shark's face.

The shark stopped—its gills flopping helplessly against the cage, its tail idly whipping back and forth to keep it afloat. I stared at the shark's eyes, keeping its gaze as I reached a shaky hand forward. Meg's fingers brushed against my wet suit from behind me, but I ignored her, entirely focused on the shark, and locked our gazes.

The shark jerked as I neared its gills, but I fought every compulsion to snap away. Nudging my hand between the shark's gills and the cage, I grunted and pushed with all my might. The shark did a small shimmy with its head before it dislodged—free. Like the swell in the ocean, my chest soared, almost bursting, beaming at the sight of the freed shark. A film flapped over the shark's right eye before it swam away with solid strokes of its tail.

My lungs burned. The regulator. I shoved it back into my mouth and took several long gulps of air. Meg grabbed my shoulder and turned me around, frantically grabbing for my hands, checking all fingers were still intact. She shoved my shoulder before pulling on the rope, signaling the boat to make the cage ascend. I rested a hand on my throat, recalling the swirling pattern of bubbles from my underwater yell.

My head breached the surface, the sun warming my skin and calming my rattled nerves. The shouts from the boat's captain, birds flying overhead, and the water crashing against the boat faded into my ears—I felt like a stranger in my own skin.

No sooner had we climbed back on board, Meg tore off her goggles and grabbed both my shoulders. "What the ever-loving hell happened down there, Cor?"

"Miss, are you alright?" The captain asked, running a hand over his bald, sweaty head. "That shark was throwing the cage around like a damned seal. Never seen that happen before."

I furrowed my brow, dropping my focus to the laugh lines bordering Meg's mouth. "I'm fine."

"I got this handled, Captain. Can you get us back to the dock as soon as possible, please?" Meg guided me to the bench and pushed me down to sit.

"You never being threatened by sharks, Cory, is one thing. What I witnessed down there was damned shark whispering." Meg grabbed her camera and held the digital screen on the back out to me.

I rubbed my lips together, eyes shifting to the screen. She'd taken several succession shots of me reaching my hand to the shark and even more when I pressed my hand on its gills and pushed. Closing my eyes, I turned away, my head dizzy and pulsing. "You can't publish those."

"No shit. I wanted you to see for yourself what you did." Meg rested the camera on the bench beside her and scooted closer to me, rubbing my arms. "How did you know it wouldn't bite your damn arm off, Cor?"

My body jostled as she rubbed, beads of water from my wet hair falling on my upturned hand resting on my thigh.

Drip. Drip drip.

"I didn't."

"Jesus. Why did you do it, hm? Why?" She switched to rubbing my shoulders.

"It was either do something or watch it die." Tears welled in my eyes at the mere thought. "You know I couldn't let that happen."

She side-hugged me, pulling me in tight. Given our height difference, I was able to rest my head on her shoulder comfortably. She placed her head on mine. "Please don't ever do it again. I couldn't earn enough money on my own. Kinda need you." She chuckled, making my body vibrate.

A smile pulled at my lips but faded.

There weren't any telltale signs of a shark's emotions. No gleams in their eyes. No thinned lips or reddened cheeks. But I knew with every fiber in my being—that fish not only understood me when I yelled but also *thanked* me before swimming away.

SIX

I'D BEGGED MEG TO come with me to the surf competition because I wouldn't know what to do with myself alone on the beach watching a bunch of surfers. As predicted, she refused and told me to concentrate on Simon. If he'd have been the only contestant, that wouldn't have been an issue, but I sat on a towel in the sand watching athlete after athlete catch the waves, and none of them were Simon. Stifling a yawn, I tilted my head back and closed my eyes, letting the sun kiss my skin.

"Already bored, huh?" Simon's voice spoke from nearby.

I popped my eyes open to find him standing over me with a snarky grin, his head partially blocking the light in the sky. "Full disclosure. I came here to watch one singular surfer."

"Oh, yeah?" Simon plopped on the sand next to me, propping his forearms on his knees. "And who might that be?"

Several beach-goers pointed and stared at us, whispering to each other. If Simon noticed, he didn't act like it.

"Some guy the media says is the biggest thing to hit the surfing circuit since the board leash." I pushed my sunglasses to my head, taking in the sight of him up close and at my level.

Those eyes of his never failed to make me feel antsy and calm all at once.

"Wow. Sounds talented." He winked at me before lightly nudging my elbow with his. "I appreciate you stopping by. If I'd known you were just showing up for me, I would've told you to come later." He chuckled and turned his glance to the waves, impatiently tapping his fingers on his bronzed forearm.

"Oh? Do they always save the best for last?" I sat up straighter, causing my hip to brush his thigh.

Both of our gazes snapped to the brief contact before meeting each other's eyes.

He canted his head to one side, taking me in. "They think it's best for publicity. I don't give a damn in what order I go, so long as I get to surf."

"You really are an aqua baby, aren't you?" I wanted to drag my fingers through his hair. Instead, I dug them into the sand.

He nodded as he leaned on the elbow closest to me, the hair on his arm brushing my skin. "If I could live in the water—" His gaze lowered to my lips before returning to my eyes. "I would."

An obnoxious foghorn sounded from the other side of the beach.

Simon rolled his eyes. "That would be my sponsor. Their delightful way of letting me know there's one surfer to go before me." He leaped to his feet and dusted the sand from his butt.

"You'll stick around afterward, right? There's a great little salad bar just down the beach." He pointed with his thumb. "And the margaritas are strong." The lopsided grin that slid over his plump yet masculine lips made the insides of my thighs ache.

"I'm not going anywhere."

His expression fell, and he stared down at me, the left side of his mouth twitching. He took a step forward but retreated, giving one quick shake of his head. "At one point, I'm going to hold three fingers above my head. That signal? It's for you."

I traced a finger over my lips. "I'll look for it."

After flashing me another award-winning smile, he trotted off, waving his arm at his sponsor. Every woman he passed on his way turned their gazes on him, watching his hardened muscles tightening and flexing with each step. A knot twisted in my stomach. I barely knew the man, yet somehow, my body still figured out a way to be jealous. I yanked the camera from my bag with a grunt, setting the shutter for the appropriate lighting.

Tossing the strap over my neck, I hovered my gaze behind the viewfinder, zooming in and taking several images of the waves. Surfing photos weren't always at the top of the list of shots my clients asked for, but a few of Simon Thalassa might be desirable.

Desire.

A lump the size of a conch shell formed in my throat, and I tightened my grip on the camera.

As the announcer's voice introduced Simon, surrounding beach-goers perked up on their beach towels. I rose to my knees with the camera perched in my grasp, spotting Simon running across the shoreline, his board nestled under one arm. The water welcomed him with every lap of the waves crashing against his calves. He flopped on his belly atop the board, swimming to where the waves broke.

He fully stood on the board as the wave curled, expertly balancing and riding the water. His right hand cut through the wave, the pipe coiling around him like an embrace. I put the camera to work, taking shot after shot one after the other to catch any subtle piece of the action. His arms flowed through the water and as I zoomed closer, the shape of a dolphin appeared, but was gone just as quickly with a furious splash.

My shoulders tensed, but I didn't drop the camera, keeping my gaze glued on Simon through the viewfinder. As he made a smooth transition from beneath the wave, he held an arm up, displaying three fingers and a wide smile.

Grinning, I took several shots of his secret message to me. Only me.

Three fingers. I blinked, my lashes fluttering against the camera—a trident.

A numbness coursed down my arms, and I sat back on my haunches. The camera would've fallen into the sand were it not for the strap keeping it hung around my neck. I rubbed the skin between my eyes, flashes of the sparkling trident beneath the water blazing through my brain as if trying to break through some mental barrier. Shaking my head, I forced my focus back through the viewfinder.

Simon surfed another four waves, not surprisingly scoring max points with the judges in every attempt. Gathering my towel and bag, I walked to the winner's circle to witness him receiving the first-place trophy. He took it with both hands, holding it above his head, the golden gleam sparkling under the sunrays. After posing for the cameras for several minutes, he turned to a young boy holding a surfboard beaming up at him.

He handed the trophy to the boy and ruffled his hair. "Something to inspire you. Never stop surfing, alright?"

The boy turned to the crowd and smiled wide, his two front teeth missing. "Thank you so much, Mr. Thalassa. I won't! I promise!"

Simon kept the same warm smile as he gave a final wave to the crowds. I crossed my arms, grinning. His gaze fell on me, somehow finding me within the mass of a hundred people shouting his name. A group of bikini-clad women armed with sharpies and ample cleavage called to him as he passed, begging for his autograph. Making his way through the sea of people surrounding me, he didn't so much as glance at them, leaving behind frowning women in his wake. I dropped my arms at my sides, gulping.

When he reached me, he held his hand out for me to take. "Ready for that salad?"

I'd never been so excited for leafy greens.

Nodding without words, I slipped my hand into his, the calluses on his palms scraping against my skin, making my toes grip the soles of my flip-flops.

Simon led me through the crowds, each fan stepping aside as soon as we neared them. He was Moses, parting people like the sea. After a short jolt down the boardwalk, we arrived at a small restaurant with patio seating. The name "Vesta's Greenery" hung over the entrance in jagged blue and green lettering.

"You pick a spot here and go order your salad at the counter. Do you have a favorite?" Simon pulled out a seat for me at a table facing the view of the ocean.

Smiling, I sat down, curling my hands in my lap. "Surprise me."

A glint flashed in his eye, and he gave one firm nod. "You got it."

Peeking over my shoulder, I caught a glance of his board shorts hugging the muscular ass hiding beneath. My cheeks burned, and I bit my lips as a smile crept over them. Seagulls flew overhead, some landing on lamp posts, others waddling the dock hoping for humans dropping food. Though there were ambient noises of children playing, people laughing, and varying forms of low-key music from each shop or restaurant—my ears tuned to the water crashing against the sand in the distance. I took a deep breath, soaking in the smell of salt hanging in the air.

"Here we are," Simon's smooth voice announced his return. He placed a wide bowl of colorful ingredients in front of me and handed me a fork.

I took the utensil with a sparkling grin and eyed the bits of orange sprouting between the green leaves. Poking one with my fork, I held it up. "Mango. A mango salad. How did you know mango was my favorite fruit?"

Simon tousled his short hair before sliding into his seat across from me. "I'm fairly good at reading people, and you seemed like a mango kind of gal."

Saliva collected in the corner of my mouth as I eyed the

rainbow salad in front of me—mangoes, romaine lettuce, cilantro, and hearty tomatoes. Gathering a variety on my fork, I slid the bite into my mouth and all but moaned.

"Did I pick well?"

I'd closed my eyes and lazily opened one. "Very well."

"Good." He smiled and cut his salad into more manageable pieces—cucumbers, tomatoes, olives, and sprinkled feta cheese.

"Greek?"

Simon had taken a bite and widened his eyes at me, shoving it against his cheek. "Me?"

Laughing, I tapped my fork against the plate. "Your salad."

"Oh, right." After a sheepish grin, he swallowed his food. "Yeah. It's the best. Less rabbit food and more beef to it without being actual beef, you know?" His gaze dropped to the heaping amount of green on my plate. "No offense."

"None taken. I love rabbit food."

Like shy teenagers, we smiled at each other, making bubbles erupt in my stomach.

"I have to ask. What got you into gaming? Especially on the professional level?" Simon leaned his arms on the table, bringing our faces closer.

It wasn't as short-winded of an answer as he'd probably thought.

"It's kind of personal." I shifted all the mango to one side of my plate in a pile, tomatoes on the other. "Are you sure you want to hear it?"

He took a sip of water, waiting for me to look at him. "Only if you want to share."

I want to tell you everything.

"I never knew who my parents were. I grew up in the foster care system and never ended up in a home with a normal family for more than months at a time. Not near long enough to feel like they were my family—even an adopted one." I traced a swirly shape onto my plate with the dressing.

"Why only ever for a few months?"

My palms clammed up. "I—" He met my gaze, not speaking but urging me to continue. "I used to talk to animals."

The sight of the shark from our cage dive staring at me before swimming away, the faintest tinge of thankfulness stirring from it, still swam in my thoughts. I couldn't tell a soul about it—not even Meg. She couldn't wrap her head around the shark allowing me to help it let alone say it communicated with me.

He tapped his finger on the table twice. "Don't most children at some point?"

I kept my eyes traced on him, ready to gauge his reaction. "I used to think they talked back."

And still do.

His nostrils flared, and he stared at me. He didn't lean away, didn't laugh, didn't so much as twitch.

"You're telling me no family would adopt you because you had a vivid imagination?" He frowned, forming deep creases leading from his nose to the corners of his mouth.

I shrugged, popping a mango chunk into my mouth with my fingers. "That was always my theory. Anyway, I ended up in a foster home with a dozen other kids. You can imagine how much attention we all got from the foster parents with that many kids under one roof."

His finger thudded against the table again. "You started playing video games to escape."

Heart. Squeezed.

"That's right," I whispered.

He cleared his throat as if choking on something and sipped on his water. "What uh—what games have you played?"

"You're going to laugh." I leaned back and crossed my arms.

He chuckled.

Widening my eyes, I held a hand out.

"Hey. That's not fair. You set something up like that you're asking for it." He made a "come on" gesture. "Spill."

I shoved a finger between my eyes and closed them. "I was obsessed with *Ecco The Dolphin* as a kid, and then it progressed into *Aquaria*, *Subnautica*, and most recently—*Tides of Atlantis.*"

He didn't laugh. Not even a snicker.

I opened my eyes to find a radiant smile playing across his lips.

"Seems I'm not the only aqua baby, hm?" He traced his middle fingertip in a circle over the table cloth.

"I imagine my birth mother had a water birth with me." I chewed my lip, getting lost in those eyes of his like a never-ending emerald meadow.

"Very plausible."

His foot brushed mine under the table, making me gasp.

"Shit. Sorry. Long legs." He rubbed the back of his head.

"They must be to reach these stubs." I pointed down.

He rested his chin on his palm, still not letting his eyes roam away from me. "Nothing wrong with being petite."

His words made my vision hazy, and I held my breath before harshly blowing it out. "I want to ask you something, but I don't want you to think I'm weird."

"Well, you're a gamer—a professional one at that—who's obsessed with fish and picks up trash for fun. Not sure how much weirder I can think you." A dopey smile pulled at his lips.

I dropped my jaw and grabbed a tomato from my plate, throwing it at him.

His hands flew up, blocking it with a glorious laugh roaring from his chest. "I'm kidding. I'm kidding. Ask away. Some may think I'm weird too." He scratched his ribs.

"Do you—believe in past lives?"

He coughed into his fist.

Anxiety swirled my brain, and I flattened my hands on the table. "I'm sorry. I shouldn't have asked."

"No." He cleared his throat. "No. I've just never had anyone ask me that before and it threw me off guard because—" His fingertips skirted mine on the table. "Yes. I do."

Breathing air suddenly didn't seem enough, and my chest ached—not with pain but with…hope.

"Why do you ask, Cordelia?"

I slid my hand away from his, the proximity to his skin sending me through raging rapids. "I should go. This has been incredibly lovely. But the tournament is soon, and I still need to practice, and I promised Meg a vacation if I win and—"

And I was stammering.

"Sure, but tournament?" He stood, moving behind me to pull out my chair.

I stayed seated long enough to ensure the jelly my legs had

turned into would hold me up if I decided to stand.

"A *Tides of Atlantis* eSports Tournament. I've been signed up for over a year." Scooping my bag over one arm, I slipped my sunglasses on.

"Very nice. Can I walk you back to your car?"

"Sure," I squeaked.

We were silent the few minutes it took to reach the parking lot. I fished for my keys, dropped them and immediately sank to my knees to retrieve them.

He met me on the asphalt, sliding a hand over my trembling one as I grabbed the keys. "Did I say something wrong, Cory?"

Quite the opposite.

"No, not at all. You've been nothing short of amazing, Simon." I slowly rose, and his hand fell from mine.

"Then, what is it?"

Finally managing to meet his gaze, I clutched the keys, wincing at the metal impressions pushing into my skin. "I'm not good at this."

"Good at what? Dating?" A tiny smile peeked at the corner of his lips. It wasn't a mocking gesture but an endearing one.

"Dating. Socializing in general."

"Hey." He cupped my chin. "We have all the time in the world. That is—if you want to see me again."

"Yes," I blurted.

Way to sound desperate, Cor.

"Good." He dipped his lips near mine and pressed a tender kiss to my cheek, pausing there for several seconds. "I'll see you soon, Jewel of the Sea."

He walked away, and I stood by my car, trailing my fingers

over my cheek. The kiss lingered on my skin, rippling like a stone disturbing calm water.

SEVEN

WITH THE TOURNAMENT THE following day, I'd spent every waking moment practicing my technique in *Tides of Atlantis* until my eyes couldn't stand staring at the screen any longer. I'd been at it so long I started to see *myself* as my character within the game. It would be the third tournament I've competed in, but the first focused on this game alone. Simon continued to text me, even with a simple, "Good morning," or "Hey Beautiful," but gave me distance, knowing I needed to practice. Most of the bigger tournaments happened in central or south Florida, but Pensacola decided to put their own foot in the ring and rented space at the Pensacola Bay Center to host the event.

I streamed the last few hours of my gameplay, inviting any subscribers in the area to watch me compete at the tournament. In exchange for their support, anyone wearing a shirt with my gamertag on it would receive a free swag pack

I'd leave with will call.

The morning of day one for the tournament, I packed away my game controller, charging cable, and headset. Some tournaments provided game-themed headsets for all to wear, but I wanted mine as a backup if necessary.

Pausing in front of the mirror, I smoothed out my fitted tee, staring at the SaucySiren logo—a cartoon version of me with a teal mermaid tail holding a game controller. I had yet to step foot into the convention center and could already feel the mixture of nerves and excitement swirling in my belly, competing for control. There was no telling if any other women gamers would be in attendance, but with how few we were at these events, it prickled an extra set of nerves. I didn't want to leave fellow lady gamers down.

My phone buzzed on my nightstand. A text from Meg saying she was here. Meg offered to drive us to the tournament, so I could focus on keeping calm and not dealing with traffic anxiety. I sent her a quick reply, telling her I was on my way downstairs, and grabbed my bag.

Pausing in front of my fish tank, I blew them a kiss. "Wish me luck, guys."

Several responded with vibrant flaps of their fins.

I made my way downstairs and crawled into Meg's truck with a smile. Given how high I had to step up to get into the behemoth vehicle, it always felt like mounting a horse.

"You ready?" Meg's brow bobbed.

"I only lost one match the last three days. Not sure how much more ready I could be." Pulling the door shut, I rested my bag in my lap and focused on my breathing.

"That's my girl. Mama needs a vacation." Meg winked at me before pulling out of the parking lot and turning on the radio.

The calming sounds of Aurora singing *Under The Water* soothed my erratic heartbeat.

"Please don't remind me. It only adds to the pressure I already feel. I can't place any lower than third to win enough money for the cruise."

Meg squeezed my knee and patted my thigh. "Relax. Sure, I'd love a vacation, but don't let that give you an anxiety attack in the middle of a match. I'm going to watch you kick a bunch of young dude's asses, quite frankly."

"That—" Placing my head on the rest, I turned it toward Meg with a grin. "—I can do."

"I've never been to one of these events. Anything I should know?" Meg grabbed her Chapstick from the center console, slathering some over her lips.

"It's like any other sports event. It lasts two days. Today consists of pools and brackets as losers are weeded out, and, eventually, only the best eight remain. Tomorrow is the actual final tournament or The Big Show with the crowds cheering for their favorite players. And they live stream it. So, don't get caught picking your nose or something." I bit back a smile.

Meg stuck out her bottom lip after beating her hands on the steering wheel. "Noted."

"There's also a party tonight." I kept my face forward, waiting for her response.

"A party? What kind? Costumed?"

"Definitely. But it's an actual party. Dancing, drinking, nerding out."

She raised one brow and slowly turned her head. "Nerds party? I had no idea."

"Oh, you really should see it. We may not frequent clubs, but get us together for an event like this? You better believe we know how to throw down." I flashed a sparkling grin at her.

She shook her head. "And to think I knew you."

When we arrived at the convention center, the *Tides of Atlantis* game logo in gold and teal hung over the building. I'd managed to dry my hands and keep my nerves at bay…until now. We parted ways once we walked inside, Meg heading for the restroom, and I following the signs for "athletes." Several pairs of male eyes followed me as I briskly made my way over the orange and blue swirly-patterned carpet, focusing my gaze forward.

A woman with fifties-style flared glasses and eye make-up to match shuffled papers at a table with a sign reading, "Registration." Her black hair pulled back into two small buns atop her head and chocolate-colored eyes beamed at me as I approached the table.

"Hey there." I gave a small wave. "I pre-registered. Cordelia Bourne?"

"Bourne. Bourne." She licked the tip of her forefinger and flipped through colored tabs, yanking out a sheet marked with the letter b. "Cordelia Bourne. Here we are. We just need your registration fee, and you'll be all set."

The tournament added a portion of the fees to the overall pool for the top three players at event's end. The additional amount donated by the tournament's sponsor, Blue Ring Surfing Supply, made for a hefty winning sum despite its smaller town location. After removing the credit card from my wallet, I held it up with raised brows.

"Let me cue up the tablet. Damn thing went to sleep again," the woman said, swiping a hand over the fingerprint-covered tablet, handing it to me to swipe through the attached card reader.

After paying and horribly signing my name with my finger on the touch screen, she held a lanyard to me.

"Lanyards too? How fancy." I grinned, slipping the teal and gold neck strap over my head.

She blew a bubble with her gum, popping it. "The first pool starts within the hour. Looks like you're in station three. Feel free to roam the showroom floor in the meantime. They'll announce it over the intercom."

"Thanks." I turned away, ignoring the steady increase in my heartbeat. "Oh, can a guest go on the floor, or is it for participants only?"

"Oh, honey, of course. The more, the merrier for those vendors. More of a chance they'll sell something." She winked at me before turning her attention to another approaching gamer.

Wrapping a hand around the lanyard, I found Meg and led her to the showroom floor. "I need you to keep me from buying everything in sight."

"You? I could barely talk you into buying fancy underwear for yourself, and you're worried about here?" Meg scanned the floor—rows of tables varying from toys, video games, authors, t-shirts, and c-list celebrities signing autographs.

"I'm nervous. And when I'm nervous, I buy things. And ninety percent of said things here make me squeal just looking at them." I gasped and darted to a table with Funko POP toys, swiping one of the Poseidon characters from the *Tides of Atlantis* game.

"Hey." Meg plucked it from my hands, gave a warm smile to the vendor, and placed it back on the table.

"But look at how cute his plastic beard looks." I conjured my best puppy dog eyes.

Meg folded her arms. "You place in the tournament, and I'll personally buy you the cute hunk of plastic."

"Bribery." I bumped my hip against hers. "I love it."

We spent the next thirty minutes perusing the tables, and I eventually shoved my hands in my jean pockets to make them behave.

"Attention, participants. The first round of pools is about to begin. All players assigned to stations one through six, please make your way and be ready to go within the next fifteen minutes. All guests, please enjoy the showroom floor as we will only grant entry to guests for finals tomorrow. Thank you," an announcer's voice boomed over the intercom.

"Oh my God." My hands instantly clammed up, and I wiped them on my pants. "What if I choke? What if I freeze? What if—"

Meg pressed a hand over my mouth, and I looked up at her pleadingly. "You are good at this game. I've watched you countless times. You play with thousands of people watching you and manage to make it entertaining. Just imagine there's a webcam and chat window. You'll be fine."

I nodded, and she dropped her hand.

"I saw a food court on the bottom level. Going to grab some grub. Text me, yeah?" She jutted behind her with her thumb, backpedaling on her heels.

"Yup," I squeaked, turning for the signs directing participants to the gaming arena.

During the pools and brackets, the setup wasn't entirely impressive—rows of monitors and swiveling gaming chairs positioned far enough apart each player couldn't see the others' screen. The final round was when they pulled out all the stops. All it was missing was a cage and it'd look like an MMA fight. I waited in the foyer for them to open the door and allow us to settle into our stations.

A younger man I didn't recognize ducked his head in front of me, scanning my shirt. "Well, well. If it isn't SaucySiren." His mop of dirty blonde hair fell over his blue-gray eyes, and he flicked his head, throwing it out of his face.

"I'm sorry. Do I know you?" I bobbed my brow.

He pointed at his lanyard, displaying the username ProteinGeyser. The player who tried to snipe me when I saved my fish from dying.

I narrowed my eyes. "Do we have a problem?"

"You got lucky, Saucy." He sniffed once, folding his hands behind his back and turning away from me. "I'm not sure what you tried to pull using the trident, but I can tell you, this is the big leagues."

Every doubt and uncontrollable bubbling of nerves I'd felt the past hours—gone.

"Absolutely. Besides, the trident takes actual skill to wield."

I lifted my chin, making myself taller standing beside his six-foot self.

He bent backward, pressing a hand over his stomach. "A girl shit talker. Oh, I'm looking forward to this."

"All players move to your stations," the announcer said.

I could've continued the verbal jabs, but I needed to focus—get my head in the game.

Especially now.

A *Tides of Atlantis* headset rested at each station. After removing my gaming controller, I sat down, wiggling myself in the seat and adjusting the height until I felt comfortable. Geyser was several stations away from me, which I preferred considering I could only ignore his death stare into the side of my head for so long.

There were several gameplay styles with person versus person—team deathmatch, capture the flag, controlling zones, but what *Tides of Atlantis* focused on—was individual "Free for All." The game unleashed players on a rotating map, unaware of where the other five players spawned in. Using your wits, listening for signs of nearby players, and utilizing attack and defense, you'd play until the first player reached twenty-five terminations.

Almost an hour had gone by the time it was Geyser and me at the top, tied each with twenty-four kills. The next would win the pool and have a reserved spot in the winner's bracket. They'd purposely selected maps with a shorter range, making it quicker to find someone and not as many places to hide. I followed the shore to help track where I was on the map but hugged the tree line to conceal myself.

"Why you hiding, Saucy?" Geyser yelled from his station loud enough for me to hear *through* my headset.

A sound similar to a hundred orca whales calling out in unison blasted through my head, making me wince, but also making me hyper-focused. A twig snapped behind me, and I rotated my analog stick in time to see Geyser leaping into the air with his sword held above his head, readying to land a heavy attack. Pressing the left trigger button at the opportune moment, I blocked him, sending sparks flying. My hands tensed along with my shoulders and I took a deep breath.

I needed to focus on something to relax my mind. Tingles shot down my arm like water rippled over them. Simon's eyes. That smile. A genuine interest in everything I said during our date. My thumbs flew over the buttons, dodging at critical moments, striking when I saw a possible clearing.

Another player attacked us from the side, trying to take advantage of us distracted by the other, but I yanked my second weapon, a xiphos from my back, and pressed the "y" button, launching it into the player's chest for an insta-kill. Geyser launched another combo attack, and I timed the deflection just right for my character to perform a move that rendered him swordless. With one push of the "x" button, I threw one light attack…and that was that.

"We have our winner. Please make your way back into the foyer and wait for instructions on stations for your assigned brackets."

Every player stopped to shake my hand once we'd left the arena with wide grins plastered on their faces and congratulating me and my skills. Geyser appeared in front of me like a looming shadow.

"You think you've seen the last of me? I'll work my way up that losers bracket to be in the final tomorrow." His thin arm lifted to point in my face.

I leaned away with a grimace. "At least you have a plan. See you tomorrow then?" Before he had time to retort, I turned with a flip of my hair.

Hopefully, it hit him in the face.

The remaining pools and brackets commenced, weeding out the weaker players, enticing anxiety and excitement packed into a singular arena with each passing hour. Geyser did as he promised, winning the top spot in the loser's bracket and gaining the last opportunity for the eight finalists. Finishing second in the winner's bracket did nothing for my nerves, but it was a guaranteed spot in the finals. I'd make up for it tomorrow.

They'd outfitted one of the many large ballrooms in the convention center to host the party for players, fans, and guests. An electronic song called *Freaks* by Timmy Trumpet blasted through the room, the bass vibrating in my chest. I'd always enjoyed the jazzy element the trumpets added to his songs. His music became a regular on my numerous gaming playlists. As I promised, there were indeed people in costume. Some were dressed as characters from the cut screen storyline of the *Tides of Atlantis* game, while others partied as generic mermaids, crabs, and pirates—which were *not* in the game.

"Mind. Blown," Meg mumbled.

I elbowed her. "Told ya."

"Do any of these players ever get so completely shit-faced they can't compete the next day?" Meg stepped aside as a giant lobster in glasses walked past, holding drinks in both hands.

"Usually not for finals, but I've heard of people missing their scheduled time for pools and getting disqualified for sure."

"I kinda dig that. Rock star lifestyle as a gamer?" Meg grinned while tapping her hand against her hip to the beat.

"The big-time pros do live like that. The game companies will pay for their lodging, shower them with sponsor gifts. Some of the big teams even have live-in chefs." I tossed my lanyard, making it do one rotation around my neck.

Meg paused and shot her gaze to me. "No shit."

Geyser stood at the opposite side of the room, glaring at me with one eye through the sea of bouncing bodies. He lifted his fists like he held a sword and slashed the air in front of him before pointing at me.

"Who the hell is that?" Meg's shoulders rolled back.

"Apparently, my arch-nemesis. Can he be any more dramatic?"

Meg shoved her jacket sleeves to her elbows. "Need me to remind him what humility looks like?"

I grabbed her elbow and coaxed her toward the bar. "I'll remind him in-game tomorrow. Trust me."

"Have I told you how much I love this side of you?" Meg leaned on the bar top, hunching forward. "I'm totally crushing on you right now." She winked before nudging me with her boot.

"Oh, be quiet and shove a drink in your face." I slid some cash to the bartender after grabbing the two beer bottles they'd rested in front of me.

After handing her one, I turned my back to the bar only

to be met with a man not much taller than me in a white toga—more like a bedsheet—a plastic trident under his arm, and a fake grey beard was partially falling off his face from failed glue.

"Are you—" He swayed as he spoke and dropped his eyes to my shirt with a gasp. "You are. Holy shit. I watch your Glitch stream every damn week. You're hellah good. And if I may say so—" He leaned in, tripping over his own feet. "Very, very cute."

Meg slid closer to me.

After discreetly waving in front of me from the stench of his beer breath hanging in the air between us, I plastered a smile. "Thank you. I appreciate the support."

"It's why I'm dressed like this. To honor your mad trident skills."

I stole a glance at Meg, who shrugged, not interfering but also not leaving me to fend for myself. "Oh? Are you one of the characters?"

"Just call me…Poseidon." He bowed, tripping again.

I bit the inside of my cheek to keep from laughing.

"What you need to call—is a cab," a deep voice said from behind "Poseidon."

Simon.

EIGHT

"POSEIDON" SCRUNCHED HIS NOSE and shuffled away, slurring words at a group of young men laughing and pointing at him.

"Simon?" I couldn't help the insanely wide grin pulling at my cheeks. "What are you doing here?"

Meg waved at him before hanging an arm on my shoulder and resting her chin on it. "Remember when he and I exchanged e-mails about the logo files? He asked me what tournament you were in, and so—I told him."

I let my jaw slack. "You two conspired behind my back?"

"It was for the most honorable of reasons, I assure you." His grin sparkled as he pressed a hand to his chest.

"I'm happy you came, but you didn't need to. I know this scene can't be much your deal?"

Meg playfully punched my shoulder.

"You making assumptions about hunky surfers again?" He

pointed at me with his thumb and forefinger.

I crossed my arms. "Hunky?"

"Am I wrong?"

His eyes never failed to captivate. This time it was enough to make me forget how to speak, so I shook my head.

"I got us seats next to each other." Meg shoved a ticket at Simon. "Cool with you?"

"Absolutely. We can look clueless yet excited together." He curled the ticket into his palm.

"Bruh, you're Simon Thalassa. I don't believe this," a thin, younger man with auburn hair past his shoulders wearing a *Halo* t-shirt and cargo pants said from beside us.

Not missing a beat, Simon jutted his hand for a shake. "Indeed I am. How's it hangin'?"

"Dude, an honor to meet you. Truly. Been following your surf competitions since I was a kid."

Meg and I didn't exist in this man's eyes as he remained fixed on Simon.

"Appreciate the support."

"Anyway, sorry to have bothered you."

"Have fun." Simon threw up a "hang loose" gesture with his thumb and pinky, the fan responding in kind with a wide smile.

"Even recognizable at gaming tournaments, huh?" I chewed on my thumbnail.

"Hey, I'm as surprised as you are. And do you think people realize telling them you've been into something since you were a kid is both flattering and depressing all in one sentence?" He let out a throaty chuckle, rubbing the back of his buzz-cut head.

I smiled, but it faded as soon as I caught sight of the time. "Simon, I appreciate that you came, but I need to head to bed. I'll look for you in the crowd tomorrow."

"Should I bring one of those foam fingers? An air horn, maybe?" He slid his hands in his pockets.

"Just yourself and a set of lungs to cheer me on, Big Guy."

"Can do."

Our eyes locked, swirling my stomach into a series of tidal waves and sinkholes. Grabbing Meg by her jacket, I forced her to force *me* from the ballroom.

"You didn't want to hang out with him more? I'm confused." Meg ruffled her hair.

"I need to focus. And he distracts me in the best ways possible but still…distracts me." I rubbed between my eyebrows.

"You got it bad, my friend. It's great to see you this—fluttery over someone."

I was a ravenous humpback whale with an endless appetite for Simon krill.

Finals day.

My nerves and excitement fought a deathmatch within my stomach. The arena had transformed overnight into a battleground spectacle fit for gaming. A center circular stage housed six walled stations with chairs, monitors, and headsets. Stadium seating surrounded the stage, filled to the brim with hundreds of fans. Jumbo screens hung from the ceiling, switching feeds from each of our screens or shots of our faces.

Whenever they'd show me, I would more than likely be furrowing my brow with my mouth wide open the entire time.

I wrung my hands together as the game's menu theme music blared through the arena with resounding bass drums and ethereal violin and cello. As the announcer called us to our stations, I scanned the seats, spotting Meg and Simon sitting dead center, smiling at me. Simon sat up straight, and his grin melted into something else entirely as we caught each other's gazes.

Before a match, I always built myself up until I felt like I could take on the world. But that look in Simon's eyes—told me I could *own* the world.

The nerves flittered away, and I took my seat, putting on metaphorical blinders from the rest of the arena as I slid my headset on. The crowd already went wild, but I'd drown them out to concentrate. Announcers would talk strategy and segments as the game progressed, but we wouldn't hear any of it.

The game began, and hours went by of sword slashing, trident striking, mythical sea creatures we'd have to kill before returning to terminating each other. It became abundantly clear that the player to beat was PudgyPop, a male veteran pro-gamer at the ripe age of twenty—that's right, *twenty*. He led the charge with six more terminations than me and was only three away from winning it all. I'd yet to run into him in-game, and planned to avoid him at all costs. Being the last kill someone needed to win *and* causing me to lose the title? No thanks.

I'd done well not coming face-to-face with Geyser either

until we neared the end. When his character stepped from behind a tree, I felt my cheeks warm. We were tied with kills, and PudgyPop only had one remaining, which meant whoever won this duel—would get second place. Processing his weak points from the several times I'd fought him, I was able to take him out within thirty seconds, with Pudgy taking first place. I finished second, but more importantly, I beat Geyser—again.

They called the three of us to a raised podium stage to announce the first annual *Tides of Atlantis* Tournament winners. After shaking hands with Pudgy, congratulating him, I bolted from the stage to Meg's awaiting arms.

"You freaking did it. I'm so proud you wiped the floor with that Geyser prick." She playfully slapped my shoulder. "Too bad you didn't get first, though."

"Pudgy is good. Really good. He may even get a sponsorship out of that performance. But, it doesn't matter. Second place is more than enough money for a cruise."

Simon approached with his hands in his pockets and a cheeky smile. "That was incredibly hot to watch."

"Oh, yeah?" I sucked my bottom lip as I bumped my knuckle against his arm.

"I especially love your concentration face." He lifted his hands like he held a controller, furrowed his brow, and stuck his tongue to the corner of his mouth.

Laughing, I glanced at Meg before turning back to him. "I don't stick my tongue out."

"Uh, you do, Cor." Meg shrugged.

"You do. Honestly, I don't think you could make an ugly face if you tried." Simon chuckled, his green eyes twinkling as he gazed down at me.

I displayed several different expressions on my face, including going cross-eyed, making the tendons in my neck bulge, and puffing my cheeks like a blowfish.

Meg and Simon shook their heads.

"Still disgustingly adorable," Meg mumbled.

Simon lowered his lips to my ear and whispered, "Have fun on your cruise, Sea Jewel. Call me when you get back, hm?" He touched the crook of my arm, a brief brush of skin that felt like grazing the body of a stingray.

He walked past me, stealing a glance over his shoulder right before exiting the arena. The man had a presence about him that could make the ocean itself bend to his will. And I apparently would be floating right along with it.

Meg whisked through the options of onboard activities, and when neither pool volleyball nor trivia struck her fancy, we headed straight for the casino. We sat in adjacent stools, the ship having shoved off hours prior. I played with the strap of my aquamarine maxi dress, bobbing the top sandal-covered foot of my crossed legs as I repeatedly pressed the "go" button on the machine. Various fruits lined up and exploded on the screen, occasionally adding twenty-five cents to my total before being taken away in the next round.

"Whatever happened to pulling a lever? This feels too much like a video game with none of the skill and all the luck," I mumbled, popping another quarter into the machine.

"Welcome to the twenty-first century, my friend." Meg's leather bomber jacket creaked every time she raised her arm. "We could always try our hand at roulette."

"I would have virtually no idea what I'm doing, but I'd gladly blow on dice for you and watch." I smiled at my best friend and hit the "Cash Out" button with extra enthusiasm. After ripping the exposed ticket from its slot, I shoved it into a pocket of my dress.

Meg fake cried, dabbing a knuckle at the corner of each eye. "You'd be my Lady Luck? How thoughtful."

I looped my arm with hers, and without batting an eyelash, she approached the first open spot at a roulette table. Shoving my clutch under my arm, I snagged two watered-down cocktail drinks from a tray as the waiter passed.

Meg slid the "cash out" ticket from the slot machines to the dealer, and he handed over the same amount in chips. Sipping on my rum and coke, I spied the table as if I knew how the game worked. Sure, there were black and red and numbers, but all the squares intended for player bets? No clue.

After Meg made her bet, she pushed her palms against the table's edge, idly tapping her boot. I slid my foot over hers, suggesting she tried not to show her nerves on her sleeve without using any words. Elbowing her, I held the drink out with a grin, wiggling it.

The small white ball sprung over the spinning wheel, pinging and panging as it bounced, finally landing on a black number seventeen.

Meg threw her non-drink-holding hand into a fist in the air. "I didn't lose any money that round, so it's a start."

"What's your criteria for stopping for the night? Profiting?" I sipped my drink, eyeing a man over the rim who was staring at Meg's butt in her skinny leather pants. And he wasn't trying to hide it.

"Profiting." She snorted. "That's rare. But I make a point to never walk out of a casino without at least half of what I started with, ideally as *much* as I started with."

The man licked his lips before swatting the man next to him in the stomach and starting a strut aimed at Meg.

I wrapped my arm around her lower back, resting my chin on her shoulder, hoping he'd take a hint.

Meg raised a brow at me. "Unwanted suitor?"

"Mmhm. Six o'clock and currently retreating."

"I shall do the same for you on this trip if you're fully invested in Mr. Surfer, but in the meantime, if you don't mind," Meg started before holding dice up that the dealer slid her.

I blew on them with a grin. "Yes. I'm invested."

She played for another twenty minutes, winning all of her money back plus a hundred extra dollars. After cashing in her chips, she turned to me with a wink. "I know what you want to do."

"Oh? Think you know me that well?"

"Topdeck. The view of the ocean must be crazy up there."

I played with my fingers behind my back, attempting to hide my antsy fidgeting. "I'm sure it's quite pleasant."

"Oh my God." She rolled her eyes and grabbed me by the crook of the elbow. "Come on, you."

After climbing the stairs several levels, the sight of the moon reflecting off that dark rippling water surrounding us drowned any breath before it had a chance to escape my throat.

"The views in Pensacola are amazing, but this—surrounded by water and not a shoreline insight is another matter entirely." I leaned my hips on the railing and threw my arms out to either side of me. I was Kate Winslet, and this was my Titanic moment.

"This is rather majestic. I have to admit." Meg joined me at the railing, bending forward and resting her elbows on it.

My phone buzzed in my clutch, and I jumped, snatching it.

Simon: Enjoying yourself? I'm sure the views are amazing from the top deck.

Furrowing my brow, I did a quick turn, half expecting to see him on board. He'd shown up at the tournament without a word until he was there. I wouldn't put anything past him now.

After snapping a quick photo of the ocean from my point of view, I replied to him, attaching it.

Me: You must be psychic.

Simon: :(Aw. No selfie with the ocean behind you?

Biting my lip, I quickly peeked at Meg, who was distracted by the view. Flashing a pearly grin, I held the phone out in front of me and snapped the photo, sending it to him.

Meg snorted.

I whipped my head in her direction. "What?"

"It's fun seeing you revert to what I'd imagine is a teenage version of yourself when you like someone." Meg bumped her shoulder against mine.

Heat pooled in my cheeks as I bit back another smile.

Simon: Positively gorgeous. :)

Whether he referred to the ocean or me, or both, would

remain a mystery. The butterflies still performed a symphony in my belly all the same.

"Time will tell but, I do have a soft spot for this guy." Curling my hair over one ear, I slipped the phone back in my clutch and lifted my gaze in time to see dolphins leaping through the water. I slapped Meg's arm and pointed. "Look over there."

Meg gasped and slid closer to me. "How cool. I'll never get tired of seeing dolphins in the wild. They look so carefree."

I've loved all aquatic animals throughout my life, but dolphins had a special place in my heart. Meg had it right. They were carefree, jovial, and playful—everything I wanted to be and more.

"How many sharks have we cage dived with and still never swam with dolphins?" I rested my head on her shoulder, still watching the pod of four as they dove in and out of the water, communicating to each other in squeaks.

"Something we'll need to rectify when we get back."

Letting out a contented sigh, I stood and faced her. "What would you like to do tomorrow?"

"I'm not a hard woman to please, Cor. So long as it isn't something I'll embarrass myself in public, I'm game for anything." She clutched the railing and leaned back, swinging her hips to and fro.

I clicked my nails against the metal, turning my gaze away, and contemplated my next words. "Did you—happen to see the flyer in the lobby? The one for the LGBTQ brunch?"

She raised one brow. "I did. But dismissed it considering that'd mean ditching you."

"It's not ditching me. We're still on the same boat and can meet up later. We have days on this cruise, Meg." I tugged on her jacket. "You might meet someone."

"But what the hell are you going to do then?" She hunched forward, resting her forearms on the railing and tapping her non-existent fingernails together.

"Sunbathe on this deck. I could be out here for hours and be perfectly happy."

The sun warming my cheeks, light whispers of the roiling water as the ship's engine propelled us through it, and the echoes of birds cawing as they flew overhead.

"Are you sure?" Meg squinted at me as if the sun were in her eyes.

I patted my hands against the metal to the tune of *Beyond the Sea*. "Yes. You'll have fun. I'm sure of it."

"Thanks, Cory." Meg side-hugged me, and we stood in silence, watching the ocean.

I'd been lying on the top deck for the better part of an hour, soaking the sunrays and rotating. I lay on my stomach, and a buzz vibrated my clutch. Resting my chin on my forearm, I smiled to myself. Either I'd begun to expect Simon's texts, or I recently developed a form of ESP. After swiping the screen to unlock it, my grin widened.

Simon: You can tell me to stop checking in on you every day at any point in time. You know that, right? ;)

I slid my sunglasses to my head.

Me: Would it scare you away if I said your texts are the highlight of my day?

Pinching my lips, I hovered my finger over the send button for an extra moment before pressing it.

Simon: Absolutely not. You don't have some weird taxidermy collection hidden in a closet somewhere or something, right?

I laughed out loud, noticing the empty benches surrounding me on the deck for the first time. Completely alone and free to make an ass of myself as I pleased.

Me: I'm a conservationist. What do you think?

Simon: Had to check. ;)

A loud explosion sounded from nearby, echoing off the ship's hull. I sat up with a gasp, clutching my phone to my chest to not drop it. Without thinking, I ran to the railing, searching in the direction of the disturbance.

Several motorboats bounced against the waves, speeding alongside the cruise liner. They all held large, slender devices in their hands but were too far away to make out what they were. A knot slowly coiled and tightened in my stomach.

Pirates.

I lost my footing as the ship lurched forward, picking up speed.

"Attention all passengers. If you are in your cabin, remain inside and do not leave until we give the clear. All others proceed to the lower decks immediately. This is not a drill," a voice said over the loudspeakers.

My heart raced, and I stumbled backward, fumbling with my phone.

Me: Pirates.

Simon: Pirates? Pirates, what?

Surely the cruise ship would be able to outmaneuver speed boats. The boats drifted further away, the vessel gaining distance, and I let my tense shoulders drop. The faintest sight of several large octopus-like tentacles curled beneath the boats in a barrage of sea foam and waves, launching them faster through the water. I gripped the railing, breaths escaping me.

Simon: Cory, why did you say, pirates?

I blinked away water beads forming on my eyelashes and shot my attention to my phone, dropping to my knees and crawling out of sight.

Me: We're about to be boarded.

Simon: What??? Find a place to hide, and do NOT leave for anything.

I slid my phone away and grabbed my tank top and shorts, slipping them on before crawling to the atrium.

Meg.

The anxiety roiling through me had me chilled and shaking.

They held the brunch on the opposite side of the ship, several floors down. I'd never make it to her in time.

Me: Meg, hide somewhere NOW. Don't come looking for me.

Meg: Are you out of your fucking mind? I'm already on my way up to you.

"Shit. Shit. *Shit.*"

The blast of several water cannons firing from the ship roared all around me. After finding a suitable corner, I pushed my back to it and closed my eyes, trying to calm myself enough to breathe normally. I hoped the sound of blissful silence would follow the thwart of the cannons. Gunfire rattled off the metal walls around me, and I clapped my hands over my ears.

In a language I didn't understand, various male voices spoke with urgency near the railing I'd been standing by only moments ago. I pressed my back to the wall as if it'd swallow me—shield me within its womb. The voices grew closer, and I shoved my mouth to my knees, suppressing the whimpers threatening to leak out.

A loud splash sounded, followed by one man yelling, several shots rang out, and I dropped to the floor, covering my head— thuds, screams, more gunfire, and then…silence.

The ship guards? Whoever it was, had no idea they saved me.

Slowly rising to my feet, I peered out the small circular window of the atrium door, my harsh breaths fogging it. Nothing. No men. No weapons. Simply a soaking wet deck.

"Cory?" Meg's loud whispers seeped through the door behind me.

Staying on my knees, I reached for the door handle, cracking it. Meg crouched through the atrium, turning circles, looking for me.

"Meg," I whispered back.

Meg's eyes widened once she spotted me, tears welling in her eyes—a rarity for her. She dropped to her hands and knees, crawling to me.

"Are you alright?" She gripped my shoulder, tremors lacing her voice.

"I'm glad you're here, Meg, but that was so stupid," I

chastised, fear coating my heart like hardened wax.

She furrowed her brow. "You can slap my hand later. I don't know what I would've done if something happened to you and I wasn't here."

More male voices leaked through the door. I sucked in a breath and slid a hand over Meg's mouth.

The language remained indecipherable, but I picked up one word—Skylla.

My hand fell away from Meg's lips, limply landing in my lap. Why did I recognize that word?

The door flew open, and a man in a full ski mask, black jacket, pants, and boots, holding a rifle, grabbed me by the hair, hoisting me to my feet.

Meg stood with an outstretched arm. "Take me instead."

The man babbled, waving the point of his weapon around. I winced at the pain surging through my skull from his death grip on my hair. I dug my nails into his hand in a panic, and he tugged harder.

"Please. Don't hurt her," Meg pleaded, holding her open palms up.

The man pointed down with the barrel, yelling over and over.

"Meg. Just do what he says. They're probably looking for a ransom." I'd gone beyond the point of fear. The anxiety ebbed away, replaced by numbness.

"Cory." Meg's voice cracked as she slowly sunk to her knees, her chest heaving.

"It'll be alright, Meg." Words meant to soothe us both—a hopeful declaration.

The corners of Meg's jaw bobbed as we stared at each other. The man pulled me to the deck, shoving me against the railing. My phone flew from my pocket, crashing to the wooden planks, dislodging the battery, and cracking the screen. Four men huddled in a circle, shouting, pointing, and dragging hands over their mask-covered heads.

Water sloshed over the side of the deck, a mirage following—a flash that resembled the silhouette of a human being. The men turned on their heels in a panic, aiming their weapons. One man panicked, his trigger finger twitching, sending a bullet flying—straight into my shoulder.

The pain shot down my arm, and all I could hear was my heavy breathing as I leaned back, the world circling into chaos around me. The blue sky dipped into view as my head fell back, followed by the rest of me.

A man roared the word "no" into the wind as I fell and fell, splashing into the murky waters below. Darkness overtook me, and I sank, the depths opening their watery cold embrace to me. A jolt sprung through my chest. Visions warped through my mind like a slideshow gone maniacal. Each flash was of myself—but not. Me in the Middle Ages, my dark brown hair falling in wavy tendrils to my knees. The Roman Empire. A Highlands battleground. Norway. Colonial America. The Old West. The Roaring Twenties—my hair cropped short, a fringed dress hugging my curves in a speakeasy.

My eyes flew open, and I gasped, sucking in water through my lungs like the gills of a fish.

I remember.

NINE

BREATHING UNDERWATER CAME AS easy as on land—the steady rhythm through my nose or mouth. My dark hair floated in light wisps, curling over my arms as the current washed over me—patches of bioluminescent blue scales scattered over my skin. Something stirred behind me, and I whirled around, dragging my fingers through the water and sending a swirl of bubbles. Simon floated in front of me, a cinch in his brow, staring at me with that radiant emerald gaze.

I knew him.

As I reached forward, keeping my gaze focused on his eyes, the specific part of him I recognized, his expression fell. It resembled someone who'd been punched in the gut but transgressed into shock and soon—relief.

He spun in the water, kicking up so many bubbles it impeded my vision. When he stopped, he was no longer the short-haired surfer I'd met on the beach. He appeared as I knew him with his long hair, falling past his shoulders and full beard.

"Poseidon?" I said, the water welcoming my words and not distorting them.

His brow furrowed, and he swam toward me, letting me touch the side of his face. No sooner had my skin brushed his, he closed his eyes with a contented sigh. "Amphitrite."

"I don't understand what's going on." I tangled my fingers through his wet beard. This was the man I knew. The god. My husband. My king.

I snapped my hand away and turned my gaze down. *Was* my husband. The suppressed emotions punched at my skull—hurt, abandonment, guilt.

"Amph, look at me." His large hand cupped my chin as he lifted my eyes to his. "We have a lot to talk about, but right now, I need to stop the rest of those pirates from taking over the ship."

That first group of pirates. The mysterious force that made them all disappear.

"You've been here since I texted you. Haven't you?" I stared into his eyes, welcoming the safety they had always exuded like our hideaway grotto.

He nodded and took my hand in his. "All things we can talk about later."

Before I could say any more, he catapulted us through the water like a great white shark readying to breach the surface. We landed on the deck. With ill-practiced sea legs, I fell to my knees, sputtering water.

A memory sizzled over my brain, my knees crashing

against the wet wooden planks of a classic tall ship. Night had overtaken the sky—a storm making thunder boom overhead, the rain pouring over the boat in droves. My soaked linen dress clung to my legs as I scrambled, my long dark hair stuck to my face. A burly man with a shaved head, his bronze skin caked with oil and tar despite the rain, barreled toward me, a toothless grin pulling at his lips. My chest pumped with erratic breaths as I backpedaled on my heels, colliding with the wooden mast, my neck brushing against the coiled rope around it. He snatched my wrists, and I screamed, pinching my eyes closed.

"Amph, it's me," Poseidon's voice soothed.

Refusing to look, I shook my head, trying to force the memory away.

"Amphitrite," Poseidon yelled.

My eyes flew open, and I stared up at him, my wrists held within Poseidon's delicate grasp, concern furrowed in his brow.

"This is all too much, Seid. So many years of memories. How am I going to filter through them all without it driving me mad?" My limbs went limp as I slumped to the deck as if defeated.

"Look at me." He tugged one wrist and slipped his fingers under my chin.

Doing as he asked, I lifted my eyes to his, my gaze blurring with tears.

"You *can* do this because you have to. You need to find Meg."

"Meg," I breathed out, wincing at my buzzing brain.

"Amphitrite. You *will* get through this. And I know because you are the strongest woman I've ever met. Even twice." His callused thumb circled my cheek.

I slipped my hand over his and a weak smile quirked my lip.

"But right now, sweetheart, I need you to *move*."

Meg. I couldn't lose her. It was enough to force me to my feet, holding onto Poseidon's arms as leverage.

"Meg is right around the corner. You'll have to go on your own. I can't have anyone noticing me." He pinched my chin with two fingers. "You're going to be alright. They won't get that close to you again. I promise you." His last words rolled off his tongue in a snarl.

"Go stop those assholes."

Poseidon backed away with the grace of the sea god I knew him to be and pointed at my arm. "You'll need to make those disappear."

"I—I don't know how to do that. I don't remember." I held my arms up and stared at the glowing scales, shaking my limbs as if that were the answer.

He delicately pinned my arms at my sides, the calluses on his palms making my toes curl. "Close your eyes and think about them disappearing. Will them back to the sea."

Doing as instructed, I let my lids shut and thought of nothing but the vast empty ocean. Calling to it, I beseeched it to hide my scales—my true self—until I beckoned for it again.

Poseidon's lips brushed my cheek, his beard tickling my skin. "They're gone. We *will* talk about all of it."

With a shaky breath, I blinked my eyes back open. "When?"

He was gone.

I bolted around the corner, finding Meg curled against the

same wall I'd been. "Meg, it's me," I whispered, trying not to startle her.

"Cory?" Meg stared at me wide-eyed before launching at me, pulling me down, and hugging me.

"I'm okay. Everything's going to be fine. We just need to stay put." The anxiety I'd felt melted away with the knowledge of who was on board, ridding the decks of pond scum.

She peeled away and touched my face, my shoulders. "I don't understand. You're soaking wet, and I *heard* that gunshot. It took everything in me not to scream."

"They did shoot but missed. It startled me, and I fell overboard."

It felt so wrong to lie to Meg. What's worse—it was the first in a forthcoming string of hidden truths. How did someone tell their best friend they were a sea goddess in a past life? A queen? The instances she couldn't explain my connection to sea life were because I could speak to them and control them.

"How the hell did you get back on deck, Cor?" Her eyes frantically searched my face, her lips thinning.

"You know I'm a strong swimmer. Besides, I knew I needed to get back for you." A weak smile tugged at my lips.

Lies. Lies. *Lies.*

Meg was an intelligent human being. The situation warranted her questioning expression, and I braced for the impact of her fiery interrogation techniques.

"Ladies and gentleman, the situation has been contained. We are turning course for the nearest port, and as a safety precaution, we ask all guests to migrate to the bottom deck for the duration of the trip. Upon arrival in San Juan, you will be given complimentary flight service back to Orlando and a full refund. We hope you'll still consider a future cruise with Calypso Cruises, and we deeply apologize for today's occurrence," an announcer voiced across the deck over the intercom.

"Let's get below decks." I helped Meg to her feet.

As we walked, Meg stayed deathly quiet, switching between rubbing the back of her neck and running a finger over her eyebrow.

"You okay?" I risked more questions asking this, but I couldn't in good conscience pretend I wasn't concerned. We'd gone through a life-threatening ordeal. It could rattle anyone.

"All things considered? Yeah. But I can't get past something." Meg shook her fist as if she played roulette again.

"Oh?" A barnacle formed in my throat.

I wasn't ready for this conversation. I'd yet to figure out things for myself, let alone explain it to someone who had no idea our world existed.

"There is no feasible way that boat could've caught up with the speed of this cruise ship. Not to mention the water cannons. It barely phased them. How?" She snapped her gaze to mine, her jaw tightening.

All valid questions. And the answers I knew lay with Poseidon.

"I don't know, Meg." I frowned and hugged her to my side.

When we reached the lower decks, hundreds of people scattered the tables they'd spaced throughout, including a dozen buffet counters with various foods and bottled water. It took several hours to travel back to San Juan and another couple of hours to fly to Orlando. With our vacation cut short,

I accepted a job offer to fill in for a tour guide who called in sick at an aquarium in Orlando. Meg hadn't complained much, considering she planned to spend the day with Mickey in the Magic Kingdom. I told her to grab me a pair of Little Mermaid mouse ears.

Donning my striking oversized blue polo with the Brizo Aquarium logo over my left boob, I led a small group of attendees. Two parents carted their twin toddlers in a conjoined stroller, an elderly couple who couldn't stop making googly eyes at each other, and two young women who spent more time taking selfies for social media than looking at the fish.

We approached the jellyfish tank, and my heart wrenched. Their anxiety pulsed through me in waves. They wanted to be in the open ocean. Their appreciation for being in the tank and out of harm's way was evident, but it couldn't compare to freedom. Gulping down the anger and irritation storming in my core, I drowned them out as best I could before I suddenly started Operation: Free the Fish in the middle of a public aquarium.

"A little known fact, but jellyfish are one of the oldest multi-organ animals, having been around for at least six hundred million years." I referenced the floating, gracefully flapping jellyfish with a hand, beaming at my tour group.

"Wow. Before the dinosaurs?" The older man asked, wrapping his arms around his wife from behind her.

"Yup. Even before the dinosaurs, before plants or fungi in fact, as well."

One of the young women finally lifted her nose with a sneer. "I still think they're aliens. They don't have brains or any other real guts for that matter."

"Fair point. But they do have an advanced nervous system. Does anyone know what all their receptors can detect?" I lifted my brows, waiting for an answer.

"Vibrations?" The mother of the family of four chimed in.

I pointed at her with a smile. "That's one thing."

When silence fell over them, I folded my hands behind my back. "They also help detect light and chemicals in the water. With these extra senses and their gravity navigation abilities, it's how they chart themselves through their environment."

"Have you heard of the immortal jellyfish found in the Mediterranean Sea?" A deep husky voice asked from behind the crowd.

Every nerve in my body sparked like tridents clashing.

Poseidon.

The small group of tourists stepped aside as Poseidon made his way forward. He was utter perfection with his hair down in wavy tendrils, sculpted full beard, Henley shirt with the sleeves rolled, exposing his tanned corded forearm muscles. I plucked at the buttons of my polo, somehow remembering flashes of our times spent together in bed. The way he rolled his hips. The feel of his beard brushing my inner thighs when he—

"Miss?" The older woman asked, making me jolt from my daydream.

"Yes. Sorry. I'm sorry. That concludes the tour. If there aren't any questions, please enjoy the rest of your stay here at Brizo Aquarium." With a quick, bland smile to reassure the tourists, I curled my hand with Poseidon's arm and dragged him to an alcove where few attendees walked.

Poseidon smiled wide, his bright white teeth shining in stark contrast to his darker beard. "You look adorable in that polo, but they didn't have a smaller size?" He chuckled, pointing at the length draped to my knees like a dress.

I pulled at the hem, feeling my cheeks warm. "How did you find me?"

His brows bobbed as he stared at me, waiting for me to answer my own question.

I palmed my forehead. "Right. I don't remember how to use my—" Lowering my voice, I leaned into him. "I don't remember how to use my powers."

"Amph, you're not going to have them all anyway. You're mortal." He rubbed my shoulder, a sympathetic pout melting over his lips.

Turning away from him, I flopped onto the bench facing the Mediterranean Sea tank. "You can't call me that in public, *Simon*."

Poseidon winced before sitting in the space beside me. "You finally realize who you are, and we still have to pretend. The irony."

"And why are you still in your true form? How is Simon Thalassa going to explain growing long hair and a beard overnight?" I ran my fingers through his blonde tendrils and gulped.

By Olympus, he was beautiful.

"I'll tell them magic. They'll think I'm being a smart ass and forget about it in a week. Guaranteed." He smirked and gripped the bench's edge, moving his gaze to watch the fish—a blue tint flowing over his features from the tank lights.

"Besides, I don't ever want to lose that look on your face when you saw the real me and *knew* who I was."

As pleased as I was to see him and as grateful as I was to no longer be stuck in the sky as a constellation, we had such a rocky past, he and I.

"I don't know where to start with this," I whispered, my nose stinging, threatening tears.

"Yeah. Not sure there's a written protocol for a situation like this, Starfish."

The nickname made my heart swan dive, and I snapped my gaze to his, tears clouding my vision.

He gave a sheepish smile, cocking his head to one side, causing his hair to fall in glorious shambles over one eye. Reaching a hand, he swiped a rolling tear from my cheek with his thumb. "We both did some things. Some—horrible things. But it was a lifetime ago. I'd like to think we're—" He bent forward, dropping his hands between his knees.

"Getting a second chance," I finished for him.

He nodded, lifting his eyes back to the colorful fish in front of us. "If we want it."

Why would anyone not want a second chance at anything? But could we honestly work through what we'd done? And more importantly, what we'd done to each other?

"What's the last thing you can vividly remember?" He played with one of several hemp bracelets on his wrist, twirling a small shell attached to one between two fingers.

"Of which life?" I huffed a breath, disorientation roiling in my brain as soon as I tried to recall all the lives I'd led.

His jade eyes found mine. "Ours."

Pinching my knees together, I folded my hands in my lap. "Zeus exiling me to the stars. Pure darkness with the occasional glimpse of Olympus until one day I just—" I paused, glancing around us to ensure no one was within earshot. "I was a child in the Middle Ages."

"Shit. Reincarnation. Is that what happened on the boat? Did you have a memory? Thought I was someone else?" He sat up straight.

I raised my shoulders to my ears before letting them flop back down. "Yes." It came out stilted. "And I keep having these random flashes like a real-time slideshow in my mind."

He slid his hand on my knee, and I zoomed to a memory of us on our thrones in Atlantis, his hand sliding over that same knee, smiling at me. When I tensed under his touch and looked away, he slid his hand to the bench.

The skin between his eyes formed a deep groove—his expression when deep in thought. "We'll figure it out, but I think this—" He paused to point between us. "Is the more immediate hurdle to overcome."

"We're a hurdle now?"

He bumped his shoulder against me. "That's not what I meant, and you know it."

"What have you been doing all this time?" I scooted backward, making my toes barely touch the ground.

He blew out a harsh breath, making his lips vibrate. "Oh, man. Well, once mortals stopped believing in us, we all had to start disguising ourselves if we wished to stay amongst them. I've donned many hats. Military diver. Dockworker. Ship captain. Even worked as an actor for a spell."

"An actor?" I pinched my lips together, attempting to hide my smile. "You?"

He playfully nudged my chin with his knuckle. "Yeah? How's that so unbelievable, miss pro gamer?"

I gasped, feigning offense with a dramatic hand over my chest, and then...I narrowed my eyes. "You're KingofFish69."

A gooey smile played over Poseidon's lips, and he lifted a palm. "Guilty."

I rolled my eyes and leaned on the carpeted pole behind us. "You knew who I was this entire time and have been so—" My gaze fell to the horse tattoo covering the inside of his forearm. "—patient."

He nodded, beating his fist against one knee. "A lot of things have changed about me, Amph." He quirked one brow and scanned the area.

"Yeah. I can tell." Feeling bold, I brushed my pinky against the hand he rested on the bench between us.

"You have as well." Poseidon eyed our skin touching, and he curled a single finger with mine. "Maybe that's what it took. Eons apart."

"Rebirth," I said on a breathy exhale.

"Go on a date with me." His green eyes sparkled.

"A date?" A fluttery laugh escaped my throat.

"If we're starting over, we might as well go all out. Besides, we never even had a first date. I sort of—" His cheek twitched.

"Claimed me?" I raised a brow.

"I'm not proud of it."

"As long as you pick me up in a car and not a dolphin, then yes." I tightened my one-finger grip on him.

He chuckled—deep and godly. "Deal."

The aquarium boss tossed me a glare as he pointed at the last tour group for the day waiting.

"Damn. I have to give a final tour." Standing, I turned to Poseidon towering over me.

"Tomorrow at seven work for you?" He slipped his hands in his front pockets.

I played a finger over the tip of my nose. "Perfect."

"Cool. I'll uh—I'll see you then." He dragged a hand through his long hair before turning on a heel and walking away, stealing a final glance at me over his shoulder.

Two gods torn apart for past selfishness brought together again in search of hope and serenity. Ages ago, the idea of it would've brought me comfort, but despite our history, it was as if we were meeting for the first time. I wasn't the same person as I was back then, and it was clear—neither was he. Still, the Fates gave us another opportunity to find the happiness we'd lost. Could we work through it? Could I deal with the onslaught of past life memories? Would they stop? All of it aside, I owed it to myself to *try*.

TEN

MEG AND I DROVE HOME the following day, and she regaled me with her time spent at the Magic Kingdom. I didn't tell her about Poseidon er—Simon showing up at the aquarium because it would've led to more lies about our conversation. A kept mistruth versus lying seemed a better alternative at this stage. When she dropped me off at my apartment, I walked up the stairs on autopilot, scarcely remembering how I'd reached my front door. Unlocking it, I shuffled my way inside in a daze, removing the mermaid mouse ears Meg had bought me, and resting it on the counter but missed. My bag ended up in a slump near my coffee table, missing that surface as well.

I was Michelle Pfeiffer after being brought back to life by a dozen cats in an alleyway, spiraling her way into becoming Catwoman. Only instead of cats—it was fish.

My gaze snapped to my tank, where all seven fish huddled together in a group at the frontmost glass. Squinting, I pressed a finger against the tank on the opposite side, making them all scurry to greet me.

"I'm so sorry I've kept you all in there." I scratched the glass, simulating a petting gesture.

Unlike the jellyfish at the aquarium, my fish were content in the tank—happy even. Less room than an entire enclosure at an aquarium but somehow, their presence with me this whole time mattered the most. I glanced at the analog clock with a seashell border hanging in my kitchen. Thirty minutes until Poseidon would pick me up. Nodding to myself, I snapped to attention. Thirty minutes until my ex-husband showed up for us to start the first day of our reconciliation…or not. My palms clammed up, heart racing, beads of sweat rolling down my neck.

Sprinting to my bedroom, I whipped open the closet doors and stared at the array of clothing. As I shoved hanger after hanger aside, panic latched onto me like a snapping turtle. I was still Cordelia but didn't feel like myself. A mind stuck between two worlds, many lives, and a being once reliant on magic now rendered almost powerless. Mortal.

Giving up on finding anything suitable for a former queen, I slammed the door shut and stormed into my living room, plopping onto my blue sofa. Dropping my face in my hands, I concentrated on slow, steady breathing, mentally announcing to the tears which threatened a visit, they weren't welcome here.

My mind fizzled, and my knee pressed into the dirt, crouched behind a round wooden shield—scents of blood, sweat, and dirt floating around me. I shouted something in a language I couldn't translate to the woman beside me, her hair pulled into knotted sections on the top of her head, middle, and at the nape of her neck. Black paint smeared over her eyes,

Knock. Knock. Knock.

With a strangled gasp, I sat up, cutting my eyes to the clock. Five minutes early. Punctual now? Poseidon was *never* punctual. Now of all times.

I headed for the front door with a grimace while rubbing my temples. The distance, in actuality, was several feet from my sofa, but the walls appeared to expand, creating a narrow path that seemed miles away. Peering through the peephole to ensure it was my fish god on the other side, I whisked open the door, hiding behind it, and peeking over the side at him.

A sparkly grin played over his lips. "Uh, hi. This a bad time?" He pressed a forearm above my head on the doorframe, waiting for an invitation.

Remaining silent, I shook my head.

He shifted his eyes left-to-right, still waiting and still grinning.

Oh, to Tartarus with it.

I pushed the door open, revealing the same v-neck t-shirt and jersey shorts I'd worn all day traveling. "I couldn't figure out what to wear. The last I remember about the true me? Well, there's nothing in my closet that even comes close." It came out far more whiny than I'd have preferred.

The smile on his face had yet to fade. "May I come in, Amph?"

I stepped aside, holding my hand out and locking the door behind him.

"There's a reason you're not going to find togas or wispy see-through dresses." He plucked the bit of hair below his bottom lip, roaming his eyes over my body before forcing them away.

Crossing my arms in a huff, I leaned against my kitchen counter. "I know I'm in the twenty-first century. I haven't forgotten Cordelia. I'm just having a—I don't know. An identity crisis?"

"You've changed, Starfish. Cordelia is more you than the oldest version of Amphitrite." He folded his hands in front of him as if he wasn't sure what to do with them.

"That name doesn't even feel like me anymore." I frowned, moving my gaze to my fish floating in the corner of the tank near me, flapping their tiny fins.

"What? Starfish?"

I cut my eyes to his. "No. That name makes me feel bubbly as it always has."

"Well, maybe Amphitrite doesn't suit you any longer." He cocked his head to the side. From the way his right knee bounced on occasion, I could tell he was antsy. He more than likely wanted to take me in his arms and pick up where we left off—when we were happy together.

Maybe I left the name Amphitrite up in the stars.

"So, where are you taking me on this date? It'll help me decide what random piece of clothing to grab from my exploding closet."

With a swagger that'd been impossible to forget, he walked in front of me. Holding up his fingertips, they turned into water, and he bobbed his brow. "May I?"

Despite the ability to breathe underwater, staring up at him with his power surging in his palms, I forgot how to breathe land air and managed a nod.

With his hands on my shoulders, a dress materialized over my chest in splashes of water and sparkles. It traveled over my hips and didn't stop until it reached my ankles, forming a flowy train. Poseidon released a raspy breath before taking a step away, urging me with a flick of his wrist to look at his handiwork.

I traced my fingers over the radiant white and silver sparkles adorning my body. A slit ran up my left leg, stopping just below my hip, and a drape of fabric hung over my chest. "This looks like—" I gasped. "Ariel's sparkly dress from *The Little Mermaid*?"

Poseidon rubbed the back of his neck. "I figured you'd be a fan of that movie—especially in modern times."

"You would be right." I grinned at him before twirling several times, making the train swish around me and the light catch the sparkles in the dress, bringing them to life.

"By Olympus, you're beautiful," he murmured, gawking at me. "No longer a constellation, but the stars are forever with you."

I gazed at him from across the room, picturing him with his golden crown, the matching trident with Atlantean symbols carved into its hilt, clutched in his grasp.

"You ready to talk?" He held out a hand.

It was a simple gesture, but in truth, his palm held the universe within it—a possibility to find the happily ever after I've always strived for but lost sight of so long ago. But it also held the potential for heartbreak.

Clutching one arm to my chest, I slid the other hand into

his. "Are you porting us there? We're not going to drive?"

"What would you prefer, Starfish?" His grip tightened on my hand as if now that he had me, he never planned to let go.

I stepped closer to him, a breath between us. Closing my eyes to let the scents of sea spray and sun spark dozens of memories—magical midnight swims, stolen kisses on Olympus, lights glinting from his majestic gold crown. "I want to feel the magic again."

He slipped an arm around my lower back, pulling me flush against him. I fluttered my eyes open, gazing up at him.

His beard tickled the tip of my ear as he whispered, "Hold on."

My dress's train circled me as a surge of water erupted around us but didn't make us wet. The water swirled in overlapping spirals, and in a shimmer of light, we appeared on a rooftop with a single table, two chairs positioned beside each other, and a dozen candles with flickering flames.

"Where are we?" My arms were still around his waist, and I left them there as I scoped the beautiful setting.

"A restaurant." He hugged me and delicately rested his chin on my head. "I wanted it to be as normal as possible but still have the freedom to talk about *everything*, so I rented the entire building for the night."

I peeled back, squinting at him with one eye. "Mighty romantic of you, but how are we getting food?"

His eyes turned to the stars. "That was the only part I hoped you'd be fine with not being normal?"

"Suits me fine. Both of us are lousy cooks."

We laughed in unison, only letting the chuckles dissolve

when our eyes met, and a flame flickered within them. I stood barefoot in my sparkly Ariel dress on a rooftop with the King of the Seas in my arms. He splayed his hand at our feet, making his shoes disappear, and skirted a sheet of lukewarm water across the concrete.

I smiled, letting my toes splash.

"Figured it'd make it feel more like home without flooding the building." He grinned, gave a quick peck to the corner of my brow, and led us to the table.

Like two teenagers with first date jitters, we fumbled to our seats. I'd been halfway to sitting before realizing he pulled the chair out for me and had to readjust with a blushed smile. He waved his hand over the table, producing bountiful plates of leafy greens with colorful splashes of tomatoes, cucumbers, and a variety of other fruits and vegetables.

"I can see you were in the kitchen all day with a meal like this." I winked at him, unfolding the white cloth napkin and placing it over my lap.

Poseidon brushed each of his shoulders. "A lot of blood and sweat went into this meal. I certainly hope you enjoy it."

I paused the fork midway to my mouth, scrunching my nose at the mention of blood and sweat.

He chuckled, never taking his eyes off me as he took a bite. After listening to the melodic crunching with each rotation of his jaw, I followed suit. We had countless moments like this at the beginning of our marriage—so enamored with each other we couldn't get enough. How had we let ourselves grow apart?

I wanted to ask something but feared killing the moment before we had a chance to develop one. Letting my gaze fall to my plate, scraping my fork across it, I derailed—for now.

"How did those pirates get on the cruise ship? I got Bloodhound Meg off the scent, but she was right to find it suspicious."

Poseidon swiped his napkin over his mouth. "Skylla."

"Skylla?" My fork clanked as I dropped it. "I thought most of the creatures were dead."

"Atlantis has been off the charts for decades. With it lacking the security it once had, it brought unwanted attention. I wanted to keep busy, but I never thought it'd be playing gatekeeper to creatures of the deep and the modern world." He smirked, bumping a tomato from one side of his plate to the other.

"I don't understand what was in it for Skylla, though. Aiding a group of sea thugs to rob or ransom off passengers on a cruise ship?"

Or surely, she hadn't been after me all this time? My dream of plummeting into the depths, tentacles wrapped around me—the sight of those same tentacles making the pirate boats move faster…

"You've got me there. If I had to guess, she probably made a deal. She's always wanted control of the seas, but she forgets a tiny detail." He leaned his chest on the table, sliding his hand across it to rest on top of mine. "She has to get through me."

Memories of us battling under the seas, protecting them, protecting our *family*—a pain twisted in my chest, and I yanked my hand away, pressing my back to the chair.

"Amph?" He frowned. "What is it?"

"How are our—" The words stuck in my throat, clinging to

it like saltwater taffy. "—children?"

I snapped my eyes to him, a trident twisting in my gut at the sight of his solemn face.

Poseidon blew out a breath before rolling a tomato between two fingers. "Triton is doing very well for himself. He's captain of a fishing boat and loves it. I'm guessing he'll stay there until him not aging becomes alarmingly obvious."

Triton. My sweet boy. Now a grown man. A god in his own right.

"*Fishing* boat?"

Poseidon threw his hands up. "Not what you think. He goes after whalers, stops them using any means necessary that won't get them flagged by the Coast Guard."

"Why use a human boat? Couldn't he use his powers?" I ran my finger over the hem of the slit in my dress.

Poseidon tapped the table with his forefinger. "He prefers working for it. Says it means more at the end of the day. Wonder where he got that from, hm?"

Tears threatened, but I forced them back.

We had another child—a daughter. Nerves coiled my lungs, squeezing the breath out of me. "And Rhode?" She was so small the last time I'd seen her, so young.

Poseidon licked his lips, casting his gaze away from me before sliding his chair closer.

"Oh my—" I clapped my hands over my mouth. "—she's not…"

"No." He peeled my fingers from my face, holding my hands in his large grasp. "No, she's not. As I told you, anomalies have been occurring in Atlantis. She'd gone to try and fix it, despite me firmly telling her no, that it was too dangerous."

"I wonder where she got that from," I said weakly, a crackle in my voice.

Poseidon didn't smile. He didn't even look at me, his grip tightening around my hands. "Atlantis took her. She disappeared."

"What?" I shouted, pushing out of my chair, toppling it over. "What do you *mean* she disappeared?"

Poseidon stood, dragging a hand over his beard. "Atlantis is the heart of altering dimensions. It has portals. One opened and…took her."

Pacing the roof's perimeter, I slapped a hand on my forehead. "And you haven't tried to find her?"

"Of course, I have. I tore apart half the universe looking for her." His voice dropped an octave, no doubt insulted by my accusation.

Panic. Pain. Fury. Anger at *myself*. It all engulfed my senses, tore at my insides.

"And you just gave up?" I stopped and glared at him from across the space. "You should've tried harder."

He rolled his shoulders back, his nostrils flaring. "And *you* should've been there. It's one of the reasons she went. To look for you."

A tear rolled down my cheek, and I swiped it away.

"As if you were always there for them. Don't you dare put this all on me." My bottom lip trembled, and I turned my back on him.

"They were children when you disappeared, Amphitrite. I *raised* them."

The stern expression on his face brought back memories of one of our past arguments. He'd been away for days performing his aquatic duties without so much as a word to me—to us. The loneliness I'd felt far too many times to count made my gut wrench.

"I knew this wasn't going to work," I whispered.

The heat radiated from his chest, pulsing against my back as he stood behind me. "What are you saying?"

"We've done too much. I'm not even sure it's repairable. And for you, this all happened a lifetime ago, a lifetime to get past it—to accept it." I turned to face him with a scowl. "For me? It was like it all happened days ago."

The memories were all so fresh, rushing through my mind, making the present mix with the future. The last argument I remembered us having pinched my brain—both accusing the other of putting the job before family.

His jaw tightened, and he sneered at the ground.

"I know about Medusa." Further torture inflicted by Zeus during my constellation prison. Glimpses of Earth and Olympus, to witness those I loved thinking I was gone.

His eyes snapped to mine, and he shook his head. "I thought you were dead. That was years after you disappeared. It was a fling, at most."

"I know. I'm not mad because you slept with other women after I was gone. It's what Athena did to her as a result." The skin between my eyes wrinkled as I imagined what agony she must've gone through, realizing she couldn't look at anyone without them turning to stone—not to mention the head of snakes for hair.

Poseidon pursed his lips. "I'm not proud of it."

"Is she still alive?"

"Yes. Though, I haven't seen her since. She's become a recluse."

I nodded, hugging myself. "You should rectify that."

"Maybe I will," he said softly, barely audible against the harsh winds that'd picked up.

"I need you to take me home, please." A sea urchin poked at the backs of my eyelids, trying to force tears out.

"We can work through this, Amph. You just need to give us another shot." He wrung his hands together, a deep furrow forming in his brow.

"I'm not saying no, but I'm not saying yes either. I need some time, Seid. I need to process this, to—"

Before I could finish my sentence, he wrapped his arms around me, and we appeared in my apartment.

"Thank you." My throat betrayed me, making my words quiver.

He stepped back, running the back of his hand over his nose. "I'll recruit a few more gods to help search for Rhode. I never stopped, Amph. You need to realize she can be in virtually any dimension or time period. It's like looking for a black speck of sand in a dune of tan."

"Thank you." I turned my attention to the fish tank.

"Take all the time you need. I've been waiting this long. I can wait an eternity if it comes to it."

By Olympus, how much my king had changed.

He stood in front of me, delicately placing a finger under my chin and turning my face to him. "Hey. Regardless if you come back to me or not, we *will* find Rhode."

He made it so damn difficult to be mad at him. To not simply throw the neglect I'd felt in the middle of our marriage, the loneliness, straight out the window. But no—as sweet and attractive as he was, he'd have to own up to it. I needed to be in the right headspace for that conversation. Otherwise, he'd be talking to idle ears.

"Text me when you're ready to talk." He slowly backed away, fighting the disappointed look on his face with tightened lips.

And with a blazing white flash and sea spray, the King of the Seas disappeared into the night, leaving only the sparkling dress clinging to my body as a pale reminder he was ever here.

ELEVEN

I'D BARRICADED MYSELF IN my apartment, missed my usual streaming night on Glitch, fed my fish but barely fed myself, and answered with vague one-word answers whenever Meg texted me. The knock on my door came as no surprise because it could only be one of two people. Considering Poseidon told me to let him know when, and if, I was ready to talk. Considering we were on thin ice prepared to crack—it could only be one other.

Sighing, I paused the movie *Fool's Gold* playing on Fox and slumped to the door.

"Open the hell up, Cor. You have some serious explaining to do," Meg's voice boomed from the other side of the door.

Bracing for impact, I said a silent prayer to my fish before greeting her with a forced smile. "Hey, Meg."

"Hey, Meg? Oh, can it, sister." She pushed past me, turning circles and all but sniffing the air of my apartment. Snapping her fingers, she pointed at the TV. "Uh-huh. Kate Hudson movies."

As she stormed past me for the kitchen, I was too weak to protest and leaned on the doorframe with crossed arms.

She yanked the fridge open. "You've been surviving on expired milk and olives for the past few days."

I canted my head to the side, noting how cute she looked in only her jeans, boots, and brown vest. I'd never say the word "cute" to her, though.

"Your hair is greasy, and your clothes have more wrinkles than a shar-pei puppy." She lifted my lifeless hair and let it drop with a huff. "What happened with Simon?"

I groaned and walked past her. Without turning, she reached behind her, grabbed my shirt, and dragged me back in front of her.

"Sit." She pointed at my lounge chair. After I obliged, she sat across from me. "Talk."

"It's tough to explain." I slouched until my chin met my chest.

"Try me." She spread her legs and leaned forward, resting her arms on her knees. "You know I've been through the seven dating circles of hell."

She had. I could attest to it.

I flicked the air and let my hand drop at my side. How the Tartarus did you explain to your best friend a godly past that not only she didn't know existed but would make you sound two seas short of a horse? "We—both have things we've done in our past that we're not sure we can accept."

"You? What have *you* done he has such an issue with? Your

one unpaid parking ticket? Running a yellow light?"

Or feeling neglected millennia ago, and rather than talking to my husband, I consumed myself with aquatic life?

"You know how much I love the ocean and fish, right?" I sat up, wiping my hair from my face.

"I have a vague idea, yes."

"In some of my past—relationships—I cared more about the seas more than humans, i.e., the men I dated." I squinted, knowing the odds were slim she'd feed into this.

She steepled her fingers between her knees and glared at me.

Dammit. She was *not* buying it.

"And Simon kind of has the same deal, I mean, he's been extremely consumed with his career." I shot to my feet. "If we were to date—we wouldn't be each other's number one."

Meg clucked her tongue against her cheek, stormed from her seat, and yanked me back to the lounger, sitting on the armrest. "Do you remember Cassandra?"

"Yes."

Meg hiked one knee on the armrest and moved her gaze to stare at the carpet. "Do you remember how she had a gambling problem in her past? We're talking, she was still in debt when I met her, kind of problem?"

This relationship ended in heartbreak, so I wasn't entirely sure where she was trying to go with it.

"I do."

"It bothered me in the beginning. Really bothered me. At any moment, she could've fed into temptation, asked me for money I would've had a hard time refusing. There was also the thought of: What else could she get addicted to?" Meg wrung her hands in her lap.

"But she didn't." I nudged her hip with my shoulder. "You broke up with her because she didn't want to commit."

"That's exactly my point, Cor." She turned and smiled down at me. "That relationship lasted for three years. And it was a happy one until it wasn't, but it had nothing to do with her past."

"You're slick, Megara. Very slick." I beamed up at her.

She slapped her hands on her thighs and stood, swiveling on her booted heel. "So. What is the moral of this story?"

"Uh, something about not letting the past ruin the possibilities of a future?" I bobbed my brow.

She blinked once. "Damn. That's better than what I had brewing in my head, but yeah."

"I get what you're trying to say, I do, but—it's more complicated than simply looking beyond it." I pushed to my feet, images of Poseidon's smile swirling in my brain. He'd changed so much, but the crippling anxiety I'd felt of all those times spent alone night after night, not even knowing where he'd gone, dug into my skin.

"It's really not." She grabbed each of my shoulders, squeezing them. "Do you *want* to give him a shot? A real chance?"

The first year after our arranged marriage had been the happiest. We couldn't get enough of each other—kissing, making love, swimming together. I wanted those exact moments forever.

"Yes," I answered, my voice garbled.

"Then text him right now. Ask him to come over and to his face, ask him on another date. If he fucks up, he fucks up, but at least you gave it a *chance*, Cor."

Slipping my phone from my pocket, I puckered my lips at her. "Have I told you lately I love you?"

"I believe you just did." She slapped my shoulder.

I opened Poseidon's text window and paused with my thumb over the screen. "Wait. This is just as much his decision as it is mine. Even if I convince myself I can deal with his baggage, who's to say he wants or *can* deal with mine?"

Meg rolled her eyes and walked to my fish tank. "Was he still giving you that dopey but handsome smile last night?"

"Maybe." I clutched the phone to my chest.

"Something tells me he'll be willing to give it a try." Meg waved at one fish, but unlike me, they only responded by opening and closing their mouths. "I don't hear those thumbs flying on your phone screen."

We could be a family again. Poseidon, Triton—Rhode. They were children when I disappeared. How did they look full grown? Would they recognize me?

I tapped the phone against my forehead, forcing the tears down, knowing there was no possible way to explain *that* to Meg. Not right now. But both she and Poseidon were right. This could be the Fates willing us another chance. There had to be a reason for my continuous reincarnations. Had to be a reason we inexplicably ran into each other on the same beach at precisely the right moment.

I started typing.

Me: Can you come over ASAP?

Simon: On my way.

"Good. I'm gonna use the head, and then I'll be out of

your hair before he gets here." As Meg walked down the hallway to the restroom, she backpedaled and pointed at me. "Proud of you."

My damn palms clammed up again, and I peered into the fish tank with a deep sigh. "Think we can do this, guys?"

Their fins waved in unison.

"Always so supportive." A small smile tugged at my lips.

Ding dong.

I stood straight with widened eyes before bolting across the room and whipping open the door.

"Hey, Starfish." Poseidon stood there in a white shirt hugging at all the right places of his arms and chest, distressed jeans, and that long wavy hair hanging over one eye.

"What are you doing here already?" I whispered, snapping my head over my shoulder to check for Meg.

His eyes narrowed. "You said ASAP. I figured I'd port over." He pushed past me, lazily pointing a finger around the apartment. "Is someone here?"

His tone sounded borderline jealous.

"Don't even go there." I raised onto my toes to poke him in the chest. "It's Meg. Care to tell me how you're going to—"

"You sure got here fast." Meg stood in the hallway with her hands on her hips.

"I was at the gas station across the street when she texted. Came right over." Poseidon turned at me and winked.

"Convenient." Meg squinted at us before moving forward.

"They are, indeed. Gas stations, I mean." Poseidon clasped his hands behind his back.

I rubbed the skin between my eyes with an exasperated sigh.

"Right. Well, I'll go so you two can talk but first, Cor, can I borrow a book? I have lifeguard duty tomorrow." She stuck her tongue out.

"Of course. You know where my shelf is in the bedroom. Pick whatever you like." I gave as warm a grin as I could. "Just don't bend the spine or so help me—"

"I know, I know." Meg held her palms up in defense before disappearing into my room.

"How are you doing, Cordelia?" Poseidon folded his arms like he didn't know what to do with them.

Hearing him call me Cordelia instead of Amphitrite gave almost as many bubbles in my stomach as Starfish.

"Better. Open-minded. You?"

"Apologetic. I thought back on it. And I was a dick to you. I honestly have no idea how I could let a 'job' take me away from someone like you." He ruffled his hair, making it bunch on the crown of his head before falling in seaweed-like tendrils.

"All things we can talk over. But not right now." I shifted my eyes toward my room.

"Right. After she leaves?"

"I was kind of hoping we could go on another date?" I one-arm shrugged.

"You know I can't turn you down." His eyes brightened. "Have somewhere in mind?"

"The Quarter? They have dueling pianos on Wednesday nights and quarter beers. Between the loud music and cheap alcohol, I figured we'd be pretty free to talk but also be on a real date?"

He chuckled and bowed his head. "Clever. I like it."

The door whooshed open. "I finally left him."

A tall, slender woman with waves of dark brown hair down to her hips, full lips, sharp jawline, and pale, perfectly almond-shaped eyes stood at the doorway. Her peacock feather necklace swung as she stopped short, looking between Poseidon and me.

"Hera?" I whispered.

"Amphitrite?" She whispered back.

"I ended up with something called *Then a Hero Comes Along*? I assume it's a—" Meg stopped short with the paperback held in mid-air, shifting her gaze from us to Hera. Her throat bobbed at the sight of her, lips parting before she licked them and forced her eyes away.

"Meg, hey. Yeah, that's a great choice."

Please, Hera, do not call me by my godly name.

"Okay, but what's going on?" Meg used the book to point at each of us, avoiding eye contact with Hera.

Poseidon wrapped his arm around Hera's shoulder, wrinkling the jacket of her black and white pinstriped pantsuit.

"My sister decided to make a surprise visit. Isn't that right, sis?" He squeezed her with a wide grin.

Hera's mouth opened, not saying anything at first, staring at Meg before finally blurting, "That's right."

Meg scanned Hera from head to toe before turning her gaze on me. "Do you know her?"

The hole grew deeper and deeper with each passing lie.

"I tracked him," Hera said.

"My phone, she means," Poseidon added.

"I've got to go, but, Cory, everything alright here?" Meg

raised her brows at me, staring me down.

I nodded emphatically. "Absolutely. Thanks for everything, Meg. I'll call you tomorrow?"

She shimmied past us, but Hera broke away from Poseidon, turning to face Meg with grace only a goddess could exude. She extended her thin hand, the gold chain hanging from it catching the glint from the sun peeking through the curtains.

"I'm Hera."

Meg stiffened before shaking her hand. "Her-Hera? Like Queen of the Greek Gods?" A shaky laugh floated from Meg's belly.

She was nervous. I'd *never* seen her nervous around anyone.

Hera held onto her hand for another beat longer before tracing her thumb over a knuckle and letting go. "That's right. But also…a goddess to the life of womankind." Hera smiled, bright and sultry, revealing her perfect snow-white teeth.

A breath pushed from Meg's nose as she traced the spot on her hand Hera had caressed. "Sorry. Guess I've forgotten a lot of mythology since high school."

"No need to apologize, my dear." Hera stepped forward, her black stiletto heel clicking against the hardwood floor. "You, yourself—" She ran a finger over her bottom lip with a sultry smile. "Are a goddess."

Meg's chest heaved, extenuating her bosom beneath the vest. "Th-thank you. I really do need to get going, but Hera, it was genuinely nice to meet you." She smiled and scanned Hera's face one last time before leaving.

Hera bit her knuckle, smiling as she watched Meg leave and shut the door behind her. She pressed her back to the door, still grinning. "She is an absolute treasure. Mentally. Physically. Who is she?"

"Meg. My best friend."

"Meg," Hera whispered, running a fingernail over her collarbone.

"Care to explain what the Tartarus you're doing here?" Poseidon's voice boomed.

Hera shook her head as if awoken from a daydream. "As I said, I left Zeus."

Poseidon and I exchanged perplexed glances.

"You just—" I flicked my wrist. "Left?"

"I at least wrote him a note, if that's what you mean." Hera pushed off the door and sauntered past us, moving to the fish tank.

"I'd love to say, 'About damn time,' but he let you? Just like that?" Poseidon threw his arms out at his sides.

Hera eyed me. "Didn't Zeus banish you to the stars?"

Tunnel-vision took over my sight, warping me to that pivotal moment in time with Zeus looming over me, shouting at me, announcing my punishment. I'd not only slacked on my duties but ignored *both* warnings Zeus had given me before finally drawing the line. How could I have been such a fool? The King of the Gods had given me chances, and I hadn't taken them.

Closing my eyes to will the memory away, I gave a curt nod. "Yes. And now I'm back—" I crossed my arms in a huff. "And don't know how, but let's not change the subject from the fact you left the King of the Gods Queenless?"

Hera bent forward, waving one finger at my fish, who

followed it back and forth. "Not my problem anymore. I'm sure he will have no issue finding another. The man can be rather convincing, as we all know."

"You were willing to give up the throne? A portion of your power?" Poseidon sat on the armrest of my lounger.

Hera sighed and stood straight, facing us. "You both know we were an arranged marriage—"

"So were we," I interrupted with a frown.

Hera held a hand up at me. "But, unlike you two, we never loved each other. We tried. But in the end, we led different lives, had countless lovers, and upheld our duties."

I spied Poseidon over my shoulder. He'd been staring at my hair and gave me one of his warmest smiles—like light rays pulsing beneath the surface of the water.

We had loved each other. So how did we drift so far apart?

"You asked if I was willing to give up my crown and part of my power? The answer is yes. I'd rather be completely powerless than unloved. I'm tired of it. I want something real." Hera dragged a finger under her chin.

"Wow." I rested a reassuring hand on her forearm. "I fully support it. But Zeus isn't going to have some outlandish backlash over this, is he? I remember how well he took it the last time you betrayed him."

"It's not like that this time. I told him it was happening, he called my bullshit as he usually did, but this time—I really did it." She patted my hand. "It's been three days. I've been laying low, and he hasn't tried to stop me. Believe what you all want, but he and I have both changed since we met. I think we *both* would be happier with other people. I just hope he isn't so pigheaded to not simply settle for the first pretty mortal who bats her eyelashes at him but truly finds someone suited for him."

"He has changed. But I'd lie if I said he still wasn't pigheaded." Poseidon snorted.

"Besides, I can finally be the goddess of women and marriage alone. It's grown tiring being known only for the goddess married to Zeus and people thinking I repeatedly let him fool around on me." She rolled her shoulders back. "It's time I make a name for *myself*."

It'd been so long since I'd seen my sister-in-law. As queens to kingly brothers, we had always gotten along, vented to each other.

I raised to the balls of my feet to hug her. "This is amazing."

She returned the embrace. "I'm happy you're back."

"Do you need a place to say?" I peeled away, dabbing the tears collecting on my lashes.

"I do still have most of my power, Amphitrite." She smiled and bumped her knuckle on my shoulder. "But you—" Her lips tilted downward. "Don't? You're mortal. I don't understand."

"In all her lives, she's been a mortal. She has to accept queenhood again with Zeus's approval." Poseidon patted the tops of his thighs. "If she desires it."

I peered at him from across the room. The memories we shared, both good and bad, had my heart swelling like a tidal wave. We'd be fools not to explore it. Not only had we been a strong alliance in both love and power, but we were an unstoppable force protecting the oceans—defending Atlantis. And now creatures of the deep threatened Atlantis.

"Ah," Hera said, slowly making her way to the door. "Sounds like you two have a lot to talk about. I shared my news, so I'll be on my way, but Amphitrite—"

I turned to look at her with raised brows.

"Would you mind telling me a bit more about Meg at some point? I'd like to get to know more about her."

"If you like her, then why not ask her yourself?"

Hera pressed a hand to her chest. "I don't—I mean, how would that work?"

It tickled me to no end to see my sister and best friend show vulnerability at the thought of each other.

"Why not?" Poseidon added, catching my gaze.

Hera grinned, chewing on her thumbnail. "I'll—think about it. You two makeup and pay my ex-husband a visit." With a swoosh of her arm around herself, she disappeared in swirls of dark purple haze.

"Well, this has been an eventful day." Poseidon chuckled as he slid from the lounger, crossing the room to stand in front of me.

"I still can't believe Hera isn't Queen anymore. It's been eons."

"I know. And I'm insanely curious to see how my little bro handles this. Twenty bucks says he demands her back after day five."

My fish danced in circles through the water, making me grin. "No deal."

"Really?"

"If my return has proved anything to me, it's that we live in an entirely different universe than before. And here—anything is possible." I turned to him, running my hands down his muscular forearm. "Even Zeus listening to something else besides his dick."

Poseidon barked with laughter, cupping a hand over his mouth. "I don't think I've ever heard you say 'dick' before, Amph."

"We've *all* changed."

"Wait a minute. You said Wednesdays are dueling pianos. That's today." He pointed at the floor with a quirked brow.

"Yes. I want to go tonight. It's been long enough, Seid. Time to clear the air. *Tonight.*

TWELVE

I'D THROWN ON MY little white dress with cap sleeves to wear to The Quarter with Poseidon. He picked me up in his navy-blue Chevy Silverado truck, holding the door open for me both in and out, and yet again as we entered the bar.

"You're laying the charm on thick tonight, Simon. Hoping to get lucky?" I elbowed him in the side.

He slipped a hand over my lower back, making a breath catch in my throat. "I'd like to think I already have, but I'd be lying if the thought of you underneath me again doesn't entice me." His beard brushed against my nape as he whispered into my ear.

I'd be lying too if I said the thought didn't ignite every possible nerve in my body.

The sight of the shoreline in the distance caused me to freeze. A pale mirage of my children playing in the tide shimmered over my mind, my daughter barely old enough to walk, her older brother helping her up whenever she'd fall on her butt. A whimper fluttered from my throat.

"Cory?" Poseidon's hand pressed between my shoulder blades, kneading my muscles.

Sniffling, I gave him a warm smile and squeezed his arm. "I'm fine. Let's get inside, hm?"

As we stepped through the doorway, the loud sounds of two pianos playing, accompanied by men singing and the murmuring crowds, pulsed in my ears.

"You want a drink?" Poseidon pointed at the bar extending the room's length except for the dance floor in the corner.

"Absolutely." I slipped my hand into his, letting him lead me through the droves of people standing near the stage, others leaning on hi-top tables with varying colors of plastic cups filled with watered-down beer.

The Quarter's décor made it feel like stepping back in time— stained glass domed lights, ornate patterns carved in the wood ceiling, framed advertisements circa eighteen hundred. Even the bar itself had old-fashioned brass fixtures for the beer taps.

"Here we go. I do believe someone mentioned cheap beer." Poseidon grinned, making his bicep peeking from the aquamarine v-neck shirt he wore bulge as he handed a blue plastic cup with a handle to me. "They had a bunch of colors, but I got us both blue."

"Thanks." I smiled, taking the cup with both hands.

All tables were occupied, so we found a vacant spot near a pole to lean against, watching the show. Two white pianos faced each other while two men sang *The Joker* by the Steve Miller Band. Each piano had a glass jar filled with cash and request cards rested at each table. Poseidon's burly arm wrapped around me from behind, pulling me against him. He let his hand rest on my hip.

"I truly am sorry for neglecting you," his low voice rumbled in my ear.

I shook my head, trailing my fingers over the masculine scattering of hair on his arm. "I'm the one who should be sorry. I should've come to you. Talked things out. Instead—"

He took my words away by pressing a kiss to my temple and gripping me tighter.

"Daddy Poseidon." I simpered. "I'll never forget the mesmerizing look on your face when Triton was born. Or the way you held tiny Rhode as if she'd wither in your arms. You looked like a Titan holding a glass statue."

Every time I brought up Rhode, it carved another piece of my heart away. But I knew there was little I could do in my mortal form. If I wanted any hope of helping to find my daughter, I *knew* what I would have to do.

"Do you remember teaching Triton how to swim?" He rested his chin on my shoulder.

I chuckled, making a strand of hair fall over my gaze. "How could I forget? He wanted to use the full course of his power before he learned to swim normally and almost took out an orca."

It was one of the last memories I had of my son, years shy of being a godly version of a teenager. And Rhode had been *half* his age.

Poseidon curled the loose hair over my ear and kissed the tip of it.

"Thank you."

"I figured your hands were tied up, and you wanted to see the show." He shrugged, gesturing toward the stage with his cup.

"Not for the hair."

"Then what, Amph?" He lowered his voice when saying my name, pressing the bridge of his nose against the side of my head.

"For raising them. I really wish I could've seen them grow up. Mature into gods." I sniffled back tears.

"You don't have to thank me for that. In all honesty, it made me more involved in their lives than I may have been otherwise." He turned my head to look at him. "And don't think they won't be ecstatic to see you. *Both* of them."

See them again—my children. A family I hadn't remembered having until only days ago. The thought excited me as much as it terrified me to my core.

A group of women at a nearby table gawked, giggled, and whispered over the man standing behind me. Poseidon hadn't seemed to notice the attention—but I did. One woman bit her lower lip, idly licking the corner of her mouth and standing as if she were coming over to pounce on him.

I wanted to kiss him—to show all he was mine. My king. My children's father. My—.

"Holy shit. When did you get back?" A man slid in front of us, blocking the woman's path. His long, dark wavy hair with blonde streaks fell past his collar bone.

Dionysos.

"You expected me back?" I raised a brow.

His dark eyes squinted at me as his lips curled into a mischievous smile. "Nothing, and I do say nothing, Pops cooks up is ever final." He winked before slapping Poseidon's shoulder. "Look at you rocking your true self. I have to say, man, the beard is where it's at." Dionysos ran a hand over his own dark facial hair.

Poseidon shifted behind me, his crotch pressing against my ass before disappearing again. "Not as if I have to ask, but what are you doing here, Dion?"

"The Quarter on a Wednesday night? Debauchery and delights to be had 'o plenty every week here." He threw his arms out at his sides, doing one full twirl. "The better question is: what are *you* two doing here?" Still smiling, he narrowed his eyes at us and slowly pointed from one of us to the other.

"I didn't remember who I was until recently. We're— working things out."

Poseidon gave me a reassuring squeeze.

"Fuck. You didn't *remember*? That's heavy." Dion scratched his chin with the tip of his thumb.

"And she's mortal," Poseidon added.

Dion bobbed his brows. "Double fuck."

"But I remember everything now. Even when I was in the stars."

"The stars. What the shit was that like?" Dion took a swig from his beer bottle.

A chill shot down my spine as I conjured those moments trapped in space and time.

"You're aware but the most relaxed you've ever felt in your entire life. Content yet—distant." My grip tightened on my cup, making the plastic squeak.

Poseidon rubbed my lower back.

Dion tapped his finger against his lips before raising his cup, gesturing at Poseidon. "Yamás."

Poseidon glared at him before tapping his cup against Dion's. "Yam—ás. What are we toasting to?"

"Your cup is now enchanted to turn any liquid into ambrosia wine. How can you two let loose and air out dirty laundry if only one can get tipsy, eh?"

Poseidon stared into his cup and sniffed it. "Yup. Ambrosia wine."

"How is getting drunk going to solve anything?" I asked.

"You two have a wicked past. Trust me. You'd be surprised what a little shield lowering will do for the soul." Pressing a hand to his chest, Dion gave a mock bow. "Now, if you'll excuse me, I have a red-head to show how to have a good time." He turned away.

"Hey, Dion. Your horns are showing." Poseidon pointed to his head.

Dion froze and felt each side of his forehead before glaring at the sea god and pointing. "Trying to pull a fast one on me, are ya?"

"It worked." Poseidon chuckled, making the rumble from his chest vibrate at my back.

"You two kids have fun." Dion scooted past us and waved his arm above his head. "Chels, over here."

We stayed silent for several moments before Poseidon cleared his throat. "We don't have to drink."

"I don't often say this, but I think Dion's right this time.

Maybe it'll help us relax and bring us back to our old selves." I held the cup in the air to toast.

"Except for the neglecting, ignoring, and refusing to talk parts," Poseidon added, raising his drink.

"Except for those."

We tapped our cups together and, in unison, pronounced, "Yamás."

An hour later…

My cheeks warmed, and my head fuzzed just enough to make me giggly. "Do you still have that pet dolphin?"

Poseidon sat on the stool next to me, slurping on his fifth ambrosia wine. "Delphinus?" He snorted. "He was never my 'pet.' I specifically created him because I knew you couldn't resist that face."

I squeezed his cheeks with one hand. "I resisted yours."

"You gave in eventually." He smiled and pretended to bite one of my fingers.

I stroked the hair on his chin. "I should've thanked Delphinus when I was up there."

"As if he could've strolled on by." Poseidon snickered as he kneaded my hip.

Making an exaggerated pout, I added, "I'm serious."

"Thank him for what, Starfish?"

"I always thought when he told me marrying you would bring peace and harmony to the seas was simply a ploy but now—" I locked gazes with him. "I realize he told the truth."

"Hm. You're right. I should've thanked him more too." Poseidon beamed with a mischievous sparkle in his eyes. "I know you said you started playing video games to escape, but if I'm being honest—it still surprises the hell out of me."

"Why is it so surprising?" I tugged his beard.

He narrowed his eyes at me, playfully poking me in the ribs, making me yip. "I know you're not the same woman I married, but I never knew you to be into games of any variety."

Letting out a rolling sigh, I rested my head on his shoulder, watching the dueling pianists. "And this is the part where I need to remind you of your continuous absence back in the day."

"Shit," Poseidon grumbled, adjusting himself on the stool, making me bounce.

Raising my head, I flicked my hair at him and poked between his pecs.

So. Much. Muscle.

"Uh-uh. You made this bed, and now you're going to listen to it." I looked skyward. "Or something like that."

He chuckled, beating his fingers against the side of my ass. "Let's hear it."

"When the kids were little, I made up all sorts of games to keep them entertained. Seashell puzzles, catch the seahorse, guess the fish. But one they particularly enjoyed—" My brow pinched, just now remembering what I'd called the game. "—was Heroes of Atlantis."

"What?" Poseidon bumped his knuckle under my chin. "You called it that?"

I nodded, absently staring at his collar bone. "I conjured play weapons for them and water monsters, and we'd fight for Atlantis." Laughing, I pressed a hand to my chest. "Usually, they'd wind up fighting each other, but those are some of my best memories with them."

"Olympus, Amph. I'm an asshole." Poseidon made a clicking sound with his teeth, his gaze dropping to my hand resting on his shoulder.

"I wouldn't have called you a full-blown asshole, Seid. More like—a work in progress. And one that I loved."

He squeezed my thigh. "I'd give anything to have had even one of those moments with the kids and you."

"I'm an adult, and I still play games. Who's to say they don't still, too?" I kissed the tip of his nose.

"You, Jewel of the Sea, are something else." His hand trailed over my lower back.

My skin burned for him, but my brain kept telling me to wait—take this slow.

Playfully swatting him in the shoulder, I slid from my stool. "Be right back. I have to use the little girl's room."

"Want me to walk you?" Poseidon turned on his stool, interlacing his hands between his legs.

"I think I can handle it, Big Guy, but thanks." I flashed him a grin over my shoulder before ascending the stairs.

The line was out the bathroom door along a railing that overlooked the bar floor. Poseidon remained on his stool and smiled to himself, tapping his fingertips against his thighs.

What are you thinking about?

A grin tugged at my lips and faded as a group of women walked up to him.

A gal leaves her guy alone for thirty seconds, and the circling lady sharks go in for the kill.

Poseidon waved his hands before pointing up, saying something to them I couldn't make out. He grabbed two cocktail napkins and scribbled his signature before handing them to the women. One pouted, another shrugged, and the third hadn't stopped smiling so wide it made her eyes form slits. Once they left, Poseidon looked up, spotting me and waving.

I wiggled my fingers at him, feeling my cheeks turn rosy. After waiting another ten minutes, forcing me to pinch my knees together and waddle like a penguin I had to go so badly, I was finally able to do my business and return to my awaiting sea god.

"There you are. I was beginning to think you fell in." Poseidon snorted, turning his back to the bar and resting his elbows on it.

"Wow. You even make dad jokes now." Grinning, I tugged on his shirt's hem.

"The next song is a requested dedication to an exceptional lady named Cordelia," one of the piano players announced.

I snapped my attention to Poseidon, who held a finger over his lips in a shoosh gesture. As soon as the first few notes played, tears filled my eyes, and my chest tightened.

Beyond the Sea.

"How could you possibly know that's my favorite song?" I propped myself on one of his knees, sitting on his lap and curling my arms behind his neck.

He slid an arm around me. "I heard you hum it. Couldn't think of a more suiting song."

As the piano players sang, I closed my eyes, swaying to the soothing melody.

"Beyond the stars. Beyond the moon. The sea really did lead us together, Starfish." His warm palm pressed against my cheek, making me flutter my eyes open.

"And it will never tear us apart again." Pressing my hands to each side of his face, I slid my lips over his.

The kiss ignited endless memories blazing through my mind, but the one which stuck out the most was the first time we'd kissed—truly kissed. Our wedding hadn't counted. It was the time Poseidon strolled on the beach with me, swam with me—made the entire day fully about me alone. The moment we realized our marriage had blossomed into something unexpected—a love for each other.

He pulled me tighter against him, snaking his free hand through my hair, massaging my scalp. The kiss began as subtle and sweet but now turned carnal and ravenous. Flutters exploded in my stomach, my skin, my body, remembering him, craving for him again. I peeled away, pressing my forehead against his. His green eyes stared lazily at me, his tongue skirting his lower lip.

"Swim with me, Seid," I whispered.

He traced my jawline with a single finger. "It's nearly midnight."

"I seem to recall midnight being the *perfect* time for a swim." I combed my fingers through his ash-blonde waves. "And the ocean has no choice but to behave as you see fit."

His fingers trailed up my spine, his hand wrapping the back of my neck. "Do you want me to give you fins?"

"I'd be disappointed if you didn't."

"Then what are we waiting for?"

Biting my lip, I hopped from his lap. He slapped cash on the bar top to cover our tab, and as the piano players brought

Beyond the Sea to a close, it served as exit music while we whisked out the door hand-in-hand. As soon as we rounded the corner to a deserted alley, Poseidon ported us to the shore.

The bright moonlight bounced over the lapping waves hitting against the sand. Without care or thought or worry, I slipped the dress over my head and opened my hand, letting it drop. Standing in only my bra and underwear, I raised a brow at Poseidon's stunned expression.

"Not what you remember, Seid?" I crossed my arms over my stomach.

His callused fingers took a gentle hold of my arms, and he slowly parted them, staring at my bared tanned midriff with a heat building in his gaze. "No. You're exactly how I remember, Amph. I'd forgotten how much I missed you." His throat bobbed as he let his eyes roam.

"I missed you too, Seid." I stepped forward, playing my fingers over his arms. "Now, take your shirt off."

He grinned—bemused and satisfied. "I like this new commanding side to you." He reached over one shoulder, bunching the fabric in his large hand before yanking it over his head and throwing it in the same pile as my dress.

Pure. Tanned. Male perfection.

Whether it'd been the alcohol fueling my boldness or the memory of how attracted I'd been to him when we were together, for either reason, I traced my hands over his beefy sculpted arms, the ridges of each abdominal muscle.

"I love when you do that," he said through a growl. Walking behind him, I dragged a finger over his skin. "Touch me like I'm Poseidon the man, not the god king."

I paused at his words, flashing a warm smile at him. A black trident tattoo started between his shoulder blades, its hilt traveling the length of his spine. "That's new."

"Oh, yeah. I couldn't be the only brother without tattoos. And I made sure to outdo them both." He winked at me over his shoulder, extending his hand to me.

"Of course, you did." As I slipped my palm against his, the moon brightened at our touch.

"You ready?" Poseidon nudged his chin toward the awaiting ocean.

"More than ever," I whispered, longing for the feel of salt and silk against my skin.

We walked to the water's edge and didn't look away from each other as the water enveloped us with each step taken. When the water reached my chest, I let go of his hand and dived in, welcoming the scales I'd commanded away to appear again. They'd glowed before but now shone with a radiance stemming from the moonbeams and my own gradual acceptance.

Poseidon joined me, smiling as his hair floated in wisps behind him. He touched my hip, turning my legs into a teal mermaid's tail. In my past life as a sea goddess, I'd often give myself a tail to swim alongside the dolphins, to keep their pace. There was something especially tantalizing about him *gifting* it to me.

Dragging my arms through the water, I flapped my fins, turning several times in a full circle, kicking up bubbles. Poseidon chuckled before wrapping a single arm around my bared stomach, twirling with me, kneading the middle of my back with his strong fingers.

"I'll race you," I flicked my tail at him.

His smile spread wide. "A mortal demi-goddess with a tail versus the King of the Seas? That's almost fair."

"You're on, KingofFish69." I flapped my tail again, sending a shockwave through the water at him.

It pushed him back, and he tightened his muscles to stop, raising a brow at me. "You're never going to let me live that down, are you?"

"Probably not. Three, two, one," I quickly counted down before darting through the water, my arms pinned at my sides, and letting the tail work its magic.

It didn't take long for Poseidon to catch up. He swam on his back beneath me, his hands interlaced behind his head, a smug grin on his lips.

"Hey there." He waved at me.

I glared at him before banking to the right, kicking the tail into overdrive.

He appeared at my side, his muscular arms cutting through the water like pushing aside clouds. With his arms wrapped around me, he tackled me. In a bout of laughter and a pretend struggle on my part, he catapulted us into a grotto. We landed on the sea bed, him on top of me, straddling me, his arms caging me in on each side of my head. I flicked my tail between his legs and gleamed up at him.

"I've missed you, Amph. Truly missed you."

I slid a hand over one of his forearms. "I mi—"

"Well, well. It must be my lucky day," a woman's voice echoed off the stone surrounding us.

Poseidon's face morphed into a predator—cold and angry. He shot to his feet, making his golden trident appear in his grasp.

Several curling dark tentacles like an octopus emerged from the shadows, followed by six limbs with snapping dragon heads on the end of each one. Attached to the tentacles was the torso of a topless woman, her long black hair shielding her breasts when it grazed over them.

"Skylla," I gasped, pushing off the seafloor and floating near Poseidon.

"Imagine my surprise when the word on the waves was that Cordelia Bourne was more than some petty mortal. Amphitrite. Queen of the Seas." Skylla's blood-red eyes glowed, her pointy fingernails clacking together as she petted one of the dragon heads. "You've somehow avoided my wrath."

Poseidon ushered me behind him with one arm. "I'd watch your tone, sea witch."

"Ah, yes. You don't know. Your lovely former goddess is the reason *why* I'm a witch, as you so graciously describe me."

It'd been an accident. I never meant for her to turn into—this.

"What the Tartarus are you barking about?" Poseidon slammed the trident's hilt against the stone floor.

"I have a chance to be something in these seas with only one sea god to contend with. And now that I know the Queen is back? I will end her while she's vulnerable before she decides to do something stupid."

Skylla let out a howl like a canine before the dragon heads snapped in our direction. Poseidon turned to me with a growl and wrapped us in a dome of water. We splashed onto the floor of my apartment, my elbows smacking against the wood. My feet slid as I stood, the mermaid tail a distant memory.

"I don't know if I can do this," I stammered, wiping away the water collected on my brows.

Flashes of war on land, on the water—swords clashing, people screaming in agony—it all punched at my mind, making me collapse to the floor.

"Amphitrite, what's wrong?" Poseidon was at my side, but the sporadic memories continued.

Each memory, each life led, scorching my brain with bright flashes of white in between. I clutched my head, screaming, trying to make it stop.

Stop. Stop. *Stop.*

"Amphitrite," Poseidon roared, shaking my shoulders.

The memories faded away, and I blinked my eyes open, staring up at Poseidon. His jaw tightened, and he rubbed my arms. Something wet collected on my lower lip, and I touched it—warm and red. Blood. My blood.

"Fucking Olympus." He held me firm, and I was glad for it. Otherwise, I may have slunk to the floor in a heap. "Are you alright?"

The question confused me. I shook my head. "I've lived so long as a mortal, Seid. Through so many lives. Battling sea creatures—real battling—dealing with the other gods, Olympus, the politics and procedure, and I—" My chest heaved, and I stared in horror at the puddles collected on my rented apartment floor.

It took several attempts to stand before Poseidon relented, letting his hands fall with a sigh. Sprinting to the linen closet,

I returned with every towel I owned, dropping them on the floor and hurriedly mopping up what I could.

"Amphitrite," Poseidon beckoned, his half-naked form moving to stand beside me.

Ignoring him and the tears welling my eyes, I continued to dry the floor.

"Cordelia." He snatched my arm, halting me.

I looked up at him, numbly holding a soaked towel in my grasp.

"If you decided to take the title back, no one is saying you'd need to battle sea creatures…unless you want to."

Whimpering, I tossed the towel to the floor and turned away from him. "It's so confusing. At one moment, I want it all back. You. The seas. Our family. Queendom. But then I remember how settled I've become in leading a semi-normal life."

"I can't sympathize. But I am jealous you've gotten to experience the beauty that's mortality." He wiped his hand over his chest, ridding it of water beads.

"I need to get some rest."

His jeans clung to his legs, making a puddle collect at his feet. Scampering for another towel, I batted his feet until he lifted them. "Let me stay here, Amph. I can sleep on the couch."

"Stay? Here? Oh, I don't know…," I trailed off, clutching a wet towel under my chin.

"Skylla threatened you. And until you work through these memories, it's better if I'm here to snap you out of them. Your nose bled this time. *Bled*, Amph."

"What is Skylla going to do? Climb up the apartment building with her tentacles in open view?"

He rested his hands on my shoulders. "If she knows, others might too. You know as well as I do, there are far more spiteful gods than not. The chance to take out a Queen before she's Queen again?" He furrowed his brow.

"This is what I'm saying. I didn't even think about that. I haven't *had* to."

"Let me stay."

I gulped, staring up at him as his fingers brushed my skin. "Fine. But we're both adults here. Just sleep in the bed with me."

"Are you sure?" He cleared his throat and rubbed the back of his head.

"Can I trust you?"

He frowned. "Yes."

"Then get in the bed, Seid."

After drying off our hair and clothes, we each took opposite sides of my bed. I turned my back to him, pinching my knees together once I felt the bed dip from his heavy frame.

"I did have one question before we go to sleep," his voice rumbled next to me.

I turned on my side, resting my head on my hand. "Yes?"

"Skylla said you're the reason she is what she is. That true?" He slipped one hand behind his head, making his bicep twitch before turning to look at me.

"It was an accident."

There was no hiding the surprised look on his face. He turned on his side to face me. "Mind giving the quick version?"

"It's silly, but—I thought you were having an affair with her. When she, you know, was just a nymph?"

"I was a lot of things, but a cheater wasn't one of them."

I patted his arm. "I know. I know. But I was so upset you were never around, and I didn't know where you were. Rumors flew. I actually believed them and got jealous." My cheeks flapped as I blew out a breath.

"It's okay." He caressed my cheek with his thumb.

"It's not okay. I slipped these herbs into one of her drinks. They were supposed to give her bad acne or gas or huge bags under her eyes." I shook my head. "And worse, it wasn't supposed to be permanent."

"Well, you're right. That's pretty messed up, but it was a long time ago. Leave it to a mythical being to hold a thousand-year-old grudge."

"Did you *see* her?"

"Then take your own advice. Apologize."

I flopped to my back. "You think that'd make her stop? She wants us *both* gone. I'm just the easy target right now."

"You don't have to be."

I turned my head with softened eyes.

"Just promise me you'll think about it more?"

"Of course, I will."

He nodded once and kissed my forehead. "Goodnight."

"Goodnight," I whispered back, numbly turning off the lamp on my nightstand.

I lay in the dark with my hands folded atop my stomach, watching the steady rise and fall of the sea god beside me. A man who could conjure typhoons and hurricanes, crash aircraft carriers, or summon any sea monster of his choosing— wanted me back. He wanted me ruling at his side. But most of all—he wanted to be a family.

THIRTEEN

I AWOKE THE FOLLOWING day with my butt nestled against Poseidon's hips, his large arms wrapped around me, and his breath scaling the back of my neck. During the happy years, there were so many mornings like this. Only the golden pillars of Atlantis would greet me versus a humble apartment bedroom. Could I go back to it? It sounded absurd, but was I still made for the life of royalty? Of a goddess?

"Is this okay?" Poseidon's gruff voice mumbled near my earlobe.

I smiled to myself, nuzzling closer and pulling his arms tighter around me. "More than okay."

"Survived the night without any more sea hags threatening your life. That's a plus." He grinned into my hair, inhaling me.

"Oh, good. You two are already sleeping together. Progress," a woman's fluttery voice filled the room.

We sat up, and I clung the sheets to my chest like I was

naked. Poseidon conjured his trident, darting all three prongs at the throat of the blonde woman standing at the foot of the bed.

Her hands splayed and waved in front of her, producing a red wall of swirling glitter like a shield. "Woah there, spinach chin. It's Aphrodite."

"Aphrodite?" I kicked the covers away and rustled to standing, smoothing my hair out. "What the hell are you doing here? And in the middle of my bedroom, for that matter?"

Poseidon narrowed his eyes, keeping the weapon aimed at the love goddess.

"Seriously, P?" Aphrodite pointed at the prongs.

"Answer her question," Poseidon barked.

Aphrodite fluttered her fingers, making the glittering shield disappear, and crossed her arms in a huff. "Yeesh. You do the family a favor and get a trident at your throat."

"What favor?" I cocked a brow.

"I'm sure you've been wondering how you got out of the stars where my dear dad so graciously banished you?"

I stole a glance at Poseidon, who didn't take his gaze from Aphrodite, his grip tightening on the trident's hilt. "The thought crossed my mind."

Aphrodite pointed at her chest. "You're lookin' at her."

"You? But why?" I tapped a finger against my lips.

"Why? I had to have a reason? I *am* the goddess of love. Give me a little cred?" She hung her thumbs from the belt loops of her pale pink skinny pants.

Poseidon grumbled, making the trident disappear in shimmering sea spray. He stood and crossed the room to stand next to me.

Aphrodite pressed her palms together, curling her hands under her chin with a sparkling grin. "I can't tell you how happy I am to see this."

"Don't get too excited. We're not *together*." Poseidon ran his fingers through his hair, followed by his beard, quickly grooming himself.

Ouch. He'd spoken the truth, and I gave him no clue to the contrary, but the words still stung like the wrath of a man o' war.

"You're right. I suppose you'd have been naked when I popped in. Poo." Aphrodite stuck her bottom lip out as she tapped her white heel against the hardwood floor.

"Are you going to explain how you did it?" I scooted closer to Poseidon, aching to feel his warmth against my skin.

"I'm rather proud of myself." She ruffled her wheat-colored locks and clapped her hands together. "With my dad's power, there are always loopholes. It keeps him from being all-powerful. He turned you into a constellation, right? Which made your organic form non-existent. To pull you straight from the stars as you were was impossible, especially the goddess part." The golden heart pendant hanging around her neck swayed on its chain as she paced.

"Go on," I encouraged, fishing for Poseidon's finger and curling mine around it once I'd found it. I caught a quick smile on him from the corner of my eye.

"It was a simple reincarnation spell. You'd be reborn as a mortal. A demi-god. And all you'd have to do is find Poseidon, agree to become Queen again, schlep on over to Zeus, and *boom*, done deal." She made explosion gestures on each side of her head. "Nifty, right?"

"As much as I appreciate what you did, did you honestly think it'd have been that easy to find Poseidon in one lifetime?" I pressed my cheek against Poseidon's arm. "I couldn't remember who I was, and he didn't know I was alive."

Aphrodite snapped her fingers. "A small oversight on my part, but with continual reincarnations, it gave you all the time you needed to come together. However, I didn't know the opposing curse annoying Athena invoked at the time." She rolled her eyes and stared at her fingernail, flicking something from it.

"What curse?" Poseidon stepped forward.

"On you, surfer boy."

Poseidon chuckled, looking at me and pointing to himself. "Me? She put a curse on one of the kings?"

"Yes. That whole Medusa business? My sister is a rather smart cookie. Medusa wasn't the only one punished for your little frolic in Athena's temple."

It hadn't bothered me. We weren't together. He didn't know I was alive. It still didn't make the green-eyed monster any less ferocious.

"Out with it, Aphrodite," Poseidon snarled.

"Okay, okay." Aphrodite held her hands up and flicked her hair. "She knew she couldn't punish you to the lengths she did Medusa, but when she heard about my spell—she cursed you. As many times as Amphitrite would be reincarnated, if you saw her, you wouldn't recognize her. Until you became a changed man—selfless, humble, loving." She shifted her weight to one hip, tapping a fingernail against her cheek. "She never did specify if it was one or all of those things."

"Are you fucking kidding me?" Poseidon clenched his fists. "I could've found Amph hundreds or thousands of years ago? We could've already been together?"

"Fraid so, P. But hey, you finally found each other, right? Though, why the Tartarus aren't you Queen again yet?" Aphrodite raised her thin, sculpted brows.

"It's complicated," I mumbled.

"I can't believe her. You better believe I'm giving Athena a piece of my mind." Poseidon started pacing, dragging his hands over his face and beard.

"Seid." I touched his forearm, willing him to stop moving and look at me. "You said it yourself. My banishment to the stars had a positive spin to it. It made you a loving father and a changed man. If we would've met before we *both* had changed—this may have never worked."

The skin between Poseidon's eyes cinched, and he took my face in his hands. "You're right."

"Okay, so what exactly is complicated about this? Do you two realize how much love is coursing through this room? It's almost strangling me."

Poseidon winced and shook his head, pressing a palm to his temple. His hands fell away from my skin with a grimace. "You've got to be kidding me. Elani has the worst timing."

"Elani? She talked to you too?" Aphrodite leaned against my bed frame.

"Yeah. She wants me to turn her. I just didn't think it'd be that quick." Poseidon rubbed the back of his head.

"If Elani's anything like my son, once she knows what she wants, she goes for it." Shooting her gaze to me, Aphrodite grinned.

"You're leaving? Right now?" I asked, trying to hide the disappointment in my voice.

"Five minutes, Starfish." He kissed my forehead. "I promise I'll be back. It's a favor for Eros." He backpedaled, holding five fingers up before he disappeared.

"Eros? What's going on, Dite?"

She played with the heart charm, working it back and forth on the chain. "My son found true love."

"Found? What about Psyche?"

Aphrodite coughed and scratched the back of her head. "Mistakes were made, obstacles overcome, but the important thing is he found Elani. She's a gem."

"And she's mortal…" I trailed off, turning away and walking into my living room.

"Listen. I'm not exactly the best to give relationship advice, but—" Aphrodite followed me, making exaggerated steps by planting her heel first.

"Shouldn't you be *the* best, goddess of love?" I bit back a smile as I trickled fish food into the tank.

"You would think, but most people find the lack of my own relationship distrusting. Go figure." She snorted. "But all I wanted to ask was why you're so afraid. You were born for this, Amphitrite."

"I know. And everything about it feels like home but—" Bunching my shirt at my stomach, I stared at the fish. "I don't want to revert to that old version of myself."

"Phi." Aphrodite tapped my shoulder, causing me to turn on my heel to face her. "You've lived over a dozen full lives. Have experienced virtually everything a mortal can. What makes you think for a moment you haven't learned from all these lifetimes? You won't do it again. And neither will Poseidon. As flawed as he was, he missed you like Tartarus."

A weak smile pulled at my lips. I *did* want to calm the seas once more with him at my side.

"And despite Zeus hounding him every other year to marry another Queen, he refused. Got pretty ugly up there on Olympus a time or two. Those two can fight like bulldogs, I swear." Aphrodite blew out a breath.

He never married again. Not even for politics's sake.

"About these other lives—" I turned to face her with folded arms. "I get flashes of memories so vivid it's as if I'm reliving them. It's damn near debilitating. I couldn't risk it happening in the middle of a fight, or when I'm addressing the council, or—what kind of Queen would I be?"

Aphrodite fluttered her lashes with widened eyes. "You remember all of them? All of your lives?"

"Yes."

"Well, shit." Aphrodite frowned and scratched her cheek. "I didn't see that one coming."

Flopping to the edge of the bed, I sulked. "I've tried to suppress the flashes, but the power behind them is too strong."

"Maybe—" Aphrodite sat next to me. "—it'd be different when you're a goddess again. You'll have the strength to fight them?"

"I don't think I should take that chance. There have been mortal lives at stake with some of the battles Seid and I have fought. I'd never forgive myself if someone died because I froze during a flashback." Balling my hands into fists, I beat them against my thighs.

"What a bummer," Aphrodite whispered, clicking her nails together before snapping her fingers. "I got it. Mnemosyne."

"The Titan?"

Shaking her head with a fluttery cackle, Aphrodite slapped my shoulder. "Olympus, no. When Dad imprisoned them, she transferred her powers to a river in the Underworld."

Gripping the mattress, I turned to her with a raised brow. "What kind of powers?"

"Memory." She grinned with her chin lifted.

I sucked in a breath, holding it until my lungs burned.

"Phi, you don't have to make a decision now, but promise me you'll think about it?" Aphrodite rested a hand on my knee, making me jump.

"Of course, I'll think about it."

"That's my girl." Aphrodite squeezed my thigh.

My mind dove into the possibilities of what life would've been like if we were to have lived mortal lives as a family. An animated image of my children surrounding the tank and feeding the fish swam through my brain. Rhode stood on her tiptoes, trying to reach it, and Triton picked her up. Closing my eyes, I pushed off the bed to stand. "I abandoned my family once. I'm not doing it again."

Aphrodite followed and gave me a side hug. "We've all done things in our formative years we regret, even if some of us would never admit it. Olympus knows I could be a real harpy back then, but I'd like to think we still all had our moments."

Chuckling, I nudged her in the side with my elbow.

"Careful. You're starting to sound like Athena."

Aphrodite gagged before giggling.

The swirls in the carpet came to life as I stared at them, transgressing into a paintbrush in my hand swirling in water. An emerald green dress clung to my legs as I raised the brush to the canvas, painting a landscape of rolling green hills and a perfectly formed stone castle against a brightly lit horizon.

"Phi?" Aphrodite's voice echoed through my mind.

The feel of the brush's handle became less and less concrete as I pulled myself away from the memory. Aphrodite tugged on my shirt sleeve, and I snapped my gaze to hers.

"It just happened, didn't it?" Aphrodite's brow furrowed as she stroked my hair.

"How long was I staring into space?"

She continued to soothe me. "A few minutes. Please, please consider the river, Amphitrite."

"I need to talk to Poseidon," I whispered, gulping.

Aphrodite nodded and stepped back after giving my arm one last reassuring squeeze. "The hardest part is over. You found each other. You'll figure it out."

"Thank you, Dite."

She smiled, sparkly and radiant. "Anytime, toots." And she was gone in a blast of glitter and rose petals.

I stepped to my fish tank, swirling my fingertips through the surface, preening as the fins occasionally brushed my skin. Closing my eyes, I whispered, "Poseidon."

In a breath, he appeared behind me, his arms enveloping my waist.

He kissed my nape and splayed his hands over my stomach.

"You rang, Starfish?"

"Everything good with Eros and—what was her name?" I sank into him, tracing my hands over his arms, still keeping my eyes closed.

"Elani. And mmhm. She's a goddess of love, and they're bonded. I did my part. Rest is up to them." He pulled me tighter against him, trailing his lips over my ear, moistening it.

"Any other interruptions I should be expecting in the next twenty-four hours?"

"By Olympus, I hope not."

Turning to face him, I cupped his cheek. "I spoke with Aphrodite about my constant flashing memories."

"Oh? Did she have an idea how to stop them?"

I let my gaze fall to the hemp bracelet on his wrist, running my fingertips over one of the shells. "The Mnemosyne River."

"I forgot it even existed." He grinned and tightened his grip on my waist. "What are we waiting for?"

"Seid, I don't know how it works. There is no way in Tartarus I'm losing my memories of the kids, of us, of my life as Cordelia? I won't let it happen." Slipping away from him, I turned my back and cupped my hands over my mouth to stifle a whimper.

His hand slipped over my elbow. "Then we'll talk to Laurel."

"Laurel?" Sniffling, I gazed at him over my shoulder.

"Apollo's wife. He made her leader of the Muses."

The Apollo I remembered was anything but selfless. His arrogance almost rivaled that of his father.

"No shit."

Poseidon let out a hearty chuckle. "I know, I thought

that too, but Laurel can get us in touch with a Muse, and maybe they can give us more information. Their mother *was* Mnemosyne after all."

A newfound hope erupted in my chest like a geyser. "Yes. Let's do it."

"Your chariot awaits." He held his hands out to me with a wry grin.

Slipping my palms over his, I slid into his arms, and he ported us away. We stood in a studio with ballet barres on three walls, mirrors on the fourth, and speakers aligned in each corner. A blonde woman with her hair in a bun stretched on one barre, gasping when she spied us over her shoulder.

"Poseidon," she breathed out, clapping a hand over her chest. "Muses, you startled me."

Poseidon pressed a hand to my lower back, urging me to step forward. "Laurel, this is Cordelia or as she used to be known, Amphitrite."

Laurel's sky-blue eyes widened as she fluttered toward us, her pointe shoes clonking against the floor. "*The* Amphitrite?"

"Yes, it's—complicated." I shook her hand.

Laurel smiled and cocked her head to the side. "You're mortal."

"As she said—complicated," Poseidon added with a smirk.

"Well to what do I owe the visit from the King and Queen of the Seas?" She folded her arms, making the black leotard on her torso tighten across her chest.

"We hoped you could call one of the Muses for us. Any of them would do. We have some questions only they can answer." Poseidon wrapped an arm around my shoulders.

Laurel closed her eyes for several moments before blinking them open. "Absolutely. Euterpe is the only available one, but she's already been summoned. Should be here momentarily."

"Thank you." I distracted myself by scanning the studio. "Is this place yours?"

Laurel nodded with a broad smile, displaying her arms at her sides. "Yes. Apollo and I bought it to have our own place to practice."

"And Apollo? How's that going?" Poseidon asked gruffly.

Laurel batted a stray piece of blonde hair from her eyes. "I couldn't ask for a better partner in virtually every aspect of life."

My emotions seemed to be on overdrive lately as the serene look on her face brought tears to my eyes. Forcing them back, I pressed a hand to my chest with a warm smile. People—even gods—*could* change.

A *whoosh* sounded behind us.

"Apologies for the delay," Euterpe started, dusting off her robes as she moved to stand beside Laurel. "I had to finish scribing the notes for a new piece before I forgot them."

"No matter." Laurel smiled and rested a hand on Euterpe's shoulder. "Poseidon and Amphitrite have a question for you."

Euterpe's eyes widened at me, and she bowed her head. "Amphitrite, I had no idea you were back."

With vigor, I shook my head and held up a palm. "No need for bowing. I'm not Queen."

"Yet," Poseidon added.

My cheeks warmed, and I smiled.

"The Mnemosyne River. How does it work exactly?" Poseidon folded his arms, his jaw tightening.

Euterpe cut a glance to Laurel before looking back at us. "You wish to have memories erased?"

"Me. Yes." The words came out as a whispered squeak.

"If you decide to drink from my mother's river, you must know this—only the memories you hold dear will remain. Be certain you know what those are, or you will lose even the happiest of memories—" She paused, making sure I looked her in the eyes before concluding. "—forever."

I stumbled backward, and Poseidon caught me, pressing his muscular chest to my back.

"Are you certain? There's no way to pinpoint the memories?" Poseidon traced his fingers over my biceps.

Euterpe shook her head with a frown. "I'm afraid it's not that simple."

"If you don't mind me asking, what memories are you trying to get rid of?" Laurel played with the string of her ballet skirt.

Did I want to lose the memories of my past lives altogether? No, not really. They were as much a part of me as Amphitrite and Cordelia, but my family—this life was far more important.

"Memories I don't need anymore." I looked up at Poseidon and slipped my hand into his.

"Do you need me for anything else, my liege?" Euterpe turned to Laurel.

Laurel bowed her head. "No, Euterpe, thank you. Go finish your symphony."

Euterpe turned to face us. "I hope you get the answers you seek, Amphitrite." After a swirl of her arm, she disappeared.

My heart thumped against my chest. "Seid, let's go to the Underworld before I lose my nerve."

"Are you sure?"

I nodded instead of answering him, unsure if I could say the words.

"It was a pleasure meeting you, Amphitrite. I hope the river works in your favor." Laurel gave a warm smile, followed by a graceful curtsy.

"Thank you, Laurel." I squeezed Poseidon's hand, urging him to port us.

Poseidon hugged me to him. "Tell Apollo it's his turn to host poker night."

Laurel laughed and tapped the wooden block of her pointe shoe against the floor. "I'll be sure to do that."

My hair flew behind me as Poseidon took us to the Underworld. It'd been so long since I was here. The chill in the air and the smell of sulfur surrounding us sent a shiver through my bones.

"It's right in front of you, sweetheart." Poseidon kissed the top of my head. "All you have to do is drink if this is what you want."

I had my forehead pressed to his chest; my eyes closed so tightly it made the skin above my nose ache. After taking a deep, calming breath, I slipped away from him and turned to the dark river water, the sconces hanging above us in the dank cave reflecting orange shimmers over the surface. Dropping to my knees, I scooped the water into my palms and held them in front of me, hovering near my lips.

FOURTEEN

ALL THAT WAS LEFT to do was sip the water cupped in my hands. One sip to stop the sporadic images flashing through my brain. One sip to bring me closer to my family. Closing my eyes, I lowered my mouth.

"Stop," Hades's voice boomed from behind me.

Gasping, I let the water in my hands splash to the sandy shoreline. Turning on my heels, I stared up at the imposing god of the Underworld. My previous brother-in-law, who I'd remembered never failing to come across powerful while remaining the most levelheaded of the brothers. I cared for Poseidon, but I'd be the first to admit he could be frivolous.

"Hades, it's what she wants." Poseidon slipped a hand over his brother's shoulder.

Hades didn't tear his glowing white gaze from mine and brushed Poseidon's hand away. "Amphitrite, I'm equally delighted and shocked to see you back. But tell me, why do you wish to terminate memories?"

Wringing my hands together, I glanced at Poseidon for backup. He gave me a curt nod, and I blew out a breath before speaking. "Aphrodite created a reincarnation spell. And it worked countless times leading me into dozens of lifetimes before being born into this current one."

Hades nodded, not appearing as surprised as the others. His floating white hair brushed against his dark robes. "And the memories?"

"At any given moment, flashes from all my past lives consume my mind. It's brought me to my knees more than once." I rubbed my stomach as nausea bubbled, remembering how it felt when my nose bled.

Hades nodded again, the flame crown surrounding his head flickering. "Living through the ages, living these multiple lives—it seems like something one wouldn't wish to forget."

"I'd rather have the chance to be with my family again." I squared off my shoulders, staring at Hades unblinking.

"Drinking that water is too risky, Amphitrite. Allow me to offer an alternative." Hades nudged his chin to the right, his pointed ears sticking out from his long hair.

"Alternative? What else is there?" Poseidon followed beside me as Hades led us along the shore.

"Thanatos's twin brother, Hypnos." Hades's voice sounded like a dozen whispers in varying pitches.

"Hypnos? The guy who helped Hera try and betray Zeus?" Poseidon quirked a brow at me.

"That would be the one. Though most only use him for his sleep abilities, he also has powers of the mind and forgetfulness.

I believe he can help you."

I quickened my steps to walk alongside Hades. "Do you know where he is?"

"Here."

Poseidon pointed down. "Here?"

"Yes. When he woke up to an angry Zeus looming over him, Hypnos asked for refuge in the Underworld. He's been here ever since."

We rounded a rocky corner to a smaller cave, its entrance glowing a welcoming orange from a lit fire within.

"He lives there. I will not be accompanying you as I have to feed Cerberus, however, explain to him the situation, and I'm certain he'll be more than happy to help."

Hades feeding Cerberus. The thought of it made a smile creep over my lips.

"Thank you, bro." Poseidon extended a hand to him with a firm nod.

Hades shook it before patting Poseidon's shoulder. "I'm glad you get to be happy, Poseidon. And Amphitrite, welcome back."

"Thanks, Hades."

After nodding a goodbye, Hades disappeared in ash and fog.

"Let me go first, Starfish." Poseidon coaxed me behind him with a burly arm.

He didn't have to tell me twice. Hypnos was a primordial god. I couldn't remember the last time I'd been around one.

We edged closer to the cave entrance, and once we were at the threshold, a voice rang out, "Who's there?"

"Poseidon and Amphitrite. Hades sent us." Poseidon spoke

to the entrance.

When silence fell across the cave walls too long for comfort, I gripped Poseidon's arm.

"Come in," Hypnos finally answered.

We moved forward, our feet scraping against the stone floor. The inside didn't look like what I imagined a cave home. It was cozy, warm, and inviting with a roaring hearth, a quaint wooden table with a bowl of fruit in the center. A modest bed with red and gold blankets rested in a far corner, while a chess set resided in the other.

Hypnos stepped from the shadows, tugging at his maroon robes as if not knowing what to do with his hands. His dark brown hair fell in waves to his hip bones, and the small black wings on either side of his head perked when he laid eyes on us.

"You'll have to excuse me as I've never had—visitors down here." Hypnos gulped and sprinted to the table, splaying his hands to make an array of meats, cheeses, and a pitcher with mugs appear. "Please, sit."

The desire to get this done and over with took a backseat to how grateful Hypnos looked to have company.

Tugging on Poseidon's shirt to let him know I was alright with staying a little while, I took a seat at the table with a smile. "You have a lovely home, Hypnos. You've made a dreary and dank cave look like a cottage on the inside."

After grumbling something under his breath, Poseidon sat next to me.

"Thank you, Amphitrite. Being alone for so long, I wanted to feel as comfortable as I could." Hypnos grinned and urged us to eat by gesturing at the wooden plates in front of us. The wings folded back, circling his head.

After scooping some fruit onto my plate, I poured from the pitcher—ambrosia wine. "I'm sure Zeus wouldn't smite you were you to join everyone on the surface again."

Poseidon coughed and discreetly shook his head at me.

"You weren't there." Hypnos frowned and plopped in the seat across from us. "His rage at what Hera and I had tried to do rattled the mountains surrounding Olympus. And I took the coward's way out by running. It's a matter of pride at this point."

"Hera left Zeus." Poseidon popped a grape in his mouth. "Pretty sure he wouldn't give a shit about you returning, Hyp."

The wings fluttered as Hypnos's eyes widened. "I'll… consider it."

I tapped my finger against my mug before scooting to the edge of my seat. "Listen, Hypnos. I need a favor if you're able and willing to do it."

"Unless you're asking me to murder someone or assist in betraying a king god, I'm all ears." He grinned as he folded his hands on the table and leaned forward.

"I've been reincarnated multiple times through the ages, not remembering who I truly was. Now that I know who I am—all those memories come pouring in like lifting a floodgate." I gripped the mug, frowning. "It's too much."

Hypnos nodded, the warm smile he'd given moments prior still present. "Ah, yes. I do believe I can help, Amphitrite."

I leaned back, flattening my palms on the table. "You can? That easy?"

"Yes. I simply need your permission to touch you as I need

direct access to your mind." Hypnos's grin faded as he cut his gaze to Poseidon as if looking for his permission moreover mine.

Poseidon glared at him.

I stood and leaned in front of Poseidon, blocking him. "You have my permission."

Hypnos cleared his throat as he stood and walked toward me, raising his hands to press all fingers on each side of my head. "All I need you to do is relax and try to keep your mind as clear as possible."

The inability to clear my mind of all thought was the precise reason I'd never been able to meditate successfully. I'd have to dig deep.

Closing my eyes, I forced my concentration on my breathing—the sound of it as it left my nostrils, the feel of my chest rising and falling, the air filling my lungs.

"Done."

My eyes flew open. Hypnos steepled his fingers and took a step back.

"Done? That's it?" I felt my forehead, checking for fever or some leftover residue or—something?

"I've had these powers for a very long time. It doesn't take much to accomplish a wanted task. I've suppressed only your alternate life memories, but they're not lost forever. If you wish to recall them, then and only then will they surface."

I'd never met Hypnos and only knew him for the several minutes we'd been here, but as tears filled my eyes, I threw my arms around him and hugged him.

"Thank you, Hypnos. You have no idea how much this means to me."

Hypnos stiffened from my touch at first before he hugged me back, the rustling of his feathers as they bristled echoing in my ears. "You're most welcome."

After I stepped back, wiping tears from my eyes, Poseidon jutted his hand. "Thanks, Hyp. You should really consider visiting the new world. You'd be quite the asset up there."

"Thank you. I will. If I can get over the shock of how much has changed, perhaps I'll pay you both a visit."

"We'd be glad to show you around. Anytime at all. I owe you a favor." I curled my hands under my chin and smiled.

Hypnos bowed his head and pressed a hand over his chest. "My dear Queen, you don't owe me a thing. I appreciate the company, but being as she's mortal Poseidon, you'll need to get her back to the surface." He frowned but urged us with a flick of his hand.

Poseidon pressed a hand to my back before pulling me against him. I rested my head on his chest, listening to his heart as I smiled at Hypnos before Poseidon ported us away.

Poseidon's nose nuzzled my cheek. "It's been a whole twenty-four hours, and you haven't had one flashback, right?"

Not in the slightest. It was a form of bliss I didn't know I missed.

"Not a one," I whispered, nestling against him with my eyes closed as we lounged on my couch.

"Good." He kissed the side of my head and lazily stroked my arms.

Fluttering my eyes open, I pulled his arms tighter around me. "When I'm Queen again, I will pull rank on any god or goddess to find one who can help us find Rhode."

"I'm with you, but—" His body stiffened, and he pushed me forward before gently grabbing my chin to turn my face to his. "Are you saying what I think you are?"

I nodded as tears filled my eyes, and I combed my fingers through his wavy hair. "Now that I remember who I am, I don't think I'd ever feel complete without accepting what I was born to do. So, yes. I'll become Queen of the Seas again, *your* Queen, and reunite this family."

"Amph," he said through a loosed breath. His chin dipped to kiss me, but I pressed a finger over his lips.

"I have but one request."

He kissed my finger. "Anything."

"The name Amphitrite belonged to a failed Queen. I want to be called Cordelia from here on out—the name in the lifetime where things fell into place. Fate." I smiled up at him, holding back tears.

This was happening. Even a goddess could be starstruck.

"Cordelia suits you." He pressed his palm to my cheek. "I've thought it since the first moment I re-met you. But I'd never say you were a failed Queen. More like…a work in progress."

I burst a single laugh, a tear rolling down my cheek before I tackled him and kissed the ever-loving shit out of the love of my life—the love of *all* my lives.

Meg.

Pulling away from the kiss with a sigh, I pressed our foreheads together. "There's someone I need to talk to first before I do this. She deserves to know the truth."

"Meg?" He secured my hair over one of my ears. "Are you sure you're ready for that? It'll be a lot for her to take in."

"Did I tell you how we met?" I grinned at him.

He shook his head, tracing one of his fingers over my cheek.

"We met years ago on a dive. Well, we were on separate dives, but she was photographing barracudas, and I was after reef sharks." I sat up, straddling him and trailing my fingers over the horse tattoo on his arm.

He grabbed my hips and pulled me tighter against him.

"Meg was so caught up in her shot she didn't see one of the sharks in her peripheral."

Poseidon smiled. "Did you beat it up?"

"Oh my—" I swatted him with a laugh. "Of course not. I did, however, bump its nose with my camera rig. When we both surfaced, she thanked me a dozen times and offered to buy me lunch for saving her life."

The memory pulled a wide grin over my lips, and I was thankful for Hypnos's help even more now because I wouldn't know what to do if I'd lost memories like this.

"I told her it wasn't that big of a deal, but she insisted, and we spent the next three hours talking about diving, camera rigs, and Disney's *Hercules*, of all things." I flicked my fingernail over the buttons of Poseidon's Henley shirt. "A month later, we agreed to be partners, and the rest, as they say, is history."

He massaged my lower back. "Sounds like you two are pretty close."

"We're like sisters, Seid. So, believe me, when I say it may take some convincing, but Meg will come around."

Poseidon kissed the tip of my nose. "You know your friend better than I do, and I can tell this is something you need to get off your chest, so, go." He bucked his hips. "Get."

Laughing as he continued to bump me off of him, I crawled from his lap. "Okay, okay. I'm going." I dove in for another kiss with a grin. "I'll be right back."

"And I'll be here waiting. Always and forever." He smiled back at me before slapping my ass. "Now. Go."

Backpedaling, I blew him a kiss and exited to the hallway.

Once in front of her door, I knocked three times. Anxious, I followed it up with repeated light taps until finally, the door swung open.

"For crying out loud, Cor. What the hell's going on?" Meg asked with wide eyes before squinting into the sun.

I hugged her tight, sending us fumbling into her apartment. She laughed and patted my back before shutting the door behind us.

"Okay, I'm all about the hugs, but seriously, what's going on?" She folded her arms, making the ribbed lines of her white tank top stretch.

"I've got something to tell you. Something—huge." I waved my arms in large circles.

She puckered her lips. "Do we need whiskey for this conversation?"

"Probably?" An anguished smile tugged at my lips, and I let out a nervous laugh.

"Alrighty. Follow me to the kitchen."

Watching Meg grab two tumblers and a bottle of Jim Beam, I drummed my fingers on the counter.

What was the best way to do this? Lay it all out in one swoop? Use analogies?

She set one glass in front of me and held hers up in a cheers gesture before taking a swig. "Let's have it, Cor." Leaning one hip against the counter, she draped an arm over her stomach and looked at me expectantly.

"Okay. So, you know how animals seem to react differently to me? For instance, you naming me a shark whisperer?" I tapped my fingernail against the tumbler, feverishly chewing on my lip.

"Uh-huh. You told me it was your experience and presence. You called my bullshit, remember?" She pointed at me with her glass-holding hand.

"I did. Scratch that because—you're right." I snapped my gaze to hers, nerves somersaulting in my belly.

She squinted at me, shifting her stance. "So…you *are* a shark whisperer?"

"More than that." I guzzled half of my drink and winced from the burn coursing down my throat.

"You know I'm not a beat around the bush type of person, Cordelia. You got something to say, say it." Meg sipped her drink.

I placed a hand under her glass and tilted it up, encouraging her to drink much more than a tiny sip. With a cock of her brow, she obliged.

"Do you believe in reincarnation?" I was tip-toeing around

it again, but I couldn't—I just could not come right out and say I'm the former Queen of the flipping seas.

"To a point, sure." She narrowed her eyes, and after scanning my face, she finished her drink.

"Meg—" I slid forward and pressed my palms against the marble top. "I'm Amphitrite reincarnated."

An invisible whale lifted from my shoulders, only to be replaced by uncertainty and fear.

"Who's Amphitrite?" She casually slipped her phone from her back pocket, averting her gaze.

This is what happened when a Greek goddess turned into a constellation—they're forgotten.

Gently taking her phone away, I placed it on the counter. "Greek mythology. Queen of the Seas."

She blinked. Her lips quivered, and she pursed them together, laughter following.

I should've seen it coming. Sighing, I turned on my heel and pressed my back against the fridge.

"Holy shit. You're not laughing. Cory, I'm more open-minded than even you are, but you're trying to tell me you're a Greek goddess?"

I didn't say anything, just locked our eyes and shrugged.

"Fuck me." She grabbed the whiskey bottle and poured more into her glass. "You mean that someone, a real person existed back then, and she was known as Amphitrite, right? That's who you're a descendant of?"

"No, Meg." I crossed the room to stand in front of her. "I am Amphitrite. I used to be a goddess, Queen of the Seas, and married to Poseidon. *Simon* is Poseidon."

She sputtered her whiskey and wiped the back of her hand over her mouth. "Wait, what?"

"It's why I kept telling you I felt like I knew him, that he already knew me. It's because we had dozens of years together before meeting again centuries later."

This was far worse than I imagined. If the roles were reversed, I'd be interrogating my friend about what narcotic I was on.

"Okay, okay, okay." Meg closed her eyes and held the tumbler up. "Let's say I'm tracking you so far. And you and Simon are star-crossed lovers reunited in modern times. Is he reincarnated too?"

"No."

Far. Worse. Then I imagined.

"I'm officially lost." Meg downed the rest of her drink.

"Let's sit down. I'll explain everything from beginning to end, and you can make it what you will. Deal?" I gestured toward the living room.

"Sitting. Yeah," she murmured, shuffling against the area rug before claiming a seat on the sofa.

"We had an arranged marriage, and it took us a while to love each other, but once we did, we were an unstoppable force. And crazy over each other." I looked at my palms resting in my lap and smiled. When I lifted my gaze, Meg had a warm grin displayed.

"But over time, Poseidon became consumed by his job, and I saw him less and less. I started to feel neglected, depressed. And I turned to the one being I knew would never let me down—the sea." I wrung my hands, sniffling. "I should've talked to him about it. But instead, I distracted myself in the sea, ignoring my duties, my responsibilities, and also…my family."

"Family?" Meg propped her head on her hand.

Oh, boy.

"I have two children. Triton and Rhode."

"Jesus," Meg whispered, pushing a breath from her lungs. "Continue."

"Because I wasn't upholding my responsibilities and had made no move to change it, Zeus banished me to the stars. I was to live the rest of my days as a constellation, looking down on those that I loved but no longer existing."

If I concentrated enough, I could dig up memories of Poseidon's face when he realized I was gone. He'd destroyed an entire atrium in Atlantis out of fury. And despite his best efforts, he couldn't make Zeus budge on his decision. They didn't talk for a decade. Aphrodite was right—he did miss me.

"That seems a tad harsh. Why didn't Poseidon get punished?" Meg leaned forward, resting her arms on her knees.

Questions and curiosity meant progress. Good.

"Zeus always knows what he's doing. He couldn't formally punish another king, but banishing me, taking me from him— was punishment enough." I rubbed my thumbs together. "Aphrodite created a spell to start my reincarnations."

"Time out." She made the time-out gesture. "Reincarnation plural?"

I nodded. "Countless times."

She tugged on her bottom lip and stared at the floor before giving a firm nod. "Continue."

"It was a matter of Poseidon and me finding each other

again. But Athena put a curse on him that if he ever found me, he wouldn't recognize me unless he'd changed as a man."

And he had in so many ways. I was proud of him.

"That's. Horrible." Meg frowned, her eyes glassy.

"It is, but we found each other. We're reunited, and that's the most important thing." I canted my head to the side, spying her erratic bouncing knee. "Meg? You okay?"

"Not really. I'm trying to believe you here, Cory. I really am. But this is all crazy to me." She shot to her feet. "But the way you talked about all of this was as if it was *your* life to tell."

She needed more, and I didn't blame her.

My scales.

Rising, I held my palms out for her to take or ignore. "Can I show you something?"

Her eyes panned to my palms before landing back on my face, and she took my hands. "Alright."

Closing my eyes, I willed the scales to show themselves— the blue radiant patches shimmering in the dimly lit room.

She gasped and tightened her grasp on my hands, making me wince.

"You're not joking." She stared wide-eyed before poking the scales on my arm with a single finger. After rubbing her fingers together and seeing no signs of paint, she shook her head. "Greek mythology is—real?"

"Yeah, Meg." I made the scales disappear before her eyes, making them widen again. "And I think you knew deep down that something was different about Simon. I could see the cogs turning in your brain from a mile away."

"Sure, but I would've never come to the conclusion he was

Poseidon. I wouldn't have even believed myself." She beat her hands against her cheeks like a drum. "This is surreal."

"I wanted to tell you the truth because I've decided to become Queen again."

Meg grabbed my shoulders, a scowl forming in her brow. "What does that mean? What does it entail?"

"When I married Poseidon and took shared responsibility of all waters, it brought a sort of harmony. In my absence, my home has become catastrophic." I squeezed her shoulders back. "I prove to Zeus I'm worthy of the title again, and I get my home, the love of my life, and my family back."

"Wow, Cory." She pulled me to her, hugging me tightly. "Just wow."

Given her newfound information about the Greek gods, should I tell her about Hera? No. It wasn't my truth to tell. That was Hera's choice when and where if she truly wanted to confess.

"Have you heard from Hera?" I peeled back, keeping one hand on her shoulder.

Meg laughed, dragging two hands through her short dark hair. "You throw me that curveball and then want to revert to peon conversation about my love life?"

"This doesn't mean we'll stop being friends. It doesn't change us as photography partners or picking up trash on the beach to promote our conservation group either. I *do* need a cover after all." I jostled her.

"We could still be friends?"

My lips parted beside myself. "Meg, of course. You're as much family to me as all the gods in Olympus."

She hugged me again, sniffling, before leaning back. "Hera

and I have had multiple phone conversations, and we're supposed to be going on a date tomorrow."

"What?" I grinned and swatted her in the arm. "That's amazing. Why do you not look excited?"

"Because I don't know how to act in front of her, Cor." She brushed past me, rubbing her eyes with her palms.

"What do you mean?"

"She makes me feel different. Flustered. Vibrant." Meg turned to face me, pressing her fingertips together. "I don't even know how to categorize it."

"Flustered?" I bobbed my brows, trying to hold back the gooey grin yanking at my lips.

"No one. Not a soul has ever made me feel like this." She ran a hand through her hair, bunching it atop her head.

I beamed up at her, letting her sort out her thoughts.

"I don't even know what to wear." Meg stared down at me like a baby seal looking for its mother. "She's incredible, Cory."

"Do you want my help?" I rubbed her arm.

She forced out a breath and looked skyward. "For the love of God, yes."

We both chuckled and spent the rest of the night digging through clothes in her closet, sipping more whiskey, and talking about my previous life. With each passing hour, she sounded more accepting and open to my being a goddess. It was the reassurance I needed for myself and her to go through with it entirely. I spent the night at her place, knowing it was my last chance to be Cordelia, her mortal friend. Poseidon and I would go to Zeus and announce that the Queen had returned and wanted her crown back.

FIFTEEN

I'D PORTED BACK TO my apartment from Meg's living room, hearing Meg gasp as I disappeared. Poseidon lay on the couch, precisely where he said he'd be waiting on me.

He stood with a grin, tossing the photography magazine he'd been flipping through to the coffee table. "How'd it go?"

"Better than I expected." I interlaced my fingers behind my back, grinning and swiveling my hips.

He stood in front of me, gazing down at me with hooded lids. "And you still want to go through with this?"

"There isn't a doubt in my mind, Seid." I leaped into his arms and kissed him.

He coaxed my legs around him, wrapping one arm under my butt while the other kneaded the back of my head. With every caress of our lips, every lap of our tongues, the familiarity settled into our veins—our bones.

Pulling away from him with a whimper, I said, "I lied. I have one more request."

"What do you need?" He adjusted me in his arms, causing my pelvis to rub against his stomach.

I bit my lip, moaning. "Be with me like this—before I'm a goddess. I want to *feel* your magic before I have my own again."

With an accepting snarl, he crashed his mouth against mine, diving us into a carnal exchange of kissing, nipping, groaning.

"No other woman could've ever lived up to you, Cordelia. I was ready to spend eternity alone." He tapped his forehead with mine, moving us into my bedroom.

"Shh," I whispered against his lips. "I'm here, Seid. I'm right here."

He searched my face, memorizing every freckle, every groove before kissing me again and pushing us to the bed. Instead of landing on a mattress, he ported us to an underwater grotto, keeping us dry within a created air bubble filling the space. I broke away from his lips long enough to grin at our atmosphere. Water walls surrounded us, giving a prime view of the aquatic life swimming around it—fish of all shapes and colors, sea turtles, and dolphins. It was as if they came to pay their respects to our reunion.

"Shouldn't we be worried about Skylla here?" I lay beneath him, gleaming up at his emerald gaze.

"She won't be able to sense us through my protection spell. And I'd pity anyone foolish enough who tried to interrupt what's about to happen." He dragged a hand through his hair, parting it from his face with a smolder capable of boiling the water around us.

"What's about to happen?" A sultry grin melted over my lips.

He rolled his hips, pressing himself against me, making me gasp. "I'm going to remind you how the Seven Seas themselves couldn't compare to how wet you always got around me."

His words alone had me soaked, and I pinched his sides with my knees. "Remind me, Seid."

With a devious curl of his lip, he pulled spirals of water from the ocean, disguising us, and circled them over my body. Every pass over my clothes made them disappear, each brush of the silky moist tendrils making me writhe beneath him. His arm turned into water, joining the spirals as they tantalized my skin in tandem. He skirted his hands up my inner thighs, yanking my knees apart to display myself for him.

His tongue lapped at the corner of his mouth as he gazed down at me, and with one flick of his head, water splashed, and he was fully naked. I sat up, reaching for him, ready to greedily roam my hands over every toned piece of him, but he snatched my wrists.

As he coaxed me to lay back, his length brushed my folds. He leaned over me, grinning like a tiger shark. "Not yet, Cory. I've got so much reminding to do first." His brow bobbed.

Hearing my new name on his lips with him between my legs was almost enough to send me over the edge right then and there.

His beard tickled my skin as he kissed my neck, traveling to my breasts, sucking on each nipple before trailing his tongue the length of my stomach, stopping right above my clit. Grinning against my hip bone, he gave my folds one slow, torturous lap of his tongue. My back arched from the sea bed, fingers tangling in his hair, holding him captive. He used the tip of his tongue to flick, switching to nibbling, sucking, lapping, and all forms in between. He pressed a firm hand on my stomach, keeping me still as I squirmed with pleasure.

He paused, hovering over me, evidence of my appreciation for his efforts laced in his beard. I propped on my elbows, panting, gazing back at him. The first time we slept together, I'd been a virgin sea nymph—nervous, afraid, apprehensive. I hadn't expected him to take the care he had, the patience. And the sex became a wildfire even fathoms below the surface through time.

Keeping our eyes locked, he lowered his lips between my legs, covering me with his mouth. His cheeks filled with warm water, rolling against my folds in partnership with his swirling tongue. I gripped the cushioned floor beneath me, my nails digging into the spongey surface. An earth-shattering cry poured from my lungs as I climaxed, shaking, bucking, and writhing.

Poseidon had no plans to let me come up for air, splashed water over his chin, crawled over me, and thrust. I gasped, throwing open my eyes and wrapping my arms around his neck.

Poseidon peered down, rocking in and out of me. He kissed the tip of my nose, my cheek, my lips. "Gods, I've missed you. I've *fucking* missed you."

Digging my fingers into his strong shoulders, I lifted my hips, making him go deeper. "I've missed you too, Poseidon."

A satisfied masculine grin played over his lips and a sparkling water surge coiled through my hair, surrounding us like a halo. As a soft satiated moan escaped my throat, I reached behind me, plunging my hand through the water wall and letting the outside salty ocean wet my fingertips. One of his hands curled under my ass as he pounded harder into me.

Sitting up, grinding myself against him, I pressed my lips to his ear. "I thálassa eínai to spíti mou allá esý eísai to katafýgió mou." After sucking on his ear lobe, I leaned back, peering at him with ravenous eyes.

The sea is my home, but you're my sanctuary.

He'd been out of my life for far too long, and now with a new taste for him—the hunger may never be satisfied.

His eyes twinkled, his hand cupping the side of my face, before he pushed off the seafloor, launching us skyward. We plunged through the top wall, circling into open water, sending fish darting in all directions. Bubbles ebbed and swirled, floating through our hair in sinewy wisps. In the water, it was akin to being near weightless. Holding onto his shoulders for leverage, I moved up and down over him, the chilled ocean water flowing over my nipples plummeting me into euphoria.

My scales appeared—vibrant and shimmering. Poseidon smiled against my lips before opening his mouth and curling his tongue with mine. He grabbed my hips, halting me, and I opened my eyes, blinking, a flash of the golden crown on his head sparking in my brain.

"Kósmima tis thálassas," Poseidon said, his strong hands guiding my hips up and down his length, those jade eyes holding our entire past and future gleaming within them.

Jewel of the Sea.

As Poseidon held me close, angelfish swam circles around us, swirling our bodies in a descending typhoon. Our feet emerged through the water wall, back to the dryness and protection of the grotto. Water bubbled under my feet, floating us down to the sea bed, our hair soaked and wavy, sticking to our foreheads—our chests.

"I chose you that day when I saw you dancing on the bank, not only because I thought you were the most beautiful creature I'd ever seen, but—" He pulled out of me, pressing his hand to my chest and backing me to the nearest water wall. "I chose you because I could see my life with you with every sway of your hips. Saw our bond with every swirl of your arms. And envisioned our children in every breath you took."

This was what I'd always wanted. This. Right. Here.

"Oh, Seid," I sighed out.

He lifted one of my legs, curling it over his hip, pressing my back against the liquid wall. He made the wall solid but alive, the ocean tickling against my skin as I rested against it. He pushed into me inch by inch, slow and delicious. "I love you. I've always loved you." Before I could say it back, he covered my mouth with his and filled me to the hilt.

At that moment, he didn't need to hear me say it back but knew *I* wanted to hear it more than anything. Words scarcely exchanged between us so long ago.

He pressed a hand above my head and made the water supporting us glow and pulse with each bonding thrust. The sweet ache pooled between my hips, building and building until it reached its peak. After several more thrusts, Poseidon reached his own euphoria, spilling inside me and growling into my nape.

I nuzzled my nose against his cheek. "I don't want to leave this place. Not yet. I haven't felt this comfortable in my surroundings in such a long time."

"We can stay here as *long* as you want," he said, the satisfaction in his tone making his voice extra raspy.

I ran my big toe up his lower back before pulling him tight against me. "You most certainly haven't lost your touch, sea god." I grinned and walked my fingers up his abs.

A deep chuckle rumbled from his chest. "Crisis averted." He slowly pulled out of me, standing and moving to the center of the grotto. "Come here."

I bit my thumbnail as I sauntered to him.

His arms turned into water as he waved them at the floor, turning it even spongier than before. He lay on his side and opened his arms wide and inviting. I lay down with my back to him, all but cooing once he wrapped his arms around me.

"Can you still do the water horse trick?" I nestled my ass against him, grinning to myself at the hardness still there.

"You insatiable nymph." He playfully nipped my earlobe, shoving himself harder against me. Without answering me, he lifted his hand, making it form the clear liquid. Gradually it took shape, morphing into a horse and galloping around the grotto. Its water mane left a sparkling trail in its wake.

I laughed, kissing his shoulder as he obliged me with the water show.

"Olympus, that laugh." He kissed my cheek, dropping his hand, the horse fading away in a wave of bubbles.

"Do you remember that shimmering negligee I conjured on special occasions?" A wicked grin fluttered over my lips.

His cock bounced against me. "You're kidding, right? How in Tartarus could I forget *that*?"

"I hope I can remember how to do it. I hope I can remember

how to do *any* of it." I frowned, curling his arm around me again. Playing with his fingers, I pushed our hands together, noting how small mine was by comparison.

"It's like riding a chariot, Cor. Once you have the power again, it *will* come back to you."

"What if he doesn't accept me?" I traced the grooves in his palm, scraping my nail against the calluses.

"Who? Zeus? I'll *make* him if he doesn't." His arm tightened, and I trailed my finger over the scattering of blonde hair on his tanned arm, calming him.

"You know that's not how it works. We have to prepare ourselves for the worst-case scenario."

"No. I won't let him fuck us over a second time." He rested his chin on my shoulder. "You've changed. He can be a prick, but he *is* a smart man. He'll see it."

"So, what other sea monsters have returned since I've been gone? Please tell me the Kraken is still dormant."

Silence.

"Seid?"

Bubbled water collected at his fingertips, and he massaged one of my breasts, making my stomach tingle and flip.

"Hm?" He lazily asked as if not hearing my question.

I moaned as his silk water touch traveled to my stomach. "Are you distracting me to avoid my question?"

"Because you absolutely hate it, huh?" He slipped a finger inside me, stirring the bubbles.

I arched against him, groaning.

"All the more reason for you to become Queen again, Cordelia." He slid another finger in me, warming the water, sending a surge straight to my toes. "We can fight them together and send them all back to their holes."

I cried out, reaching for the back of his head to hold onto something.

"Restore Atlantis to its prior glory." He flicked the water with the tip of his finger, grinding against my spot.

Moaning his name, I grabbed his hair, pulling him to me for a kiss.

After briefly kissing me he said, "And put fear into anyone or anything who tries to *fuck* with our home."

Yes. Yes. All of it. *Yes.*

After one final flick, I came undone, quivering in his arms, kissing him again. I pushed his shoulder, forcing him to his back, and straddled him.

He grinned, letting me hold him down.

"Promise me one thing. We will always be equal rulers. Where you go, I go. The seas are *ours*."

He grabbed my hips and narrowed his eyes. "I promise on Rhea's life what happened before will not repeat itself. You'll be my Queen. I'll be your King. Our thrones touching side-by-side."

A grin tugged at my mouth, wide and brimming with life. I kissed him with the soul of the sea coursing through my veins.

"Now, let me remind you of a skill of mine I remembered you *never* complaining about." My scales shimmered.

A wicked smile slid over his lips, and we made love throughout the night, re-introducing ourselves and bonding, surrounded by what we swore to protect, to control, and improve—the mysterious depths of the sea.

SIXTEEN

"HEY." POSEIDON REACHED FORWARD, tapping my knee. "We don't have to do this right now. The seas have waited for a long time. They can wait for more."

We sat in my living room, Poseidon on my couch, and I in my lounger. I'd sworn up and down when we left the grotto, I was ready to go to Zeus. To ask him to be Queen again.

"Only the seas have been waiting?" I nudged his foot with mine.

He sighed and wrapped his arms around my shoulders. "I have too, yes. But seriously, take the time you need."

"The sooner I get my powers back—my reign, the sooner we can find Rhode." I pressed my palms together, slipping them between my knees.

"It *would* help, yes." He scooted to the edge of his seat and grabbed my knees. "But I can tell you with the utmost certainty our daughter is alive and well wherever she is, and you'd be doing her no favors rushing into this."

"How can you be so sure?"

"Because she has the strength and wit of her mother coupled with the courage and fighting sense of her father. She's going to be fine until we get to her. Tartarus—" He rubbed the back of his neck. "Who knows? She may not want to come back."

My throat tightened because I knew he was right. If she were anything like me and found someone she cared about in all the time she'd been gone, she wouldn't leave it for anything.

"Way to kill my hope before the box is even opened, Seid." I frowned with a partial smile.

"I didn't mean it like that. We'll—cross that bridge when we get to it." He kissed my temple and squeezed my thigh.

"I haven't seen Zeus since he banished me." I wrung my hands together, a crinkle forming in my brow.

Poseidon rubbed my shoulders. "Zeus does *not* have full power over me. I do have veto rights. And you think Hades would vote against it? It'll be fine, Cor."

I sighed and looked to Olympus above. "I know you and Hades would have my back. That isn't the point."

"What is it?" He rubbed between my shoulder blades.

"Is it crazy I want Zeus to accept me? To *want* to give me my Queendom back?" I couldn't look at him as I squeezed my hands together in my lap.

"You really give a shit what he thinks?"

"Under normal circumstances? No. But this is different, Seid. You were right when you said he'd be able to sense if I'd changed. So, if he disagrees…" I let my voice flutter away, turning my attention to my gaming setup. I'd neglected it for days. My Glitch viewers probably wondered why I'd suddenly disappeared.

"Take twenty-four hours. Let it settle. I'm asking you. Please."

I pressed a palm to his cheek. "Alright, Seid. But would you do me a favor?"

"Anything I do for you at this point, sweetheart, isn't a favor. It's a given." He kissed my hand. "Out with it."

"Would you—make an appearance on my Glitch channel as Simon Thalassa?" I squinted one eye. "It'd shoot my ratings through the roof."

A deep chuckle roared from his belly. "That's it? Let's do this." Slapping his hands on his thighs, he stood, walking to my gaming desk.

With a grin as wide as my face, I flopped into my rolling chair, pushing the power buttons of my console, monitor, and webcam.

"Did you—want them to know we're together, or will that ruin your image?" He asked in a strained voice.

My heart sank, and I swiveled to face him. "Is a gal supposed to be ashamed of a guy like you?"

"I'd certainly hope not, but I figured ninety percent of your following are dudes, most of which undoubtedly have a crush on you." He raised a thick brow.

"Oh? You think they only watch my stream because I'm a woman and not because of my gaming prowess?" I folded my arms.

He glared at me and grabbed the back of my chair, rotating it. "You're purposely being difficult, aren't you?"

I curled my fingers around the leather strap hanging from his neck, the pewter trident pendant cool against my palm. "Maybe. But I have an idea. I can tell them I've been away getting—" My eyes lifted to meet his, and I flashed my scales at him. "—engaged."

A moan escaped his throat and he curled a hand behind my back. "And it wouldn't be a lie, would it?"

"Nope." I grinned and shook my head, leaning forward to give his lips a quick peck.

"If that's the case. You're going to need proof." He held his fist between us.

I sat back, pressing a hand to my chest.

His hand morphed into water and returned to normal after a bright shimmer. A ring rested in his palm when he turned his hand over. "I know we've technically skipped ahead and already consummated the marriage—" A wicked glint flashed in his gaze. "—three times, but what do you say we do things properly this time, hm?"

My vision blurred with tears, sinuses stinging, and I cupped my hands over my nose. Smiling at me, he dropped to one knee and held the ring between two fingers.

"Cordelia—mother of my children, my forever Queen, and caregiver to the seas—will you marry me?"

"Poseidon, for the love of Olympus," I cried out, leaping from my chair and wrapping my arms around him, sobbing.

He softly laughed into my hair and wrapped one arm around me. "Love, you didn't say yes."

"Yes," I yelled, pushing against his shoulders to stand straight. "Times every year we've spent apart, *yes*."

Grinning, he slid the ring on my finger and remained on his knee as I lifted my hand to gaze at it. A silver mermaid made up the band, her scaled tail circling it, her hair made of intricate looped metal coiling around the prongs, which held a vibrant aquamarine stone.

"Seid, it's beautiful."

He pulled me closer, his head in line with my hips. With a deep sigh, he pressed his forehead against my stomach and held me. I rested my hands on the back of his neck and lowered my lips, pressing a kiss to his head and freezing there in blissful silence.

"I should probably wait to go on camera now. My eyes are puffy and red." I sniffled and laughed.

He tilted his head back and wiggled his fingers over my face. "It's going to be fun when you have your powers back reminding you of everything you can do with them."

"Shut up." I swatted him in the shoulder, my new ring sparkling from a nearby lamplight.

"Do you like it?" He rose to his feet, pulling me to his side.

Resting my head against his bicep, I turned the ring left to right, smiling at its glitter. "It's so me it makes my heart ache."

"You ready?" His eyes lifted to my awaiting powered-up gaming system.

"Yeah. It'll be quick, promise. Just a check-in so they know I'm alive."

Nestling in my chair, I grabbed my Pelican Beach headset and the generic standard set that comes with every console, handing it to him. "You get the dorky pair."

"Aw, you're so sweet." He plucked the headset from my

fingers and poked me in the side, making me yelp. After he slipped it over his head, a strand of hair falling over his gaze, he turned to me with a raised brow. "How do I look?"

The man was physically incapable of being unattractive.

"Like the world's sexiest telemarketer."

He pumped his fist. "Nailed it."

Chuckling, I started my webcam and went live on Glitch. No need for a moderator with how long we'd be on. I tapped my fingernails against my desk, waiting for viewers to realize I'd randomly gone live.

"Oh, I should appear from out of frame, right? Make an entrance?" He bobbed his brows with such a charming ass grin I couldn't help but kiss him.

"I'm surprised you didn't think of that sooner, King of the Seas." I flashed him a sly grin.

He glared at me, pointing, and wheeled himself out of camera.

It took several minutes, but soon, the list of attendees grew by the dozens leading into the hundreds.

"Oh, wow. Hey Sea Farers." I waved at the camera with a beaming smile. "Thank you all so much for joining me on this random stream."

I paused to watch the chat feed.

MissTacoX: OMG! I thought you quit.

HufflePufflenz: You've literally been the highlight of my week. SO glad to see you back.

"Told you," Poseidon mumbled at my side.

I swatted him on the knee. "Sorry I've been absent, everyone. I've just been busy…well—" Holding the back of my hand at the camera, I shoved the ring into frame. "Getting engaged."

MissTacoX: WHAAAA Congrats!!!

FriskeeBizkit: Who's the lucky S.O.B.?!

"Some of you may have heard of him. Simon Thalassa."

Poseidon dipped his head into frame, holding his hand in the hang loose gesture. "What up, fishies?"

MissTacoX: AHHHH

HufflePufflenz: I'm legit about to lose my s* right now.**

Poseidon pointed at the comments and laughed—the jade in his eyes intensified from the camera. "And you're right Friskee, I am a lucky, lucky dude." He planted a kiss on my cheek, making me blush.

MissTacoX: Staaaahp you two are adorbs!

HufflePufflenz: If you tell me he's going to start showing up as a guest gamer on your channel, I'm going to completely lose my s*.**

Poseidon dragged a hand through his wavy locks, squinting at the camera.

MissTacoX: Oh. Dear. Gawd.

"Well, it just so happens I am. You better believe all should fear us when we team up in *Tides of Atlantis*." Poseidon pointed into the camera. "And I'm mostly talking to you—ProteinGeyser."

FriskeeBizkit: Daaaaaayuuuum!

MissTacoX: LMAO

I bit my lip, attempting to hide the shit-eating grin that so very much wanted to show.

"Yes, indeed. Stay tuned, everyone. Anyway, I just wanted

to pop on really quick to let you all know. And I promise I'll be back to my regular streaming within the next few weeks." I blew air kisses. "Keep swimming."

FriskeeBizkit: Congrats!

Dozens of other comments flew through the chat, but I didn't bother to read anymore as I cut the feed, turned off the camera, and took Poseidon's face in my hands. "Soon, the whole world will know about our alter egos."

"Why stop at the world? There's a whole galaxy out there."

Removing his headset, followed by mine, I spied him from the corner of my eye. "Let's go to Atlantis."

He coughed into his fist. "*Atlantis*, Atlantis?"

"No, *Tides of Atlantis*." I referenced the poster hanging above my desk. "Of course, I mean the real Atlantis."

"Uh—not sure that's such a great idea, Cor." He scratched the back of his head.

Folding my arms, I leaned back in my chair, swiveling. "And why not?"

"For starters, I told you it's a mess. And secondly, Skylla *will* be able to find you there." He grabbed my armrests and rolled my chair in front of him.

"I don't care how messy it is. I want to see it. And wouldn't my apology to Skylla mean more as a mortal?"

He puckered his lips. "Probably, but why risk it? You're too vulnerable right now."

"You wouldn't let anything happen to me. Besides, give me a trident, and I'll make sure I use it *if* she shows up." I tapped my fingers on my bicep.

"Oof," Poseidon responded, adjusting himself. "The thought

of you with a trident in your hand again…"

"Will you take me home, Poseidon? I think seeing it, especially if it's in the state you say it's in, will be the final push to stand in front of Zeus and ask he reinstate me."

He slowly nodded. "Alright."

I jumped in my seat, my phone vibrating in my back pocket. "It's a text from Meg."

A selfie photo of her and Hera, their arms draped around each other. I hadn't seen Meg that happy in such a long time, and Hera—possibly never. Showing the screen to Poseidon, I grinned.

"Cute. Did Hera tell her yet?"

"Give her some time. I wasn't as hard of a sell because I already knew all this existed, remember?" Moving behind him, I held the ring up between our faces and took a selfie to send back to her.

Me: I'm so happy for you, Meg.

Meg: Is that a ring?!

Me: It's happening tomorrow.

I'd made up my mind, but Atlantis was the final piece I needed to face the King of the Gods.

Meg: You're going to be amazing.

Me: You two have fun. ;)

Slipping my phone away, I lifted my gaze to an awaiting Poseidon in front of me with his burly arms folded.

"I still don't think this is a good idea," he grumbled.

"But a favor is a given?"

"I'm going to regret ever saying that, aren't I?" His beard hid the smile on his lips, but his eyes sparkled, giving him away.

"Time will tell." I took his arms and wrapped them around my hips. "Whisk me away."

He ported us underwater in the middle of the ocean. If I'd been a full-fledged goddess, the sight of Atlantis would've shown immediately. After he waved his hand in front of us in an arch, the familiar pillars and spires nestled fathoms below any unknowing human eyes or mind appeared. Kicking my feet behind me, I swam forward, gasping at the rubble of the once powerful city. The blue beacon that shone from the center tower, beaming skyward, had gotten so dim you could scarcely make it out through the murky waters surrounding our home. It didn't even have enough power for the dome shield it produced, keeping out all unwanted guests.

"You weren't kidding. How did this happen?" I gulped, swimming to a building with a giant hole in the side.

"The creatures have battled for control of it. I've stopped them every time, but without harmony, chaos is bound to ensue."

Without…me.

"I knew you wouldn't be able to resist coming back here," Skylla screeched from behind us. Her tentacles lashed out.

"Cordelia," Poseidon yelled, making a silver trident, the twin to his own but more petite, appear in my hand.

My old trident. He'd kept it.

Twirling the trident in my palm, I held it above my head in a stabbing motion. "I don't want to fight you, Skylla. Simply talk."

"Talk is so very cheap, Amphitrite. I've been waiting a long time to get my revenge. Have been ever so patient." She let out a shrill scream and launched two tentacles at me.

Using the prongs of my trident, I deflected one. Poseidon darted in front of me, stabbing his trident through the second.

Skylla let out a blood-curdling cry, yanking her tentacle from the sharp prongs, sending a spray of blood.

"Skylla, I want to apologize. I was a completely different person back then. I was jealous. Confused." I held the trident's staff above my head as one of the dragon heads on her tentacles snapped at me, making it bite the indestructible metal—Atlantean metal.

"Jealous? Over something I didn't do? And so you turned me into—into this?" She roared, throwing her large arms out at her sides.

"I didn't know the herbs would do this to you, Skylla." My brow pinched, and I tightened my grip on the staff. "If I could drop the curse, I would."

Skylla's chest heaved before all dragon heads snapped and snarled. "It isn't good enough. Nothing you say or do will *ever* be good enough."

"That is enough," Poseidon's voice boomed as he sent a sonic wave through the water with his hand, forcing Skylla back. "If you won't accept her apology, then you best make yourself scarce and *pray* she doesn't want to hunt you down when she's Queen again."

I kept the prongs pointed in her direction, furrowing my brow.

Had I thought it'd be that simple? She'd accept my apology, we'd hug it out, and the dragon heads would let me scratch them all under the chin?

Skylla's fists clenched and vibrated at her sides before she disappeared in the dark depths, a fading shriek following her. The trident fell limp in my hands, and my shoulders slumped forward. Poseidon floated in front of me, gently taking the weapon from me.

"You alright?" Despite the very recent threat on my life, his gruff voice still made my skin tingle.

"I feel terrible. How could I have done that to her?"

He scoffed. "I've done far worse. Trust me."

I cut him an exasperated glare.

"Not helping. Right." He snapped his fingers, floating tiny bubbles in front of him. "When you're Queen—you can lift her curse. At the very least, manipulate it."

"I can? But how? The herbs came from—" I bit my knuckle. "I don't remember who I got them from."

"Doesn't matter. She's a creature of the sea now, which will give you the means to control. Not to mention she was a previous nymph, like you."

I curled my hands under my chin. "I'm so ready, Seid. I am." Turning to look at a once vibrant, brightly shining city's ruins and rubble, I sighed. "And I *must* fix this."

"You will." He slipped his hand into mine, making circles against my palm with a thumb.

Lifting my head high, I nodded. "Set up a meeting with Zeus. First thing tomorrow, I'll stand before him and ask— no—*demand* my reign back."

"You're going to *demand*?" A sly grin curved his upper lip.

"Don't think I can?"

He turned to me, tugging my hand to bring me flush against him. "I *dare* you."

"Challenge accepted." I preened up at him, snaking my arms around his neck. "Spiral us."

"You better hold on tighter, soon-to-be Queen." He brushed his lips against mine, waiting for me to tighten my grip around him.

Making his trident disappear, he held onto me with one hand, turning his other into the same ocean water we floated in. After several twirls, we slowly spun in a circle, his power creating streams and helixes of bubbles around us. The momentum built and built until we spun in unending spirals toward the surface. Laughing, I'd grazed over the thought of the consistent circling making me dizzy as a mortal, but pressed my check to his to ground me.

We breached the surface and bobbed, wrapped in each other's arms. The setting sun cast purple, pink, and orange hues in streaks across the sky, reflecting in the sparkling ocean waters.

"I love you," I whispered, and we watched the rest of the sunset with the best seats in the house.

SEVENTEEN

WE STOOD IN FRONT of the Crane, Crane, and Wallace Law building in New York City. I donned the one dress jacket and pencil skirt I owned, styled my hair, and fished my black stilettos from a black hole in my closet.

"I cannot believe Zeus, King of the Gods, is practicing law," I mumbled, folding my arms.

Poseidon put on a dress shirt and slacks but refused to tie his hair back, stating his brother would have to get over it. He opened the door for me, ushering me inside. "You don't want to hear other cover jobs he's had through the years. Trust me."

"You're right. I don't. Is he at least a good lawyer?" I held my clutch in one hand and grabbed Poseidon's hand with the other.

"Unfortunately, he's the best this side of the country."

"Why, unfortunately?"

"Because he's a damn criminal defense lawyer," Poseidon

grumbled, pressing a hand to my lower back and guiding me to the front desk.

"What?" I snapped, prepared to spout unending questions when a woman my height with cropped brown hair approached us.

"Are you Mr. Vronti's three o'clock?" The woman twirled her hair as she scanned Poseidon's arms and chest.

Sliding in front of my soon-to-be-again husband, I flashed a charming grin. "We are."

"So, you're his brother, huh? The apple most certainly does not fall far from the tree. I can see the resemblance." Ruth bit her lip, leaning to the side to peer around me.

"Just what I love to hear," Poseidon mumbled.

I took one of his arms and wrapped it around my shoulders.

The woman cleared her throat and adjusted her wire-rimmed glasses. "Right this way, please.

Poseidon's mouth pressed against my ear. "Defending your territory there, Starfish?" He grinned into my hair.

"You bet your ass I am." I playfully elbowed him in the ribs.

Chuckling, he curled a hand over my hip as we followed the woman.

"I'm Ruth, Mr. Vronti's assistant. He said he's been looking forward to this meeting all day." Ruth offered a warm smile over her shoulder.

"I bet he has," Poseidon said through a cough.

I bit the inside of my cheek. "You always get so feisty when you know we're going to be around your brother," I whispered.

"He brings it out of me."

"Here we are." Ruth opened her hand to an awaiting

meeting room. "Do either of you need any refreshments while you wait? He should only be another minute or two."

"Water?" I hovered by one of the rolling chairs nestled against the long glass table.

"Of course. Bottled okay?" Ruth's perky nose perked even more when she smiled.

"Perfect," I answered before taking a seat.

Ruth scurried away, letting the glass door click shut behind her.

I sat straight, folding my hands in front of me first on the table, dropped them to my lap, and then back to the table.

Poseidon slid his large hand over both of mine and raised a brow. "Relax. It's going to be fine."

Nodding, I flattened my palms on the table. "I'm actually looking forward to the look on his face."

Poseidon snorted, and we both stiffened as the door swung open.

Ruth trotted in, setting two bottles of water in front of us. "I swear he should only be a few more minutes. He's in a meeting with the prosecution over his latest big case, and it's gone over the scheduled time. This happens often." She gave a reassuring smile before bouncing on her heels and exiting.

I blew out an exasperated breath and slumped in my chair, resting my head on the back. "He hasn't changed a bit."

"I highly doubt his punctuality ever will. He likes to make people sweat." Poseidon leaned his forearms on the table, swiping one of the bottles into his grasp.

"Oh, that has already started." I plucked my jacket's collar. "Thank Olympus, I'm wearing a jacket over this blouse."

"How many times did you practice your speech in the mirror when I dropped you off last night?" Poseidon's eyes gleamed at me as he sipped from the bottle.

"Only twice." I crossed my arms in a huff. "Okay fine. Four times."

"Want to practice? I can pretend I'm him."

I scrunched my nose. "Thanks, but no thanks. I don't want you even pretending you're him."

Chuckling, he tilted his head back and finished the water.

I stood, moving to a corner of the room, pinching the bridge of my nose, and going over in my head what I planned to say to him.

The door cracked open, and I froze with my back to it.

"I'd say I'm sorry I'm late, but then I remember the company," Zeus said as he entered, smirking and closing the door.

"How's it going, asshole?" Poseidon said.

Why hadn't I turned around yet? My heels were clearly glued to the floor.

"Eh. Things are bound to turn around eventually. Who's the babe?"

I clutched my hands at my chest.

Poseidon cleared his throat.

Rolling my shoulders back and wiping any evidence on my face that my nerves were on overdrive, I turned on one heel.

Zeus had a smug grin on his face, but it morphed into shock and anger when he locked eyes with me. "What. The fuck?"

"Surprised to see me?" I raised my brows.

"You're damn right I am." He cut his glare to Poseidon, pointing at me. "What is this all about, Don?"

"What the Tartarus does it look like? She's back. We're together again." Poseidon pushed off the table, standing and tensing his arms.

Zeus rolled his eyes and turned away from us. "Oh, for fuck's sake. Can a King god catch a break?"

Mustering every ounce of courage surging through me, I crossed the room, standing directly behind Zeus. "I want my Queendom back. My immortality. All of it."

"Oh, do you?" Zeus whirled to face me, looming over me like the rain clouds he commanded. "Tough. Shit."

His words jarred me, making my brain fuzzy. Shaking it off, I stood my ground. "Yes. I know I failed on my responsibilities thousands of years ago. But banishing me to the stars? Making me watch my family gradually forget about me? Don't you think it was a tad, I don't know, harsh?"

Zeus's left nostril bounced. "You got off easy, Amphitrite because you were my brother's wife. Would you like to know what happened to other gods who failed me?"

"Zeus," Poseidon growled, stepping toward us.

"Don." Zeus pointed at him, lightning sparking from his fingertips and flashing in his eyes. "Don't even think about it." He cut his glare back to me. "I gave you chances. Twice, in fact. You didn't heed my warnings."

"Zeus, please." Resorting to begging made me nauseous. "We've both changed. I won't turn away from my true duties again. He showed me Atlantis—the state our oceans are in. I can *fix* all of it. And I want to more than anything."

The lightning fizzled away, and he lowered his hand, his gaze faltering to the floor.

"You know there's no one more fit for this than her. Stop being so godsdamned prideful." Poseidon's chest heaved.

Zeus clucked his tongue against his teeth. "It has nothing to do with pride. The decisions I make are for the betterment of the universe. It has nothing to do with *me*."

"I will not fail this time, Zeus. I won't." My throat bobbed, thinking of Rhode. "I can't."

A scowl distorted Zeus's features as he shifted his gaze from me to Poseidon and back again. He played with one of the "Z" cufflinks on his shirt, his jaw tightening.

"Amphitrite. If I do this, and you fail again, I will make certain there is absolutely *no* way you can come back. Do you understand?" Zeus's cheek twitched, a hint of a gleam in his eyes.

"I understand."

Zeus turned his head at Poseidon. "This is on you if she fucks up."

"She won't." Poseidon shook his head.

My heart soared at Poseidon's words while at the same time raced with the intimidating god king standing toe-to-toe with me, holding my fate in his palm.

Without asking if I was ready, Zeus gripped my shoulder and closed his eyes. My back arched as the familiar power surged through me, intertwining with my bones and pulsing into my veins. Ocean waves crashed against my mind, the rough texture of shark skin brushed my fingertips, and the salty scent of the sea settled around me. Once Zeus's hand fell away, reality trickled in like raindrops on a boat deck—collecting little by little until I stood in the meeting room as myself, as Cordelia, but so much more. My very pores coursed with power, begging to be free after being suppressed for such a long time.

Zeus's glance turned toward the window behind us, where New Yorkers scurried on the sidewalk. "Are we done here?" He cracked his knuckles, tossing a piece of ambrosia to Poseidon, the glowing orange crystalline substance landing in his palm.

"I wouldn't dream of asking anything else of you, brother." Poseidon clenched the ambrosia in his fist, glaring at Zeus.

"Good. Take her to Atlantis, I want that situation fixed *today*." Zeus headed for the door.

I ported in front of him in a shimmering sea spray that matched Poseidon's. "Wait."

Zeus thinned his lips. "Oh, is there something else I can do for you, your highness?"

"Rhode. You can help us find her." I pressed my fingertips against the glass behind me.

"What makes you think that?"

"You're King of the Gods. Surely you could—"

Zeus bent forward, bringing his face closer to mine. "I'm not all-powerful. Gaea sure as Tartarus made sure of that. I can't help you. Now move."

I gulped, pushing my hands so fiercely against the door the glass cracked. "No. I *must* find her."

Zeus's eyes dropped to his damaged door, and he sighed, dragging a hand through his dark, neatly trimmed short hair. "Talk to Kairos. He won't be able to take you to her but may be able to tell *when* she is."

I blinked, half expecting him to put up more of a fight.

Zeus was…different. An older version of him would've made me grovel at his feet to gain my Queenhood back—and he would've toyed with me, possibly for days, before eventually doing it as a favor in exchange for something else. But now, he only hesitated because he was concerned I wouldn't do my job.

Had Hera leaving him rocked his world more than he let on?

"Thank you." I squinted at him as I stepped aside.

He snarled under his breath, whisking open the door. "Uh-huh."

"Zeus, are you—" I reached forward but curled my fingers back. "Are you alright?"

He paused with a stiff arm on the door. "Nothing Hermes can't look into for me." His jaw tightened. "I will expect double the work from you."

And with that, the King of the Gods prowled to his den as the mortal lawyer.

"Are you ready to finish this, Starfish?" Poseidon stepped to my side, dragging his finger over my cheek.

As a mortal, his touch electrified my skin, but as a goddess, it positively melted it.

"She's calling to me, Seid." I beamed up at him, wrapping my arms around his waist, and after ensuring the blinds were closed, I ported us to the shore.

The waves lapped against my bare feet, whispering to me, beckoning me, asking me to heal it.

"Do you remember what to say, my love?" Poseidon pressed a hand to my cheek.

Even though it'd been eons ago, I remembered saying the

words to him for the first time like it happened yesterday.

"I claim the Seas and its King, as he claims me."

He kissed me, making circles on my cheeks with each of his thumbs. Water launched around us, shooting geysers toward the skies. A watery swirl encompassed me, returning my original white robes, my trident, and finally…my silver seashell crown with three petite points. Poseidon slipped the ambrosia in my mouth and kissed my brow. A spark of light blasted through me, traveling to each neuron, tearing them apart before fusing together, binding them for eternity.

Immortality. I'd forgotten how bittersweet it felt—forever finality.

"My Queen," Poseidon whispered against my skin, taking my hand with the ring he'd given me in his and stepping back.

He appeared in his golden armor in a gusting wave—shoulder pieces, gauntlets, grieves, bare chest. His golden pointed crown gleamed atop his dirty blonde hair, and he kissed my ring.

"Let's go restore our home, Cordelia." He held his hand out, encouraging me to walk to the water's edge.

Closing my eyes, breathing the life that vapored around me from the depths of the ocean, I took my first step home. A sonic wave blasted over the surface, pulsing into the sky. Poseidon stood at my side but didn't touch me. Not yet. He let me re-familiarize myself on my own terms. With each step I took into the water, my trail glittered and glowed, warming to my touch. Once the ocean reached my hips, I twirled my hands, casting dew from my fingertips. Inch-by-inch my legs disappeared, replaced by a teal mermaid's tail. I dove in, turning to wait for Poseidon to follow me.

He grinned, circling his hand around himself, producing a golden tail. "As I told you. Like riding a chariot."

I flipped my tail, out-stretching my hands for him to take them. "I don't remember the way to Atlantis, Seid. Show me?"

Interlacing our fingers, he made us barrel roll around one another, our tails brushing.

"We'll take the scenic route. The sea, the animals, all of it— can you feel how much it missed you?"

With every swipe of my arm through the water, it pushed back like an embrace.

"Yes," I breathed out.

He tugged my hand, and swimming side by side, led me through the ocean, our crowns gleaming and glowing bright like a beacon for all aquatic life—an announcement that both the King and Queen had returned. Fish of all varieties circled our arms and tails, sea turtles brushing our arms as they passed. A pod of dolphins appeared from below us, squeaking their excitement, begging me to play with them.

Poseidon squeezed my hand and jutted his chin. "Go on. Keep following me, and they will too." He smiled at me, urging me to swim with them again with a nudge of his elbow.

With a jovial laugh, I swam between the six dolphins, matching every stroke of their tails by flapping mine. Two moved on either side of me, urging me to hold onto their dorsal fins. Grinning, I wrapped my hands around them and with the brute force of two of them together, they catapulted me toward the surface, causing me to breach. The moon above beamed down at me, making my scales shimmer before I flipped backward and dove, re-joining Poseidon at his side.

"It's amazing seeing you like this again." He trailed his fingers over my tail at the flare of my hips.

I shivered against his touch. "It's amazing *feeling* like this again."

"We're almost there. Can you sense it?" Poseidon produced his golden trident, readying to battle off any creatures that could be lurking.

Producing my silver trident, I curled it against my arm, closing my eyes to feel Atlantis's pulse. At first, it was weak, but after pouring all of my power into it, the steady rhythm like a mighty bass drum vibrated in my chest. I flew my eyes open and there in front of us, with no need to reveal this time, was Atlantis.

I wasted no time, reaching for the first pile of debris. The shambles glowed and pulled back together, sealing with a beam of blue light.

"Keep going. I'll keep a lookout and alert you if I see anything." Poseidon curled an arm around my waist and kissed my forehead before swimming up to gain an aerial view of our surroundings.

I continued to work my way around the ruins of our city, pulling it back together, rejuvenating it, giving it life and purpose again. With every completed structure, the building would sigh as if in relief at my healing touch. It'd been so long since I used my powers to this magnitude, the effort was exhausting to the point of almost falling limp to the ocean floor.

A loud growl vibrated off surrounding buildings, followed by several giant black tentacles wrapping around structures and crushing them. A pair of large glowing red eyes appeared from the shadows, its bulbous head sleek with slime.

The Kraken.

"Fucking Tartarus. Keep going, Cordelia. I'll fend it off. We need to get that beacon working," Poseidon yelled, twirling his trident and cradling it in the crook of his arm.

The sight of the monstrous squid may have jarred me—terrified me as a mortal. As a Queen, I sneered at its presence and readied my trident at my side. Lifting my hands, I continued to heal my fallen city, fighting the urge to collapse. Using the trident's hilt, I pressed it against the ground—leaning on it, touching, and stroking each piece of rubble.

Poseidon roared, swinging his trident and stabbing one tentacle before yanking it out to impale another. Tendrils of black blood clouded surrounding waters, and the Kraken's wails shook the sea bed like an underwater earthquake. The glow of the creature's red eyes pulsed, and it launched two tentacles into Poseidon's stomach, throwing him into the building I'd been mending, destroying it again.

"Honey, I'm trying to repair Atlantis?" I yelled out to him, swirling my hands to bring the fallen pieces back together once more.

Poseidon grunted, the Kraken's tentacles wrapped around him, squeezing him. "I'm so sorry sweetie, I'll be sure to ask the Kraken if it wouldn't mind tossing me in the other direction." With a snarl, Poseidon stabbed through the underside of the tentacle and the creature let go.

Zooming horizontally through the water, Poseidon aimed for the Kraken's neck, using the trident and his arms to choke it. All of the creature's tentacles wiggled, writhed, and swung in frantic movements. Poseidon leveraged his feet on the creature's shoulders, pushing away and leaning back. With gritted teeth, he growled, pulling harder and harder before yelling.

With the last building healed, I used the ounce of strength I had left, flicking my tail to meet with the Kraken face to face, my silver trident gleaming in my palms. The creature glared at me, darting its tentacles, trying to wrap around my waist. I sliced to the left, cutting off one tentacle, stabbed to the right, skewering another. Rolling my neck, I pulled energy from the ocean, replacing only a fraction of what I'd used up repairing Atlantis. Throwing my arms out at my sides, trident in my grasp, I pulsed an echo through the water as soon as Poseidon let go of it. The pulse traveled in ringlets until catapulting into the Kraken, flying it fathoms away, the darkness consuming it and swallowing it whole. My shoulders slumped, the trident falling limp in my hands as I leaned against a pillar, out of breath and woozy.

"Are you alright?" Poseidon's hand caressed my arm.

"I'm fine." A weak smile fluttered over my lips. "Just not used to exerting that much power anymore."

Poseidon smiled, curling one of my arms over his shoulders while one of his wrapped around my hips, supporting me. "I'd forgotten how incredibly badass we are together in a fight."

"Shame on you." I smirked.

"It looks better than it ever has, Cor." Poseidon swam us in circles, marveling at what I'd created.

"There's one final piece, Seid. But I'll need your help." I held my hand out to him.

Grasping it, he kissed my knuckles, and swam us to the highest point of the tallest building. We each took a side, and holding our tridents with two hands, we slammed the hilts down in unison. A bright beam of blue light flew high, serving as a road map for any worthy of its glory to find Atlantis. A blue holographic dome of hexagons formed over the city, sealing it tight.

Poseidon hugged me to his side and we beamed at the light shining at the city center again.

"Well, well. Look who got her power back," Skylla's slithery voice echoed off the stone buildings around us.

Poseidon and I turned in unison, readying our tridents at our sides.

She'd already been inside before we sealed it off.

"Skylla, wait. I can help you now." I held one palm up, spreading my hand wide.

I hadn't a clue *how* I would help her, but Poseidon said I could…

"No one can help me. You're lying in an attempt to save your own skin." Skylla's dragon head tentacles flapped and snapped.

"You should be worried about *your* skin, Skylla. You're lucky she hasn't already skewered you where you float." Poseidon spun the hilt of his trident in his grasp.

Closing my eyes, I called to my power, keeping my hand outstretched in Skylla's direction. What could I do for her? How? As if answering my unspoken pleas, my magic settled an answer over my mind like water droplets.

"Skylla, I can't make you a sea nymph again, but I can make

you a different creature. Though I can't promise you still won't crave flesh. Perhaps it won't be purely of the human variety." I kept my hand up, ready to use my power on her the moment she agreed.

"Another creature? What would be the point? All creatures of the deep are monstrous and vile." She snarled, curling two of the dragon heads to her chest.

"I can make you a mermaid." I felt Poseidon's eyes tracing over me.

Skylla scoffed. "A mermaid that craves flesh. Absurd."

"I'm giving you one opportunity to be transformed, Skylla. After today, the offer no longer stands. Would you rather be a mermaid or a half-woman, half-octopus with dragon head tentacles who sounds like a dying sea lion whenever she speaks?" I glared at her.

Take the deal.

The dragon heads hissed, rotating and gyrating as if they understood they might soon not exist.

Skylla frowned, petting one of the heads with the delicacy of touching a house pet. She lifted her chin and slowly shook her head. "No."

I blinked, dropping my hand at my side before raising it again. "No?"

"Your offer isn't for me. It's for you. No doubt, to make yourself feel better. You want to help me?" She urged the dragon heads forward, their mouths billowing fire. "Fight me."

Fighting wouldn't solve anything even if I did have the strength in me.

"I won't. Let me help you, Skylla. It's not only about relieving my conscience. It's about undoing a wrong. What can I do?" I made my trident disappear, holding my palms up at her.

"Cordelia, what the Tartarus are you doing?" Poseidon growled and swam to my side, pointing the golden prongs of his weapon at Skylla.

"There's only one thing you can do to make me happy, sea queen." She threw her hands to her sides, unleashing the ten black claws. "Die."

Welcome back, Cordelia. Welcome back, indeed.

Skylla screeched and darted forward, Poseidon darting in front of me to block her first blow. I closed my eyes, splaying my hand to pull some of the water's energy into myself—temporarily revitalizing me. Refusing to stab her with my trident accidentally, I clapped my hands together, causing a shockwave to travel through the water and catapult into Skylla. She flew into a nearby building, crumbling it again, making me grimace.

"Seid, whatever you do, please don't kill her." I grasped Poseidon's elbow, looking at him pleadingly.

His jaw tightened before he gave a curt nod.

Skylla let out a blood-curdling scream, her dragons hissing and baring their teeth. She swam toward us, and I swirled my arms, kicking up a water tornado that made her freeze in place, spinning. Every time she tried to escape, I'd push my hands forward, creating an invisible water wall.

Poseidon smirked at my side, his grip tightening on the trident's hilt.

"You're trying to best a pair of sea gods who can hold their own against the Kraken even, Skylla. Do you really think you can win?" I frowned, ignoring the exhaustion pulling at my brain.

Skylla growled, snarled, and screamed as she continued to try and escape from my swirling water.

"Either let me help you or leave, Skylla. I can't let you destroy Atlantis again." I clenched one fist, making the spinning stop, but holding her in place.

"Just kill me." The words came out of Skylla's throat—strangled.

Witnessing her anguished expression made a lump form in my throat. "I can't do that. It's not the kind of goddess I am."

The dragon heads pulled back, their mouths clamped shut and Skylla's shoulders slumped. "Put me down."

Doing as she asked, I lowered her to the ground and gently pulled my hand away, allowing her free movement. "I am truly sorry for what I did to you. We can't allow you to stay in Atlantis, but you can have whatever place you wish to make a sanctuary under the seas. And you *will* be safe."

"I'm unsure if I'll ever be able to forgive you, Queen, but I do accept your offer of sanctuary."

I nodded to her, a knot forming in my gut. "Then pick the place, and we'll do it. Poseidon will put a shielding spell over it."

Skylla cut her gaze to my king.

Poseidon went silent for a beat before he slammed the trident's hilt against the seafloor. "It will be done. You have my word."

Skylla bowed her head with a scowl, her tentacles curling through the water, pushing her through the dome shield into darkness before disappearing.

"I'm sorry." Poseidon placed a hand on my back. "I can't imagine that's the kind of closure you hoped for, sweetheart."

"It's not, but I shouldn't have expected she'd forgive me. I'm at least happy to know she'll be safe, wherever she ends up."

He kissed my temple. "We've done the illustrious Zeus's bidding. What do you wish to do now?"

I rested my head on his shoulder and sighed. "There's someone I need to see. And I hope...he wants to see me."

EIGHTEEN

THE PORT OF SAN DIEGO, California. Home to the ship
Sea Urchin when it wasn't defending the seas from the surface,
stopping whalers. According to Poseidon, the ship my son
Triton manned disguised as a mortal for the past decade. I
stood on the dock, watching crew members exit the massive
ship after roping off. Despite the weather reaching a balmy
eighty-five degrees, I shivered from bubbling nerves.

What if he was still angry with me? What if he wanted
nothing to do with me?

And I couldn't blame him for feeling any of it.

A tall man with ash blonde hair to his collar bone and a
light beard hopped to the dock, swinging a duffel bag over his
shoulder.

"See you next week, Tim," another man called out to him.

Tim was Triton. He had to be.

When we locked eyes from across the dock…I was sure of

it. He was the spitting image of Poseidon with his blonde hair and eyes the same color as the stone on my ring. And he had my nose and sharp jawline. My. Son.

Triton froze, staring at me, a wrinkle in his brow. I'd gone over this scenario a dozen times, weighing out all the possibilities. Hope fluttered in my stomach, but the scowl on his face had me reeling.

"Triton," I whispered, knowing he could hear me despite the distance between us.

The scowl disappeared, and he dropped the bag on the dock with a thud. He power-walked toward me, and I met him halfway, clapping my hands over my nose to keep from crying.

"Mom?" He searched my eyes as if trying to remember my look—trying to remember a face from when he was a child.

"Hey Turtle," I choked out his nickname I'd given him as a boy, making my scales flash on my skin so quickly the human eye would miss them. But he wouldn't.

And now I knew why my entire mortal life as Cordelia I was always so drawn to sea turtles. My subconscious had been throwing me hints at every turn. The only life I led that it ever had. Did fate know I'd finally meet Poseidon?

His black T-shirt hugged his muscular, tanned arms. Not bulky like Poseidon but lean like the body of a swimmer. "I don't understand. How is this—how is this possible?" Without warning, he hugged me, sniffling.

Tears rolled down my cheeks as I wrapped my arms tightly around him. "I can explain everything, but not out in the open like this."

"Right. Yeah. Um. I know somewhere we can go." He peeled

back, quickly turning his face away from me and wiping his cheek.

After trotting to his abandoned bag on the dock, he ran back to me, curling his arm around my shoulders with a wide grin and leading me away.

"So, let me see if I have this straight. You've been reincarnated an insurmountable number of times thanks to Aphrodite's spell, but you never remembered who you were? And even if Dad saw you, he wouldn't have recognized you if he hadn't changed because of Athena's curse?" Triton sat across from me with that same quizzical squint Poseidon did when confused.

He'd taken us to the boathouse he stayed in when docked in San Diego. It was quaint, masculine, and surprisingly well kept.

I tapped my fingers on the tackle table between us. "I gave you the short version, but yeah. Once your dad recognized me, little by little, I started to remember."

"And you two are back together? Happy? And I mean *genuinely* happy, not just pretending to save face?" Triton cocked his head to the side, staring at my expression.

No doubt trying to catch me in a lie.

"We've both changed. And yes. What we are now is all I've ever wanted." I sucked in a breath. "Him…and my family."

Triton licked his lips, smiling only with his eyes before he sulked in his chair. "Did he tell you about Rhode?"

I pressed my elbows against the table. "Yes. We're going after her."

Triton's bright eyes snapped to mine. "You know where she is?"

"Not yet. But Zeus, of all people, gave us a lead."

"I'm going with you once you figure it out." His jaw tightened.

"Triton, I—"

He held his hand up, halting my words. "And I'm not taking 'no' for an answer. She's my little sister, and I want to help. I'm not a guppy anymore, Mom." A small smile crept over his lips.

Tears filled my eyes, and I sighed, leaning back in my chair. "No, you're certainly not." I bent forward, sliding my hand over his that rested on the table. "I'm so, so sorry I wasn't there to watch you grow up."

He placed his other hand over mine. "I know you are. Honestly, it's been so long I'm not even mad about it anymore. During my teenage years? Oh, I was so angry, I'd make mini typhoons in the middle of the ocean, but—I eventually accepted it. And Dad. He really stepped up."

"I'm so glad to hear it." I squeezed his hand with a warm smile before sitting back.

"Besides, the memories I had of you when I was a kid— Mom, you were the best. I cherished those times the three of us spent together. The games. The laughing. The swimming. It was enough because I never thought you were coming back." He scratched the back of his head, revealing the small trident tattoo on the inside of his bicep. "I'm sorry. Did you want anything to drink or eat or—I don't have much, but I could conjure us something?"

I waved my hand. "I'm fine. But I do want to hear more

about the Sea Urchin. How did that all start?"

"It actually started from me almost getting caught." He smirked, beating his fist against the table. "These whalers, Mom. They're horrible news. They disguise themselves as 'Science Vessels,' but all they're doing is slaughtering thousands of whales. I attacked a ship using my powers, and one of the crew took a photo with his cell phone."

"Olympus. What did you do?"

"Made a wave crash on deck, swept the damn thing into the depths." Triton shook his head, folding his arms with a sigh.

"Quick thinking." Pride swelled in my chest over the man my son had become. "And that's why you started the Sea Urchin as a mortal."

"Yeah. I mean, don't get me wrong, I still use my powers, but not to the full extent I'd like to. Hopefully, now that you're Queen again, some of the whaling will stop."

"I'll do what I can."

"So, tell me, *Cordelia*—what have you been doing all this time in this life? Marine biology? Surfing like dad?" Triton chuckled, crinkling the skin at the corners of his eyes.

"Marine biology? Yeah, I don't think in any of my lifetimes I could've lasted through that amount of schooling." I laughed, interlacing my fingers in front of me. "I'm an oceanographer and run an ocean conservation charity with my friend, Meg."

"Not surprising in the least." He bumped my hand with a knuckle and a grin.

"I'm also a pro gamer who streams on Glitch every week." I moved my gaze to my palms, squinting.

"Did you just say you're a *pro* gamer? What game?" Triton

pressed his forearms on the table, his eyes brightening.

"*Tides of Atlantis.*"

Triton slapped the table. "Holy shit. Mom, that's amazing. Not to mention *incredibly* cool."

"Yeah? I thought you'd think I was a dork or something."

"Are you kidding? It makes total sense, too, with how much I remember you loving games. It's great you found something to make you happy besides the ocean."

"Oh, you mean the video game *about* the ocean?" I laughed, resting my chin in my hand.

"Hey." Triton threw his hands up. "It doesn't involve getting wet."

I sighed, staring at my handsome son, putting his face to memory. "I'm so proud of you, Triton."

His cheeks turned crimson, and he scratched the back of his head—another gesture he inherited from his dad. "Wow. I never thought I'd hear that from my mother again."

"Well, get used to it. I have a lot of lost time to make up for."

"As long as it doesn't involve spankings or embarrassing me in front of my friends, I'm game." He winked at me with a wide grin.

"Ah, I see. So, you're saying the next time I make a surprise visit to the docks, I should give you a big fat wet kiss on your cheek in front of your crew?" I wiggled my eyebrows.

"Hey now." He pointed at me. "The jokes on you. They'd be jealous their own hot moms aren't there."

My cheeks warmed, and I shook my head, snickering. "Oh, stop, Triton."

"I'm glad you're back, Mom. I really am. And once we find Rhode…we'll all be together again."

I sighed, closing my eyes and envisioning it. "It's all I dreamed about since the moment I remembered who I was, honestly."

"We'll find her. You don't back down on anything once you set your mind to it."

"You remember that do you?" I grinned.

A laugh swelled from his chest. "Dad certainly does."

I joined in the laughter, and it continued for a solid minute until we both dabbed tears from the corners of her eyes as it died down. "This has been nice, but I should get out of your hair. I know I showed up out of the blue and—" I stood but cut my sentence short once Triton appeared in front of me.

"Out of my hair? Mom, I haven't seen you in *hundreds* of years. The only place I want to be right now is right here with you getting reacquainted." He squeezed my shoulders before pulling me in for another hug. "And probably at least a dozen more of these."

Laughing, I hugged him back, positively beaming inside. "Alright. Deal."

We spent hours talking, reminiscing, laughing, and the reunion was everything I could hope for. We were in the middle of a game of Red Hands, trying to out-slap the other, when Poseidon appeared, sending a sea spray throughout the cabin.

"I had a lot of things in mind that I'd walk in the middle of, but my wife trying to slap the top of my son's hands was *not* one of them." Poseidon quirked a brow.

Grinning, I leaped from the table, wrapped my arms around his neck, and kissed him.

"It's been ages since I've seen it, and it's still as gross as I remember," Triton teased.

Poseidon chuckled. "How you doing, son?"

Triton threw his hand out for a shake, and the two manly gods proceeded to do what I'd dubbed the "bro hug."

"I was doing great before, but now—" Triton flashed me a smile. "Even better."

My word. He was so much like his father.

"Glad to see the reunion is going well." Poseidon wrapped one arm around Triton's shoulders and the other around my hips, pulling us both to his sides. "I have some news."

"Oh?" I peered up at him.

"I tracked down Kairos."

Gasping, I turned to look at him. "You have?"

"Yeah. We can go whenever you're ready, but I don't want to rush you both."

Triton gave a hearty slap on Poseidon's back. "If this is about Rhode, you two should go. Mom and I have plenty of time to catch up."

I squeezed Triton's hand.

"You ready then, Starfish?" Poseidon trailed his fingers down my arm.

"I'm going to tell you the same thing I told Mom. When you go after Rhode, I *am* going with you. I don't care where or when. I'm going to be there." Triton rolled his shoulders back, standing the same height as Poseidon.

"I wouldn't expect anything less, my boy." Poseidon

clapped his hand against Triton's shoulder before holding his hand out to me.

I pressed my hands together and fluttered to Triton, raising on the balls of my feet to kiss his cheek. "I'll see you soon."

"I know, Mom. Now go." He gave a reassuring smile.

I didn't take my eyes off my son as Poseidon wrapped his arms around me and ported us away.

We appeared in a front tiled courtyard of a white-washed building with green roofing. Iron lamp fixtures hung from the walls between every rounded archway opening leading inside.

"Where are we?" I asked as Poseidon led me inside.

"Morocco."

Inside, the archways continued, and a stone fountain stood in the center of the next room, surrounded by rounded pillars and benches. Further in, the tiled walking path turned into a vibrant red carpet with intricate mosaic designs. Rounding a corner, I gasped at the floor-to-ceiling shelves of books—rows and rows of them.

"A library?" I whispered, even though there wasn't another soul in sight.

"The oldest in the modern world." Poseidon squeezed my hand, leading us into a room filled with wooden tables and chairs.

"And Kairos is here?"

We moved into a room with a singular large desk at the front of the room. "He's the curator." Poseidon spun in circles, searching, and still holding my hand, bringing me with him. "Kairos?"

A man appeared with a withered red book in his hands from

the shadows. There was very little hair on his head, but what remained was stark white along with the long beard that hung to his stomach. He squinted at us through his monocle.

"How do you know that name?" The man asked, slamming the book shut, sending dust flying.

"Are we alone?" Poseidon twirled his finger in the air.

The man rested his fists on his hips. "Yes."

"I'm Poseidon."

"Uncle Poseidon. Not sure we've ever met." The man smiled, and in a swirl of torn paper and glowing numbers, he transformed into a young man with a single lock of hair draping from his forehead to his hips.

Poseidon looked down at me with a smirk before moving his gaze back to Kairos. "You'll have to excuse me if I've lost track of my brother's children."

"No offense taken in the slightest." Kairos waved his hand. "How can I help you?"

"We were hoping—" I stepped forward and paused. "Sorry, that was rude. I'm Cordelia. Formerly known as…Amphitrite."

Kairos grinned wide and pressed his fingertips together. "The King and Queen of the Seas reunited at last. How delicious. I tracked you through all your lifetimes, you know. My, my, did you have some *lives*."

I rubbed the back of my neck. "You're telling me. But we were hoping you could help us find our daughter. She got pulled through a portal in Atlantis, and we think it may have been to another time."

"It is Rhode you speak of, I presume?"

"Yes," Poseidon replied with a frown.

Kairos nodded, steepling his fingers. "I can see what the universe says to me, but I'd need something of hers."

"Something—but how could we possibly—" I started, feeling my body as if I actually had an item from her possession.

"Here," Poseidon's voice boomed, removing one of the bracelets from his wrist. A simple one made of twine with a singular cowrie shell in the center.

I touched the crook of his arm with a crinkled brow.

"When she was eight, she made us friendship bracelets, and she gave me this one saying it was hers. We've never taken them off." He smiled, but forlornness muddied it.

"Oh, Poseidon." I gulped and shoved my face against his shoulder.

"This will work nicely. Thank you," Kairos said, curling the bracelet into his palm and closing his eyes.

A circular band of glowing sparks curled around him, forming a helix before settling as a halo circling his chest. Shooting stars arched over his head followed by flaming rocks, geysers of volcanic lava, and descending numbers—they spun and spun until abruptly, they stopped.

Kairos's eyes flew open, glowing red. "1719. The Caribbean."

"That's still the golden age of piracy," Poseidon mumbled.

Fear burned down my spine. "By Olympus."

"And she's alive," Kairos added before he exhaled and his eyes returned to normal.

"I've told you all I can. And unfortunately, I have no means of transporting you there, nor do I know of any such god with the power to do so." Kairos steepled his fingers again after handing the bracelet to Poseidon.

"There has to be someone." I slapped a hand on my forehead.

"I do know of one person, but I'm not too keen on the risk we'd take releasing the raging asshole." Poseidon tied the bracelet back to his wrist, nestling it in with the others.

"Kronos? Tartarus no. I just found you again. Last thing I need is you getting eaten."

Poseidon grabbed one of my belt loops and pulled me to him. "We'll figure it out. Now that we know where she is, it'll make things that much easier."

"Can I help you two with anything else?" Kairos clasped his hands behind his back.

"You've been a great help, Kairos. Thank you." I slipped my hand into Poseidon's.

"Any time." Kairos bowed, morphing into the older man before walking away.

"Do you think she's mixed herself in with pirates?" Poseidon rubbed his chin, glaring daggers into the red carpet.

"Nah. There's far more in the Caribbean in that time other than piracy. Surely she's a merchant or scholar or…"

Poseidon locked gazes with me, and we both knew, given her powers, the likelihood of what would make an ideal cover for herself, but neither of us wanted to say it out loud.

Piracy.

NINETEEN

WE'D RACKED OUR BRAINS for days, asking dozens of fellow gods who might have the power to time travel, and continually came up empty. It was an odd feeling possessing so much power as the Queen of the Seas, yet powerless to find my daughter. I'd promised Meg my transition wouldn't affect our friendship and had already gone radio silent on her since getting wrapped up in finding Rhode.

I knocked on her front door, smoothing out my shirt as I waited for her to answer. Laughter floated from the other side—from two people. Smiling, I sucked on my lips as the door whipped open. Meg had been grinning, and it widened when she spotted me.

"Cory, holy hell. I haven't heard from you in days." Meg yanked me to her for a hug.

I hugged her back, spying the fridge door open in the kitchen with a pale hand wrapped around the handle. "I'm sorry about that. I've been—."

Wait. Meg knew I was a goddess but didn't know Hera not only knew too but was one herself. When did my life become this complicated?

"Occupied with something very important." I gave an exaggerated wink to Meg.

She leaned back until the realization slowly dawned on her, and she nodded. "Right. Yeah. Muy importante."

"Hey, Hera," I said toward the kitchen with a grin.

Hera's head popped over the top of the fridge door. "Amp— er, Cordelia."

"I see you two are getting well acquainted." Clasping my hands in front of me, I nudged Meg in the ribs.

"I guess we have been spending almost every waking moment together these past few days, haven't we?" Meg ran a finger down the bridge of her nose, looking at Hera sidelong.

Hera rested her forearms on the still open fridge door, and with her chin resting on an arm, smiling, she replied, "And I'm not complaining one bit."

Meg's cheeks turned pale pink.

I bit the inside of my mouth so as not to squeal like a teenage girl. "I hoped, if it's alright with you, Hera, I might borrow my friend for a couple of hours?"

"Of course. You *did* see her first." Hera winked, tapping her red nails on the door with a grin.

Meg choked out a laugh before bobbing her brows at me. "What'd you have in mind?"

"It's a surprise. I'll meet you out by the Jeep?"

"Sure. Okay?" Meg scrunched her nose before moving for

the door. "Feel free to stay here. Oh, and snoop around if ya want. I ain't got anything to hide." Chuckling, Meg beat her hand on the doorframe before exiting.

That would make *one* of them.

After hearing Meg's footsteps fade away, I bolted for the kitchen. "Have you told her yet?"

"Told her? Told her what?"

The fridge door creaked from her leaning on it, her bare feet shuffling on the tiled floor.

"You know exactly what I'm talking about." I squinted at her feet and panned up to her arms.

"Of course, I haven't," Hera spat in a loud whisper.

"Why are you still *in* the fridge?"

Hera clucked her tongue at the inside of her cheek. "I'm naked."

"Oh." I widened my eyes. "*Oh*. Oh, shit. Did I interrupt something?"

"No. You didn't. I'm just me, and I walked out of the bathroom like this to surprise her."

I folded my arms. "Why don't you conjure clothes on yourself?"

"Because—" She sighed and beat her forehead against her arm. "My powers aren't acting normal. Ever since I cut ties with Zeus, one day I could be overpowerful and the next practically mortal."

"That's strange. Maybe your powers are readjusting? Reverting to the way they were before becoming Queen?"

"I hope you're right." She bit her thumbnail.

"You should tell her. She knows about our world already,

which gives you a huge advantage."

Hera slapped a hand on the door. "You told her?"

"She's my best friend. I couldn't keep that from her. And she took it surprisingly well, all things considered."

"Wow." Hera's gaze fell to her knuckles. "We've had a good thing going. I didn't want to risk screwing it up."

"Tell her. Air everything out, let her process it, and I promise you, it won't change anything. What it *will* change is you one hundred percent being able to be yourself around her and most importantly––no lies." I patted her arm.

"I'll think about, Amph." She patted my hand back. "Thank you.

I snapped my fingers. "Oh, and I know it's a little thing but, it's Cordelia now. Amphitrite is a name locked in a corked bottle at sea."

Hera grinned and nodded. "Cordelia it is. I like it."

"I better go before she gets suspicious. She's incredibly intuitive." Giving her arm one last squeeze, I turned away.

"I know." Hera smiled, her eyes trailing off into who knows where. A dress materialized over her body, and she gasped. "Well, look at that."

Grinning, I left Meg's apartment and met her in the parking lot. She leaned against my Jeep, her feet crossed at the ankle, chewing on a toothpick and staring at the asphalt.

"The real reason I've been MIA for a few days is that I've been finding information about where my daughter is, Meg."

"Jesus. You have kids. I already forgot." Meg grabbed my shoulder. "Wait. You said she's missing?"

"An accident in Atlantis and a story I swear I'll explain in its entirety someday." I tugged at her jacket with a warm smile.

Considering Meg just recently learned Greek mythology was anything but myth, trying to describe Atlantis and the way it operates seemed like begging for her head to explode.

"Atlantis," Meg mumbled, staring at the ground.

"It, too, is real." After patting her arm, I climbed into the Jeep, whistling at her to get her attention.

"Before we head out, I have something for you." She shoved a pink plastic bag at me with a stiff arm.

Frowning, I took the bag, but didn't look in it. "It's not my birthday."

"Just. Open it, Cordelia."

As I peered inside, I recognized the Funko logo and gasped before yanking the box out. The Poseidon toy from *Tides of Atlantis*. It looked nothing like the real Poseidon—my Poseidon—but it was the version I knew of him in my mortal life as Cordelia Bourne. He had long white hair past his chest with an equally as long beard, blending in. Green octopus tentacles replaced his legs, making me frown at the thought of Skylla, but the usual radiant three-pronged trident would remain synonymous with the King of the Seas.

"I promised if you placed in the tournament, I'd buy it for you, remember?" She nudged my knee.

"I do." I squeezed her thigh with a grin. "Thank you."

"So, you're a goddess now? A full-fledged goddess?" Meg asked me with wide eyes as she crawled into the passenger seat on autopilot.

"I am. Queen of the Seas and all." After giving her a warm smile, I slipped my sunglasses on and pulled out of the lot.

"You don't seem any different."

"Well, good. It'd be a real drag if mortals could tell I wasn't one of them."

Meg held her hand out the window, letting the wind caress through her fingers. "Where are we going, Cor? You know I hate surprises. Especially if this is of the godly variety."

"We're going swimming."

"Swimming?"

I beat my hands against the steering wheel to the tune of *Beyond the Sea*. "Yup. With sharks. And all you need—is a tank." Cutting my gaze, I caught her expression bordering on excitement and terror.

"They don't like me. Who's to say they'll listen to you?"

"Oh, they'll listen. Sharks fear humans more than the other way around. Fear is just as potent as blood in the water." Pulling into the beach's parking lot, I moved to the back, grabbing the scuba tank and gear.

Meg shut the car door and shuffled toward me. "We're seriously doing this? What if people see?"

"They won't." I handed her the gear. "I'm going to port us away from the tourist traps and directly underwater, so check your regulator and suit up, my dear."

She took the tank and let her arms flop. "I retract my statement. You're definitely not the same."

I frowned as I turned to walk along the shoreline. "Is that a bad thing?"

"No. You're more confident. Comfortable. Like you've settled into your own skin." Meg bumped me with her shoulder.

"I have. And Poseidon he—" I clutched my hands to my chest, missing him already. "We're a force to be reckoned with now."

"A power couple. I dig it." Meg slung the tank over her shoulders after sliding into her wetsuit.

Far enough away from any crowds, I stopped, letting the water's surf lap against my toes, waiting for Meg to finish gearing up.

"Just talk like we normally do. I'll be able to hear you." I smiled up at her, going on my tippy toes to pull a piece of hair out of her mask. "Ready?"

She gave a thumbs up.

After curling our arms together, I ported us to the depths where several circling hammerhead sharks swam. Meg gasped, and I gripped her tight to keep her from fleeing on the spot.

"Trust me," I said, floating to the sharks and outstretching my hands to them.

They both swam under my touch, letting my fingertips trail over their hands and down their bodies and tail. They repeated the motion, turning around once they'd reached the end, only to get pettings all over again.

"Come here, Meg. I promise they won't bite you."

After a few deep breaths on her part, she appeared beside me with shaky hands. Gently, I took one and held it out. One shark continued to circle under my touch while the other switched to Meg.

Meg gasped and laughed. "This—this is amazing."

Closing my eyes, I willed my scales to appear, feeling more at home with them radiating from my skin. Meg smiled at me from behind her mask, her eyes beaming at the shark.

"Follow my lead." I turned on my belly, swimming in the style of a dolphin without my mermaid tail.

The sharks changed course, settling on either side of me. Kicking her flippers, Meg caught up, and we swam in tandem, each with a shark on our right.

"Woo! This. Is. Amazing," Meg screamed, shoving her fists sky high and laughing.

Grinning, I stopped swimming, tuning my ear to the familiar sound waves pulsing through the sea. A great white shark emerged from the dark shadows below us, making Meg shriek and swim behind me. The hammerheads darted away.

I curled an arm behind me, giving Meg a reassuring pat on the arm. "I promise you, you're fine. She's curious."

The great white floated up until we were face to face. She was one of the largest I'd ever seen at roughly six meters. She had multiple scars over her gills and toward her neck—some from mating, others from Olympus knows what. She had an exhausted glaze in her eyes that choked my heart.

Reaching for each side of the massive shark's head, I pressed our foreheads together and closed my eyes. Siphoning every ounce of pain and every tendril of sadness from her into myself, I passed on a fraction of the true happiness blossoming within me. My scales buzzed against my skin. Little by little, the brightness in the shark's gaze returned. I opened my eyes, smiling at her change in demeanor. After kissing the tip of her nose, she flicked her tail and swam off. When I turned to Meg, she floated motionless with eyes as wide as buoys.

"If somehow I wasn't fully convinced you were who you say

you are, there's no denying it now," she said, her eyes still wide.

I tugged on the straps of her tank. "You alright? Want to call it a day?"

"Are you kidding? Let's do this until my air supply is out."

We laughed and swam with sharks, whales, dolphins, and every other variety of animal Meg requested for the next hour. The pure delight radiating from her in unending waves gave me all the reassurance I needed that not only was Meg adjusting to the true me but accepting it.

I sat at my desk, scrolling through hundreds of photos from a recent dive, marking the first round of candidates for editing and eventually selling to magazines. Cocking my head to the side, I noticed a familiar blob in the background of one shot and zoomed in. These were taken before the cruise—before I remembered who I was, and there was Poseidon as a mirage, barely caught in the lens. He may have looked like driftwood and seaweed to the human eye, but I recognized my husband from the way his hair floated in the water alone.

"Seems I've been caught," Poseidon's voice rumbled near my ear.

Grinning, I swiveled in my chair to face him, receiving the kiss he immediately swooped in to give. "I can't believe you were there the entire time, and I had no idea."

"It was your less advanced demi-god brain." He tapped the top of my head.

I swatted him away with a laugh.

"What in the Seven Seas is—that?" Poseidon pointed at the Funko Pop Meg bought me displayed on my gaming desk.

Biting back a smile, I held the figure out to him. "Poseidon. Don't you recognize yourself?"

"This looks nothing like me. And why the Tartarus do I have sea witch legs?" The size of his hand made the modest-sized figure look microscopic.

"Just another depiction of you, hun. How would mortals know what you look like? They had to come up with something for the game."

He grunted and shoved the figure back at me. "Remind me to write the video game company a letter."

Chuckling, I snatched the figure and set it back on my desk. "I took Meg swimming with the sharks today without a cage. You should've seen her face, babe." My chest hummed.

"No kidding. It must've been some experience for a mortal. Perks to having a Queen goddess as a best friend, huh?" He bumped a knuckle against my cheek.

"I should be done here pretty soon." Lazily, I pointed at the computer monitor.

"Can it wait? There's something I need to do, and I'm afraid if I don't do it while I have the nerve built up, I'm going to back out." He cracked his knuckles.

Standing, I wrapped a hand over his wrist. "What is it, Seid?"

"Medusa. I'm going to apologize."

My jaw dropped, and he stuck a finger under my chin to close it. "But you want me to come with you? Wouldn't that only piss her off more?"

"Doubtful. You didn't do anything. I need her to see there's no foul play. I'll do all of the talking. I just need your presence there. Please, Starfish?" He rested his hands on each of my shoulders.

"Yes. Of course." I slipped my hand into his, waiting for him to take us to wherever Medusa hid.

We appeared in front of a dark cave and a chill coursed through my bones. I tightened my grip on Poseidon's hand, and he pulled me closer.

"Does Medusa's power work on gods?" I whispered, my bottom lip quivering from the damp chill inside the cave as we entered.

"Not kings or queens," he answered simply, his jaw tightening.

I curled against his side once the smoke skirted the ground from a nearby cavern. Hissing sounds reverberated off the walls as we drew near. As we rounded the corner, Medusa sat on a single wooden chair at a simple wooden table in the center of a stone room, rock formations hanging from the ceiling— jagged and deadly.

"What in the seven hells are you doing here?" Medusa roared, slapping her palms on the table and standing.

The snakeheads all snapped in our direction, hissing and baring their fangs. Medusa's face remained beautiful with deep brown eyes glowing yellow at certain angles from her power, full lips, and high cheekbones—but centuries worth of pain and suffering settled in her gaze.

"Medusa—" Poseidon started, holding up his palms. "I swear on pain of death I've come to make amends."

"Death? What would you have to fear from such a thing? You, King god, are never punished due to your status, let alone killed." She dug her long black nails into the wood, the tail from her snake body coiling around one of the legs.

"What he says is true, Medusa." I made the scales appear to prove who I was. "I can attest to it. If you'd only listen to him."

Her face softened for a fraction of a second before hardening into the same stone she turned everything else.

"Amphitrite. You were banished to the stars by Zeus." Medusa scoffed, flicking her wrist at Poseidon. "Even your own Queen was punished while you remained unscathed."

"Not true." Poseidon clenched his free hand into a fist.

"I'm listening." Medusa clicked her fingernails together, her snake body moving from behind the table.

"Athena cursed me as well after our—encounter. Aphrodite created a reincarnation spell to bring Amphitrite back, but she wouldn't remember who she was without me."

Medusa yawned, flicking a finger against the small skull at the center of the belt hanging around her hips. "This doesn't sound nearly as cruel as what she did to me."

"Until I changed as a man, as a god—I could see Amphitrite but wouldn't know who she was. She reincarnated countless times, and we kept missing each other."

Medusa paused and then let out a villainous bout of laughter, the golden metal pieces positioned over her breasts reflecting the fire from the hanging sconces as her chest bounced.

Poseidon and I remained silent. Despite how much it hurt hearing someone laugh at our lifetime of misfortune, she had to contend with her own mishaps.

"I'll admit, knowing this does help a tad, but—" She zoomed in front of us, all snakeheads rearing back and hissing at Poseidon. "You still were not turned into a fucking gorgon. You weren't forced to live a life of seclusion because you fear turning innocent children into stone—fear *killing* them."

"And that's the reason I stopped Perseus from killing *you*." Poseidon glared at one of the snakes, and it whimpered away.

He did what?

"What?" Medusa's face fell, and so did the snakeheads, relaxing.

"Hermes can be a blabbermouth when he's drunk. He told me all about Perseus' plan. The sandals he'd given him, Hades' helmet, a shield from Athena. He planned to protect himself from your sight with the shield and behead you in your godsdamned sleep." Poseidon folded his arms. "I offered to rescue his mother from King Seriphus in exchange for leaving you alone."

"I—" Medusa pressed a hand to her bosom, gliding backward until she bumped into the table, leaning against it.

As if I couldn't love this man anymore.

"That day in front of the temple, I was furious with Athena. You were there, and I knew you desired me as soon as our gazes met. I asked. You agreed. But I should've known Athena would've been a spiteful harpy that it happened in her temple. And for that, I'm sorry. She cursed us both, and I apologize for all of it." Poseidon let go of my hand and made a scroll appear in his palm, approaching Medusa with it.

Medusa leaned away as if Poseidon would hit her, shielding her face with a forearm. "What is that?"

"A peace offering. A cursed man exists. Anything he touches turns into gold. To further the curse, he was made immortal, so he has to live with it for the rest of his unnatural life."

"So?" Medusa shrugged.

"He can't turn you into gold, and you won't turn him into stone when he looks at you."

The snakeheads of Medusa fell limp, framing her face and simply dangled, shifting against one another. She traced a finger over her lips, staring up at one of the sconces.

"If you decide you want to meet him, this scroll will tell you where he is at all times, whenever you desire." Poseidon held the scroll out to her. "Take it. Please."

Locking gazes with Poseidon, she slowly slid the scroll from his grasp, holding it out in front of her as if it'd catch flame.

"I hope you can find happiness and companionship. You don't deserve living like this." Poseidon bowed his head and turned away, returning to my side and ready to port us away.

"Poseidon—" Medusa called out.

We froze.

"Thank you," she whispered.

Poseidon nodded once and whisked us away.

We were back in my apartment, and I jumped into his arms, kissing him deeply, trailing my fingers through his blonde hair. He held me against him even when we pulled away.

"I knew you changed, but Seid, you have *changed*."

"A man gets a lot of time to think when he loses the love of his life and doesn't know he'll have the chance to make her fall for him all over again."

A tear fell down my cheek, and I hugged him. "We could

be torn apart and thrown in each other's paths a thousand different times, and I'd fall for you each and *every* instance."

"But thank Olympus—we don't have to. This is it right here, Cor. This is it."

TWENTY

"YOUR THREATS ARE AS empty as your hands. Because I keep taking the sword from them." Poseidon roared with laughter.

I peeked over my shoulder at my husband. We'd outfitted him with a corner of my apartment to situate his own gaming setup, complete with a monitor, console, controller, chair, and better headset.

"You're really getting into this, aren't you?" I spoke through my headset's mic since we were in a party chat through the game.

"It's crazy, Cor. I *live* this life and yet playing it through the game gives it a whole other angle. Does that make sense?" His controller's triggers made clacking sounds as he feverishly worked the buttons.

"I'm sure your prowess against the AI players and consistently high scores has nothing to do with it, hm?" In the game, I swung my trident around my head before stabbing it into the next approaching enemy.

"You know me so well." Poseidon chuckled as his character, whom he created to look as close to himself as possible, threw the trident across the map like a javelin, skewering the enemy into a nearby stone wall.

"Think you've had enough practice? Ready to take this live and play against other gamers?" Pausing the game, I turned in my seat, letting one arm dangle off the back of the chair.

"We did promise your audience. I'd hate to disappoint them. But first—" Poseidon hooked his foot under my chair and pulled me toward him as he took his headset off.

The armrests of our chairs bumped together, and Poseidon widened his legs, encouraging me to shimmy between them. Pressing my palms on the seat, my fingertips a breath away from his crotch, I bent forward to kiss him.

"I appreciate you doing this, Seid."

When I leaned, it made my shirt billow open. Smiling, he slid a finger inside and trailed his touch between both breasts. "How appreciative?" A growl laced his words.

"You're bad." I slapped him in the shoulder with a grin. "Very appreciative, but we do that now, and I'll be all forms of distracted. I need complete focus."

He frowned, still lazily running his finger over my chest. "I'd hate to be the reason you lose subscribers. You'd never let me live it down."

"And eternity is a long time, Seid." Combing my fingers through his hair, I smiled wide.

He jutted his head at the monitor. "Let's spin this up. The

sooner we own enemy players, the sooner we can get to the 'appreciation' portion of the evening." After kissing the tip of my nose, he spun in his chair, scooting himself closer to the desk and sliding the headset back on.

After pulling everything up, I drummed my fingers on my desk, waiting for the moderator to start the chat. It didn't take long for several familiar names to join, and after taking a deep breath, I started the webcam.

"Hey, Sea Farers! I know I primarily stick to free for all mode in *Tides of Atlantis*, but tonight I thought we'd switch it up for a bit of Team Deathmatch." I grinned, waiting for comments to flood the screen.

FriskeeBizkit: Does this mean what I think it means?

"If you haven't guessed, this Wednesday, as will be every third Wednesday of the month, I will have a guest gamer. Everyone, please flap your fins for Simon Thalassa." Clicking into the webcam situated on Simon's monitor, I brought our faces side by side in the corner of the screen.

Poseidon waved, his green eyes popping like gleaming emeralds. "Hey there."

MissTacoX: Sultry, I know he's your soon-to-be husband but pardon me for saying…he's HAWT.

Poseidon chuckled, and my cheeks warmed.

"I couldn't agree with you more, MissTaco. You all ready to see double trident team action?"

HufflePufflenz: This is going to be epic!

My heart raced as a surprising bout of nerves fluttered in my stomach. I'd always played alone. This would be the first time live with a partner—in more ways than one. When the first map loaded, I grinned. I knew it well.

"Simon, head right, and I'll take left. There's a wall some players always climb on top and try to snipe with arrows. We'll beat them to the punch."

Poseidon smiled at me through the camera. "I like your style."

MissTacoX: I can't even with these two.

Just as predicted, another player waited at the top, bow aimed, waiting for the first sap to run below.

"On my count, charge your trident, so it makes a sound and gets their attention, then crouch." I had my character waiting around a corner, careful not to show myself too early.

Still grinning, Poseidon did as I asked, his gold trident bursting with white light as it charged. The opposing player's character turned its back on me, launching an arrow at Poseidon, but he crouched in time, avoiding it.

Holding down the right trigger button, I charged the trident for a heavy attack knowing it'd take several seconds for their bow to reload. As the opposing player turned around, I hurled the prongs of my trident into their chest, and they dematerialized to respawn elsewhere in the map.

FriskeeBizkit: You say epic, I say legendary.

We'd spent the next hour double-teaming other players and dominating the scoreboard with every passing match. We worked like a well-oiled machine, the cogs aligning with every strategy and fighting combination we tried. It made me miss the days we battled together in real-time, but I appreciated the safety which accompanied the silence of the seas.

After saying goodbye and signing off, my arms were around

Poseidon's neck before his headset hit the desk, my mouth covering his. He chuckled against my lips as he pulled me against him.

"I truly didn't believe you could get any more attractive," I said through heavy breaths.

"I strive to keep you guessing, Starfish."

In a swirl of shimmering spray, I ported us to Atlantis. A massive bed outfitted with gold embossed sheets rested in the center of a room surrounded by windows of blue holographic hexagon walls. I created it for privacy with a clear view of the surrounding ocean waters, including the marine life.

"This is new," Poseidon mumbled as he scanned the room.

"I thought I'd do a little redecorating." I held my palm up, wiggling my fingers, creating interlacing tendrils of water. They spiraled around Poseidon, coiling around his arms, his neck, and through his hair.

"Mm. I'd forgotten how good this feels." He closed his eyes, his muscles tensing with each swipe I made with the water.

"The water?"

He returned his heavy-lidded gaze to me. "Your magic."

"Intertwine with me, Seid," I whispered in his ear.

His nose brushed my cheekbone, a low purr vibrating in the back of his throat. As he trailed his fingers down my arm, his magic bubbled from his palm, turning our limbs into water. I kept swirling my power around us, the spray misting against our cheeks. Our bodies continuously morphed from water to flesh when we kissed, causing my insides to writhe. Like falling back into an awaiting pool, I pulled him toward me, porting us to the bed and landing on my back naked.

He landed on top of me, caging my head with his arms, his blonde tendrils skirting my forehead. "Welcome home, Queen."

As if cementing the declaration through action after his words, he plunged into me, rocking his hips against mine. Our water powers had their own reunion, making patterns in the air—figure eights, helixes, sunbeams. Light spilling from the ocean waters around us cast blue shadows through the holographic windows, a manta ray darkening the room for the few moments it took to pass with each flap.

Pinching my knees against his sides, I arched into the sheets, turning the bed beneath me into water, cushioning me, and tantalizing my skin. I flashed my eyes open, staring up at the King of the Seas—my equal. Morphing my fingertips into water, I traced over his lips, leaving a sparkly trail that disappeared with one lap of his tongue. I dragged my fingers down his chest, making goosebumps sprout with each passing touch.

He furrowed his brow with a grunt. "You keep doing that, and I'm going to come undone, Cory."

"Come undone with me then." Sucking his earlobe, I continued my torturous liquid touch, circling right at the base of his shaft.

His lips became a liquid stream as he dipped to kiss my neck, shooting vibrations through my skin and straight to my core. Gasping, I willed my fingernails to return, digging them into his back as I cried out, tensing around him. As I'd asked, he joined me, shaking and rattling through his release. After trailing a feather-like kiss over my lips, he slid behind me to his side, pulling my ass against him.

Smiling, I watched a family of sea turtles swim past and cooed within Poseidon's arms. "Do you think the shield will hold now against the sea monsters?"

"One could only hope. Though I wouldn't mind battling off one or two with you again." He nibbled my shoulder.

"I'd be lying if I said I didn't wish the same." I laughed and trailed my finger over the hair on the back of his hand.

His nose rubbed behind my ear. "Now that Hypnos has allowed you to control your past memories, is there one that sticks out the most to you?"

"The Viking Age." It took only a passing thought to recall it—the smells of blood and sweat, the weight of my shield in my grasp, longhouses in the distance with moss growing on the roofs.

"Shit, really?" Poseidon sat up on one elbow. "Tell me."

I turned on my back, peering up at my husband with a small smile. "I was a shieldmaiden."

"Not surprised by that in the least."

"The memory that keeps rolling through my head is us leaving our village to conquer land. I had a husband—a blacksmith. He'd spend the entire time I was gone forging weapons and would be the first on the shoreline when our boats docked, ready to greet me." Cutting my glance to Poseidon's eyes, the glare I'd expected cut through his gaze.

"I hope we do find someone who can port us to different times so I can kick this guy's ass." Poseidon hugged me to him tighter.

Laughing, I nudged him with my shoulder. "Very long time ago. We didn't know each other existed. Remember?"

"I know, I know. Still." Poseidon kissed the side of my head. "Did you die in battle in that life?"

My heart grew heavy, remembering the distance I'd felt on my deathbed. "No. I got sick. My husband put a sword in my hands, but I remember shoving it back at him because I didn't want to go to Valhalla without him. And he wasn't a fighter."

"That's—wow," Poseidon mumbled.

"I'd do the same for you, Seid. If there were such a place gods would go—Chaos, perhaps? I'd want to make sure we ended up there together. I married you for eternity." I cupped his cheek in my palm.

He kissed me—delicate and sweet before brushing our noses together. "I'd follow you to the stars now, Cor."

A blue portal appeared at the foot of the bed, making us both jolt to attention. A dark-haired man with a full beard sporting a duster jacket toppled out of it. We both sat up straight, Poseidon snapping his fingers to make a white flowing dress appear over my body.

The man's arms flew up in an "X." "Bloody hell. Were you two—?"

"Take a wild guess, Heph," Poseidon grumbled, not bothering to clothe himself as he moved from the bed.

"Hephaistos?" My brow shot up. "I haven't seen you in ages. Even before I was banished."

Heph clicked his teeth. "Can't say I've been around the 'ol stomping grounds enough to socialize with the pantheon elite. So, no offense taken."

"I wasn't—" Poseidon shot me a look that suggested I'd be wasting my breath if I continued that sentence.

"What are you doing here?" Poseidon folded his arms.

Heph took one step forward and dropped his gaze to Poseidon's bare lower half. "You know, this is the second time I've been in this situation in less than a year. I severely question my life choices." Wiggling his fingers, Heph produced a square device from a jacket pocket.

Sliding from the bed, I clutched my hands to my chest, hope tingling my skin, giving me goosebumps.

"Word on the waves is—" Heph spun the device in his palm, making another portal appear behind him. "—you two need to do a tick of time travel."

Poseidon and I exchanged glances, a glint sparking in our gazes.

"We better grab Triton." Poseidon took my hand.

Hang on, Rhode. Your family is on their way.

THE
CONTEMPORARY MYTHOS
WILL CONTINUE

ZEUS

COMING SOON

Catch the first book in the Contemporary Mythos series:

HADES

The King of the Underworld may have found a woman truly capable of melting his cold, dark heart.

HADES (Contemporary Mythos, #1)
BUY IT ON AMAZON

EXCERPT FROM

ZEUS

NEXT IN THE
CONTEMPORARY MYTHOS
SERIES:

ZEUS

SHE DIDN'T THINK I heard her slip out of bed in the middle of the night. Didn't think I saw her nab a twenty from my wallet before ducking out with a light click of the door. At least she had the decency to look at my ass peeking from the sheets before leaving. It *was* a nice ass.

She also probably didn't think I remembered her name. Elena.

I didn't bother locking the door behind her. In fact, it'd be entertaining for someone to barge in and try to kill me. The King of the fucking Gods. It'd been far too long since I'd seen the terrified look on a mortal's face when they realized who I was. Any attempt to announce it in the modern age…they'd look at me like I was insane. Fucking mockery.

And I know what you're thinking. This scenario isn't

surprising. Dickhead Zeus sleeps with yet another woman, cheating on his wife. Shocking. There *is* more to that story, but I digress.

This time…I'm not the asshole. This time, I fucked her fair and square. Hera left me. Gave up her Queendom, sneered at me, and left.

And I let her.

Despite the humiliation. Despite the absolute fury. It hadn't been the first time she rebelled against me, only this time I didn't care. Because in a bizarrely fucked up way…I admired it. It grew old and tiresome pretending things were as they'd been all those ages ago. She changed. The world changed. And most importantly, hold onto your asses, *I* changed.

I shook my head at the notion, rattling away whatever fog clouded my brain.

Besides, I couldn't remember the last time I was single—a bachelor. She may have unleashed a monster. A short-lived one anyway.

I crawled out of bed, slipping on the boxers I'd haphazardly tossed to the floor earlier, making my way to a back room. Lightly touching the knob, I cracked the door open, greeted by a large wet black nose.

"Come on, boy," I said to my white Labrador, Levin.

He forced his shoulders into the door, sprinting down the hall, slipping and sliding with each passing step. I smiled to myself, patiently following him. No woman I'd ever brought here deserved to meet Levin. He was the only being in the universe who'd ever see past all the bullshit, didn't give a fuck about my past, and loved me unconditionally. When I rounded the corner, he was already making circles on the bed, finding a suitable spot to curl up and sleep for the night.

Before crawling in myself, I paused at the edge, taking his large head in both of my hands, scratching behind his ears. His wide pink tongue flopped to the side of his mouth, panting.

"Good boy." After turning off the light, I climbed into bed and felt Levin's furry warm body shoving against my back after only thirty seconds.

Morning seeped through the cracks of the black curtains in my sleek downtown New York apartment, making me grumble. As much sleep as I got and never seemed to be enough. Ironic considering I'm a god, right? It's what happens when you partially hold the entire cosmos on your shoulders—always on your mind. The important thing was to *never* show it on your face in front of your people. And I hadn't for millennia.

Ruffling my hair, I shoved my face into the pillow, ignoring the scent of Elena's shampoo, or fragrance, or whatever the fuck it was she'd left behind. The metal statue of an eagle in mid-attack, appearing to protrude from the wall stared down at me from above. Levin was sprawled on his back, curled to the side with his legs spread, sleeping away. And I let him. Slipping out of bed, I paused to stretch my arms to Olympus, leering at my reflection in the mirror—cut, toned, tanned, and immaculate. A physique that never changed, and I had to do absolutely nothing to maintain. Perks to being a Greek god.

My face. The closest semblance I could replicate to the true me. Unless, of course, I enjoyed the sight of each mortal I passed on the streets catching flame. A younger, more ruthless me may have grinned at the thought. But no, I've learned to marvel at the poor bastards. My mortal guise was a version of me that existed before fighting for and *earning* the right of chief deity. But my eyes...those would never change.

Where was I? Ah yes. My small window of bachelorhood. Thanks to the overpowerful bitch of a grandmother of mine, Gaea...there's a stipulation to my Kingdom. At all times—there must be a Queen. If the expiration date lapses, I not only lose my title but part of my power to go with it. We couldn't have that, now, could we? And to be honest, I'd never given the clause much thought. There'd only ever been Hera. I didn't think she'd give up her crown. At any rate, I'd take the next few nights to "live it up," so to speak, and then pick the nearest mortal woman who was pleasing to the eyes to be my Queen. Done deal.

Any and all of them would pine over the idea of it. And why wouldn't they? To become not only a goddess but an immortal Queen? Not to mention I could walk down the street and have each and every one of them if I so desired. Fuck—if I had a thing for man-ass, I could have that too. The world was my oyster, and I'd shucked my share. But I'd be lying if I said the ease of the conquest on the rarest of occasions never felt...hollow.

Sneering, I turned for my walk-in closet, the light automatically illuminating as I entered. Hundreds of pristinely hung suits lined the walls, dozens of glossed dress shoes resting on matching shelves. Displays held a different Rolex for each day of the week and several shined and glinting pairs of silver and gold cufflinks.

I could conjure clothes with a snap of my fingers, but for as long as I'd roamed the earth one starts to appreciate the smaller things—things mortals take for granted. A uniquely tailored suit created to fit you like a glove. The feel of it as you slip it on like liquid sex. Even the scent of the fabric calmed me far quicker than any steaming hot shower. And I never wore the same suit twice. Ever.

Donning the light grey ensemble with a white shirt and dark blue tie, yes, I did up the tie as well every time. Peering into the full-length mirror, I did the necessary overlapping and pull- through to secure the perfect knot in the silk tie, smoothing it down. I turned my face to the side, running a hand over the light beard on my chin. My godly King form was far less…clean. Ironic that between my brothers and I, Hades' true self was the only beardless one.

Upon securing the gold Rolex on my left wrist, I attached the gold "Z" cufflink to one sleeve, a lightning bolt on the other, and paused to stare at the New York City skyline through the wall of windows near my king-sized bed. Mortals of all varieties busied the streets, appearing as ants in a structured maze. Chins tilted down, eyes glued to their phone screens, missing half the world around them. It was no wonder they didn't believe in us anymore. They were far too busy worshipping technology and the media. Eons ago, I may have asked Poseidon to wipe the slate clean by making Earth's oceans swallow it whole, but I no longer interfered that deep. There was an entire universe to oversee, and if you think the Greek gods are the only deities from "mythology" in existence—you'd be sorely mistaken.

I turned to Levin, who was still snoring, fast asleep on the bed. With a smirk, I snapped my fingers, making raw meat chunks appear in his dog bowl in the kitchen. Levin's body writhed and his head shot up, nose sniffing the air. He jumped off the bed and scurried over to me, sitting but shaking, waiting for permission to eat. Crouching, I scratched under his chin and gave a quick kiss to the top of his head.

"Be good. Go on." I motioned with my head at the kitchen, and with an excited yip, he trotted off to eat.

New York. I've lived in many, many places. Aside from Olympus, aside from Greece, New York felt like a kingdom to be ruled—even if they had no idea who walked amongst them. Slipping my hands into my pockets, I made for the elevator and began my daily stroll to the firm's building. I could've had a chauffeur, *me* knows I could afford it. Could've even simply ported there. But there was something about feeding on the energy of mortals—their expressions. Their reactions, as pure raw power, waltzed right past them. A pity they didn't believe in the old gods anymore. We could all have *so* much more fun.

It was time to don the mask. A façade forged through the ages that mortals molded and adapted to fit their own needs. Their own agenda. Same old song and dance. It'd become as much a part of me as the warmth of a perfectly aged scotch settling in my stomach. Could I have taken the time to convince a world there was more to me than the endless parade of women? More than the meddling king god who cared for nothing or no one else but himself? Sure. But I had an entire fucking kingdom to oversee. Hundreds of gods beneath me and seemingly more even within the last few months. We'll get to that tiny detail later. There were far more pressing matters to deal with over a reputation I've grown to accept. If it gave them comfort to hate me, I'd be their sounding board because I'm a leader. The alpha. A godsdamned admiral.

STAY TUNED!

WWW.CARLYSPADE.COM

WANT TO DONATE TO A REAL OCEAN CONSERVATION GROUP?

I'm currently partnered with Blue Ring, Inc. and ALL proceeds made from my contemporary shark romance (with a hero based on Shark Week's Paul de Gelder): THE OTHER TIDE are donated to them. Please consider checking out the book (Kindle Unlimited counts as well) or going directly to their website to make a donation!

CHECK OUT THE OTHER TIDE:

mybook.to/TheOtherTide

BLUE RING'S WEBSITE:

bluering.blue

ACKNOWLEDGEMENTS

FIRSTLY, TO MY HUSBAND who will forever be my "co-op" partner for life in any and all gaming! I'm so fortunate to find a partner who enjoys video games as much as I do.

To my parents for forever being my truest and biggest fans ever!

To PeachyAenne, thank you so much for your input on game streaming and competing in eSports tournaments! You really helped keep the story afloat. (Ohohoho! Get it?) Be sure to check her out on Twitch! @sharkyaenne

To my critique partner AK, thank you for working Poseidon in so quickly while simultaneously reading through Zeus as well. Your input is always super appreciated and as you've been with this series from the start, it was super important to me!

To my beta readers, I can't believe this series is almost over and you've all been with me from the beginning with Hades. Your feedback continues to make this series better and you've also helped thicken my skin as a writer with your honesty. You are all seriously the best.

To my continued readers, thank you sincerely, from the bottom of my heart, for believing in me enough to trust my interpretations of the Greek gods and myths. And to all the new readers who started with Poseidon, welcome aboard. Thank you. And I hope you stay for the journey.

ABOUT THE AUTHOR

CARLY SPADE is an adult romance writer who has been writing since she could pick up a pencil. After the insanity of obtaining a bachelor's and master's degree in cybersecurity, creating worlds to escape to still ate at her very soul. She started writing FanFiction (which can still be found if you scour the internet), and soon felt the need to get her original ideas on paper. And so the adventure began.

She lives in Colorado with her husband and two fur babies, and revels in an enemies to lovers trope with a slow burn.

Find her online:

WWW.CARLYSPADE.COM

Printed in Great Britain
by Amazon